MARSTOWN

the beginning

Lee Michaels

ISBN 978-0-9903223-1-3

This book is for you, the reader, from me.

The characters in this book and the events that take place are fictional. Though several real locations and public figures are mentioned, any similarity to people—living or dead—is purely coincidental.

I'd like to thank the people from Norwood and Marshfield Scrap for sharing their experiences and knowledge with me. You helped me see the shadows in the corners.

I hope you enjoy reading this book as much as I enjoyed writing it.

Lee

Contents

You, yourself, have got to see

that there is no just

interpretation of life

except in terms of

life's best things.

No pleasure philosophy,

no sensuality,

no place nor power,

no material success

can for a moment

give such inner satisfaction

as the sense of

living for good purposes,

for maintenance of integrity,

for the preservation of self-approval.

MINOT SIMONS

Chapter 1

Go Dons Go

"Honey, you'll love it. When I went here back in the eighties, everyone wanted to be a Don. Wearing a Columbus letter jacket was *the* status symbol. We had the best football team around and there were so many kids we had to share lockers. It was a riot of fun. We used to hang out all over that track." Her mom pointed as their SUV pulled into the parking lot.

Samantha wrinkled her nose. "This is a private school?"

Her mom nodded. "That's right."

"It's so...small. The track isn't even paved. Where does the football team practice? There is no way that is a real field."

"We never had our own football field; we shared with Marshfield High. But the Dons will always be the best...in my heart."

"Well that sounds like a *riot* of fun, making them share a football field. Somebody got shanked." Samantha gazed at the long, low brick building, the windows paneled-up save for one section at the bottom which remained glass. She could see the slanted roof of the gym, and what looked like a giant chimney going up the back of the building. "This place looks like a prison camp."

"Wait until you see the lobby. It has gorgeous wood paneling, and the trophy cases are stuffed. My class rocked this place back in the day."

"This building is not normal."

After parking, they walked down the sidewalk to the school's front doors. Except for Columbus's navy blue color running in a glaring line just beneath the ceiling, the lobby's bleach-white walls were devoid of any wood paneling or trophy cases. Fluorescent lights beat down on a life-sized, two-toned wooden crucifix between the doors to the gym. The stained-glass entrance to what could only be the school's chapel looked wildly out-of-place in the corner. To their immediate right, the door to the front office stood ajar, next to a dusty flat-screen television that Samantha doubted worked.

"My God..." her mother whispered, "what have they done to this school?"

Samantha noticed two wide hallways flanked the lobby. "Which way?"

"I think it's to the right. Of course, I could be wrong." Her mother led the way to the Principal's office and knocked.

"Come in," came a voice.

Mrs. Symanski pushed the door open. "We're here for the meeting regarding Samantha Symanski's enrollment?"

The office was as small as a coffin, with wood-paneled walls—they must have matched the lobby at one point—laden with old photographs. A pair of diminutive wooden chairs huddled in front of a desk that was probably built inside the office. Samantha felt claustrophobic squeezing in behind her mother. A middle-aged woman with bangs cut straight across her forehead filled the chair behind the desk.

"Hello Sandra," the principal said, her voice like ice.

"Hello Barb," replied Samantha's mother in an even icier tone. She slid into one of the chairs, tense and ready to pounce.

Samantha rolled her eyes. "How do you two know each other?"

"Barb and I graduated together," Samantha's mother explained.

"She was Salutatorian, if I recall; I was Valedictorian. We used to be very competitive, didn't we, Barb?" Mrs. Symanski laughed.

"Oh yes. You haven't aged a day," Barb observed. "Who's your surgeon?"

"I can't handle knives," sighed Samantha's mother, "or forks. A problem we don't seem to share."

Barb's face flashed something akin to mortification, but she said nothing. A tangible silence drowned the room. She put on a pair of wire-rimmed glasses and sorted through a file on her desk, then pulled out a paper. "I have Samantha's transcripts from out east. River Hill High School faxed them over. Is that where you've been for the past twenty years?"

"Washington, D.C.," Mrs. Symanski nodded. "Danny was employed at the NSA for a while before we divorced. I've been working with various defense contractors in consulting. It's challenging work, but very fulfilling."

"Interesting." Barb's gaze fell on Samantha, who frowned. "I'm surprised to see you've come back to little old Marshfield. Miss the Wisconsin winters?" She said it to Samantha.

Samantha raised her eyebrows. "I've actually never been here before." Barb looked somewhat furious and turned her gaze back to Samantha's mother.

"The atmosphere in D.C. took a turn in recent years," Mrs. Symanski elaborated. "I felt it was better to raise my children in my hometown, where it's safer. It will be a strange transition with Samantha being a sophomore this year and Brandon going into fifth grade. But you guys will learn to love it." She nudged Samantha with an elbow. "They'll be able to play outside for once! We'll just have to drive to Chicago or fly out east to see the museums and the shows. An unfortunate trade-off." Samantha felt her stomach drop at the flicker of disgust in Barb's eyes.

"As principal of this school, I must say we're delighted to have a girl with such an *interesting* upbringing joining our student body."

Samantha could feel the impending danger and waved her hand. "I'm not that interesting, really." Barb ignored her and continued.

"She'll bring an element to our student body that we haven't had in some time. Your daughter looks just like you—minus the eighties perm."

Samantha gazed at her mother. "You had a perm?" Her mother smiled sweetly at Barb.

"She's really nothing like me. In fact, she's a lot like Danny. You'll probably pick up on that more as the year progresses. By the way, what happened to the lobby? Are you teaching nursing now?" The tension in the air thickened until Samantha thought she would choke with her every inhale.

Her mother's smile was offset by a thunderstruck Barb, who pulled another paper from the file. "This will be Samantha's schedule for the year. Obviously we are on a different pace than your old school, but you will be caught up by junior year." Samantha took the schedule from Barb with a soft "thank you." Barb looked back to Mrs. Symanski.

"Make certain she follows our dress code. You should remember: no jeans, no tops with cuts below the collar bone, no unnatural hair colors, no tattoos or piercings except one in each ear. No gauging or bars. The rest is listed in the student handbook. I'd like Columbus Catholic to stay the pinnacle of decency in this community."

"How are the Dons playing these days?" Mrs. Symanski smiled. "It's been a long time since I've been to a high school football game. I'd like to have my son get involved in the youth football program as soon as possible."

"They're the Rockets now. We don't have enough boys to form our own team currently, so we share a single team with Spencer High School. Youth football started weeks ago." Barb forced a smile. "Have a good day, you two. See you tomorrow Samantha."

Samantha and her mother left the cramped office, and crossed back into the lobby. "I cannot believe what has happened to this place in twenty years," Samantha's mother whispered. "It's like I'm in some alternate universe. The Dons used to own this town. Now, it looks like Detroit."

"You're the one who decided to drag us here, mom," Samantha

hissed back.

"Well, we're all just going to have to make the best of it. It was time for a change anyway."

"You shouldn't have talked to her like that." Samantha frowned. "You acted like you didn't know she was the principal."

Her mother huffed. "Well, I didn't. I called and set the appointment through the secretary. I never thought to ask for a name. That's why there's a nameplate on the desk."

"You two must have been mortal enemies."

"Yeah, well, she said some things, I said some things, she slit her wrists, and even that didn't work out for her. Now here we all are."

"What did you do, mom!"

"Oh, come on. It's high school. People get over that stuff." She unlocked their vehicle.

"Not when you still work at the school where it all happened. She's going to take out her hatred for you on me," Samantha murmured as they climbed into the SUV and shut the doors.

"You know what you should do?" Samantha's mother turned the key.

"What?" Samantha pulled a water bottle out of her cup holder.

"You should be a cheerleader."

Samantha almost gagged as she took a swig. "You're kidding. I haven't done anything physical in my entire life. How am I supposed to cheer? I can barely run."

Her mother ran a hand through her hair. "Honey, you can run. I saw you do it once when you were eight. You never forget how to run. You'd be a great cheerleader. The school is obviously dying. They'll be desperate for more girls on the squad, especially cute ones like you. Who knows? You may even encourage more boys to switch schools. They'll have to start up the football team again, the Dons can come back, money will flow into the school because of the team, and life will be fabulous! All because you took a chance and did something different!" Her mother beamed at her.

"I can't talk to you when you're like this." Samantha pulled out her smart phone as her mom's smile faded. "Why did you drag us back here?"

Mrs. Symanski sighed. "Honey, Marshfield is the safest place for you."

THE HOUSE WAITED IN THE DARK as Levi drove past in his rusted Chevy pickup: six-six-two Pecan Parkway. A little yellow dwelling with green shutters, flowers, and an American flag mounted by the front door, it hid in plain sight behind its meticulously-crafted veil of averageness. He drove a block and parked in the Lincoln Elementary School lot, flicked off his headlights, and sat in the silence of the neighborhood. The night air rustled leaves with the gentle warmth of summer's last breath.

He glanced at his companion in the passenger seat, a navy blue gym bag. Innocuous enough. Unzipping it, he pulled out his lock picks and tucked them into the pocket of his jeans. He slipped on a pair of latex gloves, then tied a black bandana around his face, obscuring everything below his eyes. A black cap and flipping up his hood completed his disguise. He pulled a sheathed knife out of the bag, clipped it to a belt loop on his jeans, then slipped a wooden stake into his pocket.

Stepping out of the truck, Levi pushed the door until it closed, trusting the breeze to carry the sound away. He was thankful it was a Tuesday. Everyone would be home, asleep. No one would be glancing out windows this time of night.

He walked briskly down the sidewalk, putting as much distance as possible between himself and his truck. Before he knew it, he stood in front of 662 Pecan Parkway. He took a deep breath and strolled in a relaxed manner up to the front door. He turned the knob, determined it was locked, then pulled out his picks. In a second, the door creaked open, exposing the dark interior.

Levi could barely make out a sofa, lamps, and a darkened television in the corner. Thick-pad carpeting muffled his steps as he entered. Through his bandana he could smell something putrid, metallic. Dried blood. There must be a lot of it. Eyes adjusted to the darkness, he scanned the room again. Pristine paneled walls, lace-curtained windows, and matching doilies on the coffee table, but no bloodstains. Still, the odor filled his nostrils.

He made his way over to an archway leading into the kitchen, pausing where the carpet became linoleum. Voices. From beneath his feet. Two men were speaking, rather calm, interrupted by the gasps of a woman. The men stopped talking, and her gasping turned to pleading. Levi had to find a way into the basement. As he moved through the house, he could hear her. "Stop it! Leave him alone! You demons! Leave us—" He spotted light from under a door.

"Shut up!" A man's voice cut her off. Levi found the doorknob and his heart skipped a beat as he pulled it open and looked down the stairs. At the bottom, a gray-haired man in a Packers sweater lay in a pool of blood. Another man crouching over him licked red smears off his fingers after having dipped them in the puddle. As he pulled his fingers from his mouth, he looked up the stairs and locked eyes with Levi.

A pang of horror struck him as he recognized the man. "Lancaster," he whispered to himself. Mr. Lancaster's eyes flashed, thick eyebrows coming together as his goateed mouth twisted into an unholy grimace. Levi felt his legs go numb as he pulled the stake from his pocket. Lancaster charged him, barreling up the stairs. Levi shoved the stake at him, but Lancaster threw himself through the door, exploding into a cloud of bats. Screeching and chaotic, Levi could only watch as they disappeared out the open front door into the night.

"Shit," he muttered. He turned and ran down the stairs because he was supposed to, then looked to his left where the basement continued. There, an old woman sat in a dining room chair, roped to a support pole. Another man loomed behind her, his teeth buried in her neck, hand over her mouth. Drunk on her blood, he didn't notice Levi approach him until the stake plunged into the crux of his neck. Levi forced it down until he hit the heart. The man slumped over, his hand falling from the woman's mouth. She gently sobbed as Levi pushed the body backwards onto the floor, freeing his stake.

He unsheathed his knife and slashed the ties that held the woman to the chair and pole. She slumped forward, weak, and he caught her.

"It hurts," she whispered, holding her neck, blood leaking between her fingers. Levi frowned. She wasn't going to live, but he needed information.

"Ma'am, I have to ask you—"

"My husband," she choked.

"How did they get in?" Levi pressed.

"We had them over for dinner. A social evening," she cried. "They wanted to see Phil's Packer collection, so we...we took them down here..." Levi glanced around and noticed the green and gold memorabilia everywhere. "They turned on us. They tied us up. They bit us, over and over again."

"Over and over again? What time did you have dinner?" Lumped clots dripped from her neck. She smelled of rot and perfume.

"About five, what's it matter?" she frowned. "I have the most horrible feeling...I'm so hungry..." Levi felt his blood run cold, and his hand drifted back to the stake in his pocket.

"Ma'am, your husband..."

"My husband seems to be doing better," she said. Levi turned around to see the man in the Packers sweater standing right behind him, smiling, canines twice as long as they should be.

"How's dinner coming, honey?"

"Dinner's ready." Her canines grew longer as she smiled back, her eyes turning black. Levi felt a surge of adrenaline as he staked the man in the heart. The wife leapt onto his back as her husband disintegrated into a pile of ash. Slamming into everything to shake her, Levi stumbled around the room as she screeched in his ear. Her weight threw him off-balance, and he tripped over the body of the other man.

He felt her head smack into the dining room chair and then into his own. Stars exploded in front of his eyes. Her nails dug into his shoulders, refusing to let go. He felt teeth graze his neck and in a thrill of terror grabbed her hair and pulled as hard as he could. She shrieked and flew across the basement, landing in a corner. Levi leapt to his feet, stake in hand. She paced like a caged animal, black eyes searching for an escape.

"You can't transform," he panted. "You let him take too much blood. If you try, you'll become a bunch of bats passed out on the floor, and I'll take my time with holy water, killing you piece by piece."

"You're a sick little shit," she hissed at him. "This was supposed to be a conversion."

"This waste of oxygen and Thomas Lancaster? You and your husband have been busy."

"It was Lancaster's idea, not mine. Let me go. I'm not the one you should be worried about."

"Are you kidding? You killed that poor dumbass over there on the floor!"

She glanced at the body. "No boy, *you* killed him with *your* stake. He didn't drink enough blood to become a vampire yet. He was human when you staked him." Levi felt his stomach drop. "Didn't you notice his body is still solid? You're a murderer. How does that feel, vampire slayer." A demonic laugh bubbled from her lips.

Levi threw the stake as hard as he could, embedding it in her chest. She gasped, glaring at him with pure hatred before turning into a pile of dust.

"How did *that* feel? Rude bitch." Levi picked the stake out of the dust pile. He focused his attention on the body in the basement. Blood flowing from his neck mixed with the other pool of blood by the base of the stairs. He turned the man over to see his face. He didn't recognize it.

"Wherever you are now, I hope you've figured out what a bad decision this was. Why couldn't you have just changed jobs? Or moved? Why this?"

Levi looked around at the Packer collection, a jumbled mess with blood spatters from the old woman. The dust piles on the floor, the dented dining room chair, the slashed bindings—he couldn't leave the place looking like this. A Packers clock on the wall told him it was two in the morning.

"Great, now all I gotta do is clean this up, dispose of a body, shower, change, and get to school on time…" He sighed. This year was starting out rougher than the last. He crossed to the stairs to find some cleaning supplies.

SHOWING UP AN HOUR EARLY, Levi made his way to the boys' restroom, where he tried once again to get all the dirt from under his nails. He hissed through his teeth as he rinsed, the water running into stinging cuts and overheated blisters.

"A night of heavy-duty shoveling can do awful things to the hands," he said to himself. All that damage and he didn't get the hole deep enough yet. The body still lay out in the open, badly hidden in McMillan Marsh. But he had bigger problems. Lancaster was a vampire. He also ran the funeral home off of Veterans Parkway. He had access to dead bodies, grieving family members, and had a good reputation in the community. Everyone knew him. Everyone trusted him, even Levi.

Until last night.

Levi worked at the Lancaster Funeral Home the previous year, cleaning the embalming room and arranging flower displays. It was base work, but it forced Levi to get over his fear of death, and of being around the dead. Over the past year, his slaying skills improved, mostly because he could finally ignore his apprehension, and go in for the kill.

But now, Levi abandoned his inhibitions, and a man was dead. A lunatic, but a man nonetheless. Since he had no identification and Levi did not recognize his face, he would have to wait for the missing person report to circulate before he would know the man's name.

Levi scrubbed soap under his nails and rinsed in the large wash fountain, tossing a bloody paper towel into the bin. He walked out of the bathroom and glanced up at the hallway clock. Forty minutes before the first bell. More students filled the lobby. Levi turned and walked down the senior hallway, to the row of lockers at the far end by the tech shop.

These lockers were never used, and most didn't have working locks—since the school had almost twice as many lockers as students. He opened a locker, pulled out a spare change of clothes that smelled a bit musty, and headed back to the bathroom. He changed in a stall, careful not to get too much dirt on anything. He glanced in the mirror. A pair of khakis, a black polo shirt, and a gray hooded sweatshirt complied with the dress code. From the neck up, he looked like a zombie: tousled hair, dark circles, and a stubborn smudge of dirt on his cheek. He splashed water on his face, rinsed his hair, pulled it forward, and flipped his hood up. With some luck, he might get through the day without acting too much like a stoner.

SAMANTHA TOOK A DEEP BREATH as she stood in front of the doors of her new school, the giant cross and statue of Christopher Columbus towering over her. The air smelled like cow manure; she wrinkled her nose. Other students walked past her on their way in, glancing over their shoulders, whispering about the "new girl." She felt a shudder go through her. There would be nowhere for her to hide.

She tossed her blonde hair and walked up to the building, the khaki pants hugging her like soulless, scotch-guarded skinny jeans. A red shirt and a black leather jacket matched her backpack. She pulled her schedule and locker information from a pocket. Students littered the wood benches around the lobby, all eyes on her. With more effort than she ever put forth before, she walked slowly, methodically, down the left hall, and followed the locker numbers to her own. She spun the dial, keeping her eyes trained, while her ears picked up surrounding conversations.

"Who is that?" "She looks like Marissa." "She does not look like her." "Is that the new girl?" "Ya, duh, look at her. She's from out-of-state." "Can't you tell? She's overdressed." "Must be really rich." "The B's gonna get on her for that blouse for sure." "Why? There's no cleavage showing." "Funny funny…lol." "Omg, did you just say lol?"

It was going to be a long day.

IF THERE WAS ONE THING Levi was grateful for, it was hallowed ground. He could sleep anywhere on the property of the Catholic school and not worry. No vampire could come closer than the sidewalk. Unfortunately he didn't live in the school, or on hallowed ground. Sleeping anywhere else made no sense. Once he figured out which room his first class was in, he sat in the back corner, leaned against the wall, and allowed himself to slip away for the half-hour prior to the first bell. He was also grateful to be one of those fortunate people who rarely dreamed; he could shut down like a computer and turn back on later. It gave his brain a chance to relax and stop thinking about Lancaster.

When the bell rang in its obnoxious 1956-style way, Levi was forced to stay half-awake in power save mode. He closed his eyes and listened as students filed in and the teacher busied himself at his desk.

Other students were whispering, but it wasn't about the usual "I did blah blah blah over the summer" thing. It was about a "new girl." No surprise there. New kids were novelties—there were so few of them in the Catholic school system, they were practically foreign-exchange students. Usually they transferred to the public high school after only one or two months of concentrated drama. Levi tuned out the conversations as someone sat in the desk next to his. He glanced over. An unfamiliar blonde girl in a red blouse pulled out her notebook and deliberately didn't make eye contact with anyone in the room.

"Good morning Columbus Dons," came Barb's voice on the intercom. *"I hope your summer was enjoyable. Now we're back for another year of intellectual stimulation. I trust you are as excited about this as I am. Let's make it a great year. A reminder that cheerleading tryouts will be held after school at Spencer High. Ladies, we would appreciate some participation."*

The blonde girl next to him scoffed to herself and shook her head. Amusement tugged at Levi's lips. The teacher stood and cleared his throat. The class continued to murmur.

"Good morning everyone," he said with the enthusiasm of a pocket protector. "Welcome to Honors Psychology. You're going to learn a lot this semester as we delve into the human mind and discover what makes us tick. I'm looking forward to exploring this amazing topic with all of you. But first, we're going to have an introduction. I'm Mr. Becker. It may seem redundant to introduce myself as I know most of you from other classes, but we have a new student with us. Samantha, would you come to the front of the class please?"

The girl next to Levi froze for a moment, then slid out of her desk and walked to the front of the room. Levi could see her jaw tense slightly, her fingers curling and uncurling. She faced the room, and he saw her focus on the back wall.

"Hello, my name is Samantha Symanski, and that's a mouthful, so I understand if y'all butcher it at first, but I won't forget to butcher yours right back." She smiled at them, but nobody responded. Someone near the windows coughed.

"*Y'all?*" Levi couldn't help but snicker a little.

"What a wonderful accent. Where are you from?" asked Mr. Becker monotonously.

"I'm from Washington D.C., but my parents are originally from Marshfield, so it's kind of like getting back to my roots—my mom's roots. It's a lot quieter than I'm used to, so…major culture shock."

"Definitely, definitely," nodded Mr. Becker. "We're always excited to have new people join us, so welcome. Please have a seat."

Samantha nodded, her blonde hair falling in a shimmer around her shoulders. Levi spotted a couple of the guys' heads turn as Samantha crossed back to her desk. She was going to be the biggest thing to hit this school since Patrycia from Poland. She sat down as Mr. Becker turned off the lights and turned on his slides. He listened as Samantha let out a long, quiet breath.

"Great acting up there," he whispered. She rolled her eyes, then focused on the slides as she clicked her pen. She began to scribble. Levi could barely register the words on the projector screen. A warm dark room first thing in the morning was impossible to resist.

"I'm gonna sleep, can I get the notes from you later?"

"Take your own," she muttered.

"I'd really, really appreciate it." She glared at him. He shrugged and closed his eyes, leaning deeper into the wall as Mr. Becker droned on. It was only day one. His lecture wouldn't be important anyway.

HOMEROOM FOLLOWED PSYCHOLOGY; then Samantha had three classes in a row with that stoner who always sat in the back, somehow beating her to each desk she bee-lined for. She wound up introducing herself in every class, and—by now—must have said her name to half the school. The other half knew her name via gossip. She didn't speak to anyone except that stoner, and that created a new problem. Where on earth was she going to sit during lunch? She didn't know a single person, and even though the faces were already familiar, she had no idea where she fit in the social scale.

She got in line and surveyed the cafeteria's four long stretches of benched tables. It reminded her of the Great Hall in Hogwarts— minus the floating candles and the charm. As the lunch line moved along and the tables filled, the social order of the school revealed itself. Most of the freshman girls clumped together at the third table, their overly made-up eyes cast in the direction of the senior guys sitting together at the far corner, the obvious kings of the cafeteria in their navy blue letter jackets. The rest of the groups were harder to figure out as the dress code kept the students looking alike.

As the lunch lady slapped a piece of hideous square pizza on her tray, Samantha noticed Stoner sitting near the cafeteria entrance, practically passed out. Well, he *was* the most familiar person she saw so far today, and the other students had given him a wide berth. She grabbed a carton of chocolate milk and dressed her salad before walking with composure to where he slept. In an act of desperation, she plopped down across from him. He was snoring. Right there. In the open. She rolled her eyes and began to eat.

Samantha felt eyes on the back of her head; they must be wondering why she sat with this guy. A flush came to her face as she realized how odd it must be, her and a stoner sitting alone together. The judgment hung in the air, inescapable and heavy. She needed an excuse to be there. She needed to demonstrate she wasn't a stoner too, that she chose to sit here for some benign reason. She finished her salad and sipped her milk, contemplating. She poked him. He sat up so fast the table scraped across the floor. The cafeteria hushed.

"Hey." Samantha forced herself to focus entirely on the boy across from her. "Did you still need my notes from Psych this morning?"

"Actually yes," said the boy. "That would be awesome." He leaned back down and prepared to sleep some more.

Samantha had to act fast. "Would you like them now? I could grab them from my locker."

"I guess," he mumbled.

"What's your name?" Samantha asked.

He looked up at her. "Huh?"

"What's your name?"

"Levi Mauer." He sort of half-smiled at her. Samantha couldn't decide what to make of that face.

"You must be…tired." She tried to mask her disdain.

"You have no idea," Levi replied. "Can I borrow your notes at the end of the day? I'll give them back tomorrow."

"Yeah," Samantha said. "That's fine." She could feel the audience eavesdropping. "Did you want this? I'm not into square pizza."

"Sure," Levi shrugged. Samantha slid her tray across the table and stood up. "Where are you going?"

"To the girls' room." Samantha left without looking at him. She walked out of the cafeteria and down the hall to the bathroom, which was miraculously empty. She sighed and went to the mirror, fixing her hair as she pulled out her smart phone. "Only fifteen minutes left to kill." Samantha continued to play with her hair as the minutes ticked by, taking pictures of her reflection in the mirror and deleting them. It was nice not to feel the scrutiny of others. She would upload the best picture to Facebook later, for her friends in Washington D.C. She hoped they would see how happy she wanted them to think she was.

Two giggling girls burst in—a brunette and a redhead.

Samantha's eye twitched before she refocused her attention on her reflection.

"Hey." The redhead stood next to her and pulled a compact out of her bag. "My name is Natalie. This is Jennifer." She moved over as the brunette cut between them.

"I love your hair," Jennifer commented, staring at herself in the mirror. "I've thought about going blonde, but my hair is so dark it would turn brassy and awful." She flipped her large curls over her left shoulder, then her right.

"OMG, look at us!" Natalie gasped. She pulled out her cell phone and snapped a picture of their reflections. "A blonde, a brunette, and a redhead walk into a bathroom. This needs a punch line."

"You're a punch line." Jennifer pouted her lips and pulled out some gloss.

Samantha faked a smile. "L-O-L." She began searching her mind for an excuse to leave.

"You're very pretty," Natalie prattled. "You should come to cheerleading tryouts with us tonight. We're going to ride with Becca up to Spencer to join the squad."

"What?"

"Spencer. That little town just north of here?"

"I don't know what you're talking about." Samantha glanced at the door.

"You know how we share a football team? We also have to share cheerleaders."

"Last year there were only four of us," Jennifer said. "I'm trying to triple the size of the squad this year. We're nonexistent compared to Marshfield High."

"Our dance team for basketball season is kickin', though," Natalie bounced in place. "Just about our whole grade is in it. And a couple older girls."

"Thanks, but I don't think I can help you." Samantha frowned. "Not a gymnast."

Natalie wagged her finger. "It's not like we're doing round-off backhand springs and pyramids. This isn't *Bring It On*. Twelve girls

16

who are too drunk to drive are not going to get on top of each other stacked three-high. Unless we're at Dylan Moede's house."

"Shut your whore mouth." Jennifer pinched Natalie in the arm.

"Don't touch my arm fat," she squealed. "And I'm not the whore. Marissa was eating his face in the hot tub for twenty minutes. Here, I think I got a picture of it."

"OMG you little skeaze! Show me," Jennifer commanded. Natalie scrolled through the phone as Samantha backed up towards the door. Jennifer snagged her sleeve.

"We're not leaving without seeing Dylan's stomach," she growled. "It's legendary."

"Found it!" Natalie chimed. She flashed the picture.

"Look at Marissa's face," Jennifer snorted. "It's like she's at an all-you-can-eat buffet."

"This is way too much for me to see on my first day." Samantha's face turned as red as her blouse. "I'm going back to lunch."

"You gave your pizza to Stoner. You have no lunch." Jennifer smirked. "What are your thoughts on this?" She tossed the phone to Samantha.

"It's so chiseled," Natalie observed. "He's got, like, an ironing board."

"You mean washboard." Jennifer adjusted her earrings.

"Who's this Marissa chick?" Samantha asked. "Someone said I looked like her earlier today."

"She was in the Catholic school system since second grade, but last year she got pregnant and transferred to Senior High." Jennifer laughed. "Don't worry, it's not Dylan's baby. He's got ninety-nine problems but she ain't one. Sexting, however…you don't even have to send pics back. It's insane. But then he got into Snapchat and now I have so little evidence."

"He never commits though." Natalie pulled out her lip gloss and started retouching in the mirror. "He's too focused on getting drafted to the NBA. He's never had a real girlfriend."

Samantha couldn't hide her disdain. "He's a player."

"In every way," sighed Natalie. "He's sooo much fu—" She

turned and glowered at Samantha. "I lied. He reads, he's boring and always does his homework."

"Anyway, you want to come with us tonight?" Jennifer locked Samantha's gaze. "I don't cast invites like this to everyone."

"I'll think about it." Samantha tossed the phone back to Jennifer, who passed it to Natalie.

"Let me know by the end of the day," Jennifer flipped her hair, "or I will find you." She stared Samantha down. "Seriously, I will find you." The bell rang and Samantha escaped the bathroom.

SHE FOUND a group of boys in blue letter-jackets blocking her locker. "Excuse me," she said. They parted a little for her and resumed talking as she opened her locker and pulled out her books. One of the taller boys leaned on the locker next to hers, and stared at her. She took a breath and turned to look at him.

Dark hair, brown eyes, and a glowing summer tan greeted her. Thick eyebrows and well-shaped lips contorted as he smirked. "Hi, I'm Matt."

"Matt who?" Samantha replied, feeling her heart flutter a little. Hello dimples—and what a sudden onslaught of eye contact.

"Matt Stauber. I'm on the football team. I'm hoping you're going to join the cheerleading squad. We need more girls to pump up the crowds for us. Has Jennifer talked to you yet?"

Samantha groaned inside, but smiled at him. "Yes, and I told her I'd consider it." She pulled more books from her locker and took out her schedule.

Matt lingered. He snatched the paper from her hands and scanned it. Then he grinned down at her indignant face. "We have Spanish together next. Walk with me."

"I can find it by myself. This school has, like, three hallways."

"Cool, cool. I just figured it would be less awkward walking there next to you if you agreed to come with me."

"It's okay to walk alone," Samantha countered. She shut her locker, snatched the paper back, and headed down the hallway to her class. Matt was right next to her in lockstep, having grabbed his backpack off the floor without losing pace. She tried not to look at him, but the way he strutted was distracting her. He was enjoying every sideways glance, she could feel it. The Spanish room was the last one on the right, and Samantha found on arrival it was mostly full. Matt held her up so long the back desks were unavailable.

She was resigned to sit in the middle, and Matt plopped down in the seat next to her. As much as she didn't appreciate the invasion of space, she couldn't stop her pulse from racing, nor ignore his movements. She glanced at him, but he was opening his notebook, pretending he didn't notice her. She couldn't help the flustered look on her face as the teacher walked in with a *"silencio por favor."* Samantha turned to face the front of the room.

"Pssst!" She glanced to her right. Matt handed a note to her. She rolled her eyes and took it, unfolding it discreetly as a syllabus was slapped on her desk. She glanced up at Señorita Black.

"I don't recognize this one," she said.

"I'm new," Samantha replied.

"I know." Señorita Black peered at her. "Finish reading that note by the time I'm done passing these out. After that, it's mine." Samantha nodded, the color draining from her face. She looked down at the note as Señorita Black moved along.

"Que es tu nombre de telefono?" Samantha read in a whisper. She clicked her pen and scribbled her cell down before handing it back, heart pounding. She tried to watch Matt out of the corner of her eye as Señorita Black began writing her name on the board. He stared ahead, but his thumbs were gliding on the surface of his phone. She felt a little rush in her stomach as he glanced at her. She slid her phone out of her bag, thanking God it was on silent, and watched as his message appeared.

'Notice she won't translate her last name.'

She blinked at the screen. Unable to think of a response, she dropped her phone into her bag as Matt snickered. Señorita Black whirled around and glared.

Samantha knew he was going to be trouble.

LEVI LEANED against the stone wall just outside the front doors to the school, waiting for the new girl to make an appearance. Students flowed out of the building, running to parents' vehicles. Levi's truck was parked on the opposite side of the building by the tech shop garage entrance. Still too young to legally drive it, he always waited until the other students left to avoid notice. It gave him more time to nap. But he needed the psychology notes as well. Then he saw her with Jennifer, Natalie and Becca in tow.

"I said I'll think about it," she huffed as she came out the doors.

"Hey!" Levi called. They all stopped and looked at him. "The notes?" Jennifer glowered at him like he was trash.

"Oh, yeah, hang on." Samantha pulled a notebook out of her backpack. "I want it back tomorrow before class."

"I'll make sure you get it. Thanks." But she didn't respond. The girls already crowded her up to what could only be her mother's SUV. Levi watched as words were exchanged through the open window. The girls squealed and dragged Samantha down the sidewalk as the SUV drove away. "They stole her."

JENNIFER RIPPED OFF SAMANTHA'S BACKPACK and shoved her in the back of Becca's red Dodge Neon. Natalie sat on her left, and Jennifer called shotgun. In the driver's seat, Becca's chin barely reached over the steering wheel. "So girlies, we're going to stop at Laderia's casa, and then we're off to Spencer for cheerleading tryouts. It's going to be delicious-o."

"For serio," Natalie chimed in as they laughed. They pulled out of the lot.

"Who's Laderia?" Samantha pulled sunglasses from her bag.

"The richest girl in school," Natalie twirled her hair. "She is soooo much fun!"

"And soooo fat." Jennifer popped her gum.

"She always cuts gym class," Becca explained. "We're picking her up. Her family got back from the Bahamas this morning."

Jennifer tisked and slid on her own sunglasses. "Roll down the windows, bitches." She pulled a CD out of a huge leather case and put it in the player. "We're going to be pimpin' this track." She hit play, and *Blurred Lines* came on.

"This song is so old now." Samantha's comment was inaudible beneath Robin Thicke's voice and pounding bass. The girls' hair blew wildly in the wind. She wrinkled her nose; the air smelled like cows. "Kill me…" She put a hand over her nose and mouth in a sad attempt to block out the world. They were crossing town, exploring places new to Samantha. She found herself looking out the window in interest. Taking 5th Street down to Peach, they took a right on Blodgett, a left on Hume, then a right onto Fillmore. Jennifer punched the music off. Becca made an indignant noise.

"Park so we can show Sammy Symanski Laderia's pimpin' casa," Jennifer commanded.

"Please don't call me that." Samantha groaned as Becca pulled over.

Jennifer jumped out of the car and stood on the curb. "Becca, where's your Zippo? Hustle, Sammy!"

"Better do what she says." Becca gave Samantha a knowing smile before opening her door. Samantha rolled her eyes and got out. They stood on a long, green swath of land with a house-lined street on either side that ran to the edge of town and ended at a manicured hill. Samantha thought it resembled a mini version of the Washington Mall, and felt a huge pang of homesickness.

"The richest girl in school lives in one of *these* houses?"

"No, in the Fillmore Estate." Becca pointed to the hill. Jennifer puffed on a cigarette; she tossed the lighter to Becca. Samantha squinted behind her sunglasses. She could barely make out the many peaks of what appeared to be a large brick house.

"Isn't it cool?!" Natalie bounced.

It certainly wasn't the Capitol Building.

Jennifer ground her cigarette into the grass. "Let's get Laderia so we're not late for tryouts."

Piling back in the car, they drove to the end of Fillmore Street where it intersected with Galvin. There, the pillar-flanked private drive of the Fillmore Estate began, at least a city block long. By the time the driveway ended, the house loomed over them like an overblown Howard County McMansion. Samantha's gut wrenched with wistfulness for the D.C. metro.

Parking in front of the double doors, they rushed up to ring the bell. A shrill voice pierced the wind. "I'm coming bitches!"

They heard a pounding of feet, then suddenly the front doors flew open. There stood Laderia, shorter than Samantha, but as wide as she was tall, with deep tan skin and thick black hair. Her clothes hugged her body tight, her dark eyes glittered with fun. "OMG, it's New Girl." Samantha thought Laderia would eat her for lunch.

Unsure of what to say, she held out her hand. "Samantha Symanski."

"Laderia Malaria." Laderia shook her hand with vigor and what could only be described as a chortle. "Is your name for serio?"

"Is yours?" The awkward pause broke under the weight of Laderia's laughter.

"Of course not, I'm just mocking you! Laderia Valdez. Like, Exxon Valdez."

Samantha's brow furrowed. "You're named after an oil spill?"

"She's named after a ship," Jennifer drawled. Natalie giggled. Laderia's smile faltered for a moment.

"Your house is very cool." Samantha looked around. "Reminds me of a castle."

"You're a sweetie." Showing teeth, the larger girl convinced Samantha she could eat her in one gulp. "Want a tour?"

"You'd have to step aside first." Natalie struck a pose. "I need to use the bathroom." She pranced past Laderia into the house and disappeared. Laderia pouted her lips and called after Natalie. "Your bladder is smaller than your brain!"

"We have to get to Spencer. Now!" Becca looked at her phone. "Tryouts start in half an hour."

"I'm ready." Laderia slung a bag over her shoulder. "Got my uniform."

"You're a cheerleader?" Samantha blurted the question in shock before she could stop herself.

"I'm also on Dance Team."

Samantha could feel Jennifer's disapproval permeating the air.

Natalie reappeared at Laderia's shoulder. "Ready." They piled into Becca's car. Samantha, Laderia and Natalie squeezed into the back, and they were on their way.

"I can't see," Becca huffed, fiddling with the rearview mirror at a stop light.

"I'm not sorry that my awesomeness takes up your entire view," Laderia countered.

"I am," Natalie squeaked, squished to the door. Samantha was too squished to say anything.

They started moving again. Jennifer turned the radio off, grabbed the rearview mirror and looked Laderia in the eyes. "Didn't your dad make a deal with you about getting a car or something?"

"Yeah, if I get below two-hundred pounds, I get a new jeep. If I get below one-fifty, I get an Audi TTS convertible. In hot pink."

"So why aren't you *working* on it?" The car was silent except for the wind whistling through the windows.

"Because…if it wasn't for my fat ass, you girls would have nothing to orbit and dance around in your stupid routines. I hold that shit together." Laderia snapped her fingers as she glared at Jennifer in the mirror. Samantha burst out laughing. Becca turned the station and reduced the tension. The sign for Spencer flew by, and soon they were parking at Columbus's sister school.

THE GRAVEL OF MEADOW LANE kicked up and clattered against the underside of Levi's truck as he pulled onto the restricted road leading through the marsh, hoping he was out of sight. McMillan Marsh was alive with the droning of insects and birds chirping. He grabbed the shovel and gloves out of the backseat and shut the door. Ten feet through the growth on the right lay the shallow grave he managed to dig for his wannabe-vampire much earlier that morning. He had placed the dead man face-down in the hole to keep those lightless eyes from looking at him. He pulled his collar up over his nose.

The sun baked the body all day and the smell was terrible. Flies coated everything. He suppressed his urge to vomit, knowing it would be better not to leave piles of his DNA around a makeshift grave. Levi shoveled dirt onto the corpse's back. Insects buzzed in an angry cloud with each toss. He tried to think about other things.

Levi's mind wandered to the new girl, Samantha. He wondered if he would have time to copy the notes for class before returning her notebook. The stink brought him back to the task at hand, the air heavy with the smell of feces. Levi knew bodies released the contents of their bowels upon death, but he didn't realize just how intense it would be when mixed with the normally-horrid smell of the marsh. No collar or bandana over the face could shield him from the stench. But as he shoveled, he thought his nose detected something else.

Something smoking.

Pot?

His stomach dropped as he stood up straight and whirled around. Standing four feet from him was a kid with spiked blonde hair, wearing a black leather jacket and jeans. A joint smoldered in his fingers.

"Dude, what the *fuck* is that smell?" said the kid.

Levi felt a surge of heat in his ears and forehead as panic took over. He whipped the shovel like a club, startling the kid back.

"Geeze man, cool it!" The kid turned tail and ran. Levi could not let him get away. If it took two deaths to preserve his cover, oh well. It was either that or let Marshfield go dark.

Levi pounded after the kid, who bolted down Meadow Lane as fast as he could, and felt a surge of power as he realized he was almost on him. He leapt onto the kid's back and tackled him to the ground. They rolled across the gravel, small stones ripping their flesh, leaving cuts and scrapes everywhere. Levi pinned the kid to the ground. One hand gripped the kid's throat, the other fished for a stake from his pocket. A stab of disappointment hit him as he realized he left all his stakes in his sports bag. He settled for his keys.

"Wait Levi! Stop!" The kid caught Levi's arm as he was about to plunge the keys into his neck. Recognition pulsed through Levi, but he couldn't put a name to the face. He paused. The kid took the opportunity and punched him in the jaw. Levi fell backward, stunned.

The kid rolled away. Standing up, he pulled a gun from his pants pocket.

"Stay the fuck down, Levi Mauer!" The gun shook in his hands, his glazed eyes wide. "Don't move," he sputtered.

"Tim?" Levi felt the adrenaline rush ebb as the blood began to pound more slowly in his ears.

"Shut up! I saw that body. I saw it!"

"Tim, what are you talking about?"

"The dead guy!"

Levi scanned their surroundings. The road remained vacant except for his truck, about a hundred feet back. There was no sign of anyone else around. "How did you get here, Tim? Did you follow me?"

"No, man. I-I got kicked out of history for wearing jeans. I had a smoke in your truck bed…and fell asleep."

Irritation colored Levi's voice. "You've been using my truck as a smoke den?"

"Hold off, Jet Li. To be fair, I thought that piece of shit was the next tech ed fixer-upper." Tim reached for his ear, scratched the back of his head, and lowered his gun. "I dropped my joint somewhere over there." He glanced back to the truck, disappointment covering his face. Levi stood up. Tim pointed the gun at his head. "Don't fuck with me, man."

"Tim, why the hell do you have a gun?"

"Dealing demands a certain level of protection." Tim ran a hand through his hair. "You never know who's going to beat your ass for a gram of coke."

Levi rolled his eyes. "And they think *I'm* the stoner…"

"Yeah," Tim chuckled. "You're a murderer instead."

Levi kicked the gun out of Tim's hand, propelling it into the air and caught it. Tim rubbed his hand and made a face. Looking the gun up and down, Levi muttered, "You had the safety on." He clicked the safety off and aimed it squarely between Tim's eyes. Tim started to tremble.

"Listen to me, Tim," he said calmly, "that man was a psychopath, and he got what was coming to him. You could tell the cops, but I doubt they'd believe a druggie like you. But now you know where the body is, and that's a problem."

"Please don't kill me," Tim whispered, his eyes closed tight. "Please, Levi."

"No, Tim, I won't kill you today." He paused. "You're going to bury that asshole. Got it...accomplice?" He lowered the gun.

Tim opened his eyes and wiped his cheeks on his leather sleeves. "Huh?"

SAMANTHA FLOPPED face-first onto her bed, breathing in the familiar smell of her comforter. "My body aches..." Brandon came strolling into her room.

"You're a pansy," he said. "It's cheerleading. That's just girl stuff."

"It's not the cheerleading that hurts, it was getting squished by Laderia in Becca's clown car." She rolled over and stared at the ceiling. Her eyes traced a lone crack that wound its way past the light. "I'm never riding in the backseat again."

"Suck it up, cupcake. You don't learn to drive until next year," her mother's voice chimed from the hallway. "Did you get any big homework assignments?"

"No. I took a lot of notes and my English teacher is making us read *Julius Caesar*, but I read that *last* year. I told her I didn't want to read it again, and she said 'Oh, it should be easy for you, then.' Screw her."

"Watch your mouth!" came the sharp reply from the hallway. "Your brother is only ten years old!"

"I'm eleven!" Brandon yelled back. "Geeze mom, when are you gonna remember that? You're so stupid! You're stupid all the time!" He stormed into his room and slammed the door shut.

"Wow, touchy," Samantha observed. "I think he's mad at you."

"He is not." Mrs. Symanski strolled into the room with a laundry basket under one arm and a box under the other. "He's frustrated. He's not good at football. But that will change as long as he keeps going to practices." She plopped both the box and the laundry basket on the bed next to Samantha. "Here's some more of your stuff. You should find places for it. Tonight. So I don't have to come in here and see a mess." She pulled the clothes out of the laundry basket and began folding them. "Talk to me, Sam. How was your first day?"

"Mom, this move was a bad idea." Samantha grabbed a shirt and helped fold. "I don't know anyone but they all seem to know me. I don't get their jokes, and they don't laugh when I tell mine. Their music is, like, six months behind—at best—and every other station is country, '80s, or Christian rock. Pandora and Spotify are my only hope."

"That's the culture shock talking. You'll find your groove. There's more to this town than there seems. At least none of the houses are clones."

"We stopped by the mall after practice. It's the size of the food court in the Columbia Mall, and half the stores are empty. They don't even have a Victoria's Secret."

"There used to be," her mother frowned. "If I remember correctly...maybe not."

"Mom, you dragged us into the middle of nowhere. You know that Spencer High School is about the same size as Columbus? Both schools put together don't make up a grade at River Hill. That's not healthy."

"Stop it Samantha. If you keep your mind closed like that, you're going to isolate yourself. In a town this small, that's the worst thing you can do. Tell me something you liked about your day."

"Well, I talked to a football player," she said with a flush. "He's gorgeous, and not a meathead."

"Uh-huh." Her mother smiled. "Not all bad, then."

"No, you're right, not all bad. How was your day?"

27

"I spent a lot of time moving furniture and unpacking boxes. I want to paint some rooms, but I have to figure out how to take wallpaper down first. It's not very inviting."

"There's a lot of wallpaper," Samantha agreed as she shoved clothes into her dresser drawers. "Maybe we could paint my room first. I hate white walls."

"We'll have to find a color that shows off your butterfly collection. Speaking of, they're in that box right there." Her mother stacked the remaining folded clothes in the basket and proceeded to Brandon's room.

Samantha sorted through the box her mother brought, and pulled out a bunch of her collectible glass butterflies and lined them up on her bookcase. She retrieved a photo album, settled on her bed, and flipped through it. She stopped and studied her parents' wedding photo. It was the earliest one she had of them together, taken as they kissed in front of the priest. She noticed a wooden castle towering in the background inside the church behind the altar. Scrawled handwriting on the bottom of the photo read 'Daniel and Sandra Symanski, St. John's, Marshfield, WI.' She felt a hitch in her throat as her fingertips traced the picture.

"Mom!"

"What!" came the distant reply.

"Can we go to St. John's for church on Sunday?"

"No, we're registered at Our Lady of Peace. Since when did you want to go to church anyway?"

"I heard it was pretty. Let's go on Sunday!" She heard footsteps coming down the hall and she quickly shoved the photo album under her pillow. Her mother appeared in the doorway, face covered in Noxzema.

"You really want to go?"

"Well, we don't have to if it's that big of a deal." Samantha crossed her arms.

"I'm just surprised. We'll go. Mass is at nine instead of ten, though, so if you're not up early we'll have to go to Our Lady of Peace."

"I can get up."

Her mother laughed. "I'll believe it when I see it."

LEVI'S TRUCK RATTLED as they sat at the light at the intersection of Central Avenue and McMillan. Tim winced next to him, rubbing his raw, dirty hands.

"I hate red lights," Levi moaned. "There's nobody around."

"Run it," Tim shot back.

Levi glanced in the rearview mirror. "Nah, I can't. That cop from the Walmart parking lot is behind us now."

"Why don't you just turn yourself in?" Tim nursed his blisters and calluses. "I need a joint or something." The light finally turned green and they headed down Central, going exactly the speed limit, the officer close behind.

Levi's palms began to sweat as they passed another police car sitting at the entrance to the Shopko parking lot. "Marshfield's got too many cops."

"It's because of the Clinic. With all that money—they want cops, they get cops."

"Why would they want so many?" Levi glanced over at Tim, who stared out the window at the massive gray buildings looming on the hill in the middle of town.

"Weird shit happens here, in case you haven't noticed." Tim gave Levi a strange look. "For instance, you killing a guy and making me bury him in the marsh."

"You wouldn't understand," Levi grumbled. "So I'm not going to explain. Where do you live?"

"Why? I thought you were going to drop me off at school."

"Change of plans." Levi pulled out Tim's gun as the cop behind them turned off onto Veterans Parkway. "Tell me now, where do you live?"

"Fuck man, I'm sick of you pointing that thing at me..."

"I'm not fucking with you, Tim, my ass is on the line here. You think I committed some horrible crime. You want me to go to jail."

"Because that's justice," Tim muttered. "You kill someone, you lose your life on the outside. It's fucking justice."

"You're a moron!" Levi yelled, clicking off the safety and pressing the gun to Tim's temple. "I've already killed once, Tim. Do you need any more proof than the body you buried and this gun to your head that when I ask you something and you don't answer, there won't be fucking consequences?!" Tim held very still as they drove. They stopped at the 4th Street intersection. "Where the fuck do you park your sorry ass at night?"

"I have an apartment. It's above the Red Cross office. Across from the Holiday Inn."

Levi put the gun down. "That's better."

They drove to the Red Cross office, a lonely building with gravel parking and a billboard decrying porn wedged on one side. Levi pulled into the lot and parked his rattling truck. He flicked off the lights and turned to face Tim, who was white as a ghost. "What's your problem?"

"You're going to make me overdose in my bathtub or slit my wrists to make it look like a suicide, or—"

"Stick your own gun in your mouth and blow your head off?"

"No, that would make too much noise," Tim frowned. "You're not *that* stupid."

"You're too kind." They got out, Levi scrutinizing every move Tim made. They went to a door in the side of the building. "What are you waiting for?"

Trembling, Tim took out his keys. "You promise you won't kill me?"

"I promised I wouldn't kill you back at the marsh, Tim. Open the fucking door." In a moment it was open, and they went up a flight of stairs to what had to be the oddest apartment Levi ever saw. The walls were canary yellow, and so were the cabinets, and so was the sink. The crown molding and ornate window casings flaked white paint. The Berber carpet was layered with off-colored stains.

"Did Big Bird explode in here?"

"The yellow hides the watermarks." Tim walked over to a ratty-looking couch and fell into it face-first. "Ahh, so good to be

30

home…" Levi wanted to disagree, but after such a long day, he had to admit there was something about the place that made you want to close your eyes and never wake up.

"Where's the bedroom?"

"I have two." Tim lifted his face up. "Next to the bathroom."

"Do you live alone?" Levi raised the gun, looking down the narrow yellow hall with three doors. He carefully opened the first one which revealed a bathroom as hideously yellow as the rest of the apartment.

"I used to live with my brother," Tim replied from the living room. Levi opened the next door and found the switch. The light barely illuminated a small bedroom with a worn-out mattress and no bed sheets. "That was his, and the first room I painted yellow. He hates that color." Tim let out a dark chuckle.

Levi rolled his eyes and moved to the final door. It creaked like it was being opened for the first time in a hundred years. He couldn't see, so he felt for a switch. His fingers grazed it, then stars exploded in front of his eyes. He flew forward into the room as everything went black.

Chapter 2

Back to Life

Levi woke to a pounding headache. He tried to rub his temples, but found his hands bound behind his back. He was in a yellow room, wrapped in duct tape, his face pressed into a nasty carpet. He rolled onto his back and awkwardly sat up. This was Tim's living room, and judging by the brightening sky, school would be starting soon. He felt his pulse accelerate. He hated being late.

"Good morning." Tim strode in, yawning, gun in hand. "How'd you sleep, motherfucker?"

"Let me go." Levi wriggled in the tape. "We'll be late for school."

"Tardiness is your biggest concern right now? You're a psycho." Tim sat on the couch. "Psychos don't need school."

"I need to be at Columbus."

"Why? Rubbing elbows with the daughter of the Chief of Police make murder extra hot for you or something?"

"I don't give a fuck about Jennifer," Levi murmured. "Besides, everyone knows you're in love with her."

Tim flushed. "I am not."

"I'm guessing you get off on selling discounted drugs to her."

"I do not." Tim turned away, red to his ears. "You say that like you know so much about me, but I know a lot more about you. I know you killed a guy."

"You don't know who he is."

"I know where you buried him."

"Technically *you* buried him."

"Because *you* forced me to." Tim began pacing.

"The cops are not going to believe a gun-wielding drug peddler over a guy tied up in said peddler's apartment." Levi was calm.

"I made a citizen's arrest."

"You've got no case. If you turn me in, you'll go to jail instead."

"Damn it Levi." Tim flopped back onto his couch. "Why does it feel like we keep having the same conversation over and over again?"

"Because we are. Either let me go or change the subject."

Tim shrugged and sighed. "Who was that guy?"

"What guy?"

"The motherfucker you made me bury."

"I don't know yet," Levi replied.

"Really? You mean you just killed some poor random?" Tim peered at him. "Just because you felt like it?"

"I thought I had to."

"The voices told you to do it, right?" Tim chuckled.

"I thought he was a vampire, shithead." Levi waited for Tim's reaction. Tim continued chuckling.

"Everyone knows vampires aren't real," he replied. "If you'd have said he was a werewolf, I'd give you some credit. Those are some scary motherfuckers. But a vampire? Who do you think you are, Biff the Vampire Slayer?"

"More or less," Levi said. "But as it turned out, he wasn't a vampire—"

"Obviously." Tim studied the gun in his hand.

"Yet. I killed him before he turned."

"Bullshit," Tim shook his head. "I'm calling bullshit."

"Call it what you want."

Tim squinted at Levi and leaned closer. "How would you even become a vampire?"

"You have to drink the blood of a vampire to get the curse. Untie me."

"I thought they just had to bite you."

"Wrong again, shithead. They drink blood to steal people's remaining years, so it's not like they need to bite people all the time. That's why you never really hear about it. And, of course, because I do a damned good job."

Tim let out a hollow laugh. "How many vampires have you killed?"

"Five. Untie me."

"Whatever. How many werewolves?"

"I've never seen a werewolf. Just vampires. Untie me. Now!"

"There are no vampires in Marshfield."

"Yet again, you're wrong. They live regular lives like you and me." Levi thought for a moment. "Well, maybe we're not such good examples. But vampires age for a while, fake their deaths, then come back to drink blood to regain their youth. Then they pose as someone from the next generation. It's a fucking *long* process to figure out if someone is a vampire."

Tim stared at Levi for a good minute, the cogs in his head straining. "Okay, I'll play. Do you think I'm a vampire?"

Levi rolled his eyes. "Of course not."

"That's good news. I don't believe you're a... whatever it is you think you are. But I think you believe it."

Levi stared at Tim. "What the hell is that supposed to mean?"

"Prove it," Tim said finally. "If there are vampires in Marshfield, I'd like to see it for myself."

"You may not live through it." Levi shrugged. "But I can do that. It may take some time to find one, so you'll have to come with me when I do the rounds."

Tim nodded, lost in thought.

After what felt like five minutes of waiting, Levi cleared his throat. "Tim, we're late for school. Untie me."

"Oh... right, okay."

SAMANTHA LOOKED WITH FURY at the empty desk to her right. Mr. Becker was droning on about ethical principles of psychology, and here she was, in the darkened room, writing her notes in the back of her algebra notebook.

It was completely unacceptable.

Her phone vibrated in her purse, and she wanted to check it, but the light would be too easy for Mr. Becker to see. She clicked her pen and sighed.

"LEVI, YOU KNOW BETTER than this," Barb glared over her glasses. "As for you Tim, I'm pleasantly surprised you decided to join us at all." They were sitting in her cramped office.

"You know I love you Babs." Tim cracked a smile that melted under her heated glare. "I'm sorry, Principal."

"You should be," she said. "Coming to school in *jeans*?! Are you completely devoid of decency? Do you have another pair of pants in your backpack?"

Tim shook his head.

"In your locker?"

He shook his head. Barb's lips stretched into a thin line.

Levi could feel what was coming, and he had to stop it.

"Well, Tim, maybe you should go home, change and then come ba—"

"I have an extra pair in my locker," Levi jumped in. "He can borrow them for the day and return them after classes. We're about the same size anyway."

Tim's face fell.

Barb's gaze shifted back and forth between them. "Tim, go wait in the hall. I want to speak to Levi in private."

Levi felt his blood pounding as Tim got up to leave. What if Tim reported him? What if the cops *did* listen? What if—?

"What are you doing, Levi Mauer?" Barb slid her glasses off. "Driving your truck here just before school started! People saw you park. You're fifteen years old—a sophomore. What if someone turns you in for driving without a license? The repercussions—"

"Barb, I've got a lot on my plate right now," Levi interrupted.

"Levi, I've been more than accommodating. As a young vampire slayer, you've got a lot of odd responsibilities. Which leads me to my next question. Why are you hanging out with a drug addict?" Barb's eyes were penetrating. "He's only going to add to your troubles."

"Tell me about it," Levi said dryly.

Barb's lips disappeared. He felt her committing every scrape on his face to memory. "What happened?"

"I had to take care of something," Levi replied. "Tim saw everything, but he doesn't understand what he saw. Now he keeps threatening to go to the police. I have to keep him close."

"Good Lord. What did he see?"

Levi was silent.

"Levi?"

"It's better that you not know."

Barb leaned back in her chair. "I hate to do this, Levi, but you've left me no choice. If you cannot keep your affairs sufficiently under wraps, you'll have to be home-schooled."

"Principal Barb!" Levi's jaw dropped. "I *have to* protect this school."

"Levi, *I* have to protect this school." Barb shifted some papers on her desk. "We are on hallowed ground. We don't need your slaying skills past the sidewalk. I cannot show any sort of favoritism toward you, and I cannot have the school implicated if the police find you *driving* underage. Especially if other students begin making wild accusations against you. We are, after all, a private school, and we're not doing as well as we had in the past. We can't afford a lawsuit."

"Barb, my family has been attending this school since it opened. My tuition is paid in full for my entire high school career." Levi couldn't believe his luck today. "I need the protection of hallowed ground. If you kick me out, I'll never get any sleep."

"Levi, you have a home."

"It's not secure."

"That's ridiculous. Your parents wouldn't be living there if it wasn't secure." Levi had to force himself to stay seated and silent after her comment as Barb evaluated him. "It's my right as head of this school to ask students to leave when they disrupt—"

"If you kick me out, you owe me fifteen thousand dollars of tuition."

Barb shook her head and raised her hands in the air. "I am not throwing you out right now. If you can find a way to handle the situation with Tim that won't harm the school or the student body, I'll let you stay. Is that fair?"

Levi thought for a moment. "So I can't kill him."

"Absolutely not," Barb murmured half-heartedly.

"What do you mean exactly, when you say the situation is *handled*?"

"As long as I don't get a call from the police or a parent regarding Tim or yourself, you're good."

"And if Tim does something stupid that has nothing to do with me?"

"You better hope he doesn't."

"That's *not* fair and you know it as well as I do." Levi glared at her. "I'm completely serious about the money." He leaned forward in his seat, daring her to continue.

"It's as fair as I'm getting," Barb replied, unimpressed. "Go get that kid into a pair of khakis and get to class before I change my mind."

SAMANTHA ROLLED HER EYES when Levi entered English class, nodding to the teacher. He took an empty desk a row over. Samantha made sure to send him a withering glare. He glanced at her, nodded, and began taking notes in a tattered notebook.

When the bell rang, she tailgated him out of the room.

"So."

"So…" He gave her an awkward stare. She found it infuriating.

"Guess what I took notes in today in psychology?"

"A notebook."

"My *math* notebook." She glowered up at him. "You said you'd give my psychology notes back before class. Keyword *before*."

"Ya, about that… I still haven't had a chance to copy the notes. I'll get it back to you at lunch."

Samantha huffed. "I guess so. But you can find someone else to get notes from if you're going to keep pulling this."

"It's the first time. It won't happen again. I had something come up," Levi groaned. "Women today…"

"Ugh!" Natalie popped up out of nowhere. "Good gravy, Sammy Symanski, is Stoner being sexist?"

Levi headed off down the hall.

"Good gravy?" Samantha raised an eyebrow. "Is that a common expression here?"

"About as common as *y'all*," Natalie shot back. "You don't take the Lord's name in vain. OMG, don't be so naive. Hmm, he's walking with Tim. Stoner and Dealer finally meet. That might cut into Jennifer's stash."

"Whatever." Samantha walked to her locker, Natalie at her heels. "What do you want, Natalie?"

"Jennifer sent me to update you on the plan for tonight."

"Why didn't she just text me or something?"

"The B took her phone away. She's gotta wait until the end of the day to get it back. Anyway, we've got cheerleading practice, then we're going shopping. We need cool clothes for Color Week—"

"What are you talking about?"

"Shopping. You know, going and purchasing something you like? As opposed to something you don't, which we call errands."

"I get *that*. What's Color Week?"

Natalie gasped out loud. "OMG, they didn't have Color Week at River Mill?!"

"It's River *Hill*. Define 'Color Week.'"

"It's, like, the best week of the school year!" Natalie gushed. "We have a different dress-up theme each day, games and competitions between grades, and a pep rally with tons of posters where we scream at each other like it's a big deal! It's awesome!"

"Why?"

38

"O-M-G! Because at the end of the week is the Homecoming Game and then HOMECOMING!"

"Oh," Samantha shrugged. "It's Spirit Week."

"No, it's *Color* Week. Each grade has a different color. Last year we were yellow. Freshmen are always yellow—like cowards."

"Right, the whole first-year jitters kinda thing."

Natalie nodded. "Sophomores are green, because, well, too old to be cowards and too young to know much. Juniors are always red, because, um, ya, and seniors are blue!"

"So we're green?"

"Ya! And we have to dress up in costumes for five days!"

"What about mass Tuesday morning?"

"We change in the bathroom after mass. Did they *really* not have Color Week at your old school?" Natalie frowned.

"It's possible. I guess I never noticed."

"Wow, that's sad. Didn't they have Homecoming?"

"Of course."

"What did you wear?"

"I don't remember," Samantha lied.

"A strapless gold metallic dress that came down to my knees and black heels, with a little golden flapper hat, and a white faux-fur shawl," Natalie answered, even though Samantha hadn't asked.

"That sounds...well...what was the theme last year?"

"Mobster Mash!"

LEVI'S HAND ACHED as he hurriedly copied Samantha's notes in study hall. His head pounded, but he wasn't sure if it was from Barb's threat, Samantha's attitude, or from Tim knocking him out the night before.

"This bites," he muttered. Tim sat across from him at the table. Columbus held study hall in the library—if one could call it a library. Bookshelves that hadn't seen new volumes since the 90s took up one half of the room, and a collection of computers and tables dominated the other half. Mrs. Hansen busied herself behind the librarian's desk, crocheting some monstrosity from pink and orange yarn.

"You know what else bites? Vampires," Tim snickered. Levi kicked him under the desk. Mrs. Hansen cleared her throat and shot them a glance without missing a stitch.

"That comment wasn't necessary," Levi murmured.

"Neither was the kick. You'll get my pants dirty."

"*My* pants."

Tim slouched back in his chair. "So what did big, bouncing, beautiful Babs say to you, all alone in her tiny little office?"

Levi flipped a page. "She threatened to expel me."

"But this is your first time being late," Tim squinted. "She didn't start that until like, my tenth time."

"There was no threat of police involvement with you."

"Not true. She almost caught me smoking. You wouldn't believe the lie I told her to get out of it."

"I don't care."

"I told her the smell was Father's new incense. She was snooping around the chapel and his office for weeks. I'm pretty sure he still doesn't know why."

"I'm almost done with these notes," Levi said. "Shut the fuck up."

"Don't burst a blister on my account. Still taking me on the rounds tonight?"

"Ya."

"What exactly are *the rounds?*"

"Sorting through obituaries, staking out new graves, mild stalking, the usual."

"Sounds fun, Biff."

AT LUNCH, Samantha sat with Jennifer, Natalie, and Becca. "Where's Laderia?"

"She's in the front office," Becca said.

"Uh-oh. Why?"

"Waiting for a delivery from China Chef." Natalie filed her nails. "It's Chinese Food Day today, right Jennifer?"

40

"I'm starving." Jennifer pushed the salad around on her tray. "She better not have forgotten my honey chicken."

"Y'all get Chinese food from Laderia?"

"Sure, she's really generous. You should give her your order next time." Becca shrugged.

Samantha's phone vibrated—a text from Matt. Jennifer narrowed her eyes and snatched the phone from her hands. Samantha made an indignant noise and felt a flush across her face.

"Why's Matt texting you?" She snickered a little and slid the phone back across the table. "He says 'meet me by the pop machine.' You'd better go."

"Make sure no one takes my food." Samantha grabbed her phone, stood up and walked out of the cafeteria, rounded the doorframe and bumped right into Levi.

"I was looking for you." He smiled down at her. She crossed her arms.

"What is it?" She eyed him curiously. He had a blonde boy by the collar, and the boy held a notebook in his hands.

"Give it to her, Tim." The boy named Tim handed her notebook back and Levi nodded to Samantha. "Thanks. You're a lifesaver."

"Better than a Sour Patch Kid, I suppose," she tucked a lock of hair behind her ear. "You're welcome. You can have my salad if you want." She pushed past them before he could thank her.

Matt leaned next to the art-filled trophy case by the soda machine. He met her gaze and grinned. She felt a thrill run up her spine and smiled back.

"My girl."

"Hey!" She mentally kicked herself for the over-enthusiastic tone. "What's up?"

"After the game on Friday, Dylan Moede's having a party." He looked around as if anticipating an interruption. "You should come."

Samantha barely remembered Natalie and Jennifer mentioning him in the bathroom the day before. "Where's the party?"

"Dylan's house. His parents will be at the racetrack, so it's pretty much unsupervised."

"Um, I don't know where he lives."

"He's just out of town on County Road H, you could ride with me. He's got a pond to swim in, and there's gonna be a bonfire. It's always a good time."

"My mom probably won't let me," she frowned. "But I'll see if I can make it. That's the best I've got right now."

"Cool." He beamed. "If you need a ride, let me know."

"YOU CAN'T HAVE IT," Jennifer said flatly. "She told us to guard it."

Levi grimaced. "Come on Jennifer." He released Tim, and the boy promptly turned and power-walked out of the cafeteria, disappearing down the hall. Levi felt his stomach drop and turned to go after him.

"Leave him alone," Jennifer commanded, putting a wonton in her mouth. "Laderia, where's the honey chicken?"

"I got sweet and sour." Laderia pulled it out of the bag.

"I said *honey*." Jennifer scowled.

"I'll take it." Levi threw up his hand.

"You *are* damn picky." Laderia narrowed her eyes at Jennifer. "Not coolio." Natalie's eyes were round as saucers as Jennifer's face grew cold.

"And you're a damn fatso. Here Levi, take the chicken, and the salad." She stood up. "I'm done. Where's Tim going anyway?"

"I don't know." Levi hoped against hope Tim hadn't called the police.

"You're useless." Jennifer left in the same direction Tim had gone.

"I hate it when she's low," Natalie sighed. "She's always so edgy."

"I don't get what her problem is," Laderia said, shoveling in rice. "I buy her everything."

"She's just stressed," Becca replied. "Her dad's threatened to get her drug tested again. Like he'd follow through."

"So I can take the chicken?" Levi asked.

Laderia nodded. "It's coolio."

MEMBERS OF THE SPENCER HIGH BAND interrupted cheerleading practice, insisting they would be performing during halftime at the Homecoming football game. When Jennifer demanded to know the song the band would play, their blank stares confirmed they had no idea. Feeling victorious, they resumed practice. Half an hour later, the sound of the gym doors flying open stopped them mid-routine and an auburn-haired girl stormed in.

"What's Kaeli Edwards doing here?" Natalie whispered to Samantha.

"As if I'd know," Samantha shrugged. "Who is she, anyway?"

"The star of the Columbus choir," Becca chimed in, words laced with venom. "She thinks she's Beyoncé or something because she has more trophies and awards than any senior."

"Hey girls." Kaeli's air of polite condescension communicated instantly to Samantha that this girl knew she was about to get her way. "I'm here because I heard there was some disagreement about who's performing the Homecoming halftime show. To clarify, it was already promised to the choir and the band."

"Oh really," Jennifer stated, arms crossed.

"Absolutely." Kaeli smiled and met Jennifer's glare without blinking. "The Homecoming game draws more spectators than the rest of our games put together. The band and choir show more support than a handful of cheerleaders with a boombox, don't you think?"

"You don't want to know what I think." Jennifer raised an eyebrow and Kaeli smiled wider. "But I'll tell you anyway, you presumptuous c—"

"Kaeli," another girl cut Jennifer off. "Jennifer and I spent all summer preparing this routine. We selected the perfect track to fit the Homecoming theme—"

"Nikki, I'm sure you did, but you know we have thirty band members per school and thirty-five choir members already prepared. You can't deny the privilege of the performance to so many other students. Comparatively speaking, your performance would make the school look bad. Both of our families want Columbus to succeed, and *my* way will show more school spirit than you girls ever can. I am sorry if that sounds…too honest." Kaeli put a hand on her chest. "I don't mean to hurt anyone's feelings. Have a great practice, girls!" She turned and walked through the gym doors, the dark cloud of oppression lifting when she vanished.

"If there's one girlio who will kill your spirit, it's Kaeli," Laderia announced.

"Well, now what do we do?" another girl asked. "This routine is useless."

"We can salvage it," said the girl named Nikki. "We'll just use it during a different game—"

"Are you really handing over the halftime show to Kaeli?!" Jennifer fumed.

"I am." Nikki sighed. "She's got a point. More students involved looks better for both Spencer *and* Columbus. As squad co-captain, we should take advantage of it."

After a somber practice, they were off to Goodwill to scrounge up costume materials.

"What are the dress-up days again?" Becca asked as they turned onto McMillan Street. "And what's the theme? I forgot to get a dress."

Natalie groaned. "I told you to come with me to get one *two weeks* before school started! The seniors picked 'Can't Fight the Moonlight.' Dumbest theme ever, but my silver strapless is gonna rock!"

"Are any of y'all on Homecoming Court?" Samantha asked.

"You know it!" Natalie bounced in her seat. "I was the freshman representative last year, and this year I'm going to be on it again!"

"Cool," Jennifer said in a perfect imitation of Mr. Becker's droning voice. "What are the dress-up days this year?"

"Vacation Day, Geek Chic Day, Duct Tape Day, Old People Day, and Color Day. Very uninspired if you ask me."

After purchasing their outfits, they dropped Samantha at her house. She walked up the steps to the front porch and entered the wood-paneled foyer.

"Mom, I'm home!"

"It's about time!" The reply came from somewhere in the house. "Where were you?"

"We had to get supplies for Spiri—um, Homecoming—Color—whatever-it-is Week."

Her mother appeared on the stairwell landing in a paint-covered t-shirt, her hair up in a bun. "Well, a call or a text would have been helpful. What if you were kidnapped?"

"I noticed you didn't call me either," Samantha replied. "You couldn't have been *that* worried."

"Don't you talk to me that way," her mother wagged a paint roller. "Now get up here and tell me what you think of this paint color in your brother's room." Samantha obliged and trudged up to see her mother's handiwork. They stood in the doorway looking into the green room.

"It's very…"

"I love it Sam. It's so peaceful and soothing. It should help calm Brandon a bit more. He's been so—feisty—these past few days. I think this is a really tough transition for him. He's not used to all the stuff kids do here. It would be so much easier if your father were around to teach him how to play sports. Anyway, I read a couple articles on color theory and moods. I spent all day at Menards and Sherwin Williams picking out colors. Walmart's were okay, but the brands didn't impress me. I'm doing the dining room in raspberry, the kitchen in off-white for contrast. I've been thinking of painting your room a lilac-gray, what do you think?"

"Can I go to a party after the football game on Friday?"

"Oh come on, Samantha," Mrs. Symanski sighed. "I spent all day working on this. The very least you could do is tell me your opinion. You're not even going to do that?"

"It's very…green," Samantha said. "Which is the sophomore color for Homecoming."

"Yes it is," her mother smiled. "We still have to get you a Homecoming dress! Want to go shopping on Saturday? We could go while your brother is at practice. Have a girls' day!"

"Actually mom, I'm already going with Jennifer and Laderia on Saturday."

"I could drive you guys."

"Becca's driving us."

Her mother's face fell. "Will you be home for dinner?"

"I don't know, maybe."

"What would you like? How about roast beef? Or lasagna? That was always your favorite."

"I haven't liked lasagna since I was six," Samantha wrinkled her nose. "You haven't really cooked since then. You were always too busy. Why start now?"

Mrs. Symanski shrugged. "Why not? We finally have a big kitchen, in a nice house, and my job is all online work now. I finally got the time. What do you want to eat on Saturday?"

"I just want to know if I can go to the party on Friday."

"Only if you have dinner with us on Saturday."

"It's a deal. Pork chops."

ST. JOSEPH'S HOSPITAL loomed over Hillside Cemetery. Most of the windows were dark, the flashing lights at the top casting the graveyard in alternating hues of red and green. Tim yawned as they sat by the fresh grave in the far corner of the cemetery. Levi looked at his watch. "It's only midnight. You sleepy?" His voice was muffled from his bandana.

"Y-yes and no," Tim whispered through the black bandana obscuring the lower half of his face. "I'm scared."

"Why?"

"I'm in a cemetery guarding a grave with a lunatic who believes in vampires, after hours. I saw four cops go by—I'm getting cramps from hiding behind these tombstones, man."

"You're a big baby."

"Isn't it weird how half the headstones have little LED lanterns? Ghost lights. I'm kinda nervous the old man will actually pop out of there and get us," Tim shivered. "What if he just, like, lunges at us and rips my throat out?"

"Then it's a good thing the emergency room is across the street."

"Har-dee-har-har," Tim said. "And then there's the alternative. What if he doesn't come out of there?"

"Then he's just plain old regular dead instead of undead, and all my research was wrong," Levi shrugged. "It wouldn't be the first time."

"So…so then you're just out here all night for no reason?"

"Most of the time."

"When you could be having a social life?"

"Pretty much."

"What a bummer," Tim sighed. "Your life is depressing. I'm surprised you're not one of my customers. Can I have my gun back after this?"

"I'll think about it." Suddenly the soil shifted. Levi felt the hairs on the back of his neck rise. Then the soil was still. Maybe he imagined it. No, there it was again! Something moved under it.

"Tim, grab the holy water and get your ass over here." A groan answered him, and Tim hauled over a large pot of holy water.

"This doesn't actually work you know," Tim said. The surface of the ground began to bulge and dip. "What the hell is that?!" he gasped.

A horrible, ominous feeling took over the graveyard as the sound of crumbling, sifting soil grew more fervent. The whole grave heaved downward and upward, as if the earth was trying to vomit.

"I'm gonna piss myself," Tim whispered.

Levi shushed him. New sod ripped as nails tore at the underside of the grass. Fingertips began to show, the nails like shark fins in the dirt. Then it stopped. They waited with baited breath on the side of the grave.

A gnarled fist burst through the sod and soil, and then another. Tim squeezed Levi's arm so tight he thought it was going to fall off. Levi clamped his hand over Tim's mouth, stopping his scream from escaping.

The arms wore dirty, stained suit sleeves. A head began birthing its way out of the ground. Levi felt Tim try to run, but he held him down.

"Not yet," he whispered. "It's all in the timing."

Letting out a growl like a tiger, the old man began to haul himself out of the grave, fingertips raw and bleeding, his face slashed from the rock and dirt. He was almost halfway out when Levi threw Tim aside, grabbed the pot of holy water, and charged at him.

With a roar, he threw the contents of the pot at the old man, who hissed, revealing long canines and blackened eyes, before bursting into flame. His arms buckled; his corpse flaked chunks of burning flesh. Levi pulled a stake from his jacket and thrust it into the vampire's burning chest. The vampire let out a strange retching noise, and Levi staked him again, and then again. He raised his arm, about to stab the old man once more, but the vampire disintegrated into soggy dust, extinguishing the flames.

Levi panted, wiping the sweat from his forehead, and turned to look at Tim, who stared at him, mouth agape.

"Dude...you're my hero."

"Give me the shovel." They spent the next hour filling in the hole the vampire crawled out of, returning the grave to its pristine condition before driving off into the night.

"I'll drop you at your apartment," Levi broke the silence.

"Nah, can I crash at your place?" Tim asked. "It's gonna be a hard walk to school in the morning after all this excitement. You're a beast."

"No."

"Come on! You can't show me a real vampire and expect me to sleep in an apartment above the Red Cross by myself! Sometimes they have blood drives. That's like living in a vampire deli!"

"Fine," Levi grumbled. "You can spend the night at my place."

"Where do you live, anyway?"

"Out of town." They took Central Avenue north to County Road E, and drove on empty country roads, past the newly-built doctors' houses that cropped up on the outskirts of Marshfield in enclaves. Farms rolled on in every direction.

"Dude, this is werewolf country," Tim murmured. "They come

back through these parts by McMillan."

"You keep talking about werewolves," Levi shook his head. "It's irritating."

"I cannot believe a man of your experience does not believe in werewolves!" Tim punched Levi in the shoulder, making the truck swerve a little.

"They don't exist."

"Oh?"

"It's not like you've seen one, Tim."

Tim pounded on the dashboard. "Do you wanna hear *my* story?"

"We got time."

"Okay, well, a while back I had to meet one of my clients out at the McMillan town intersection. The only stuff there is the fire station, the ballpark, the white church with the neon cross, and the pond, right? Well, I'm trippin' a little—"

"I don't want to hear about your drug-induced hallucinations."

They turned onto a gravel road, small pebbles kicking up and clinking on the underside of the truck. They pulled into the driveway of a dilapidated brick farmhouse, its windows lifeless eyes.

The headlights illuminated a large pile of rubble slumped in the field next to the house.

"What happened to your barn?"

"It burned down years ago." Levi put the truck in park and flipped off the headlights. They got out and went in the house's back door, coming into the kitchen. Levi flicked an old light switch, and a single bulb came on in the ceiling fan over the dining room table.

"You've got one light bulb in the whole downstairs." Tim pointed at the empty sockets.

"Ya, keeps the bills low," Levi replied. "I should plug in the fridge." He rummaged around the kitchen. Old and rickety, yet surprisingly neat—except for the pile of dishes in the sink and two full trash bags by the door. A wood-burning furnace stood in the corner, completely dark. Tim took the time to scope out the downstairs. A microwave, but no time displayed. The oven had the same problem.

"You guys don't plug in any of your appliances?"

"After dad died, I figured it would make payments easier," Levi shrugged. "Less than twenty bucks a month for electricity, no gas bill with the wood furnace, and we're on well water out here."

"What do you have to eat?" Tim patted his stomach. "I got the munchies."

"I got bread, peanut butter and jelly, and cereal. Milk's in the fridge," Levi pointed to a cabinet and the cupboard. "It's probably a little risky now. Don't touch those microwavable mac and cheese packets, I'm not offering those."

"I bet you got steaks," Tim cracked a grin. "Get it? Steaks? Stakes?"

"Uh…ya."

"You know, for being a slayer, you sure live a lot like a vampire." Tim rummaged through the cabinets. "All alone in a creepy house with no light and no food."

"I'm a man on a budget," Levi frowned.

"Lighten up, vampire hunter," Tim sighed. "I was right, you do have a ton of stakes. And boxes of latex gloves. Why do you keep this crap in the cabinets?" He poured a bowl of cereal and grabbed a spoon from a drawer.

"There's room."

"Only because all your dishes are in the sink." Tim chuckled. "And you slammed my apartment for being yellow!"

"I'm going to bed, man. School starts in less than six hours." Levi proceeded down a hall to a staircase by the front door. He found the switch for the light in the stairwell. "There's a spare room upstairs. Come on, I'm not leaving the lights on longer just for you."

Tim shoveled the last of his cereal into his mouth, left the bowl on the counter by the sink, and followed Levi up the steps. "You said your dad died. So where's your mom?"

"She died the same time he did," Levi replied.

"I didn't know your parents were dead."

"I'd prefer that nobody know." Levi opened the bedroom doors.

"Ah. So you're avoiding the foster care thing too?"

"If people found out they died, government agencies would ask questions that I can't answer. Here's the guest room." It was impossible to miss the thick layer of dust on most of the furniture.

Tim flopped on the bed. A musty odor filled the air along with the now-airborne dust. "This place is crap," Tim announced, "and you're alone."

Levi set his jaw forward. "Shut up."

"I'm serious, man. Who mows your lawn? It's gotta be a whole acre."

"I do, once a month."

Tim coughed. "That's why it looks condemned."

"Shut your mouth! I grew up here. I take care of this place!" He banged his fist on the doorframe. "I'm getting by!"

"Are your property taxes paid?"

Levi paused. "In full, until I turn eighteen. My dad was pretty good with money and planning. He thought I could make it on my own if need be. He was right."

"Man, not to bash on your father, but your place is falling apart. At least my place gets plowed in winter, and it's closer to the cemetery and all that other creepiness you have to handle."

"I don't have a place to crash in town," Levi said.

"Then just move in with me. We'll be roommates."

"That's a stupid idea. Then I'll have to pay bills at two places." Levi raised an eyebrow.

"So don't pay the bills here. You have to drive too far—you can save on gas! My place is closer to everything, and you'll be out of werewolf territory."

"Good night." Levi turned off the light and disappeared down the hall.

MORNING ROSE over the rubble pile behind the farmhouse and found Levi kneeling next to it, a hand on the stone, lost in thought. He looked around at the overgrown yard, the rut-ridden gravel drive, and the worn brick house.

"I've been trying," he murmured to the pile. "I balance the checkbooks, ration my supplies, do homework during school, cut back on sleep…I know I can do this alone, but it's harder than it should be."

"Hey!"

Levi rose up and pulled a stake, whirling around. "Don't fucking sneak up on me," he snarled.

Tim pulled out his cell phone. "My alarm went off, and I didn't factor in the extra time to get to school from here. We should probably go now." He turned in the direction of Levi's truck. "We don't want to be late again. Babs already has a hard-on for us."

Levi put his stake back and wiped the dirt from his hands on his pants. "My answer is yes."

"What?" Tim squinted.

"To your question last night. I'll move in with you."

"Hot damn!" Tim clapped his hands. "I knew you'd see reason! We're gonna be thick as thieves—maybe not literally—okay, maybe literally." He laughed.

"Don't get ahead of yourself." Levi's brow furrowed. "This is a trial period only."

FRIDAY NIGHT was the third football game of the season, but only the first during the school year. The Spencer-Columbus Rockets were up against the Cadott Hornets, who appropriately wore black and yellow. The Rockets wore red and white. The lights of the Spencer High football field burned bright as the dusky sky darkened and the crowds cheered. Samantha stood in the little cluster of cheerleaders from Spencer and Columbus, decked out in her red and white uniform, her skirt letting way too many mosquitoes bite her legs.

"These things are awful," she slapped her calf. "They're so large, and there's so freaking many. Don't y'all spray for them?"

"What are you yammering about, Sammy?" Jennifer asked, blowing her gum into a little bubble and popping it loudly in her teeth. "Not making friends with the state bird?"

"They have West Nile out east," Samantha said. "Every year they spray all the lawns with a chemical and it kills most of the mosquitoes. I've never been bitten so much before."

"Maybe it's because you've never really been outside." Brandon popped up behind her.

"Go away, you little worm. Sit with mom." Samantha ran a hand through his hair and spun him around, shoving him in the direction of the stands.

"I don't have to," he turned around and grinned. "Mom said to give her some privacy to work on papers, so Josh and I are playing hide and seek right now."

"She brought work to the game?" Samantha looked up in the stands, and sure enough, her mother was parked, glasses on with her laptop out, on the top row. "So who's supposed to be watching you?"

"I'm eleven, duh!" Brandon gave her a deploring stare. "I don't need watching."

Samantha rolled her eyes as Brandon wandered off, and turned her attention to the field. The Rockets and the Hornets were lining up and squatting, ready to go. She scanned the numbered uniforms, looking for Matt. She didn't have to look hard; he turned his helmeted head in her direction and waved two fingers in a sort of salute, right as the whistle was blown. He was promptly tackled. She face-palmed.

"You're distracting him," Becca groused. "He'll bring down the whole team. That won't be good for our record."

"How are we doing this season?" Natalie asked.

"We're oh-and-two right now, but if Stauber keeps this up, we'll be oh-and-three."

"Who's Stauber?" Samantha asked.

"Matt," said one of the cheerleaders from Spencer. "You seriously didn't know his last name? He's our wide receiver!"

"I don't know what that means," Samantha said with complete unabashed honesty.

Becca let out a "whoo!" and shook her pompoms as the teams

lined up further down the field. "We're gaining yards now! Come on boys! Get some touchdowns! Don't you dare embarrass me!"

"We didn't practice that one." Natalie shook her head.

"She used to live in Cadott," Laderia said. "For her this is a big dealio."

"You're a big dealio." Jennifer popped her gum in her teeth again. "Let's just fucking cheerio."

"For serio." Laderia grinned and tossed her hair. "Get in line, bitches." They lined up in front of the stands and spelled out words that Samantha didn't care about, getting about half the crowd to respond.

DYLAN MOEDE'S HOUSE reminded Samantha of a small airplane hangar—with massive windows thrown in for fun. It lay at the end of a very long gravel driveway, overlooking a large man-made pond with a small sandy beach. Throngs of students meandered, swam, and drank by the impressive bonfire. Samantha could only shake her head as Becca parked on the grass along the driveway at the end of a trail of cars.

"This is it!" she declared. "We're getting wasted tonight!"

"It's weird seeing all these people outside of Columbus." Samantha squinted at the students wandering around the bonfire and the pond. "Is the whole school here?"

"Most of them. Some are from Spencer," Laderia informed her. They hopped out of the car. The party raged, music audible even from their distant spot. "Looks like we're fashionably late. I want to swim."

"Why? So you can step in and cause a tidal wave? I hope you didn't wear your bikini." Jennifer popped her gum in Laderia's direction.

"Too late, it's already on underneath this sweater." Laderia grinned.

"You barely fit in it."

"That's the point." Laderia shimmied her shoulders. "Jealous much?"

Jennifer scoffed and unzipped her navy Columbus hoodie, revealing her own flowery bikini top. "This is perfect with my short-shorts."

"Where's Matt?" Samantha asked, scanning the crowds.

"Probably by the keg," Becca said. "Dylan usually sets it up in the garage."

"He drinks a lot?" Samantha frowned a little.

Jennifer shrugged. "Somebody's gotta hold people's feet up for the chug. Stauber's the one that does that."

"I'm going to pretend I understand what you're talking about." Samantha walked down the gravel driveway toward the bonfire, the girls trailing her. "What is this? Follow the leader?"

"Ya, blondes first," Natalie smiled.

Samantha got the same feeling she had on her first day—many, many eyes on her. She focused hard on walking like she didn't care and scanned the crowd. People smiled or nodded, even though she had never spoken to them before. It was bizarre. She saw Dylan Moede, towering above the other senior boys by the bonfire, shirtless and drinking. It was true, his abs were incredible. She watched him chug another beer and estimated his washboard would be gone forever in nine months.

"Yo, Moede!" Jennifer flipped her hood up and walked sultrily up to him, and he flashed a goofy grin down at her. Samantha rolled her eyes and looked over at Becca, Laderia and Natalie, who slipped away to the pond.

She turned to the garage and sure enough, Matt stood there, laughing with another football player. She couldn't hear what they were talking about over the thrum from two towers of speakers flanking the garage.

Matt glanced over, holding her gaze as he continued talking to his teammate. Samantha flushed a little and smiled. He smiled back, and waved her over.

"Hey, you made it!"

"Yeah," Samantha said. "Got a ride with the other cheerleaders."

"So how about that game, huh?" Matt stretched, the hem of his shirt lifting and revealing his abs. "Our first win of the season. I knew you'd bring us luck."

"You don't need me, I was distracting you." Samantha's eyes widened as Matt stood so close they were practically touching. She couldn't help but look with longing at his lips and brown eyes. "You caught some great passes tonight."

"I had to impress you somehow," Matt smirked. "Let's see if I can keep up that winning streak." He leaned in to kiss her. Samantha felt a moment of panic and turned her face so he caught her cheek.

"You smell like beer," she covered. "Are you drunk?"

"No," Matt shrugged. "Just feeling the buzz of victory."

"Well, congratulations." Samantha punched him in the shoulder. "That's the only contact you're getting from me, Sir Quarterback."

"I'm a wide receiver."

"Whatever. Y'all did a good job." Samantha waved her hand. "I didn't have to yell 'defense' more than three times."

"I love your accent." Matt tucked her hair behind her ear. "It's so sexy. Let's go chill by the fire."

"Well, that's a paradox. How do you chill by a fire?" Matt gave her a strange look. "It's a joke, Matt. I know what you meant." They walked over to the bonfire and sat in a pair of vacant lawn chairs. At least twenty ringed the fire. Jennifer's laughter came from across the flames.

"It's warm out tonight," Jennifer said, leaning into Dylan.

"You could always take the hoodie off." Dylan was practically licking his lips.

"I could cool you off," another senior boy said in a thick German accent. "I have got a story to give you chills."

"No," groaned Matt. "I hate scary stories."

"Be a man, Stauber," Jennifer said icily. "Sammy, do you like scary stories?"

"I know a few myself," Samantha said. "But I'd like to hear—" She gestured at the German.

"Stefan," the boy supplied.

"—Stefan's story."

"Ladies first," Stefan grinned, sitting down on Samantha's other side.

"I can't really tell it over the music." Samantha shook her head, glancing at Matt's borderline stricken face.

"CUT-THE-MUSIC!" Dylan bellowed. Somebody in the garage turned the music off. A general groan rose from the party goers. Other than the sound of laughter and splashing echoing through the air and the crackling of the fire, it was quiet. Samantha gave Matt an apologetic look.

"Scare me," Stefan leaned forward.

"Okay, well, this is one my mom told me. Just thinking about it gives me chills."

"Oh great," Jennifer rolled her eyes.

Samantha leaned closer to the fire. "We used to live in the D.C. metro area, and she worked with a bunch of people in the intelligence sector. There were rumors of this psychic, a woman in the woods of Virginia, just outside the metro. She lived alone in a trailer, with lots of cats. She was completely freaky. When she told the future, she was never wrong. Businessmen would make the drive from New York to see her and ask about the stock market; politicians would ask about campaign strategies, and war tactics, the usual."

Dylan leaned in. "Nobody ever asked about the lottery?"

"Y'all shut up while I'm telling my story." Samantha glowered at him. "Anyway, a lady in the FBI got a job offer from a private company, and she couldn't make up her mind. Should she take it or not? So, she drove out to the woods to see this crazy old woman. She paid the psychic the usual fee for one question, and she was taken into the trailer. The woman wasn't sure about the job, so she just said 'I want to know my future.' The psychic stared at her for the longest time. She took a paper and a pen, wrote something down, and stuffed it in an envelope. She handed the envelope to the lady, and said 'In this envelope is your answer. Don't open it until you get home.' So the lady took the envelope, got into her car, and started the drive home."

"I'm terrified," Jennifer popped her gum. "What happened when she got home?"

"She never did," Samantha murmured. "She was killed in a head-on collision with a semi-truck a mile from her apartment. When the investigators found the envelope, they opened it, pulled out the note, and read it. It said 'You have no future.'"

"I got goosebumps." Matt chuckled, holding up his arm for Samantha to see. She grinned with more than a little satisfaction.

"Ahh," Stefan murmured. "Vat is a psychic?"

Dylan bellowed with laughter. "A psychic knows the future, or talks to the dead—some bull like that. Like that lady in town, King Lear."

"Wait, there's a psychic in Marshfield?" Samantha looked at him.

"Ya, she's a loon. About five foot flat, with a huge hat and she wears enormous sunglasses all the time, even at night."

"She walks around with a big stick, like she's hiking," Matt said. "I see her on Central sometimes."

"Her name is King Lear?" Stefan scratched his chin.

"No, but she always quotes that stupid play," Matt corrected. "She's a wreck. I heard she used to be a stripper or something. They say that one night, the devil himself came to see her dance, and she's never been the same since."

"Still not as bad as Scary Gary," chuckled Dylan.

"Scary Gary?" Samantha laughed in disbelief.

"This is a fucked-up town, Sammy," Jennifer said, leaning her head on Dylan's stomach. "You'll see. Weird stuff is always happening in boring little Marshfield."

A lone howl echoed over the party. Everyone stopped and listened. Samantha felt her heart skip a beat.

"I think I just heard my first wild wolf."

"The moon's getting bigger." Dylan gestured to the star-studded sky. "Wait until next week. We'll have a full moon on Homecoming Night. That's why our theme is 'Can't Fight the Moonlight.'"

Samantha nodded, filing the information away to share with Natalie. The wolf howled again, accompanied by a collection of other howls. The whole party looked around at the woods and fields surrounding Dylan's house.

Samantha looked at the faces around her. "That's a lot of wolves."

"Nearby, too." Dylan stood, Jennifer tumbling off of him. He looked to the sky and howled back. Matt jumped up and howled with him. Everyone else howled. The howling lasted a good ten seconds, and the wolves were silenced. Dylan let out a cheer, and everyone relaxed. Someone started the music again.

Matt sat down by Samantha. "Who's taking you to Homecoming?"

"I haven't been asked yet," Samantha shrugged. "So I figured I'd hop a ride with Laderia. Why?"

He wore a mischievous grin. "Just wondering."

"I vant to tell you my scary story now," Stefan said. "Have you heard of the Marquis de Sade? So there vas this really rich lord vith a sick fetish—"

"Oh no you don't." Matt grabbed Samantha's hand and said in her ear, "I'm dancing with you."

"DAMN LEVI. That was a lot of shit to move." Tim flopped on his grotesque sofa. "But look at this place! A fresh coat of paint really made a difference!"

"Yeah, fresh yellow is better than smoke-stained yellow," Levi commented. "But now the kitchen looks like it belongs in a Packers collection." His mind flashed back to that house—662 Pecan Parkway—the basement memorabilia. The body buried in the marsh. He fought off a wave of nausea.

"We can paint the cabinets white some other time." Tim scrutinized them after he looked the avocado fridge up and down. "I like your furniture in here. It fills the empty spots. Feels more like a home. Even though you unscrewed half my light bulbs and stuck that weird ass cabinet with all your weapons over there." He gestured to the tall armoire that now occupied a corner of the living room.

"Think of it as mood lighting," Levi said.

"What mood? Poor?" Tim ran a hand through his spiked hair. "I'm covering the electric bill—just so it doesn't feel like *The Walking Dead* in here."

"I hate to admit it, but it turned out good." Levi looked around. "The drive to school is only a few blocks instead of several miles."

"A real improvement." Tim stretched out. "When are we going to get new carpet?"

"I'm not replacing this crap just so you can ruin a new one with your druggie stank."

Tim sat up, raising his hands. "Where am I supposed to smoke then?"

"Somewhere no one will find you doing it," Levi grumbled. Tim squinted in thought.

"Okay, the graveyard it is."

"What?! No, that's my zone."

"Levi, you're the only one who goes there at night. The nurses from the hospital stand by the sidewalk and smoke all the time. I saw piles of their butts all over the place. Not to mention the cigarettes on the ground." Tim couldn't stop laughing.

"No."

"Hey, I'm offering to give up smoking in my apartment for you!"

"Because you're afraid of being alone above the Red Cross now that you know vampires are real. Thanks for that."

"Listen Biff, I helped you move in, and we missed the football game! I usually can get in five good-paying deals during a game. That money could have covered the bills *and* munchies."

"Always thinking with that crackpot brain of yours."

"Anyway, I want to help you slay vampires."

"No."

"Why not?"

"I don't have time to train you," Levi explained.

"I'll learn on the job. Observation and shit. Come on, you can't expect me to give up a bad habit without putting a good one in its place, do you?"

"I don't see why cleaning couldn't become your next habit."

"This from the one whose house is coated in an inch of dust." Tim shook his head.

"Whatever man, I'm going to bed. Goodnight."

"YOU'RE INTO COUNTRY MUSIC?" Samantha felt her smile falter as Matt turned up *Big and Rich* over the roar of the car.

"Yep. I'm a farm boy," Matt winked. "Grew up on this. But if this is too much for your ears…" He turned the dial to 95.5 and Nicki Minaj began. Samantha turned off the stereo promptly.

"Maybe I should have gotten a ride home from Becca."

"She was drunk," Matt shrugged.

"Worth the risk."

A finger thrust into her ribcage. She jolted before smacking Matt in the shoulder. "Why would you do that?!"

"You're being a princess."

Samantha wrapped her arms around herself and huffed, looking out the window as they came back into town. Streetlights burned bright, but they were the only car on the road. The sidewalks were also dead, not a soul to be seen.

"This place is so *empty*."

"The cops are all on Central, and everyone else is asleep." They turned onto Park Street. The moon flitted through the highest leaves of the trees.

"Which one is your house?" Matt slowed the car down.

"I'm three-eleven." Samantha pointed to the brick house with the large front porch on the corner of Park and Spruce. The outside lights were on.

"The old Doege House." Matt whistled. "It figures you'd live here."

"What makes you say that?"

"Doege was one of the original doctors who founded the Marshfield Clinic. He built this house. It has history—not very pleasant."

"I don't want to hear about it." Samantha covered her ears. "It's a perfectly nice house."

Matt laughed. "A doctor's house. Your family's in the money."

"We're not rich," Samantha said. "We're normal."

"For Beverly Hills maybe." Matt eyed her. "I'm driving you home in a 1973 Hemi 'Cuda. What does your mom drive?"

"A Cadillac Escalade, but it's five years old," Samantha snapped. "Honestly! Y'all are so into appearances and money. Don't put that off on me. And I went to *River Hill*, not Beverly Hills!"

"Where's this coming from? I was trying to prove a point." He made a U-turn and parked in front of Samantha's house.

"What's the point, huh?!" There was a long pause.

"You should come to Homecoming with me." Matt's face was half-lit by the porch light spilling across the yard. "Ride with me instead of Laderia. You'll have room to breathe."

Samantha felt warmth in her chest. "Okay. I'll ride with you."

"I'm glad I have the car," Matt said, "or I wouldn't have gotten this far tonight."

Samantha watched the expression on Matt's face change. "What do you mean by 'gotten this far tonight'?"

Matt waved a hand. "I know you pretend to like me for the car."

"I don't know a thing about cars." Samantha glared at him. "But I know this one is pretty."

"An admission." Matt leaned closer to Samantha, his eyes smoldering. "So what can we do in this car?"

"*I* can get out of it." Samantha swung her door open. "What did I say earlier?"

"That you'd go to Homecoming with me." Matt smiled with satisfaction. "So what color corsage do you want?"

"I'll text you about it." Samantha swung her legs out of the car, but Matt caught her left hand and kissed the top of it. She narrowed her eyes at him. "What was that for?"

"I'll see you Monday," Matt let her fingers slip out of his, "Princess Samantha."

Chapter 3

Can't Fight the Moonlight

"Who's in there?" Becca poked Samantha in the forehead with her Oriental fan.

"Me," Samantha's voice was muffled.

"Good gravy, Samantha, where are you going on vacation?" Natalie tilted her head, her fruit headdress threatening to fall off.

"Dubai." Samantha exposed her face. "Isn't this burqa pretty?"

"I thought they were supposed to be all-black, not blue and green." Jennifer tied up the bottom of her Hawaiian shirt to reveal her midriff. "At least I'm going somewhere worth visiting."

"Hey, Dubai is pretty cool." Tim chimed in as he walked by.

"Where are you supposed to be going on vacation?" Becca looked Tim up and down, eyes narrowing at his jeans and long-sleeved shirt.

"Michigan. Geisha wanna come? Me love you long time."

"As if."

"Suit yourself, babycakes. Hope that fan's more fun than it looks." He continued down the hall.

"What a skeaze." Natalie crossed her arms in disapproval.

"Don't look now, but here comes the B." Jennifer opened her locker and hid her gum. "Bet she'll give me crap for my outfit."

Barb rounded the corner, looking positively livid. "Ladies." She stopped and looked them up and down, her lips almost disappearing as she pressed them together. "Just because it's Homecoming Week does not mean our standards have gone out the window. Symanski, cover your face."

Samantha draped the veil back down.

"An improvement. You and Rebecca are fine." She turned her glare on Jennifer. "Cromwell, bare midriffs in Catholic schools is the resulting burden on our culture from Britney Spears. Hide it."

"But I'm supposed to be going to Hawaii," Jennifer countered. "This is perfectly conservative for the beach!"

"You heard me." Barb's lips barely moved.

"You're just trying to ruin my costume so our class scores lower than the seniors."

"Don't make me send you to the office, Miss Cromwell." Barb raised a finger. Jennifer crossed her arms. "I wonder what your father would have to say." Grumbling, Jennifer untied her shirt, covering herself. Barb scrutinized Natalie closely. "Miss Devereaux, you're relatively decent this year. A pleasant surprise. But there's still four more days to go. I'll be watching." She continued down the hall, students parting like the Red Sea for her to pass.

"What a B," Natalie muttered, fussing with her cha-cha dress.

"She's not that bad." Becca helped Samantha flip her burqa.

"She's a favoritist lesbian skank. You're the only one she calls by their first name—and that's just because you skipped a grade. Who does think she is, threatening me? I don't care what my dad thinks." Jennifer reopened her locker.

"Then why did you comply?" Natalie hiked up her bosom.

"I'm not speaking to him." A piece of gum disappeared into Jennifer's mouth and she shut her locker once more.

"The silent treatment?" Becca snapped her fan shut. "He threatened drug tests again, didn't he?"

"None of your business."

Samantha rolled her eyes. "Jennifer. Don't bring it up if you're not willing to share. It's rude."

"Who asked you, New Girl?" Jennifer stalked down the hall.

"I think it's drug tests," Becca shrugged.

Natalie nodded. "Hey, has anyone seen Laderia?" On cue, Laderia walked up behind her.

"Hey Nat," she grinned. "How'd my costume turn out?" She was wearing what appeared to be a giant globe.

"You're...Earth? O-M-G! Nominate her for Best Dressed," Natalie commanded. "We'll win for sure!"

Competitions were held around lunch hour and judged by the faculty. The junior class, somehow in charge of the events, had designed them to reduce every other class's chance of winning. Monday's contest consisted of a jump rope melee in the lobby. Matt, dressed for a luau—sunglasses and all—won the competition.

The seniors seethed and shouted. "This game was fixed!" "Stauber cheated!" "Everyone knows our class sucks at jump rope!" "Jump rope is dead!"

Samantha, for her part, was amused by how much everybody got into the games. None of it really mattered, after all. She did learn that Mr. Becker could jump with the best of them as he took on Matt and the students screamed and cheered. Matt came over to Samantha after the competition's spectacular conclusion.

"I saw you yesterday, St. John's," he looked at her over his sunglasses. "I thought you went to Mass at Our Lady of Peace."

"I wanted to go to St. John's," Samantha blinked, "just to see it. My mom and dad got married there."

"So did mine. How'd you like it?"

"It's really nice. All the stained glass and candles. Probably the prettiest church I've ever seen." Samantha briefly imagined herself sitting in the pews again and inserted her parents, twenty years younger, at the altar.

"I went to the elementary school next to it. Rumor has it the playground was a graveyard for nuns."

"Stop! Do you guys have a freaky story for everything?" Samantha shook her head. "I don't like feeling creeped out."

"You were the one who made me feel things I didn't want to

feel," Matt whispered in her ear.

A flush spread across Samantha's face. "I love the castle things by the altar," she said quickly. "That's what I'd like to think about—not a bunch of dead nuns under the playground."

"The high altar, ya. Sacred Heart used to have one too, but they got rid of it. What color corsage do you want? You never texted me."

Samantha smiled. "Anything that goes with white."

He smirked. "You're going to love it."

"I THINK THEY IDENTIFIED your victim," Tim announced, dropping a paper on the wooden table. Levi looked up at him, stricken.

"We're in the public library," he whispered, "use some damn discretion."

"It's the front page," Tim whispered back. "Headline news."

Levi scanned the other patrons in the library. Satisfied no one was eavesdropping, he turned his attention to the headline. "'Search for missing resident begins.'" He felt his heart pound as he looked at the man's photo. "Holy shit, this is him."

"It says his name was Arthur Harris. He worked for Mr. Thomas Lancaster, owner of several area funeral parlors." Tim slid into the seat next to Levi, pointing to the sentence. "Didn't you used to work at one of his funeral homes?"

"Ya," Levi breathed. "The new one, last summer. I had to forge a work permit to get that job. It was stressful."

"This guy probably had your job after you left," Tim said. "Freaky, huh?"

"Why is that freaky?"

"You guys have a connection. He's not just a random dude."

"I never met him before the night I killed him." Levi leaned back in his chair, pondering. "Not that I would call that much of a meeting…"

"It says here he recently moved up from Chicago," Tim pointed to the paper. "He brought his family. They live in town."

"He had a family?" Levi's hands shook as he pored over the

article. "Wife and two kids…fuck. A husband and father…and I killed him."

"Poor dumbass." Tim sighed, rocking on the back legs of his chair. "I wonder why Mr. Lancaster hired some guy from Chicago when he could've gotten any idiot around here. He even got you."

"That's a really good observation."

"Are you admitting you're an idiot?"

"Why would Lancaster hire someone from so far away?" Levi's brows came together as he ignored Tim's dig. "Even more suspicious is that Harris came here. I'm sure there's mortuary work in Chicago. Their murder rate is outrageous. How does that justify a move to Marshfield? He must've had another reason for being here. Maybe he wanted something. Something that Lancaster has—" Levi stopped himself. He looked sidelong at Tim, wondering if he should tell him.

"Maybe we could raid the funeral homes or break into Roddis Manor. The Lancasters live there now."

Levi thought about his lock pick kit, sitting in the gym bag in the backseat of his truck, and his fingers itched to use it. "You're a cretin, but you may be onto something," he murmured.

"I'm not on anything right now," Tim retorted.

Levi punched him in the shoulder.

"OW!" The chair fell backwards. The librarian looked over from her round desk in the middle of the room, and loudly shooshed them. Tim grumbled, got up and lifted his chair back onto its legs.

"We should start with Harris's family first."

"Why do we care about them?" Tim frowned, rubbing his shoulder. He winced. "You need to freakin' relax. If somebody sees the bruises you give me they'll think I'm being abused 'n shit."

"You're getting close to it," Levi growled.

"SAMANTHA'S GOT A DAAATE, Samantha's got a daaate." Brandon ran through the house. "Samantha's got a daaate, too bad she'll be laaate."

"I hope that doesn't mean what I think it means," Mrs. Symanski said from the dining room. Samantha rolled her eyes.

"I don't think he knows what any of that means. He's a little runt." Samantha sprawled on the couch, texting Matt.

"Samantha, why don't you help me decide where to put this stuff instead of just denting my furniture with your butt?" Sandra strode into the room with yet another box, grunting from the weight of it. "When did we get all of this junk?"

"Mom, that's the good china for Christmas. It goes in the kitchen."

"Help me carry it."

"Why? You already got it."

"I suppose I could carry it myself," Mrs. Symanski huffed. "It's not as bad as when I carried you, for nine months, six in the heat of Florida, and suffered through labor, need I remind you, for twelve hours. In an army hospital with no immediate family to—"

"Fine! I'm coming!" Samantha stood up and grabbed the box from her mother. "Good gravy mom, why do we even have this junk?" Her arms were shaking under the weight.

"See, this is why I asked for help. It's not because I'm trying to be a nag." Her mother grabbed the other side and they walked the plates into the kitchen. "So, were you texting that football player?"

"Yes."

"What about?"

"Just planning our Homecoming Night." Samantha shrugged, trying to be nonchalant. "Nothing big."

Mrs. Symanski chuckled. "Did you pick out a dress yet?"

"She got it on Saturday mom." Brandon flew into the kitchen. "Don't you remember? Sheesh!"

Samantha held her breath as her mom's face went through several emotions before finally settling on frustration. "Nobody tells me anything. How am I supposed to know?"

THEY DROVE SLOWLY down Arnold Street, searching for the right house.

"That's it." Levi pointed at a dark-colored house with the glow of a lamp in the window. "That's where the Harris family lives."

"They're awake," Tim frowned. "That's not going to help us."

"We can still take a look around." Levi turned onto Purdy Street and parked. "Put your bandana on. Let's go."

"Levi, I dunno," Tim said evasively.

"This was your idea." Levi's eyebrows furrowed. "You're going through with it."

"You would've done it anyway," Tim replied, tying the bandana. "You're guilting me into this shit." Levi grabbed his lock picks.

Getting out of the truck, they shut the doors quietly. They rounded the corner and walked past the house before ducking into the neighbors' darkened yard. The grass crunched dryly under their feet. Distant laughter floated through the air.

"Levi, do you hear that?"

"Shhh!" Levi's hand traveled to the knife in his belt loop. He fingered the handle, looking around the yard. The laughter was growing. Levi heard multiple voices. His hair stood on end. They held perfectly still, not breathing. He could sense movement from somewhere to his left, but it was too dark to see.

"BOO!"

In one swift motion, Levi grabbed the person by the neck, threw them onto the ground, straddled them and held the knife to the obscured throat.

"Ow! Jesus, it's cool, it's cool!" The boy wheezed, wrapping his hands around Levi's wrists. "Let me go, let me go."

Levi's face burned as he saw the panicked brown eyes behind the ski mask and the rolls of toilet paper bouncing across the lawn. He slid the knife back into his belt loop, but did not release the throat. He pulled the ski mask off.

"Matt Stauber," Tim whispered, coming to Levi's side. "Let him go, Levi. What the hell are you doing out here?" Levi released him.

"Toilet papering, what do you expect?" Matt sat up, rubbing his throat. "What the fuck are you doing out here with knives?"

"Meeting a client," Tim said smoothly, rubbing his hands together. "Levi's my new bodyguard." Levi shot Tim a look. "For tonight."

"Holy hell, your grip, Levi." Matt's eyes were watering as he massaged his throat. "Why are you wearing bandanas?"

"Same reason you have a ski mask," Tim shrugged. "You crying?"

Matt blinked back the tears. "I'm not crying, that fucking hurt. We're hiding from the cops. They're cracking down on the TPing this year." The sound of girls approaching made them silent.

"Not a word about this," Levi deadpanned Matt.

Matt nodded. He stood up, clearing his throat.

"Stauber, where are you? Your girlfriend is worried." Jennifer tiptoed through the grass towards them. There was a loud clang as she stumbled. "Shit! Who sticks a gutter in the yard?"

"Nice," Matt said.

"I'm more graceful than you." Jennifer punched him in the chest. "Who are these two?"

"Stone—I mean, Levi and Tim." Matt rubbed the back of his head. Levi and Tim exchanged glances.

"You boys should keep your bromance private." Jennifer's hoarse whisper was condescending. "Sammy, he's over here."

Samantha stumbled out of the shadows, blonde hair glinting in the moonlight. Levi narrowed his eyes as she cast him a strange glance.

"You exist in real life," she said. "Not just Psych, Math, and English. Go figure."

"Ya," he replied. "So…"

"So…" She stepped closer to Levi. He felt a warmth creep up his face until she stopped next to Matt and looped an arm through his. He felt a wave of disappointment at that gesture. He didn't breathe, hoping it would stop him from saying something stupid.

"How are the notes in psych? I saw you sleeping in class again." She peered at him with that strange look. "Will you need to borrow them from me tomorrow?"

"This isn't the time," Levi replied as Jennifer huffed.

"Tim, I need to talk to you." Jennifer grabbed Tim's arm and dragged him away. Levi was left with Matt and Samantha.

"We got time now." Samantha tucked a long blonde lock behind her ear, glancing up at Matt. "What happened to your neck? It's...really red. I can see it in the moonlight."

Matt met Levi's eyes. "The ski mask rubs me raw."

"Oh. Good thing you took it off." Samantha looked around. "Laderia's coming with the bag. We can put the ski mask in it. Where are your toilet paper rolls?"

"I dropped them when I ran into Levi," Matt murmured, and turned to look for them. He wandered across the yard. Levi felt a rise of confidence and straightened his shoulders as Samantha turned her questioning gaze back to him.

"I didn't see you dress up for Geek Chic Day today. Are you going to Homecoming?" she asked.

"Might be," Levi muttered. "You?"

"Matt asked me," she said, crossing her arms, tucking her hands into her armpits. "It's chilly out tonight. I thought this black shirt would be enough. You guys toilet papering too? Who you hitting up?"

Levi opened his mouth to respond when Matt returned with a couple toilet paper rolls. "I think that's the Harris place," he whispered. "Did you hear what happened to that guy?"

Samantha shook her head, her hair shimmering. Levi glanced back and forth between them.

Matt handed Samantha a roll. "He just disappeared one day. Heard he was really into witchcraft and devil worship. Was in a vampire gang down in Chicago for a while before he got married."

"Where'd you hear that?" Levi demanded. "That wasn't in the paper."

"It was in the police report." Matt raised his hands and backed up instinctively. "Jennifer heard it from a cop that works with her dad."

"That's screwed up," Samantha whispered. "There are some gangs in Baltimore who drink blood too. He lived right there?"

"With his family, ya, but he's been missing since the first day of school." Jennifer trudged back with Tim by her side. "Probably killed himself or something. Where's Laderia and Becca?"

"Natalie not out tonight?" Tim looked around.

"No, her parents have her guarding their house from the seniors." Jennifer rolled her eyes. "Let's get out of this yard before we wake the owners up."

They hurried onto the road as a group and looked around. Down the street, a short thin figure and a fat figure were walking slowly toward them.

"There they are." Samantha waved. They ran to meet Laderia and Becca.

Tim and Levi looked at each other and then back at the group.

"We should follow them." Tim scratched his head and looked at Levi. "They know stuff."

Levi glanced at the Harris house. "I don't think so. They gave us really good information on Arthur Harris, but that's probably it. Former vampire gang mem—" Tim dragged Levi by his hoodie toward the group.

"They're inviting us along, let's go!"

Levi groaned. "This is a waste of time."

"We got better info in five minutes with them than we got from scoping the library all day. We're going." They jogged to catch up with them.

"Where are we going next?" Becca asked.

"*Ay*, I smell like *un gato muerto*." Laderia complained, the sweat pouring down her face shimmering in the streetlight. "Only one more house, then I'm going home."

"We're hitting up Barb's house." Jennifer grinned. "She lives one block over. It's time for some payback."

"Are you serious? No one ever gets Barb's house. It's not worth the risk." Becca shook her head.

"What risk?" Samantha met Levi's eyes again.

He half-smiled. "She'll make the whole school clean it up."

"Or give everyone detention. I wouldn't put it past her," Tim agreed.

"Don't you guys have a deal to handle?" Matt asked.

"Mind your own business," Jennifer snapped. Tim chortled.

Aside from Laderia's heavy breathing, they walked in silence to Barb's house, which sat on a corner lot surrounded by huge trees. In the moonlight, the old maples resembled ghostly weeping willows. The whole house seemed to move with the breeze.

"Wow! Somebody did a very good job." Matt caught Samantha's hand. Levi watched her furtive glances up at Matt and the small smile that she flashed him.

"No way! Who beat us to it?" Jennifer fumed.

"Let's not do this," Becca frowned. "Someone is going to be cleaning this up, and it won't be Barb. I don't want it to be me."

"Someone said she'd make the whole school clean it up," Samantha whispered. Levi watched the way she leaned into Matt. Perhaps if he just shoved them apart...violently...

"I don't care," Jennifer retorted. "We're adding to it. Laderia, toss me a roll." Laderia, huffing loudly, tossed Jennifer two. She tossed the extra to Levi. He caught it without noticing. "Come on, Stoner, let's see your throwing arm. They forgot the highest branches." She pointed to the very tops of the trees, which were untouched and green.

Levi tossed the roll back. "I'm in enough trouble with her."

"Chicken shit." Jennifer scowled, tossing the roll to Becca. "You're up, favorite."

"This is really too much," Becca sighed. They stepped into the yard, and she tossed the roll as high as she could. It arched in the air, leaving a long white trail, but fell to the ground without passing over a single branch.

"Pathetic," Matt leered. He went for the roll, rewound it, and tossed it high. It sailed clear over two trees.

"Wow, good arc on that—excellent tail," Tim commentated. "And the cardboard never hit the ground. Ten for ten."

"Nothing but the best," Matt flexed. "Samantha, wanna give it a go?"

"Ahh," Samantha moped, "I've never done this before."

"No pressure," Matt said in her ear. Levi felt an inexplicable heat in his neck. He was tempted to remove his bandana.

Samantha shrugged with a luminous smile. "Why not?" Laderia tossed her a roll. She unwound it a little for the tail, and stepped toward the house. Levi heard her soft inhale as she wound up her arm. She hurled it as high as she could, and it arced over the roof. "Yes!" She pumped a fist in the air, and suddenly light flooded the yard.

Everyone scattered. Tim and Levi took off down the street, running as fast as they could, panting. Levi's heart pounded louder than he thought it could. As they reached Arnold Street, a laugh escaped his chest in spite of himself. He doubled over, practically dry-heaving.

"Holy…" Tim panted through his chuckles. "That was awesome! We gotta get out of here. If I know Babs, the cops are coming."

Levi gasped for air. "Tim. Tim, that was…hilarious…I've…"

"That was the most fun you've ever had, right?" Tim cackled. "You need to get out more. Did you see her on the porch? Babs caught New Girl red-handed!"

"THAT WAS A THOROUGH JOB," came the sarcastic voice from the passenger seat. "You must have been out there for hours, with over a hundred rolls by yourself."

Samantha didn't take the bait. She sat in the back of the police car, head leaning on the window, gazing at the passing houses. She suspected Barb decided to come along for the ride with the police officer as he took her home so she could confront Mrs. Symanski. Her heart pounded at the thought of her mother's reaction.

"I know you didn't act alone, Symanski," Barb's voice scolded. "But you're going to clean the entire place up alone if you don't tell me who else was involved." Samantha bit her lip, concentrating hard on the sidewalks zooming by. She could feel Barb glaring at her from the other side of the cage-like mesh. "Well? Don't you have anything to say for yourself?"

"It would be best to address her parents and let them handle this," the officer spoke to Barb from the driver's seat. Samantha heard Barb shift in the passenger seat. "Miss Symanski, you didn't see Jennifer Cromwell out toilet-papering, did you? Chief Cromwell said you, Jennifer and several others were supposed to meet up at the Fillmore estate. He would be very unhappy to hear his daughter was engaged in such activities." He looked at her in the rearview mirror. Samantha turned and met his reflected gaze.

"I decided…to…go alone." She watched his eyebrows rise. She knew it sounded unbelievable as soon as it left her mouth. Who would go toilet-papering alone? Samantha had to think up something, anything to validate her story. "Principal Barb was being unfair to my class, denying us points for Homecoming Week. She disqualified our best costumes to favor the seniors—"

"I did no such thing!" Barb replied sharply.

"—so I decided to get even." Samantha felt particularly proud of herself for that lie. "Everyone wanted to do it, but apparently I was the only one brave enough to try."

"I see," said the officer. The remainder of the drive was silent, and due to Marshfield's small size, it didn't take very long. They pulled up to Samantha's house, the only house on Park Street with lights still ablaze downstairs. "Your parents know we're coming?"

"No, my mom's always up late, working," Samantha said. "Does *she* really have to come?"

"I want to speak with your mother," Barb's voice was edged with frost. The car parked and the officer got out and came to Samantha's door. He escorted her out of the vehicle. Barb stepped out as well, her windbreaker zipped tight, unable to disguise the pajama pants and fuzzy slippers as the three trudged up the front walk to the porch.

The officer rang the doorbell. It was the first time Samantha heard the doorbell at her new house—one of those creepy older rings. She made a face. Maybe the Doege House was a little eerie…

Mrs. Symanski opened the door, wearing a bathrobe with Noxzema slathered all over her face, curlers in her hair.

"Officer, why on earth…Samantha! Barb!" She looked from Samantha to Barb and the police officer. Her face grew stern under her mask. "What happened tonight?"

"Your daughter was caught out past curfew, trespassing on private property, committing vandalism, and littering," replied the officer.

"Oh, it must be Homecoming season," her mother shrugged. "Whose house did—" She glanced at Barb. Samantha watched in horror as her mother gave Barb a sickly smile. "Oh Barb, I'm *sooo* sorry."

"Sandra, you may not remember, as you've been gone for so long—but in high school, you toilet-papered my home *seven* times. Since you've been gone, there have been no problems at my house. This is the first time in eighteen years of working at a school that this has happened to me. As a middle and high school principal, you might expect high numbers, but I have maintained a level of control and respect in my school that exceeds expectations." Barb was livid. "My property was *thoroughly* vandalized—by *your* offspring. What do you have to say?"

"You're still living in the house on that corner with the big trees?" Sandra asked. "How *thorough* was it, exactly?"

"You're missing the point! Your daughter claimed she felt the need to act out against me personally. An attitude like that was probably fostered in the home, Sandra!" Barb's fists were shaking. "I cannot believe your attit—"

"Ladies, keep it civil," said the officer sternly. "Emotions are high right now."

Barb rustled her jacket and glowered at Sandra from under her severely straight gray bangs. "If you don't deal with her attitude and handle this situation like an adult, then I will press charges against her. I'd hate to see her record ruined because of a costly and completely unfounded, irrational outburst."

"Actually, this will drop off her record when she turns eighteen," the officer added. Barb looked Samantha up and down, searching for a sign of weakness.

Samantha didn't breathe, but watched with wide eyes.

"She's banned from the Homecoming Dance." Barb looked to

Sandra as Samantha gasped audibly, suddenly on the verge of tears.

"No, please," Samantha choked.

"This—this behavior is not conducive to the environment that I wish to foster at my school. I won't have it."

"Oh," the officer gave her a stunned look.

"Really, Barbara Bennett, I cannot follow your reasoning! Let me look at this like an adult," Sandra said stridently. "You know as well as I do that toilet-papering is a tradition in this city at Homecoming, at both Columbus *and* Marshfield High. You also know—as well as this officer here and I do—that there will be plenty of students at the dance who have done more and worse toilet-papering around town, to other teachers and fellow students."

"I fail to see the relevance—" Barb began, but Sandra cut her off.

"To exclude Samantha while including others who are known to have done worse is an entirely personal attack. She's new to this community and is still getting acclimated to the social expectations here. Peer pressure is a factor you are failing to consider. Believe it or not, not everyone gets to experience toilet-papering as part of a school tradition, and not everyone understands immediately who is off-limits."

"Everyone is off-limits! It's breaking the law! You don't expect me to allow her to go to the dance because of—"

"If you deny her on these trumped-up allegations, I will not only pull her from Columbus, but expect the money back for the paid tuition, tomorrow. Then I'll march down to the courthouse with my attorney and file a lawsuit for violating her Constitutional rights." Sandra put her hands on her hips and narrowed her eyes at Barb. "Don't think I won't." The principal was visibly stricken, and her eyes darted, searching for options.

"Alright, I'll allow her to go to the dance," Barb said finally. "But she *will* be cleaning up the mess after school."

"That's very adult of you," Sandra nodded, the Noxzema running down her face. "Samantha, come in the house now." She pushed the door wide enough to reveal the fully-furnished and newly-painted foyer, the wood trim gleaming with fresh polish. Samantha felt envy radiate off of Barb like heat from a stove. "We have a lot to discuss young lady. Thank you officer. Principal Bennett." Barb headed back to the car.

The officer lingered on the porch. "Ma'am, about the—"

"I was just about to ask you officer. Did anyone actually see Sam do it? Throw the toilet paper?"

"No," responded the officer. "We could only charge her with trespassing and a curfew violation." The officer took a step closer to the door and raised his voice, obviously hoping Samantha could hear him. "The other charges were just to scare her. Next time she's out toilet papering, I suspect she'll be more careful, so she won't be caught."

"Oh, that's not the right thing to encourage, officer," Sandra grinned.

"Your daughter's a little too ready to sacrifice herself for others. You might want to keep an eye on her."

"Is she now?"

"She couldn't have done that job alone." A smile tugged at the officer's lips.

"Oh, it must really be something," whispered Sandra.

"Best one of the year," chuckled the officer. "Have a good night."

Sandra shut the door and locked it before turning around and staring at her daughter. Samantha averted her eyes.

"Samantha Rose Symanski," breathed her mother, "did you get pictures of her house? I want pictures."

"GOOD MORNING, COLUMBUS DONS," Barb's voice crackled over the speakers. Levi's eyes opened at the sound of her malevolence. *Today is Duct Tape Day, and already some fine costumes are being nominated for Best Dressed. Keep up the spirit. Today's football practice will be held at 3:30. The entire sophomore class is to report to the Father Hugh Deeny Auditorium for an impromptu discussion with me immediately after final bell.*

Word got around about the toilet-papering of Barb's house, and that Samantha Symanski took the heat. Speculation about the true culprit grew; by lunch, a dozen theories circulated about who could have done such a fantastic TP job.

When it came time to file into the gym, there was no doubt in anyone's mind what the after-school discussion was about. Barb strode back and forth in front of the bleachers holding the entire sophomore class hostage, glaring at them occasionally until the gym was silent.

"I am here to let you all know Samantha Symanski has confessed to the police that she toilet-papered my property last night. Symanski, stand up." Levi's heart pounded as she complied and a part of him regretted running. He looked over at the open gym doors. Other students were leaning in, listening. Barb continued.

"Samantha will be cleaning up all the toilet paper today, starting in about an hour. I know for a fact she did not do the entire job on her own. I want to point out it is unfair for you other guilty parties not to help her. This is an opportunity for the rest of you to do the right, Christian thing and come forward. Clean up the mess you made. I expect it completed today. Dismissed." Barb was the first to leave the gym.

It was silent as students slowly exited, giving Samantha a wide berth. Levi looked at Tim, who shrugged. They stepped down the bleachers, pausing to look at Samantha. She was pale and staring off into space. They stepped into the lobby, where discussion was already breaking out.

Samantha entered the lobby last. Levi locked eyes with her. He had to talk to her. As he approached, Laderia cut in his path, and gave Samantha a monstrous hug.

"Chica, you've got the biggest balls of any man I've ever met." She shook Samantha dramatically for emphasis. "For serio!"

"I can't breathe." Samantha patted Laderia's back. Levi felt himself smile and joined in as Laderia started clapping for her. Soon the whole lobby was clapping, and Samantha, beet red in spite of herself, bowed before heading to her locker.

"Hey Stoner." Laderia turned to Levi. "You're coming to the cleanup."

"I have other things to—"

"It wasn't a question. We're going to clean up Babs's place with Samantha. The whole grade. We're making a statement against this oppression."

Levi frowned. "I'm under threat of expulsion—"

"If we're *all* there Babs can't do anything. She can't expel the entire sophomore class. If you don't come I will turn both of us in." She poked him in the chest. "Then you'll be expelled for serio."

SAMANTHA STOOD IN THE YARD in front of Barb's house, looking up at the toilet paper fluttering from the trees down to the ground.

Her mother left after dropping her off, but not before pulling out her camera and snapping a half-dozen photos. "Even more magnificent in the daylight! Have fun honey," she chimed, leaving Samantha with a pile of black garbage bags and a pair of gloves.

With a sigh, Samantha grabbed a billowing trail of toilet paper off a tree and shoved it into a bag. It was then that cars started pulling up—at least a dozen, each containing four or five students. They hopped out, pointing in amusement at the toilet paper stretching between the trees and arching over Barb's roof. Laughter rang out, cameras clicked, the whole property coated in students.

Becca's car pulled up. Natalie, Laderia, Becca, and Jennifer came over to Samantha.

"I missed out last night," Natalie took off her sunglasses to look at the spectacle. She pulled out her phone and took some pictures. "For posterity. I haven't seen a job like this since...ever. Great job, Sammy."

"I didn't do—"

"I told you it was coolio." Laderia beamed.

Jennifer popped her gum as she put her phone away. "Sammy, Matt's at football practice, but he wants you to know he'd be here if he could."

"Yeah, he texted me," Samantha lied.

"If it's any consolation, Stoner and Dealer are coming," Laderia raised her eyebrows. "Two-for-one tradeoff."

"Matt should still be here. He did contribute." Becca shrugged.

Samantha pulled on her gloves. "Grab some toilet paper and a bag. We can probably get this done in an hour." She looked around at her classmates picking up the toilet paper. Most of them she never talked to. A warmth crept into her chest as they occasionally glanced at her with smiles and waves.

A distant rattling noise followed by the slam of two car doors quieted the yard. Levi and Tim strode down the block toward them. Samantha noticed how everyone stared at them. It wasn't the same sort of stare they gave her over these first two weeks of school. It was decidedly more hostile.

DYLAN MOEDE CHARGED through a fog-machine-induced haze into the gymnasium, holding an enormous silver and black flag on a stick. ACDC's *Thunderstruck* pounded in the background as the senior class roared after him, clad in blue.

"The gym's going to be silver and black for the dance," Natalie informed Samantha. "The seniors chose the colors." The senior class filled their designated bleachers section, cheering and stomping their feet in unison to the music until Barb got on the microphone in the middle of the gym.

"Stop it or your class money will pay for new bleachers." The stomping ceased. Barb handed the microphone to Mrs. Black.

"Welcome, Columbus Dons, to the Homecoming Pep Rally!" An enormous cheer erupted from the four grades, the middle school, and a large group of alumni. "To start things off, we're going to have a little competition to see which class can cheer the loudest. Show your spirit and scream your color out, freshmen!"

"Yellow!" The freshmen bellowed vaguely.

"Sophomores!"

"Green, green, green, green!" Samantha joined the chanting.

"Juniors!"

"Red, red, red, red, redredredred—"

Barb snatched the microphone. "Enough! Seniors!"

"Blue! Blue! Blue! Blue!"

"It's the seniors for the win!"

The rest of the gym groaned as the seniors cheered.

"We're extremely excited for the Homecoming Game tonight, aren't we?" Cheers mixed with applause. "Welcome the Spencer-Columbus Rockets!" The football team strode in, their red uniforms jarring against the blue padding and white walls. Dylan, Matt, and several other boys ran from the stands to join them on the gym floor. "Players from both schools, unite to give us a team! Let's show them our gratitude." Obligatory applause commenced. "Now, we are going to see an encore performance of the winning acts from last night's Lip Sync Contest to get us in the spirit. Then the band will perform while the faculty judges the poster contest to determine the winning class."

"Since when was 'Heaven is Blue' a class motto?" Samantha narrowed her eyes at the seniors' posters. "They've got no pride."

"Technically, pride is a sin. Not good for a Catholic school," Natalie corrected.

"Who cares?" Jennifer popped her gum.

"We're not allowed to put down the other classes with our posters," Natalie explained to Samantha. "That's why they took down the freshmen's poster of the banana beating all the other fruits in a foot race."

"And Barb had Mrs. Black take down the juniors' poster of the exploding red thermometer because it was too sexual." Laderia pointed to the empty spot on the wall of red posters.

"Are you kidding?! What did it say?" Samantha asked.

"'Too Hot to Handle'," Laderia fanned herself with her hands.

"Does anyone else think this borders on ridiculous?" Samantha threw her hands up in the air in exasperation. "What's the point of Color Day if it isn't to get the grades to team up against each other and melee for the hell of it?!"

"The sole purpose is to get students riled up against each other and then put them down for giving in and hating on the other grades," Tim leaned in from the upper bleachers. "There's some Catholic lesson in there somewhere."

"Beat it, Tim." Jennifer shot him a fierce look.

"I'm looking for Becca."

"She's a junior, so try the other side of the gym." Natalie glared at Tim until he left.

Jennifer tossed her green-streaked hair. "Like it or not, Dealer's right. That's how the B does it. Divide and conquer, with a little shame thrown in for good measure."

"You're a grim bitch sometimes." Natalie adjusted the dozens of green beads around her neck. "Grim, grim, grim."

"You look like a leprechaun," Jennifer retorted.

"We all look like leprechauns," Laderia huffed. "I'm Hispanic and dressed like I'm Irish."

"And it's your best outfit all week," Jennifer droned.

"I was partial to the globe," Natalie bounced.

"I can't believe the seniors haven't had a single poster taken down." Samantha glowered. "Look, none of their posters are cool or funny. They're all very boring and safe."

"That's why they'll win," Natalie said matter-of-factly. "Their class is very competitive. They play the system and win. We did manage to beat them in the tug of war last year, but we have eleven more people in our class."

"That was the only win we had last year." Laderia adjusted the enormous green top hat adorning her head. "And it's the exact same thing we won this year. It's pathetic. I think the B has it in for us. The freshmen won three events this week! It was worth cleaning up that toilet paper. I wonder who did it, anyway."

"Some closet rebels, daring to fight the system, obviously." Jennifer popped her gum loudly. "I think it was the senior class. She trusts them too much. I bet they did it."

After the Lip Sync recap ended, Barb read a list of the winning classes and competitions, ending with the poster competition, which the seniors won.

"Told ya so," Natalie bumped Samantha. "Now they'll announce Homecoming Court. Be prepared, ladies!" She disappeared.

Jennifer popped her gum. "Whatevs."

Mrs. Black and Barb got on the microphone again after the band stopped playing. "Now, ladies and gentlemen, we will reveal this year's Homecoming Court. Your Freshmen Representatives, Brian Sullivan and Ellie Miller." The freshmen ran in dressed as bananas as the whole gym laughed; Barb's face darkened.

"Your Sophomore Representatives, Jacob Bauman and Natalie Devereaux." After some careful maneuvering, Natalie and Jacob came in—very tall and overly muscular for his age, he carried her in on his shoulders. She shimmied her shoulders and cheered, her beads shaking like maracas. The gym cheered back. As they reached the center of the gym, he let her down. Barb gestured to Señorita Black, who swooped in and took the beads from Natalie.

"You know what they do at Mardis Gras to get them," Barb scolded as the sophomores booed.

"The Junior Representatives, Matt Stauber and Kaeli Edwards." The two walked in, arms linked. Samantha felt a stab of jealousy. A great movement in the juniors' stands drew everyone's attention. Two boys brought out a great red bundle, and unrolled a red carpet across the gym floor. Matt and Kaeli walked on it as the rest of the junior class pulled out their cameras and phones and took pictures, swarming the gym floor like paparazzi.

"Oh, Natalie's turning green in the face," Laderia pointed. "She doesn't like being shown up."

"Now she really looks like a leprechaun," Jennifer pulled out her phone. "This moment will be on Facebook forever."

"Don't do that," Samantha sighed.

"Why not? It's funny," Jennifer retorted. "That expression could go viral. Hell, that outfit could go viral. She'd make a great meme."

"And now the Senior Representatives," Barb said. "Dylan Moede and Nikki Becker!"

"Oh no way! Y'all, is that Mr. Becker's daughter?" Samantha looked at her hard. "She has his nose and eyebrows. I never noticed!"

"It's weird how those features look so much better on a girl, isn't it?" Jennifer snickered.

BEELL STADIUM swelled with Marshfield High School students and fans. Samantha didn't understand why the girls wanted to see the other high school play, but at least she didn't have to wear her cheerleading uniform.

"That's the public high school?" Samantha pointed to the odd building rising behind Beell Stadium. All-brick save for a smattering of windows, its white-capped astronomy tower reached to the nearly-full moon.

"The public *middle* school," Becca corrected without taking her eyes off the football field. "When my dad was a kid, his older brothers went there for high school, before they built the new school, then my dad moved to—"

"Shut up Becca, the Tigers are tied!" Jennifer snapped.

"It's taller than I thought it would be," Samantha ignored Jennifer. "Do they use the astronomy tower? That would be—"

"Who'd want to come to school at night?" Jennifer rolled her eyes. "Just to climb a bunch of stairs and stare at specks in a telescope. Holy goodness, run, run, RUN!"

She was on her feet and screaming at the field as the Marshfield Tigers charged. Samantha and the other girls joined in Jennifer's scream as the crowds roared in the stands, the air electric. The player flew to the end zone, football in hand.

He tripped on his feet and fell face first into the ground, two yards from the end zone.

Jennifer shrieked. The football bounced away, and a player from Menasha scooped it up and ran the other way.

"Losing to the Bluejays again!" Laderia glared at the field as the crowd moaned in horror.

A Tiger suddenly leapt onto the Bluejay. They landed in a heap at the 35-yard line.

"They lost so much field!" Jennifer wailed.

"Look on the bright side," Samantha said, "there's a whole quarter to go, and they're tied."

"You idiot, we're in the first quarter. That means three more quarters after this," Jennifer glowered at her. "That's not good. If

Menasha pulls ahead early, we never catch up to them. This is, like, the most important quarter."

"Why do you care about this team anyway? It's not your school," Samantha frowned. "Our homecoming game isn't until tomorrow afternoon."

"Sammy, Columbus's dating pool is small. You need to keep your options open."

ROARS FROM THE CROWD echoed across the middle school campus. The night sky was bright from the moon and the blaze of stadium lights behind them.

Roddis Manor dominated a huge corner lot on Fourth Street, massive trees edging the property and flanking the house like sentinels. Levi and Tim skirted the perimeter, peering at the darkened windows.

"This place always gives me the creeps." Tim rubbed his hands together.

"Really?"

"Ya, it looks like the Amityville Horror house and Scarlett O'Hara's mansion had a lovechild," Tim nodded to the gambrel roof. "If I was a ghost and had to pick a house to haunt, this would be it."

"Whatever."

"Am I really the only one who sees it?"

Levi glared at Tim.

"Oh, I guess I'm the dumb one here. You probably never even saw those movies, so of course you wouldn't—"

"Shut up, Tim." Levi punched him in the shoulder.

"Ow! Can you tell if Lancaster's home?" Tim whispered through his bandana.

"Not from here," Levi whispered back. "We gotta get to the garage. We can check if there are cars." Tim nodded. They hustled past the trees, following the cracked driveway to the detached garage behind the house.

They stepped into view of the windows as they tried to peer into the garage. Levi felt the hairs on the back of his neck stand on end. He glanced over his shoulder at the house, searching for any signs of—not life—movement. He saw nothing, but couldn't shake the feeling he was being watched. He turned to look into the garage windows.

"Do you see anything?" Tim was barely audible.

"It's empty."

"Good," Tim breathed. "My heart is pounding. Let's go home."

"No. We're going in."

"In the garage?" Tim's voice cracked.

"In the house," Levi nodded to the back door by the porte-cochere.

"No."

"Yes."

"Why? How would that even help you?" Tim leaned on the side of the garage. "It's not like Lancaster's a vampire. Harris was."

"Harris wasn't actually a vampire, he only wanted to become one," Levi said slowly. "I…um…killed him before he got what he wanted."

"Exactly. So why break into Lancaster's house?"

"Tim, I should have told you earlier, but I didn't want to freak you out."

Tim slouched forward, tensing as if to break into a sudden sprint. "Tell me what?"

"I didn't think you'd believe me…"

"What?"

"Lancaster *is* a vampire." Cheers from Beell Stadium interrupted the moment of silence.

"Levi Mauer," Tim whispered, "I watched you slay a man who crawled out of a grave across the street from the Marshfield Clinic. I believe you, man. And that is exactly why I'm *not* going in."

"But it was your idea."

"When I was high," Tim hissed. "You can't expect me to make good decisions in that kind of altered state. That's like having Lindsay Lohan as your designated driver."

"You weren't high, chicken shit," Levi muttered without much certainty before darting directly to the back door, hiding in the porte-cochere's shadow. He looked back at Tim, standing in broad moonlight by the garage and shaking like a leaf. He waved him over. Tim shook his head, pointing vehemently at the spot he stood on.

Levi grunted. He turned to the door, palms sweating as he reached for the latch.

To his own surprise, it wasn't locked. He pulled the door open slowly, hoping the noise from the football game drifting in the air would mask the creaking. He only opened it wide enough to slip inside.

Stepping into a dark hallway, he shut the door behind him. Searching for obstacles, his shoes skimmed the surface of a rug. After five steps, his toes discovered a stair. The thud of his foot on the wood made him catch his breath. He held still, trying to hear over his pounding heart. Nothing happened. He put out his hands, letting his fingers trace the wallpaper as he took the steps up to the main floor.

Though he found several light switches, he decided against turning them on. It would give away his position, he reasoned. Besides, the streetlights spilled enough light into the windows in the living and dining area to allow him to make out chandeliers, ornate trim, furniture and even the patterns in the area rugs. Radiators lined the walls of many of the rooms. The loud ticking of a grandfather clock taunted him from a dark corner. It never crossed his mind just how old that house was until that moment.

He moved into the living room, scanning for anything unusual. He wasn't sure what exactly that would be, but he knew he had to look. Quick and quiet, he went through the drawers of three end tables and a desk. Nothing.

Off to the dining room to search the china hutch. Nothing. He proceeded to the kitchen, and after what must have been thirty minutes of clattering and breath-holding as he raided the cabinets, he determined it ordinary.

The entire main floor was fairly boring. Unsure of whether or not that was a good thing, he stepped toward the grand staircase that led to the upper floors, debating an ascent. There was a lot of house to search, and it would take more time than he had to search it properly.

The tinkering of keys on a piano sent his adrenaline into overdrive. He turned around, scanning the dark house from the base of the stairs. He gripped the stake in his jacket. The ticking grandfather clock sounded exceptionally loud as he tried to listen for other noises. There was something else in there with him.

Panning the room, he tried to remember which way he came from. "Porte-cochere, side door," he mouthed to himself. Kitchen, no. Dining room, no. Living room, yes. That way. Levi went in that direction, as quickly and silently as he could. A sudden rush of pittering feet. He halted, eyes wide. It was close. Very, very close. He looked around. No one. Goosebumps on his arms stood up until they hurt.

Was Lancaster here? Was he watching Levi from some obscure corner that Levi neglected to search? Was he toying with him? Playing with his food? Levi wasn't going to wait around to find out. He pulled the stake from his jacket, his arm flexing as he gripped it tight.

He proceeded to the narrow hallway that led back outside, eyes wide. Stepping carefully down the tiny flight of stairs, a sudden rush of darkness by his feet made him curse out loud. He froze as two glowing green eyes stared up at him from in front of the door. He was about to kick at the thing, when it let out a soft 'meow.'

Levi blinked. "You're a cat. A black cat."

The cat stared back at him.

"What a stereotype." Levi broke the staring contest and stepped past the pair of glowing eyes. He opened the door slowly. The cat darted between his legs, through the gap, and bolted across the yard, disappearing into the shadows. He felt the color drain from his face as the roars from the football game echoed in the air. "Oh shit."

Tim hissed from the shadows by the garage. "There's a car coming! Get over here!" Levi bolted next to Tim in the shadows, just before the car turned into the driveway.

"Behind the garage!" Levi dragged Tim through the shadows, avoiding the beams of the headlights. The sound of the garage door going up as they sat down and leaned against the white wall made Levi sweat.

"Slay him as he comes out," Tim whispered as the car pulled into the garage. "He won't suspect—"

Levi clamped his hand over Tim's bandana-covered mouth. They tried not to make a sound, listening as the engine stopped, keys jingled, and the door opened and shut. The sound of dress shoes clicking on the concrete was almost indiscernible against the noise of the football game floating through the trees.

"Buttons," Lancaster's deep voice floated through the air, "how did you get outside? You naughty creature!" The cat's yowl curdled his blood. Levi wasn't certain how Lancaster managed to catch the feline so quickly. He had to see what was happening. He took his hand off of Tim's face and twisted around. Mindful of every rustling blade of grass, he crept to the edge of the wall, and glanced around the corner.

Thomas Lancaster stood partly in the shadow of the porte-cochere, his shoes reflecting the white house. The black cat writhed to escape his hands. "You're going back inside," Lancaster held the cat high, looking into its eyes. He opened the side door and tossed the cat in before taking a step into the house.

Levi leaned on the wall of the garage, and the old structure creaked loudly. His stomach flipped.

Lancaster paused, turning his head in Levi's direction. He shut the door to the house and walked over, dress shoes clicking with each step. Levi ducked back around the garage, heart in his throat.

Tim was gone.

Paralyzed, Levi listened as Lancaster's steps came to a stop on the other side of the garage. He debated bolting through the bushes and trees to the neighbors' yard. He could keep running until he got to his truck in the middle school parking lot.

"Levi Mauer," Lancaster's voice filled the air, "I know you were in my house." Levi fought the urge to run. He wouldn't give away his position. "I don't know what's happening to you, Levi. I called your parents to offer you another job this school year, and your phone line's been disconnected." Levi figured the vampire was pacing in the driveway by the clicking of Lancaster's shoes.

"We should talk about the…incident last week. I'm not sure what you think you saw. I'm concerned for Arthur Harris's whereabouts. He was my employee, and he hasn't shown up for work lately. The police tell me he's…vanished." Lancaster stopped walking.

Levi felt a bead of sweat run down his nose. He knew the vampire was waiting for a response, movement, anything. A light breeze rustled the trees. Lancaster's shoes clicked toward the house. Without a second thought, Levi bolted through the bushes and trees, and sprinted through the neighbors' yards until he reached the parking lot. It was empty. The game was over. Levi's truck was gone.

He felt for his keys. He didn't have them. He looked around the deserted lot, panic surging through him. Glancing over his shoulder at Roddis Manor looming through the trees, Levi could see Lancaster looking out from the back balcony, the interior light coming through the glass doors casting him in a menacing black profile.

He ran into the shadow of the massive school building and cut behind Beell Stadium. He had to get away. He reached 8th Street and headed toward Central Avenue. He was only ten blocks from the apartment.

Resigning himself to jog the rest of the way, Levi's mind raced with ways he could kill Tim. A rattling behind him made him turn around. His truck lurched its way up the street toward him.

"Tim," he grunted, "I'm going to kill you."

The truck pulled up next to him, jerking to a stop. "Levi," Tim said out the window, "I was coming to pick you up. Where were you?" Levi ignored him and climbed into the passenger seat.

"Move over," he said through gritted teeth.

"I can't really drive anyway." Tim chuckled nervously, wiping a hand across his face. "You probably noticed." Tim and Levi switched spots. "You dropped your keys, if you're wondering."

"What the fuck are you talking about?" Levi stepped on the gas.

"That's how I got it started. I was gonna circle around so you could just run to Felker Street, but by the time I got there you were gone."

"You asshole," Levi growled. "I could have been killed."

"I was just trying to help," Tim shrugged.

"Stop trying to help me!" Levi slammed his hand on the steering wheel. "I need you to listen to me, not rescue me, dammit! I'm the slayer! I'm the one who does the rescuing!" They pulled into the apartment's gravel parking lot. Levi shut the truck off and they sat there.

"I'm not sorry," Tim said after a while. "You need help and I'm helping you. I admit I should have told you—"

"You should have," Levi snapped back. "You left me there."

"Not to die," Tim untied the bandana around his neck. "You had some eavesdropping to do, remember? What did you learn from Lancaster—besides the name of his cat?"

"He knows I'm onto him," Levi muttered. "He could tell I was there. He's been trying to find me."

"Well, it's a good thing you moved in with me, isn't it?" Tim remarked. "He'll never find you here."

"He saw me in the parking lot." Levi shoved Tim. "He knows—"

"He knows you had a ride that ditched you. He still doesn't know what you drive, does he?"

"No," Levi acknowledged. "I don't think so."

"If the truck would've been there, he'd know. You should be thanking me, Levi Mauer. I saved your ass, whether you like it or not."

"I LOVE IT." Mrs. Symanski smiled as she leaned in Samantha's bedroom door. "It's so elegant."

"You think so?" Samantha adjusted the single golden strap on her white dress.

"It reminds me of what I wore." Mrs. Symanski crossed her arms. "Our prom theme was Grease—the movie, you know. Everybody said I looked just like Olivia Newton-John. Your father even asked the band to play *Look at Me, I'm Sandra Dee*, but Mister Sister unplugged the speakers after 'lousy with virginity.'"

"That's one theme we're definitely *not* using." Natalie marked something off a list in the notebook in front of her.

"Glad to know I'm keeping with tradition," Samantha turned and looked at herself over her shoulder. "But what about my hair? I want to put it up—"

"No, are you nuts?!" Natalie gasped from Samantha's bed. "You didn't get an appointment at a *salon*—you can't just put it up by yourself! You need professional help."

"Truer words were never spoken," Mrs. Symanski laughed and walked down the hallway. "Just don't look like a slut!"

"Ugh! I can't believe she said that to me. What should I do with it?" Samantha pouted her lips as she looked at herself in the mirror. "I've got no time for anything really formal."

"You're in a white one-strap a-line cocktail dress." Natalie gave her a nonplussed look. "And you're a natural blonde. Volume, shine, and leave it down. Duh."

"How do I make it look silky smooth and perfect?" Samantha asked. "Your hair looks like a shampoo commercial."

"That's because I'm French…and went to a salon this morning." Natalie winked. "You gotta plan these things better, Sammy."

"You really love Homecoming."

"Second time on Court." Natalie held up two silver-tipped fingers. "I'm still mad that the B took my beads away. Just thinking about it makes me wanna TP her right now."

"Ha ha ha," Samantha said.

"So how many friend requests did you have on Facebook after that cleanup?" Natalie stood next to her in the mirror.

"One hundred and four. I only accepted half so far."

"OMG," Natalie breathed. "You're on Homecoming Court next year for sure."

Samantha shrugged. "It doesn't matter to me. I just want to look nice tonight and dance with Matt."

"A little horizontal rumba," Natalie's blue eyes glittered with mischief. "I saw the way you looked at him during the pep rally."

Samantha blushed. "I barely know him. I'm not doing anything like that."

"You totally want to," Natalie laughed. "Hey, you know what's awesome?"

"Matt's lips. No, no, I'm joking."

"Liar. What I was going to say was that I have a silver dress, and you have white and gold. Silver and gold. OMG! That could work!" She rushed back to her notebook.

"What are you doing?"

"Coming up with Homecoming ideas for our class. Themes, songs, colors, everything."

"You got a couple years." Samantha slipped out of her dress.

"It's not enough time! Last year was 'Mobster Mash,' this year it's 'Can't Fight the Moonlight.' Who knows what's coming next? I have to top all of them! I want us to be the best!"

"Well, good luck. Get your makeup and dress on. We gotta meet the boys in a little bit." Samantha entered her bathroom to work on her own hair and makeup. After almost two hours of fuss, she decided she was satisfied. She put a final layer of gloss on her lips, put her dress back on and stepped into strappy gold heels.

"Oh Sammy, you look beautiful." Natalie waited in the foyer as Samantha came downstairs.

"You do too." Samantha gushed as Natalie stood up in her silver strapless, her silver shoes and blue makeup sparkling. "You look so celestial."

"That's an adjective I don't hear often," Mrs. Symanski commented as she walked in. "Why Natalie, you look lovely, the yearbook pictures will be great! Oh Samantha Rose! You are stunning! Let me get my camera!"

The doorbell rang. Samantha rolled her eyes at the creepy tolling.

"That'll be Jacob Bauman. I'm going back to my house. My mom wants a couple shots before we go to the dance." Natalie answered the door. "Laderia! What are you doing here?"

"What are *you* doing here?" Laderia shot back. "I'm here for Samantha. She's riding with me, unlike some people I know." Laderia gave Natalie a pointed look.

"Oh Laderia, I'm sorry!" Samantha frowned. "Matt asked me to ride with him last Friday, and I forgot to tell—"

"What?" Laderia's mouth hung open. "Are you seriously not going to ride with me either?"

"He asked if we could take his car," Samantha replied.

"You knew that for a whole week and didn't bother telling me?" Laderia snorted. "Fine, but you're missing out on a limo ride. We got an unrestricted wet bar."

"No you don—Ow, don't pinch my arm fat!" Natalie squealed.

"Then it's just Becca, Jennifer, Stefan, Dylan, and me. Later, selfish bitches." Laderia huffed, and stormed back to the limo parked in front of the house, her tight white dress barely billowing in the breeze.

"What was that about?" Mrs. Symanski returned with a camera.

"Nothing," Samantha and Natalie said in unison.

"That didn't seem like nothing." The limo pulled away and another car pulled up.

"That's Jacob. I'm going! See you at the dance!" Natalie waved and was out the door.

"What a silly girl...Smile!" Mrs. Symanski said, taking several shots of Samantha as she barely posed and rolled her eyes. "Samantha, you've gotta work with me on this. You're not even trying to work it!"

"Mom, I don't want to," Samantha whined. "We never take pictures of anything, why start now?"

"Because I'm home all the time and we can." Mrs. Symanski held up the camera. "Come on Samantha. Please?"

"No," Samantha shook her head and walked into the living room. "Who's going to see them anyway? You—when you're old and decrepit. Why should I care?"

"Well Samantha, I would hope you'd care about your old and decrepit mother," Mrs. Symanski said quietly. "It's a commandment to honor your father and mother."

"Ugh! I wasn't talking about you, I was—whatever. You don't even honor your own parents."

"Samantha Rose Symanski!"

"They're dead and you never visit their graves or anything! You just sit in the house all day like a hermit, harping on me to do this or that!"

"Why the sudden outburst?" Mrs. Symanski snapped. "It's Homecoming Night. All you have to do is take some pictures for posterity, and then go and have a good time! What's so complicated?!"

"This is all for you! You turned my life into some stupid remake show for you!" Samantha shouted. "I suddenly have to look like you, be popular like you, hate Barb like you—"

"You don't have to do anything! Your life is perfect!" Mrs. Symanski roared back. "I pay the bills, paint the house, drop you at school, let you go wherever—"

"No!" Samantha's face reddened. "Don't make it sound so generous! You're supposed to do that stuff, you're the mom!"

"And I am doing it, so why are you mad?!" Mrs. Symanski was inches from her daughter's face. "You talk to your mother with respect, young lady!"

"I don't respect you!" Samantha screamed. The house was silent as Mrs. Symanski's face went white. "I don't...I-I saw the slingshot in your trunk."

"What?"

"You know exactly what! I know you toilet-papered Barb's house. The only way you'd get it so high in the trees was with that oversized slingshot."

Mrs. Symanski began to laugh. Samantha didn't think her face could feel warmer, but it proved her wrong.

"It's not funny! She blamed me! She told that policeman she saw me do it, but she probably saw you outside! I had to lie! She embarrassed me in front of my whole class—"

"Oh, stop it Samantha. You're the most popular girl in school now and you didn't even have to do anything for it. What do you care?"

"I don't want to be popular!" Samantha yelled, but she saw her mother was suddenly immune to the volume. "I just—"

"If you weren't popular, would that boy have asked you to Homecoming?" Mrs. Symanski raised an eyebrow.

"Don't put that in my head," Samantha's voice darkened. "He asked me before the toilet-papering."

"Trust me, there are perks to a good social position," Mrs. Symanski said with finality. "You'll come to appreciate them."

The doorbell rang.

"That's Matt." Samantha turned away from her mother. She opened the door. He smiled down at her. She felt her knees weaken a little.

"Hey babe, you look amazing."

"Thanks," she said, looking him up and down. "A white tuxedo..."

"I figured we should match. Are you gonna let me in?"

"Yeah, come in."

"Oh, here's your corsage." He produced a clear plastic container.

"Red roses," she murmured as she opened it. "They're beautiful."

"Of course," he shrugged. "Hi, Mrs. Symanski."

"Hello, you must be Matt." Mrs. Symanski flashed her pearly whites. "It's nice to meet you. You're very dashing."

"Mom," Samantha hissed as Matt slid the corsage onto her wrist.

"Let's get a picture of you two together. Stand by the base of the stairs!" Samantha finally submitted to the camera, but it was pleasant with Matt there and his hand on her side.

"Perfect! You kids have fun." Mrs. Symanski shooed them out of the house. "But not too much fun!"

"We're going to eat with my parents before going over to the school," Matt called as they stepped off the porch. "My mom wants pictures too."

"Oh, that's fine." Mrs. Symanski watched and waved as they got into Matt's clean, glittering Hemi 'Cuda.

Samantha had to admit she preferred Matt's car to a limo. "It looks so nice."

"I washed it when you said you'd be wearing white," Matt said proudly.

"Thoughtful," Samantha nodded. They started driving. "Roll the windows up or my hair will be destroyed."

Matt's grin faded. He rolled up the windows, and they were covered in water droplets. "Now it's going to dry all spotted," he muttered.

"Why roll them down in the first place?"

"I like fresh air."

Fifteen minutes later, they arrived at Matt's farm. The gravel crunched under Samantha's feet as they walked up to the white farmhouse. With a nod, Matt opened the door for her, and the smell of steak drifted out. The kitchen could barely contain Matt's family among its old cabinets and new appliances. The Staubers stared as Matt and Samantha came in.

"You didn't ask Kaeli?" exclaimed a gray-haired woman who could only be Matt's mother. Samantha felt a touch of fury. "Hi, I'm Mrs. Stauber. That's my husband Randy over there, Marie and Joel. Sit down! Have a plate! We'll take pictures after you're done."

"Umm, okay." Samantha was practically forced into a seat around the kitchen table. Matt sat down opposite her and winked. She hoped her makeup would hide her blush.

"So how do you like Matt's ride, little lady?" Mr. Stauber asked after they said grace.

"It's a nice car," Samantha replied. "Very loud."

"It's my pride and joy," Mr. Stauber beamed. "Matt begged me to let him borrow—"

"Dad," Matt cut in. "Thanks for letting me borrow your Cuda."

"I didn't let you borrow it." Mr. Stauber leaned toward Samantha. "I'm charging him monthly installments. Kind of a rent-to-own situation. Only twenty thousand dollars to go!" He roared with laughter. Samantha raised her eyebrows at Matt as she put a piece of steak in her mouth. His jaw was clenching. Matt's mother coughed and changed the subject.

"So Samantha, I hear you're new this year. How do you like Columbus?"

"It's alright," Samantha shrugged.

"Just alright?"

"There are some things I don't like. They censor everything, and the dress code is ridiculous—I haven't been able to wear jeans in weeks. I don't know how y'all put up with it."

"It's not that bad." Mrs. Stauber sipped her beer. "When I went there, Columbus still had nuns, and nuns had rulers and corporal punishment. But, we managed to have fun. I guess it must seem very conservative after being in a place as liberal as…"

"Yeah." Samantha ended the conversation. An awkward silence ensued and they ate quickly. After supper, Mrs. Stauber made them pose for pictures by Matt's—or rather, Matt's father's—car. They turned on the porch lights as the dusky glow in the sky faded. Mrs. Stauber kissed her son on each cheek, wished them a good time, and they were off to the dance.

"I'M BORED." Tim watched their classmates enter the school from the grassy field across the street. He rolled his shoulders and leaned back and forth. "Is it alright if I go in? You can stand out here alone."

"I thought you wanted to learn on the job." Levi glared at him. "Or are you trying to run away again?"

"I'm insulted. And I'm bored."

"Uh-huh."

"Didn't you hear me? I'm insulted, and bored. It's Homecoming Night, Levi, and I'm insulted and bored."

"You whine like a girl."

"I gotta fill the silence somehow," Tim responded as a group of students piled out of a limo, laughing as they walked past the flagpole to the front doors.

"It's getting cold out." Levi glanced at the cloudless sky and zipped up his black hoodie. "The crowd is picking up. Be alert."

"What if you wanted to go in? You didn't even dress for it." Tim shook his head.

"I think it's weird that you did. I'm going to stand out here all night and watch for vampires. Why do I need to wear a tux?"

Tim hit him on the forehead. "To go undercover, jackass. You'd catch more vampires if they didn't suspect you were a slayer."

"Nobody expects a slayer in a town like Marshfield. I'm undercover enough," Levi replied. "Besides, the school's on hallowed ground. No vampire can get past the sidewalk. And I hate monkey suits."

"It was worth a try." Tim grunted as he tugged on his white dress collar. "So itchy…fuck this bowtie. Why are watching for vampires at Homecoming at a school they can't touch?"

"Believe me, Lancaster will come here to find me. He's already been trying." Levi turned his attention back to the glowing front of the school. "I'm gonna be ready for him."

"Why wouldn't he just swing by after school any day of the week?"

"He's got a business to run. And now with a missing employee, any variation from his normal schedule will look suspicious."

"Listen. I wonder who that could be." Tim didn't hide his sarcasm.

Matt Stauber's Cuda pulled up, rumbling and roaring as he searched for a parking space.

"That's Samantha Symanski with him." Tim squinted as the car parked next to the sidewalk by the school. "She looks awesome."

"So what?" Levi murmured, his eyes not leaving the girl in white as Matt walked her to the entrance. His pulse quickened as he watched her lean into Matt's shoulder, Matt's hand sliding down to her hip.

"What do you mean 'so what'? You telling me you're unaffected by hot girls? You just wanna get me all alone out here with you, don't cha?" Tim grinned mockingly as Levi scowled at him. "Oh, don't go making those bedroom eyes at me, sir. I'll slow dance if you want—" His comment was interrupted by a punch to his gut.

"I like you better when you're high. You talk a lot less," Levi said into Tim's ear as Tim bent over and gasped for breath. He leaned against a tree and watched the door close as Samantha disappeared into the building.

"You're a prick." Tim massaged his sore stomach. "A royal prick."

"And you're a flighty bastard," Levi shot back. They fell silent as the wind rustled the trees and grass. The moon, eye-level in the sky already, cast odd shadows that faded in the streetlight.

"Dude, the moon is full." Tim held an accusatory hand up at the sky. "I don't wanna be out tonight. It's not safe."

"There's no such thing as werewolves, Tim."

"CAN YOU BELIEVE THAT BITCH?" Jennifer muttered into Samantha's ear as they stood on the edge of the gym watching the Homecoming Coronation. Matt and Kaeli Edwards linked arms and stood on the dais with the rest of the Homecoming Court. "She's so into him it's disgusting." Jennifer downed her punch.

"No she's not." Samantha crossed her arms and narrowed her eyes as Kaeli tossed her auburn hair and laughed at something Matt said. "Okay, maybe she is."

"What are you going to do about it?" Jennifer glanced at her.

"What can I do, tell her off? That's not classy." Samantha ran her fingers through her hair, lost in thought as the students playing the evening hosts went through a lousy routine of bland banter over the sound system.

"You gotta get him out of her clutches *somehow*." Jennifer gave her a look. "Believe me, if she was hitting on Dylan like that, I'd take out Miss Edwards with a stiletto in one hand and a straight razor in the other."

"Holy anger management, Batman," Samantha whispered.

"What?"

"That escalated quickly. How much punch did you have?"

Samantha glanced at the punch bowl, where Laderia and Stefan stood nonchalantly with a brown paper bag, pouring in Everclear little by little when the teachers were distracted.

"Only four cups," Jennifer teetered. "How about you?"

"None. I don't wanna spill on my dress."

"Why not? It's just an excuse to take the dress off," Jennifer hissed.

"I'm not that kind of girl," Samantha insisted.

"Hey ladies." Tim showed up on Jennifer's other side, Levi in tow. "How's the grand ceremony?"

"Boring," Samantha said through gritted teeth, glaring at the dais.

"Samantha's upset with Kaeli," Jennifer corrected. "She's being a skeaze."

"According to your friend Becca, I'm a skeaze too." Tim raised an eyebrow at her. "That hurts my feelings."

"Ooh, whatever." Jennifer popped her gum. "Get me more punch." She thrust her cup at Tim.

"I was hoping to get you alone." Tim pouted. "I got something you might like." He patted his pocket.

"I can't believe you." Jennifer walked away with him as LeAnn Rimes began to play. The Homecoming Court stepped off the dais to lead the dance. Matt and Kaeli put their arms around each other.

Samantha watched the other students pairing up as if about to board Noah's Ark. Some lingered around the edge of the floor with her, including Levi, who was decidedly not dressed for the occasion. She looked him up and down as he stood, arms crossed and uncomfortable, two feet away.

"Hey," she turned to him.

He looked at her, his half-grin barely there. "What?"

"Dance with me." Samantha stepped toward him.

"I don't know how—"

"Just do it, or I'm never lending you notes again," she muttered under her breath as she set her arms around his shoulders. "Put your hands on my waist. Make it believable." He did. They began gliding side-to-side to the beat, and slowly turned in place.

"The gym looks nice," Levi glanced around.

"Whatever." Samantha rolled her eyes. "You wore jeans and a hoodie?"

"I wasn't planning on coming."

"Tim dragged you here."

"Better than listening to him talk."

"He's a funny guy. Lighten up." Samantha looked into Levi's eyes. His face relaxed and a soft smile graced his lips. She broke the gaze.

"This is simpler than it looks," Levi said as she leaned into him.

"Uh-huh." Samantha turned her head sideways to rest it on Levi's chest, scanning for Matt as they turned. She locked eyes with him as he spun Kaeli. She smiled. He returned it with a flick of his tongue across his teeth. She blushed from a mix of thrill and revulsion.

Suddenly the music sped up and began to thump. Pairs turned into groups. Samantha released Levi from her grip.

"Thanks for playing along." She smiled as Matt came over and held out a cup of punch.

"Ya," Levi grunted. "Sure thing." He disappeared into the crowd.

"Thanks." Samantha took the cup from Matt.

"I couldn't wait to get back to you," he stood over her. Samantha flushed and focused on drinking her cup. "You look so damn beautiful tonight."

"I'm glad we get some time together now." She finished the punch and set the cup down.

"Let's get out of here." Matt took Samantha's hands in his own. "I don't want any distractions."

"Okay." The butterflies in Samantha's stomach lifted off at once as they left the school and headed to Matt's car. She barely noticed Levi leaning against the flagpole when she passed him.

LEVI WATCHED as Samantha got into Matt's car, which promptly revved up, whipped onto the street and roared away. The taillights turned a corner and the sound of the engine finally faded. He turned his eyes back to the entrance of the school as Tim and Jennifer emerged.

"Stoner." Jennifer nodded as she leaned against the stone wall holding up the statue of Columbus. Tim leaned next to her, and without taking his eyes off the school doors, pulled a joint from his tux jacket, and lit it behind his back. Levi watched as the little glowing speck exchanged hands and Jennifer took a long puff and held her breath.

"How is it?" Tim asked.

"Oh, that hits the spot." She let out a slow exhale and passed the joint to him. Tim took a drag and turned his head to the sky, the smoke escaping his mouth little by little.

"You want some?" Jennifer nodded to Levi and then to the joint in Tim's hand. Tim glanced at him.

"No," Levi said. "I gotta stay sharp."

"Too late, you're already dull," Jennifer replied. She grabbed Tim's wrist and brought his fingers to her lips and took one last drag on the joint. She strolled up to Levi and blew the smoke in his face before walking back into the school.

"That was so hot." The smoke in Tim's lungs muffled his voice.

"You've got strange taste."

"How so?" He exhaled through his nose and came over to Levi.

Levi nodded to the school. "She's nuts."

"You know what they say about crazy girls." Tim leaned on the flagpole next to Levi. They looked up at the moon. "I still haven't told you my werewolf story."

"LET'S ROLL DOWN THE WINDOWS," Samantha said. "I'm warm."

"You gotta do it manually—" Matt gestured as they accelerated onto the country roads. The wind exploded into the car as Samantha rolled the window down. Her hair billowing, she laughed as she caught the whiff of dairy farms. It didn't bother her tonight. She leaned out the window a little and looked at the moonlit road. She howled into the night air.

"You're so hot." Matt grinned at her as she ducked into the car. "We're gonna have a lot of fun."

Samantha pretended she couldn't hear him over the wind. She rolled up the window. "Where are we going?"

"McMillan," Matt said. "To my favorite spot."

"Really, now?"

"I wanna show you something."

"THIS DANCE WAS PRETTY SUCCESSFUL." Tim thumbed through the wad of bills in his hands. "The after-parties are gonna be good."

"Do you hear that?" Levi looked up in the sky. "That sound?"

"Bats." Tim pointed in the direction of the high-pitched squeaking. "Coming over those trees."

"Go inside, Tim." The swarm emerged and swooped towards them.

"Holy—" Tim bolted. Levi furrowed his brow as the swarm passed over him and banked around to spiral in the field across the street. Out of the spiraling bats, Lancaster stepped forward. The bats vanished. Levi's pulse quickened as Lancaster walked across the street, his dress shoes clicking, stopping on the sidewalk edging the school grounds.

"Levi Mauer, we need to talk," Lancaster's voice dripped with venom. "Is this a bad time?"

"No, this is a perfect time." Levi stopped just over an arm's length away from Lancaster. "What do you want, vampire?"

Lancaster's eyes flashed. "You're a slayer."

Levi forced his fear back down and ignored the accusation. "It doesn't take a genius to figure out what you are. Especially after what I've just seen."

"What can I say?" Lancaster chuckled.

"How long have you been a vampire?"

"Since my days at Kansas City Community College."

"How many have you killed?"

"I've killed no one, Levi," Lancaster replied. "This is still my first life. I'm aging normally, and I won't kill—"

"Shut up," Levi snapped. "I don't believe you—you're going to kill. You have and you will."

"Don't condemn me for crimes I haven't yet committed, Levi Mauer," Lancaster said. "I'm not a bad person—"

"You're not a person," Levi corrected. "You're a parasite. You prey on the lives of others to sustain your own so-called life. Don't tell me you haven't killed. I know how it spreads. You have to kill after you're turned, or your body will rot. You're not rotting."

"I think this is the most we've ever talked." Lancaster walked along the sidewalk, his hands folded behind his back. Levi kept pace in the grass. "Alright, I'll admit, I killed once."

"Who was it? Or don't you remember."

"Irrelevant." Lancaster looked down at Levi. "I'm more interested in what became of Arthur Harris. He never came back to work. I can only assume you killed him."

"Didn't expect the prey to become the predator, did you?" Levi glared. "You set me up. I would've been his first victim."

"Would've, could've, should've—you killed my friends, by the way." Lancaster radiated disapproval. "I work very hard to find the proper vampire material in this godforsaken town—"

"God didn't forsake this town," Levi squared his shoulders and stood straighter. "I'm still here, despite your trap."

"And that complicates things," Lancaster huffed. "Levi, I like you. I really enjoy your spunk. But you're a pain in my ass. It's a wonder the police haven't caught on to you yet."

Levi felt his veiled threat. "If they did, you'd end up at the station too. The thing is, you wouldn't show up on camera. You'd be a floating suit. The invisible man. Nothing like blowing your cover."

"No, but I can destroy yours. I could make an anonymous call, tip them off about Harris, tell them to search your house, interview your parents—but oh," Lancaster tisked, "that's right, your parents are dead." Levi felt his fists balling up. "They'll take you away, put you in a foster home if they don't decide to institutionalize you."

"I'll tell them to search your house," Levi threatened through gritted teeth, "look in your basement, see the things you've got hidden down there."

Lancaster paused, his thick eyebrows drawing together. "You

don't have anything on me, Mauer."

Levi spotted Lancaster's bluff. "I'll have them dig through your financial records," he pressed on. "They'll corroborate the outliers with what they find. Then they'll raid the funeral parlor, the graves—"

"Well, Mauer," Lancaster waved a hand. "It seems we both have enough bombs to drop to ensure mutual destruction." He leaned as far over the hallowed ground as he dared. "Let's come to an agreement."

"IT'S SO CLEAR." Samantha looked up at the full moon staring down at them. "I can see the craters, the streaks—every detail."

"Ya, it's something." Matt stretched next to her. They sat on the trunk of the car, parked on the highest point of a sloping field edged by scraggly woods a quarter-mile away. "I love coming out here."

"Very…romantic. In a country sort of way. Oh! Did you see that shooting star?!" She pointed at the sky. "I'm getting chills!"

Matt had the keys in the ignition and the windows down, an Oldies station played in the background. He took a swig of brandy and made a face. He offered her the bottle. "It'll keep you warm."

She shook her head, eyes wide. "I'm not drinking."

"You had the punch at the dance. What do you think was in it?"

"Don't boys usually offer their *jackets* to keep a girl warm?"

"Not in Wisconsin."

Samantha nudged him. With a snicker, he took off the white suit jacket and draped it over her shoulders.

"It suits you."

"I can't believe you drove your dad's car into a field," Samantha kicked her legs back and forth, her bare feet lightly touching the bumper. "Won't he be pissed?"

"I knew you only wanted me for my car." Matt glanced sideways at her.

"Assuming I even want you—egomaniac." Samantha leaned on his shoulder to hide her face. She suspected it was red, but couldn't tell if it was from his flirting or the spiked punch. "I'm having a really nice time."

"Did you have a nice time dancing with Mauer?" Matt leaned his head on her head, which made it difficult for her to shake her head no. "Seemed like you did."

"I had to dance with someone."

"You didn't have to," Matt muttered. "Nobody forced you to."

"Are you mad at me for dancing with another boy?"

"Wait, what? No I'm not—"

"That's the sound of guilt—OMG, you are!" Samantha's jaw dropped. "Why?! Y'all started it, dancing with what's-her-nuts—"

"Kaeli."

"What's-her-nuts," Samantha emphasized. "I didn't say a thing to you about it."

"It bothered you?" Matt looked surprised.

"It still bothers me! She could've gotten her own date and done the same thing! I wanted your first dance tonight to be with me!"

"Oh." Matt looked smug. "That can be arranged."

She rolled her eyes. "It could've been arranged, but guess what? It already happened; we can never recapture the moment."

"We can make a new moment. Right now."

"What?" Samantha blinked at him.

Matt was on his feet already. "We got the music and the full moon. Here in the field. Let's dance."

"But my shoes are still in the car—"

"Ever walk through a country field barefoot?" He held out a hand to help her off the car, the brandy bottle in his other hand.

"I hear it's a great way to get ticks," Samantha shot him a look.

"Don't be such a girl, Symanski." He set the brandy down on the trunk next to her with a clang and glared at her expectantly.

"I'm certain you prefer me as a girl, so I'll ignore that comment." Samantha pulled his jacket tighter around her shoulders, and didn't look at him. His eyes didn't waver, and she eventually met his gaze and sighed. "Fine."

She took his hand and he helped her down. The long grasses tickled her feet and legs. They walked into the field, just on the edge of the music. Matt put a hand around her waist and took her other hand in his, and they began to dance as *Hopelessly Devoted to You* came on the radio. Samantha rolled her eyes involuntarily as an image of her mother popped in her head.

"What was that face for?" Matt asked.

"Nothing," she said. "You're a good dancer."

"You're just worse at it than me," Matt said in her ear as they began to spin.

"If there's a way to kill the mood, you'll find it."

"Shut up," Matt whispered and pulled her closer.

"Don't tell me to—" The air was pierced with a long howl. Samantha felt the hair on her neck stand on end. "That sounded close."

"Full moon tonight," Matt shrugged. "No big deal."

"Something isn't right." Samantha dropped her hold on Matt and looked out over the field to the trees in the distance. "The crickets stopped."

Matt scanned the tree line, slipping a hand around hers. "Don't worry, wolves are more scared of us than we are of them."

"You haven't seen *The Gray*, have you?"

There was a sudden rustling in the trees on the edge of the field. Samantha and Matt watched as dozens of deer charged silently out of the woods straight for them. Samantha yelped and clutched Matt as the deer bolted around and past them to the woods on the other side of the gravel road behind them.

"What's happening?!" Samantha pressed against Matt.

"I don't know." He held her tight.

A growling sound grew louder. Samantha looked for the source of the sound. A large pair of glowing yellow eyes approached them.

"Matt," she whispered. "Matt, what is that thing?"

Matt turned slowly to look at it. Samantha heard his breathing stop. "Go back to the car," he said, barely audible.

"It's watching us." Samantha twisted her fingers into Matt's white dress shirt as the thing stalked closer.

The moonlight illuminated its dull gray skin; thin, patchy black hair coated its head and trailed down its back. Its shoulders were high and broad, its back hunched. Two sharp ears swiveled toward them as it moved forward on long, powerful legs. It stopped, sniffed the air, then its ears pressed flat to its skull. The thing let out a guttural growl unlike any animal Samantha ever heard.

"When I tell you, run to the car."

"My legs feel like rubber," Samantha breathed. "I can't."

"You can." Matt's muscles tensed. "And you will. Ready?"

"No."

"Three—"

"Matt—"

"Two—"

"I'm not—"

"One. RUN!" Matt threw Samantha toward the car. Letting out a primal roar, he raised his arms high and charged at the beast. Samantha scrambled in the grass, her balance suddenly gone. She stumbled to the car as fast as she could as roars exploded behind her. She flew into the driver's seat.

She looked out the window. Matt was rolling through the grass on that thing's back, trying to hold its mouth shut while dodging its claws as it reached to throw him off. Heart in her throat, she screamed his name. "MATT!"

The beast seemed distracted for a moment. Matt tried to get away, but it sank its teeth into his leg. Samantha gasped as he screamed. She hit the car horn and held it. The beast released him. She hit the horn again, and used her other hand to turn the keys.

"Come on," she cried as the keys refused to turn. She stomped on the three foot pedals. "Come on, come on, come on, come ON!" With a foot on the far left pedal, she managed to turn the keys and the engine roared to life. She turned on the headlights, and revved the engine, honking the horn.

The beast threw its head back, letting out a long howl. Her blood ran cold. It charged.

She rolled up the window as fast as she could. The beast stood up on its hind legs, and raked its claws over the roof of the car; the whole vehicle rocked violently. Tears rolled down Samantha's face as she looked at the gear shift.

"What do I do?!" she screamed at the three pedals on the floor. She grabbed the gear shift and wiggled it back and forth, feet hitting multiple pedals at once. The beast swung its claws at the window. She covered her head just in time as glass shattered across her.

The Cuda began to move, and Samantha hit another pedal, her arms covering her head. The car suddenly lurched forward.

The beast fell off the side and turned back to Matt, who was limping in the field, white shirt and pants stained with large patches of red.

"Matt!" she yelled out the window. She grabbed the steering wheel and turned it hard; the car fishtailed in the grass and dirt. "Gas pedal, gas pedal," she hit the one on the right, and felt a surge of adrenaline as the car responded by going faster.

The beast was in the beam of the headlights, and so was Matt. The thing looked at him, jaws open, long yellowed teeth bared. It stood up on its hind legs again, and towered at least three feet over him. It raised a paw to strike. Samantha closed her eyes as the car jumped at the collision.

Her body slammed into the steering wheel, knocking the wind out of her. The horn blared. The beast gave way and came smashing down on the hood of the Cuda. The windshield cracked, sending more shards of glass flying. The car rolled to a stop. The headlights flickered. The engine sputtered.

Everything was still. Samantha lifted her head off the steering wheel, her abdomen sore. She squinted through the web of cracks on the windshield at the beast, laying inches in front of her, immobile. She leaned forward to get a better look.

With a grunt, it slipped off the hood of the car, limped toward the woods, and disappeared into the trees. Her heart pounded, and she leaned back into the seat, gasping for air. She glanced back outside to make sure it was gone. A thud on the passenger side made her scream. She looked at the bloody arm that fumbled with the door latch.

111

"Matt," she whispered, and leaned across to open it for him. He fell into the passenger seat, crying quietly, his breath short and desperate.

"I need to go to the hospital." He clutched his stomach with both hands. "Please, I don't wanna die."

"It's okay, you're fine." Samantha felt a burning sensation in the back of her throat as she saw the blood seeping from between his fingers with every shortened breath. "I'll call an ambulance—" She suddenly couldn't recall where her phone was.

He whimpered and sobbed. "I think I'm holding my intestines."

"Try not to talk, y-you'll only add pressure," Samantha's throat felt raw from screaming. "I-I need you to tell me how to drive, okay? If you can do that, we can get to the h-hospital."

"WHAT KIND OF AGREEMENT?" Levi narrowed his eyes at Lancaster.

"The kind where both of us agree not to interfere in each other's lives again," Lancaster replied with a level of calm that Levi instantly hated. "I don't turn the police and social workers on to you and you don't interrupt my operations."

"You honestly think I'll stop slaying?"

"Only insofar as it interferes with my business."

"Slaying *is* my business," Levi countered. "Why don't you move your business somewhere else? We're diametrically opposed—"

Lancaster grabbed Levi's collar, dragging him closer until their faces were inches apart. "I do not tolerate interference with my business." Lancaster's arm began to sizzle.

Levi pulled the stake from his pocket.

Lancaster threw him back onto the Columbus lawn. "If I ever catch you snooping around my home or business again, I won't just kill you, I will *destroy* you." Lancaster turned away and then exploded into a cloud of bats that screeched into the sky and out of sight.

Levi massaged the back of his head as he stood and walked back to the front doors. He was careful to stay on the grass and cut through the flowerbeds to the flagpole. Tim burst through the doors.

"What the hell!" The spiky-haired boy grabbed Levi's shoulders. "He knows where you go to school?!"

"Of course," Levi shot Tim a look of disbelief. "Before I knew he was a vampire, I worked for him, remember?"

Tim squinted at him. "You've got one of those deep and brooding expressions again."

"He's hiding something," Levi responded. "Something big. He's got something—probably evidence of what he's up to—lying around in his home, the funeral parlor—"

"What is it?"

"I don't know yet." Levi furrowed his brow. "He didn't spill any details. He told me that if he ever caught me snooping, he'd turn me into the cops for the Arthur Harris murder."

"Well, you did kill the man."

"Shove it, Tim."

Tim scratched his head. "Lancaster knows for sure you're the one snooping. You'll have to stop."

"No, I just can't get caught." Levi looked Tim in the eye. "I have an idea."

SAMANTHA LIFTED HER HEAD off the hospital bed and watched Mrs. Symanski burst in, no makeup on, her eyes red and wild. "Samantha Rose, are you alright?" She came to her daughter's bedside and lightly gripped her bandaged hand. "They wouldn't let me in any sooner."

"The doctor said I'm fine," Samantha replied. "I'm not so sure."

"Your face," Mrs. Symanski stroked her daughter's cheek. "My baby. You have cuts all over." Her hand touched the larger bandages on Samantha's arms. "You might have scars."

An image of Matt's trembling hands pressed over his bleeding stomach flashed through her mind. "I was lucky."

"What happened?"

"An animal. I don't know what it was—"

"Did they give you a rabies shot?"

"Yes, mom." Samantha couldn't keep the bitterness out of her voice.

"I was told you drove Matt here." Samantha wasn't sure what to say next, so she just looked down. "Honey, you should have called an ambulance."

"What did you want me to do, mom? He was bleeding too much," Samantha's eyes burned. "I couldn't just sit there! What if it came back?!"

She dropped her shoulders and winced as the bandages pulled on her skin. "I was so scared he was going to die in that car with me. He said…he could feel…his intestines." There was a pause as her mother absorbed the information.

She pulled up a chair. "Have they updated you on Matt's condition?"

"No. I-I brought him in and they separated us. I don't know anything."

Chapter 4

The Tunnel

"Lancaster called." Tim sank into the seat next to Levi. "I…I got an interview with him. Tonight."

A smile tugging on the edges of his mouth, Levi struggled to maintain his stoic composure and continue writing notes. "Hmm. An interview with a vampire."

"I could hardly speak. I think my voice cracked like Justin Bieber hitting puberty—"

"Awesome. That's…that's really awesome."

"You're about as excited as I thought you'd be." Tim drummed his fingers on the wooden table. "Somehow that makes it worse."

Levi flipped a page in the textbook in front of him. "If we weren't in the school library, I'd be jumping up and down."

"If you're happy, it must mean I'm a dead man." Tim crossed his arms on the table and buried his head. A muffled moan escaped the confines of his arms. Mrs. Hansen shushed them from her perch at the librarian's desk.

"Relax, it's not like people will care if you go missing." Levi patted Tim's back. "Not like Stauber."

"He isn't missing, he's just holed up at St. Joseph's Hospital, recovering." Tim turned his head enough to glare at Levi with one eye. "From a werewolf attack."

Levi punched Tim's elbow. Mrs. Hansen cleared her throat. He lowered his voice. "It was a bear with mange. That's what Samantha told the cops."

"No she didn't," Tim shot back. "I talk to Jennifer, you don't. She knows what's in the report because her dad's the police chief. Besides, how is comparing my situation to Stauber's supposed to make me feel better about working for a vampire?"

"Hey, you said yourself that we live above a vampire deli." Levi raised his eyebrows. "Should be comforting to know where the vampires are at all times."

"That's what I'm worried about," Tim sighed. "I'll be on his radar now. What if he follows me home one night, and sees I live with Marshfield's own Biff the Vampire Slayer? He'll kill me for sure."

"He won't," Levi replied. "The last thing he needs now is to have two employees in a row disappear mysteriously, especially if one is a good little Catholic boy."

"Like people would give a shit if I disappeared."

"I wasn't trying to inspire hope, man." Levi flipped through the biology textbook. "I just meant the media would run with it—like they always do when middle-class white kids vanish—and it would spur on the police, and then he'd be questioned at the station. His cover would be blown."

"Why would he hire me then?" Tim put his hand to his forehead. "I can't be any help to whatever dark master plan he's cooking up if I'm not even disposable. What kind of villain has henchmen he has to worry about? He's gotta know that I could stumble onto something. It makes no sense."

"He's going to use you to watch me," Levi muttered, transposing the definitions into his notebook.

"What?"

Levi glanced up at the clock and down at his notebook. "He knows we go to school together. He'll probably ask you questions about me." His hand was cramping as he tried to write faster. "Keep up on my whereabouts, the gossip. It's a small school. You're bound to know something."

"And how should I answer those questions?"

"Vaguely. And make me look awesome."

Tim leaned over. "What are you writing anyway?"

"Notes."

"You're doing an extra set. And they look a lot better than your other notes." Tim narrowed his eyes. "I see. This is all part of *your* master plan."

"What plan?"

"With me doing all the dirty work, you're using the extra time to focus on school and raise your grades. Diabolical, man."

"My grades are fine," Levi said. "These notes are for Samantha."

Tim raised an eyebrow.

"She's been gone for a week, she'll be way behind." Levi focused in on a definition.

"So?"

"She hates being behind." He pulled out a highlighter and began going back through the notes. "Or having her routine disrupted."

"You don't have time to be doing homework for two," Tim hissed loudly. Mrs. Hansen shushed them even louder. The other students in the library turned and looked at them. Tim leaned in, lowering his voice. "Why do you care?"

"I owe her."

"HONEY?" Mrs. Symanski knocked on the bedroom door. Samantha glanced over her shoulder at her mother, then turned back to her phone. "Samantha Rose, you missed school again. Are you ever going to get out of that bed?"

"I don't want to."

"The accident was a week ago, Samantha."

"It wasn't an accident!" Samantha sat up. "How many times do I have to tell you? It was an attack!"

"Don't you take that tone of voice with me!" Mrs. Symanski pointed at her. "I brought you into this world, I can take you out!"

"Go ahead! I'd rather be dead!" Samantha wailed, throwing

herself into her pillows. "I can't take it!" Her voice was muffled by the pillows, and her mother snickered. "It's not funny!"

"Yes it is." Mrs. Symanski came into the room and sat on the edge of Samantha's bed. "One day, when you're older, you'll look back on all of this and laugh."

"I will not." Samantha glared at her mother's amused face. "Matt was mauled by some creature and no one knows what it is or where it went. It's still out there!"

"Honey, the police said it was probably a bear with mange."

"Bears don't howl."

"What do you know about bears? You're a fifteen year old from the Bal-Wash. Besides, you're safe."

"That was the reason you moved us to this crappy place! Safe? Yeah right." Samantha's eyes were burning.

Mrs. Symanski sighed. "You lived through it, your cuts are healing very nicely. You even saved Matt, apparently. I don't know what else you expect."

"I'm just so frustrated," Samantha balled her hands into fists, the adhesive on the bandages pulling her skin. "We've been texting. He says he's getting better, but his parents don't want him to see me anymore."

"Why not?" Mrs. Symanski raised her eyebrows.

"They think it's my fault." Tears slid down Samantha's cheeks. "The police saw the alcohol bottle in the field—his parents think it was mine. They said if he was sober, he might have gotten away."

"You were drinking?!"

"No! Of course not!"

Samantha's phone buzzed. Her breath hitched in her throat.

"What did he say now?" Mrs. Symanski stood up.

"He said 'I have to think about it, I'm sorry,'" Samantha looked at the floor. "I think...I think he's breaking up with me."

"Were you even going out?"

"Mom, please, this is not the time to grill me!"

The doorbell's long, eerie song echoed through the house. Samantha couldn't stop herself from groaning. "It's like the Addams

Family."

"Oh, that gives me an idea." Samantha's mom left to answer the door. Samantha chucked her pink pillow at her closet before turning back to her phone.

LEVI HEARD FOOTSTEPS coming down a flight of stairs as he stood, waiting, on the old brick house's wide porch. The trees rustled in the cool breeze and he felt a shiver. The door creaked open.

"You raaaang?"

"Ya," Levi said awkwardly. "Mrs. Symanski?"

"Yes," nodded the blonde woman at the door. "Are you here for Samantha?"

Levi tugged on his backpack strap for emphasis. "I got notes for her. She's home from the hospital, right?"

"Yes she is—what was your name?"

"Levi."

"Okay, hold on. Let me see if she's up for visitors." Levi watched as Mrs. Symanski walked back into the foyer and yelled up the stairs. "Samanthaaaaa, Levi's here with your school notes!" He didn't hear Samantha respond, but Mrs. Symanski gestured him in anyway.

"She's in her room." Mrs. Symanski pointed up the stairs as Levi let the door close behind him. "Go surprise her."

"Uhh…" Levi glanced back at the front door. "I shouldn't do—"

"She needs to stay caught up," Mrs. Symanski said sternly. "You came to help her, right?"

Levi nodded and walked up the stairs. He paused on the landing and looked at Mrs. Symanski. "You're alright with a boy in your daughter's room?"

"After the way she's been acting, I'd pay you to take her off my hands." She laughed a little. "So that's the purpose of a dowry. Now get up there."

Levi turned and walked the rest of the way up the stairs. Samantha wasn't hard to find. He leaned in the doorway. She was lying on her bed, facing away from him, her blonde hair draped across a pillow. He knocked.

"Go away, mom." She turned to glare, but her eyes widened in shock. "Levi? What are you doing here?"

"You've been gone for a week," Levi muttered. "I got your notes. Psychology, English, Biology—"

"You're not in my biology class." Samantha sat up.

"I borrowed Ellie Miller's notes and copied them for you," he said. "Can I come in?"

"Y-yeah." She was still staring at him like he had three heads. He wanted to leave until she patted the bed next to her. "Sit with me."

His pulse quickened as he took his backpack off and joined her.

"Have I missed a lot?" Samantha tucked a lock of hair behind her ear.

"You'll catch up," Levi shrugged. "You're a nerd."

"I am not."

"Before you moved here, you were. I could tell on the first day."

"Whatever." She touched the bandage on her cheek, the flesh around it turning pink. Levi smirked in spite of himself. "Stop mocking me, Stoner."

Levi looked around her room. As tidy as he expected it to be. Glass butterflies adorned the walls and alighted on books battling each other for shelf-space on—not one—but two bookcases. The shelves sagged under their load. "You have a lot more books than I thought."

"It's a nerd thing," Samantha laughed. "Nothing beats the feeling of turning pages."

"What's your favorite?" Levi asked.

"Right now, *East of Eden*," Samantha pointed. "John Steinbeck. Have you read it?"

"No," Levi admitted.

"Oh...well, you should sometime. It's about a guy who falls for some crazy woman who doesn't love him. I mean bat-shit crazy." He watched as she walked over to her bookcase and pulled the volume from the shelf. "I could lend it to you."

"No, I better not," Levi shook his head. "It could take me months to read. You might not get it back."

"Fine, turn down a perfectly good offer," Samantha replied, shoving the book back in its place. "You'll regret it one day."

"I'll rent it at the library," Levi said. "I'm on my way over there."

"Really?" The look of doubt she cast him was mildly offensive.

"I go almost every day," Levi shot back.

"And you read? What's the last thing you've read?" Samantha crossed her arms. "The obituaries in the Marshfield News-Herald?"

Levi was at a loss as he stared at her. "No, your biology book."

"Oh." Samantha sat back down on the bed. "I'm sorry, I'm being a bitch." Levi chuckled. She frowned. "It's not funny."

"Not at all." Levi forced his expression back into neutral and took her bandaged hand. "What happened?"

"Everyone knows what happened," Samantha said bitterly. "A mangy bear attacked Matt and me."

"That's what I heard." His fingers traced the bandages. "Tim has another theory."

"Oh, and what would Dealer's theory be?"

"You guys were attacked by a werewolf."

She looked like a deer caught in headlights. "What would give him that idea?"

"People have been saying the bear howled. He says bears don't howl." He reached for his backpack. "Did it really howl?"

"Jennifer's been running her mouth," Samantha fumed.

"Don't blame her, Tim probably believes in aliens too."

"Are you calling me crazy? It did howl." Samantha leaned closer. "It had gray skin, patchy hair, and the head of a wolf—but sort of sick, deformed. It stood up on its hind legs and was almost twice Matt's height. It had shoulders." She gripped Levi's shoulder. "Broad ones, like a man." Her hand stayed there.

"Could have been a mangy bear." Levi lowered his voice, his face inches from Samantha's. "Like the cops said."

"No," Samantha held her ground. "It wasn't."

"Was it a werewolf?" Their noses were practically touching.

"I know it sounds crazy," Samantha whispered. "Werewolves aren't real. But if I didn't know better, I—"

Her words were silenced as Levi pressed his lips to hers. She tasted like candy. He pulled away, his face hot as he looked into her wide, horrified eyes.

"My mom's downstairs. What do you think you're doing?"

"Felt like the right thing to do. Kind of instinctual, you know?"

"I cannot believe this." She rolled her eyes and threw her bandaged hands in the air. "My first kiss is with the school stoner!"

Levi felt his face drain of color. "Your first kiss?"

She huffed. "Levi, I just want you to know that although you're a super nice guy, I'm interested in Matt. Okay?"

"Like I said, it just seemed like the right thing to do," he grumbled.

"It wasn't." She shook her head, her expression full of pity.

He let out a sarcastic grunt as he stood up, unzipped his backpack, and pulled out the packet of notes. He plopped them on the bed next to her. "I just came to give you these." He zipped up the backpack and swung it violently over his shoulders.

"Listen, Levi—" Samantha was next to him in a second. He whirled around and looked her in the eyes.

"No. You listen to me," he growled. "I was only doing you a favor because you did me one. I'm not apologizing for anything that happened, because I'm not wrong. See you in class." He stormed out of her room and down the steps, not acknowledging Mrs. Symanski as he passed through the foyer and out the front door to his truck. He slammed the door and started the engine, then sped toward the public library.

"I take it things went badly?" Tim said from his place in the passenger seat.

"WHY DID HE RUSH OUT of here like that?" Mrs. Symanski's voice floated from the kitchen. Samantha came to the stairs.

"That—that *loser*—kissed me, and got mad that I got mad! Can you believe it?"

Samantha could hear her mother's soft chuckle. "Bold kid."

"How are you not freaking out?! That was a total invasion of my

122

space!"

"I don't know why you're so distressed. He's kind of cute." Mrs. Symanski walked into the foyer again and looked up at her.

"In what universe, mom?"

"Did he hold you down?"

"No."

"Did you tell him no before he kissed you?"

"…No."

"He left, didn't he? It's not like he tried to kidnap you or force you. You're just upset that it's not working out with Matt and you took it out on that poor boy."

"Don't psychoanalyze me! Ugh!" Samantha stomped back to her room. She stopped and stared. The pages of notes Levi left were torn and scattered all over the bed and the floor; bits of paper were still floating through the air. "BRANDON!"

"WHAT DID YOU DO?" Tim pressed.

"Shut up!" Levi slapped the side of his head. "You know how this goes." He turned to stare at the grave.

"Ouch! Don't be such a hard ass, what happened?"

"You don't need to know," Levi mumbled into the bandana.

"Fine. Then ask me how my day went." Tim punched Levi in the shoulder.

"How did your—"

"I hung around Lancaster for hours, man." Tim sounded pretty satisfied with himself. "He showed me around the big new funeral parlor on Veterans. Did you know there's a huge basement area where they dress the bodies? There's a bunch of different rooms—"

"I used to clean down there, ya," Levi muttered. "What about it?"

"There's refrigerators for dead bodies," Tim was practically shivering. "And an embalming machine—"

"So what?"

"There's also a room," Tim whispered. "A room with a steel door that he keeps locked. I asked about it and he said that's where the chemicals are kept."

"Uh-huh."

"Levi, I suspect there's more in there than chemicals."

THE MOVIE PROJECTED ON THE SCREEN failed to hold Samantha's focus as paper planes soared overhead. The freshmen giggled and gossiped without a teacher in the room, and she couldn't help zoning out. She found herself replaying that night in her head over and over again. Matt's grin. The alcohol on his breath. The deer running. The thing. The horrible gray-skinned thing with glowing eyes, towering over Matt. The anger in the beast's eyes matching the anger in Levi's eyes. His eyes that could see so much about her without even asking. His instincts that felt her wants, his lips that—

A light buzzing from her bag snapped her back. She cast a furtive glance around before pulling her phone out. A text from Matt. Her heart. She held the phone under the desk and opened the message. *We need 2 talk.'* Samantha felt her stomach churn.

Several other cell phones were buzzing. Suddenly the room hushed. "Matt Stauber's back! April just texted me!" exclaimed a girl. The class burst into chatter. "Sean says he's in English class right now!" "Is he healed enough to be back?" "I don't think so, Ellie." "I thought he wouldn't be here until next week!" The glances in Samantha's direction became solid stares as Ellie came over from the opposite side of the room.

"You were there," Ellie said flippantly. "How bad was it, Sammy? Was he really almost ripped in half?"

"I heard his foot was attached by only one tendon!" said a boy nearby. "The police said it was the most gruesome bear attack—"

"It wasn't a bear," Samantha gritted her teeth. "Y'all can ask him yourself."

Mrs. Golding came in, looking ragged and exhausted as usual. "Put your phones away right now," she pleaded. "I don't want to have to take them all to the front office!" Some phones disappeared, but the chatter didn't die. Mrs. Golding sat behind her desk and pulled up Solitaire on her computer while paper planes continued to whiz through the air. The bell rang, and everyone scrambled for the door. Samantha felt a pressure in her chest as she walked to her locker, like her heart was expanding. She couldn't tell if it was hope or fear.

"Dude, I wanna see your scars!" Dylan Moede cackled with a group of letter-jacketed boys near her locker. Matt stood in the middle, laughing with them like nothing had happened. He looked flawless.

His eyes locked with hers. Samantha approached with caution.

"Oh gallant Sammy Bear!" Dylan gave her that stupid grin. "Your damsel in distress is finally out of the hospital! Maybe you can sweep me off my feet next and rescue me from a dragon. Be my knight in shining armor." He laughed until Matt stepped nose-to-nose with him.

"Don't be an asshole, Dylan."

"You flirty thing," Dylan sneered. "Not the time or place, man."

"Leave her alone," Matt said calmly.

"I just said Sammy Bear—"

Matt shoved him backwards. "You enjoy antagonizing me?"

"Don't talk to me like that, junior." Samantha watched with surprise as Dylan stepped back. "You need to chill the fuck out. Just because you were eaten by a bear doesn't mean I won't kick your—"

"Did I just hear that filth and violence come out of your mouth, Moede?" Barb rounded the corner, her fat face looking especially sour. "Come with me to my office. Why are the rest of you standing around making noise in my hallway? Go to the cafeteria! Half the school is still in class." She stormed off with Dylan's tall figure sullenly following. The boys disbanded and went to the cafeteria. Matt turned his attention to Samantha.

"So, you umm…you wanted to talk?" Samantha bit her lip as she put her things away.

Matt nodded. "But not here. It's too small in here. There's no air. Let's go to Wildwood."

"I've never been to Wildwood. We'll go after school?" She shut her locker.

"We're going right now." He grabbed Samantha's hand and

pulled her down the hall to the parking lot doors.

"This isn't an open campus." Samantha tried to slow them down, but Matt pulled her so hard her shoes squeaked on the floor, leaving black skids.

"I don't see your point," Matt quickened pace. They went through the doors to the parking lot. "We're out and it was that easy." He dragged her over to a dusty Cutlass-Supreme.

"Is this your new car?"

"It's one of my dad's backups," Matt said. "He kept it in the machine shed on the farm."

"I am so sorry about the 'Cuda," Samantha spilled as Matt unlocked the doors to the sedan. "I know your dad loved that car. I didn't mean to damage it, but—"

"Don't apologize for saving my life." Matt opened the door for her. "Makes it sound like you didn't mean it." He stopped her as she moved to sit. "I hope you did mean it. You wanted to save me, right?"

Samantha felt a righteous fury. "What, you think I wanted to take that monster home with me?" She sat in the car, shut the door and waited as he came around and got in.

"When I saw the headlights moving, I thought you were leaving me," he said quietly. "I thought you were going to let me die."

"I would never do that! The only reason I got away at all was because of you. You think I could live with that kind of debt to a dead guy when I could have saved him?" Samantha slapped his shoulder, then gasped and rubbed it. "I didn't hurt you, did I?"

Matt chuckled and lifted up his polo, revealing a firm stomach with a fine bit of hair running down the middle. "No, not a scratch left." He ran a hand over the muscles. "The doctors were stunned. They said my internal cavity had almost no support, that I shouldn't have lived—"

"But you walked to the car." Samantha couldn't take her eyes off his stomach. "You said you were holding your intestines."

Matt looked down at his stomach and rubbed it again. "I'm a medical miracle. The only difference is that once it healed up I grew more hair. Now I'm supposed to record what I eat, go in for checkups every month, do blood tests—"

"How strange." Samantha frowned as Matt lowered his shirt. He winked, started the car, and whipped them around so fast that Samantha screamed.

"Grab the oh-shit handle and buckle up." Matt grinned devilishly as he squealed the tires and they shot out of the parking lot.

"Slow down." They fishtailed left onto Lincoln without stopping at the sign. Matt ignored her and flew through the school zone. "Where are the cops?!" she yelled as Matt passed another stop sign and into the path of a semi-truck. They missed it as he turned left onto 17th Street, lined with houses and apartment buildings. She saw the speed limit sign blur by and gulped. Matt brought the car to a halt on the side of the road, in front of a park with soaring trees and a large playground. Fountains spouted water in a pond in the distance, filling the air with sounds of splashing. "What was that about? Are you trying to kill me?"

"This place is empty during the day." Matt got out of the car. "All the brats are in school." Samantha followed him.

"It's pretty," she said as they walked into the playground area, the massive blue and green equipment silent and still.

"Wanna swing?" Matt ran over and jumped onto one, standing on the seat and holding the chains.

"Okay." Samantha sat in the swing next to the one he stood on. She began to kick her legs and gain air. "So what did you want to talk about?"

"I wanted to talk about us." He rocked his body to go higher.

"I didn't think there was an 'us' after what your parents said." Samantha looked past Matt to the pond fountains.

Matt's swing syncopated with hers. "We don't know each other very well, but we've been through some pretty sick stuff together."

Samantha worked her body into the kicks, soaring up past Matt. The air was crisp even with the sun on her face. "What are you trying to say exactly?"

"I think my parents are wrong." Matt thrust forward off the

swing and landed ten feet away on his feet. "I wanna see where this thing goes, between you and me."

"Are you asking me to be your girlfriend?" Samantha watched him standing there as she kept swinging. "Because if you are, you have to ask. I'm not going to assume we're dating."

Matt nodded. "Will you be my girlfriend?"

"Hang on while I think about this." Samantha swung back and forth a few times before finally jumping off and landing a couple feet from him. "First I want a couple real dates. Like, in real places. Then you can ask me properly. Okay?"

Matt growled. "You have to make everything difficult." He rubbed a hand through his dark hair and nodded. "Fine princess, I'll find a way to ask you that will meet even your approval."

"Let's go back to school." Samantha turned to the car.

Matt snagged her hand. "We're going to the zoo."

"What zoo? We're hundreds of miles from the nearest zoo."

"There's a little one in this park. It's free." Matt pulled her along as they walked toward the pond with its fountains, then followed a dirt path to a black chain-link fence gate. A narrow concrete bridge led them over a foot-high waterfall spilling from a duck-filled pond. A pair of mountain lions lazed in a large cage ahead of them.

Samantha gasped. "I love cats." She pulled out her cell phone and snapped a couple pictures. She walked around the cage, and one of the big cats raised its head and regarded her. Samantha smiled. "Hello gorgeous."

It flared its nostrils, turned its gaze to Matt and sprang to its feet, teeth bared. Samantha backed up. The other mountain lion woke and tensed, then joined its mate. The cats ran to Matt. Springing up on their hind legs, they snarled through the cage, their claws clinging to the chain link. Matt stared at them and didn't move.

"Let's go." Samantha tugged his arm. "This was a bad idea." The cats roared. "I wanna go now!" Samantha felt her breath coming shorter. She hit him in the back, hard. He finally moved.

"Okay," he said, not taking his eyes off the big cats. Samantha pulled him through the zoo's entrance toward the car.

"YOU KEEP DOING THIS. I want an explanation." Mrs. Symanski gazed at her daughter across the dining room table. "You're better than this, Samantha. Why on earth did you cut class again?"

"I'm not behind in any of my classes. It's not a big deal." Samantha pushed the pasta around her plate.

"Like hell it isn't. You're fifteen years old. Your *only* job is to go to school and get good grades. You did that just fine at River Hill."

"You're the one who decided to move us here, for no good reason."

Mrs. Symanski ignored the comment. "I know Matt's encouraging it. Barb has been more than happy to keep me updated on the situation." She grabbed a roll off a serving plate. "It's embarrassing. You know how much I despise dealing with her." Samantha rolled her eyes, and she felt her mother's anger flare across the table. "You really think this boy is going somewhere? The first time you let him take you out you were almost killed by a bear."

"It wasn't a bear." Samantha twirled the pasta in her fork and took a bite.

"I'm not having this argument again." Mrs. Symanski buttered her roll as she analyzed her daughter. "You're already grounded for a month, need I remind you. No football games or cheerleading practice, no hanging out after school, no going out on weekends. I don't understand what would compel you to keep doing this."

"Maybe because there's nothing else to do." Samantha glared at her mother. "I didn't even want to skip the first time. He made me."

"He didn't make you do anything, you went along with it." Mrs. Symanski pointed with the butter knife. "You didn't try to stop—"

Samantha pounded the table. "I wanted to talk to him, okay?! He's the first guy I've ever liked, and the last time I saw him he was almost ripped apart!"

"Why couldn't he talk to you at school?" Mrs. Symanski threw up her hands. "There's absolutely no excuse."

"Being inside too long makes him sick! And you grounded me, so that's the only time I get to see him! We're dating now!"

"No you're not!" Mrs. Symanski yelled back. "You're too young!

Remember Romeo and Juliet?"

"I'm not stupid, mom, I won't kill myself for him."

"No, you're just throwing away your future. That's *so* much better." Mrs. Symanski crossed her arms. "You're getting swept up in him. Listen to me. You'll break up, and it will devastate you. First relationships never last."

"So what! You can't even let me go through the process like a normal human being!" Samantha's fork clattered onto the plate. "You always have to spoil everything!" She stood up to leave the room. "Eat alone, you're used to it."

"Samantha Rose Symanski, you sit back down! This is a family dinner. You're not excused from this table!"

"Why do you even want me here? So we can fight some more?" Samantha remained standing, but did not leave the table. "Brandon isn't here either."

"He goes to class every day. He gets to go to sleepovers on Friday nights," Mrs. Symanski replied.

"Some family dinner." Samantha sank back into her seat.

"The point of the family dinner is to get family talking again. We need that, obviously." Mrs. Symanski twirled pasta onto her fork. "We'll do it more often."

"It's your fault dad isn't here."

Mrs. Symanski's face flashed with fury and hurt before settling on a passive expression as she locked eyes with her daughter. There was a heavy silence. "Go to your room."

"I thought I wasn't allowed—"

"You're excused." Mrs. Symanski stood up and began gathering the dishes. Samantha stood as well. The chandelier began to rattle, the crystal jingling lightly. She scrutinized it as the light fixtures began to flicker throughout the house.

"What's wrong with the lights?" she asked.

"It's an old house. They always do this," her mother replied without looking at her, taking the dishes into the kitchen. Samantha walked out of the dining room and up the stairs to her bedroom with a growing sense of unease replacing her anger.

"I LOVE THIS CRAPPY SOFA." Tim flopped onto the couch in his apartment.

"No burials or deaths today." Levi shrugged, leaning on the counter in the kitchen.

"What are you going to do with your night off?"

"Double check the supplies and go to bed."

"Levi, I'm afraid I've been thinking," Tim said in a sing-song voice.

"A dangerous pastime—"

"I know." Tim cut him off. "But I have some questions for you."

"Ya, shoot." Levi walked over to the armoire full of weapons.

"This makes no sense to me, but you're the slayer, so you should know." Tim kicked his shoes off onto the floor. "How is it that vampires can't go on hallowed ground, but they get buried in a graveyard, which *is* hallowed ground?"

"They'll fry if they get out of the perimeter of their plot." Levi sifted through the collection of stakes. "Burying a vampire taints the ground. Because of that, there are plots scattered throughout the cemetery that aren't hallowed anymore—obviously. They can never use the same plot twice, because the rest of society thinks there's still someone's body in each empty grave. If the plot gets blessed again, then it's returned to a sanctified state...so I keep a list of grave names that need to be blessed again and occasionally slip it into the rectory."

"That's what she said."

"Vampires gotta dig straight up and out. When they get to the surface, they fill in the hole, go batty, and find a victim. Didn't I have twelve stakes in here?"

"So there's a bunch of empty graves scattered through Hillside Cemetery." Tim shuddered. "That's a lot of vampires for a small town."

"Not really," Levi went through the armoire again. "It's usually the same vampires digging out each generation. But for every empty grave, there's someone who paid the price."

"Let me guess—the blood price."

Levi pulled out a box of ammunition. "They need to kill to become young again...generally a younger person, like us, so they can steal their years."

"Vampires don't age." Tim shook his head. "I've seen the movies."

"Yeah, because Hollywood is always right," Levi scoffed and returned the ammunition to its designated place. "They age like a normal person does—only difference is they're not a person. When they get old, they fake their death, then rise up, find some sap, drain their blood until they're dead, and become young again. They start a new life and repeat the process over and over. They're weakest when they rise again. That's why we stake them at the graveyard. Before they take their next victim and grow younger and more powerful."

Tim squinted hard as he processed the information. "Granny Gertrude gets buried in her nineties, so nobody suspects a thing when a young blonde long-lost cousin named Gretchen suddenly shows up. Nobody remembers that a young Gertrude and a young Gretchen look exactly the same."

"That's the general idea." Levi found the missing stake in the wrong drawer.

"What about photographs?"

"Vampires don't show up on film, so there are no pictures to prove it." Levi flipped the stake between his fingers. "Actually that's not entirely true. They do show up on film, except they look like the invisible man. Clothes, sunglasses, even makeup will show up if it's thick enough." Levi shook his head. "I've been thinking of all the things they might come up with to thwart a camera."

"So it's possible the chicks wearing too much makeup doing duck faces on Facebook are just vampires trying to show up on camera and look normal?"

"Brilliant, isn't it?"

"So that's why we have to go to the cemetery to chase every single obituary." Tim watched as Levi continued to flip the wooden stake around his fingers.

"We can't eliminate anyone from the list of potential suspects.

You never know who's walking around pretending to be human until you scope out the grave." Levi set the stake back in the armoire. "My dad taught me that."

"Your dad was a slayer too." Tim stretched. "That's bad-ass. A slayer lineage."

"It's kind of awful, actually."

"How? You're a real-life hero. You save people. Like a firefighter or police officer."

"It's a lot of responsibility." Levi's fingers trailed the stakes. They were sharp and firm. "You have to stay in one place your whole life and constantly monitor everything, or you risk letting them slip through. You stay on the edge of society so you don't draw attention—that means no social life, or the vampires will track down your family and kill them—or worse."

"How did your parents die, anyway?"

"I told you we're not talking about it." Levi closed the armoire.

"I know it has something to do with the vampires."

"You must be psychic," Levi said dryly.

"I have my moments. Oh, and speaking of moments, guess what I got?" Tim reached behind the sofa and pulled out a plastic bag.

"I don't smoke." Levi waved his hand.

"I wouldn't share pot with *you*. I got us walkie-talkies." He pulled them out of the bag and tossed one to Levi.

Levi considered it with a guarded expression. "Why?"

"Because you don't have a cell phone. If we're going to investigate the funeral homes, then we need a way to stay in contact with me inside and you outside—or vice versa. I think I prefer it with you inside, actually."

"That's what she said."

Tim's face fell. "I'm a bad influence on you." He put two fingers to his temple and pretended to shoot himself.

THE LINE IN THE CAFETERIA inched forward. "Have you heard? Someone's cows were ripped apart last night." Samantha listened to the freshmen behind her.

"Where was this?" asked another.

"I heard they were found gutted in a grazing field off of Highway 97."

"Oh, that's so sad!" gushed the freshman.

"Moede told me the head was completely off the body! The other cow had its four stomachs stretched out over a field. Blood and guts were everywhere."

"Sick! Did they find what did it?"

"No, but I heard it was a pack of wolves. It could be a bear, too."

"OMG. Like the same bear that mauled Matt?"

Samantha grabbed a tray and a fork, a warm wet feeling rising at the back of her throat.

"Chili?" asked the lunch lady. Samantha wrinkled her nose in disgust and got a salad instead. She grabbed a milk carton and headed for the table.

"Look who's here." Laderia narrowed her eyes at Samantha from across the lunch table. "Not going out for another lunch date today?"

Samantha plopped her tray down and took her seat. "Matt's at the hospital. Appointments and stuff."

"We haven't seen much of you lately, Samantha." Natalie crossed her arms and saturated the blonde with contempt. "We haven't hung out, we haven't gone out. You haven't been to cheerleading practice or any games in weeks."

"I'm grounded." Samantha glared back at Natalie. "You remember that, right?"

"From cheerleading practice?" Jennifer looked up from her phone. "It's for school. You could bargain with your mom. No, we know you're ditching us."

"I've been at home every night." Samantha jammed her fork into the salad and took a bite.

"Because you skip classes every day," Becca retorted. The girls all nodded. "You never hang out with us anymore."

"Matt's been back for three weeks." Samantha rolled her eyes. "And I only get to see him during school."

"Because you two keep cutting." Natalie's eyes were filled with frustration. "He took you to Wildwood, to the Daily Grind for coffee, to Hub City Ice Cream, to El Mezcal—"

"So? It's for an hour each day." Samantha took another bite of salad.

"And you haven't had enough time with him? He's a boy toy." Laderia pulled a chicken leg out of her KFC bucket.

"He is not! We've been through a lot together—"

"You've been through an animal attack," Natalie cut her off. "*One* animal attack. Now you're suddenly attached at the hip?"

"He got seriously injured saving me—"

"Bullshit. He has no scars," Jennifer said to Natalie. "Dylan saw him in the locker room. Not a scratch. That doesn't match the story you guys have been spewing." She tossed her brunette locks and looked at Samantha. "I think he rolled the car and you're both lying to cover it up."

"Is that what y'all think?" Samantha looked from one disparaging face to the next.

"You could just tell us the truth," Natalie reached across the table. "We won't judge."

"We tell you our secrets," Laderia picked apart a chicken wing.

Samantha set her fork on her tray. "I can't eat with people who think I'm a liar," she said finally. Her heart pounded as she swung out of her spot and grabbed her lunch. Natalie and Becca gasped in horror while Jennifer rolled her eyes.

She walked with measured steps to where Levi and Tim sat, the eyes of every student on her. Levi looked up at her in surprise as she took the seat next to Tim.

"Hey doll," the spiky-haired boy grinned. "Come to sit with the men, have you?"

"There are no men at this table," Samantha began to eat. "What are you losers talking about?"

"Embalming," Levi replied evenly; his gaze made Samantha feel decidedly unwelcome. "What do you want?"

"She's obviously escaping from the Flawed Squad," Tim noted, glancing back at the girls who were whispering among themselves and casting them woeful glares. "I see they're deliberating your social fate as we speak. What made you take the walk of shame?"

"They think I'm a liar," Samantha said. "They think Matt and I rolled his car on Homecoming Night."

"He shouldn't have recovered that quickly from an animal attack." Levi drank his milk.

"The doctors don't understand it either," Samantha shot back. "It doesn't mean it wasn't an animal attack. They documented all his injuries. I swear. I'm not making it up."

"Wait, wait, wait." Tim raised his eyebrows. "I have the answer."

"Here we go." Levi looked at the clock.

"What does Dealer think?" Samantha rolled her eyes.

"Try being a little respectful when you ask for wisdom and maybe you'll get some, babycakes," Tim glowered.

"Fine, fine, why is Matt healing so fast?"

"He's a werewolf," Tim concluded. "I should tell you my own werewolf story." Levi's mouth became a thin line as he glared at Tim. Samantha caught the look and laughed. She felt a tap on her shoulder and turned around. Jennifer loomed over her.

"Long time no see, gorgeous," Tim beamed.

"Listen up, Sammy Symanski," Jennifer said. "On Halloween Night, we're having a little to-do in the old Norwood barn. You're coming with us."

"Oh. On Halloween? I can't guarantee I'll make it." Samantha looked at her salad. "You know I'm—"

"Grounded, whatevs," Jennifer popped the piece of gum in her mouth. "Your mom's taking your little brother trick-or-treating, right? We'll just pick you up from your house while they're gone."

"But what if they're back before me?"

"You claim you're already grounded from everything, including cheerleading. How much more trouble could you possibly get into?" Jennifer stroked Samantha's hair and walked back to the girls.

"Ooh, the Norwood Experience," Tim grinned. "That's some scary stuff."

136

"Really?" Samantha looked at Tim and Levi. "What's Norwood?"

"Norwood is the mental hospital," Levi said.

"There's a lot of medical stuff in this town," Samantha shook her head. "It's like having Johns Hopkins in Smallville. They want to hang out in the mental hospital's barn?"

"The old one out on Galvin Road. It's supposed to be haunted," Tim explained. "Some patients died there. Symanski, you're going on Halloween?"

"I don't know if I should," Samantha glanced over at the girls, who looked away quickly. "They want me to go."

"But that's trespassing." Levi frowned. "It's a little soon for you to be doing anything dangerous at night, isn't it? You were caught toilet-papering, attacked by an animal—"

"Who are you, my mother? I don't care what they think they're going to do." In spite of her blush, she stared into his eyes.

Levi didn't back down. "They might—"

"What, scare me? I've already seen worse than some crummy old barn this year."

"They might ditch you there."

She shrugged. "If they take me along at all."

BARE TREES CREAKED in the cold wind. The magnificent homes alongside Fifth Street, decked out in full Halloween regalia, had lines leading up to every front door. Narrow sidewalks couldn't contain all the costumed children and parents snapping photos. Policemen regulated the vehicle traffic as the sound of throbbing music droned behind the laughter and chatter of the crowds. Levi and Tim meandered their way down the sidewalk, getting jostled on all sides.

"It's like someone dropped off a gymnasium full of goblins," Tim grumbled. "Look how packed this street is! You never see this many kids trick-or-treating anywhere else."

"I haven't been trick-or-treating in years," Levi said, his breath fogging in front of his face, the warmth of it like a kiss as it was blown back on his skin.

"You know it takes almost a half-hour to get to the front porch of the Anderson house from the back of the line?" Tim pointed. "That's like going to Mount Olympus or Six Flags, without the roller coasters."

"Look how cool the houses are this year," Levi nodded toward one with giant speakers and projectors filling the front lawn with ghostly effects. "It's worth the wait. People on this street know how to do Halloween right."

"That's because they can afford it. The cops are stupid. They should close the street." Tim eyed an SUV crawling by as children and parents jaywalked. "I'm walking faster than these people are driving."

"There will always be idiots who drive where they shouldn't." Levi rubbed his knuckles together. "Fact of life."

"This from the kid who drives with no license. Tell me, how do you plan on sorting the vampires from the common crowd?"

"I don't."

"So why are we here? We could be at the cemetery."

"Aren't you as sick of sitting around in the dark as I am?" Levi stretched as they walked. "Nobody got buried today. It's nice to see what's going on around town sometimes. Do what normal people get to do."

"Mauer! Kerner!" a voice called out. Levi and Tim turned.

"Here comes the definition of normal," Tim said sarcastically.

Dylan Moede walked toward them, Jennifer on his arm. They wore matching black cat suits. "Nice costumes," he sneered. "You guys going as yourselves?"

"Random pedestrians, actually." Tim rubbed his hands on the sleeve of his leather jacket. "Aren't you cold in those nylons?"

"I'm hotter than you, shrimp."

"He's just jealous, Moede." Jennifer ran a hand over Dylan's muscled chest and stomach, her eyes not leaving Tim's. "You two looking for a child to steal?"

"I was just about to ask Dylan the same thing, but he already has you," Tim said coolly.

"For serio, why are we doing this?" Laderia huffed as she came up behind Jennifer and Dylan. She readjusted her pumpkin suit. "I should have worn something less orange."

"I told you to wear a cat suit like they did. They're slimming." Natalie walked up, wearing a red devil suit and holding a pitch fork.

"You really wanna see *this* in something skin-tight?" Laderia ran her hands down her body. "That'll be the day I get my pink Audi. Where's Becca and Stefan? And whatever happened to Stauber?"

"They're in line at that house with the cauldrons everywhere." Natalie pointed her pitch fork. "Matt's been three blocks ahead of us all night."

"I thought there was something happening at Norwood tonight." Tim looked at Jennifer.

"There is."

"What's going on?"

"We're waiting until we see Mrs. Symanski show up with the runt." Jennifer popped her gum.

Levi felt a burning sensation in his chest. "Taking Samantha out to Norwood on Halloween. What are you planning?"

"Nothing."

Levi watched a sly grin spread across Jennifer's face. "You're a liar."

"And you're a loser." She pulled a long brunette lock forward, the curl springing back as she released it. "But we all got our faults. Don't look so upset, Stoner. What are you gonna do, tell on us?"

"Your dad's the police chief," Levi replied. "You should be more careful."

"Like they'd listen to you," Jennifer's smirk disappeared. "Let's go, Moede. That's Mrs. Symanski over there."

Levi turned, and indeed, Mrs. Symanski was walking up the opposite side of the street in the mob, a boy dressed as Iron Man jumping along next to her. They got in line at the nearest house. She turned to scan the crowd, and Levi looked away to avoid eye contact.

"Wait for me!" Laderia yelled as Dylan, Jennifer and Natalie ducked down the nearest side street.

DREW BARRYMORE'S BODY strung up on a telephone pole lost its shock value after the first time she watched the movie earlier that week. "So over *Scream.*" She flipped the channel to the *Friday the 13th* marathon, and rolled her eyes as Jason stalked a teenage girl. "Ancient." She flipped to the *Nightmare on Elm Street* marathon. "Icky." She pulled her knees up to her chest and curled on her side, flipping yet again. The *Saw* marathon. "Ugh! How'd that get on TV?!" She flipped to some black and white channel, and *The Twilight Zone* was rolling. She jumped a little when the doorbell rang, its long, creepy toll echoing in the empty house. She stalked over to the front door where a bowl of candy sat on a round table in the foyer. The doorbell tolled again. She opened the door to the cold night, irate, and glared down at a bunch of little ghouls holding up bags of candy.

"Trick or treat!" they said, their breath a fog.

"Don't mind if I do." She reached for a little girl's bag. The girl pulled it away, eyes wide with horror. "Just kidding." She held out the bowl, and glanced back into the foyer at the clock. "Take as much as you want." They each grabbed tiny handfuls, and looked up at her meekly. "Take more. More. What are you, chickens? Fine, that's enough. Now get out of here."

She shut the door and turned to the living room. The lights flickered faintly. She felt the hairs on her arms and neck stand on end and hugged herself as she walked slowly to the couch. As she sat down everything went out.

"Dammit." Samantha stood up, glaring at the faded black glow from the television. She turned to head to the kitchen to get candles out of the cabinet, and the lights came back on. Turning around, she watched the television come alive, its menu displayed. "Nothing to watch anyway." She grabbed the remote and turned the television off. The doorbell rang again. Grabbing the candy bowl, she opened the door. A crowd of even younger kids stood at her feet, their mothers down the porch steps huddled together, talking.

"Trick or treat," the kids chimed. Samantha crouched down and began to hand them candy.

"Can you believe this? They didn't do anything for Halloween this year." Samantha listened as the mothers spoke in audible whispers.

"Do they need to? The history of this house alone is frightening."

The first mother cut her off. "It's such a troubled place. I didn't even want to bring them down this street."

"But the kids get more candy here," replied another mother. "And who needs Halloween decorations on a house like this?"

"I suppose it's scary enough that it's still standing."

"Can I help you?" Samantha asked them loudly. The women looked at her, aghast she had addressed them.

"Thank you! Happy Halloween!" The children scurried off the porch to their mothers. Samantha felt herself suddenly aware of how alone she was as the group walked down the sidewalk, their laughter echoing in the cold air. The street was practically empty, the grass gray and crunchy with a light frost. She shut the door and leaned on it, looking up the dark stairwell.

A creaking sound made her heart stop. She held her breath and shifted positions. Another creak. She took a tentative step into the foyer. It happened again, only this time it was louder. Her pulse raced. "Okay, it's probably just me—or the house shifting. I'm just psyching myself out. Breathe, Samantha, breathe." She took a long breath and exhaled slowly.

The sound of screaming in the living room made her heart skip a beat. She walked into the light from the television to find Jason slashing another frightened teenager to bits.

"I turned you off," she said to the television. "Why aren't you off?" She grabbed the remote and clicked the television off again. She turned to head to the kitchen, when the lights flickered and the screaming resumed. She whipped around, her hair flailing her face as the television blared. Jason was stalking another girl in the woods.

"I wasn't even watching this," she whispered, turning the television off. A creak echoed through the house. She held perfectly still, listening hard. The silence was conscious, active. She turned to look back at the darkened stairwell in the foyer. Overcome with a sudden dread, she walked closer, waiting to hear the floor creak under her own feet. It didn't. She stood at the foot of the stairs, her blood racing.

A rapping sound behind her made her turn and scream.

"Samantha, we're here!" "Bitch, it's cold! Come on!" "Let's go, Sammy!" The voices came from the other side of the door. Samantha glanced back up the stairs, and couldn't help but feel that something menacing was lurking in those shadows. She opened the door, relieved by the sight of Natalie, Jennifer and Laderia.

"Oh, you're wearing jeans and a sweater! Smart!" Natalie exclaimed, rubbing her pale, bare arms beneath her red cape. "Got a jacket I could borrow?"

"What took you?" Jennifer popped her gum, her eyes narrowed.

"Help me get rid of the candy." Samantha grabbed the bowl. "I can't leave with it full. My mom will know I didn't—"

"Give me the candy, bitch." Laderia snatched the bowl and dumped its contents into a bulging pillow case.

"Aren't you gonna share?" Natalie frowned. "Ouch, don't pinch my arm fat!" She yelped as Jennifer released her.

"That arm fat isn't really helping you, is it?" Jennifer replied. "Don't bother adding to it." She cast a sidelong glance at Laderia.

"For serio, it does help," Laderia replied. "So does having a costume with fabric on it." She shook her pumpkin.

"I wanted something with cleavage this year!" Natalie glowered. "It's not my fault Mother Nature doesn't cooperate!"

"Be grateful it's not snowing already." Jennifer tossed her hair. "Back to the vehicles. Hey Symanski, Natalie's riding with me, Dylan, and Laderia. You're with Becca, Matt, and Stefan."

"Matt's coming?!" Samantha couldn't stop the smile from spreading across her face. Natalie and Laderia rolled their eyes and walked with Jennifer to Dylan Moede's Lincoln Navigator. Samantha shut off the porch light, locked the door and walked over to Becca's dirty red car.

"Hey beautiful." Matt grinned as she climbed in the seat next to him.

"Hey," Samantha buckled up. "I missed you."

"That cutesy talk is killing my boner," Stefan said in his heavy German accent.

"Eww, shut up," Becca said. They pulled away and followed Dylan's Navigator as it flew down Central Avenue, turned right on Veterans Parkway and headed out of town past the dragon statue.

"SHOULDN'T WE WARN HER MOM?" Tim asked from the passenger seat. "What if they—"

"They won't do anything," Levi said, more to himself than Tim. "They'll walk around inside, and just try to scare each other. Nothing bad will happen." They turned onto Central Avenue, heading back to the apartment.

"I dunno man, have you heard the stories about that place?"

"Yes," Levi replied. "They'll probably fill her in on all the gory details. Hold on a fucking moment." They were stopped at a red light. "Do you see that?"

"What am I looking for?"

"The apartment windows." Levi nodded to the Red Cross building on the next block. "The lights are on."

"Don't blame me." Tim raised a hand. "I always turn off the lights now that you're all nuts about the electric bill."

Levi glared at Tim. "Who's in the apartment?"

"It's not Lancaster, is it?" Tim's face twitched.

"No, we got the crucifixes on the doors and windows now. He couldn't get in. It's gotta be a person. You expecting anyone?"

Tim shrugged. "One way to find out."

AFTER PARKING BOTH VEHICLES behind a random shed in the industrial park, they trekked the couple blocks to the Norwood Barn on the very edge of town. The barn loomed over them on its wide patch of land. Long-cut, frosted grass ran from its towering brick walls toward Galvin Road. They shivered in the cold, looking back and forth at each other, then at the road to make sure no cop cars were driving by. Not a tree obscured them from view. The road's far-flung street lights illuminated empty concrete and an undeveloped business park.

Samantha wiggled her knees to keep warm. The gravel crunched under her shifting feet. Dylan clicked on his flashlight, its high-intensity beam shooting up to the sky like a light saber. He lowered it to the wall in front of them. The barn's walls were covered in shriveled vines, its great steel door shut.

"Well? Who's going to open it?" Natalie clutched her red cape around her body.

"I've never been in a barn," Samantha muttered, glancing at Matt. He shook his head slowly in what she could only suppose was disbelief.

Dylan's flashlight beam washed back and forth across the bare property. "I'm having second thoughts. I heard the construction company stuck cameras around the place to catch trespassers—"

"Come on, Moede." Jennifer smacked him on the shoulder. "Be a man."

"I am a man," he shuddered. "That's the problem."

"You're wussing out on me? People break into this place all the time. It's not a big deal."

"I'm eighteen," he replied. "If I get caught, that shit stays on my record forever. You guys are all younger than me. You get your records wiped clean when you become an adult."

"I wouldn't call you an adult." Becca shook her head. "Matt, why don't you open the door? You live on a farm."

"So do you," Matt nodded.

"We have a stable, not a barn! My parents have horses."

"Oh, cut the baby shit," Stefan said in his ridiculous accent. "I brought a clipper." He slung the giant shears over his shoulder.

"If you get caught, you'll get thrown out of America," Laderia commented.

"*If* I get caught." Stefan turned and winked at her. She raised a black eyebrow. "Give me light." He swaggered over to the door, grabbed the handle, and pulled. The door rattled thunderously, and slid about a foot to the side. "Oh, look, it's not locked." He turned and mocked them. "Breaking and entering an unlocked barn! Vaah, I'm scared. Pussies." He turned and stared at the black gap he made in the barn's façade. "Somebody else can go in first."

"Oh, now who's chicken." Becca let out a little laugh.

"I have no flashlight," Stefan shrugged. "Dylan, you first."

"Fine, but nobody fucking touch me." Dylan growled as he charged to the door. He stuck the flashlight in, waving it around a bit.

"What do you see?" Samantha asked.

"The byre," Dylan reported.

"What's a byre?"

"Someone who buys things," Natalie whispered.

"No brain surgeon, a byre is a cowshed." Matt snapped. "The room with all the cow stalls."

"But there's no stalls," Dylan said. "It just goes all the way back, empty. Fucking creepy."

"They probably gutted it after the place shut down." Matt walked closer. Samantha followed him, a step behind. The others drew near as well, but stopped a few feet back.

"Can we slide the door open further?" Samantha asked, trying to see around Dylan's broad back.

"Then we'll really attract attention," Dylan huffed. "I'm going in."

Matt turned on his flashlight. "I'll follow you. Samantha, stay close." Samantha nodded, and slipped her hand into Matt's.

"You're so warm, Matt." He squeezed her fingers. They waited as Dylan waved his ultra-bright flashlight back and forth and stepped in slowly. The icy breeze died as they passed through the door. The air within was stagnant and chilly, but still warmer without the wind. Empty, black doorways to other rooms stared at them from both sides.

Samantha's tennis shoes brushed against the floor, its concrete covered in a layer of dust and dirt. Dylan pressed on into the byre, its length rivaling a bowling alley. Random pieces of siding were set up against the walls.

"They use this for storage now." Matt aimed his yellow-beamed flashlight at a stack of siding panels.

"So far, my house is scarier than this place." Samantha couldn't understand the fascination with the old barn. "Is there a second floor?"

Matt nodded. "Let's go find it."

They looked into the doorways to the left. One had old, rusted gauges. "Must be the control room," Samantha commented. Matt chuckled. "What's so funny?"

"'Control Room.' You make it sound like NASA. It's the circuit breaker and electrical equipment," Matt explained. "Boring and dangerous at the same time." He pulled her over to the second doorway. "This is what we want." His flashlight revealed a set of concrete stairs turning as they went up. Spider webs clung to the corners and crevices of the room. Matt took the first few steps up to the landing where the staircase switched back.

Samantha listened as the rest of their group entered the barn, their whispers and footsteps killing any hope for a spooky mood. Matt aimed the flashlight at her and she winced, squinting at him.

"There's a huge room up here," he said, his voice amplified by the dead air. "Probably connected to a hay loft. Come on!" His footsteps sounded gritty on the concrete and Samantha followed him to the second level.

The stairs continued to a third level, but she wasn't about to go up that dark flight alone. She followed Matt through the doorway into a room where the concrete floor stretched out wide, creating a great hall. He aimed his flashlight up, its weak beam dimly illuminating a vaulted ceiling over twenty feet high.

"Wow," Samantha whispered, pulling out her phone and aiming the light around. "If you hung a chandelier you could throw a ball in here." The pieces of siding leaning against the walls towered over them in great stacks. "A construction company owns this thing now?"

"Ya," Matt replied. "It used to be part of the old Norwood complex, years ago."

"That's the mental hospital, right?" Samantha walked around, her eyes constantly drawn up into the darkness. "Why did they need a barn?"

"Look who beat us here!" Natalie's voice echoed as she scampered into the room, her flashlight on. Stefan, Dylan, Jennifer and Becca followed.

"Where's Laderia?" Samantha asked.

"I'm hoofing it for serio," Laderia gasped as she came in, her flashlight out and her pillowcase of candy swinging. "No wonder people went crazy. These fucking stairs. Is it warm in here?"

Jennifer's eye roll was practically glow-in-the-dark. "So Sammy, is Stauber here giving you the grand tour of the old Norwood barn?"

"I vant to see vat's up there," Stefan boomed, aiming his flashlight back at the wooden scaffolding that held up a third floor on the other half of the barn. "Anybody coming vith me?"

"I thought you didn't have a flashlight. You lied!" Natalie glared.

"I vill go alone," Stefan said. "I vill vave at you cowards from up there." He turned and vanished back into the doorway.

"That guy's a weirdo," Laderia said, unwrapping a Reese's. "Completely delerio."

"No go!" echoed Stefan's voice. "The stairs end at the landing." His flashlight beamed down from above. "The floor up here is rotted. Dangerous. I am coming down now!" The light disappeared.

"Über creepy," Becca said.

"Uber-goober creepy," Natalie concurred. "Hey Laderia, you got any Goobers in that bag?"

"Back the fuck off," Laderia snatched the pillowcase. Stefan rejoined them.

"Well, this was cool," Samantha cast one last look around the huge room. "Are we done now?"

"That's a pretty light reaction," Becca observed. "I thought you'd be more freaked out by this place since it's your first time."

"You guys come here a lot?" Samantha sensed a red flag.

"We went a couple times over the summer," Natalie nodded.

"It's scary the first time," Laderia said as she chewed a candy bar.

Matt frowned. "Why get us all here if you did it already?"

"Because tonight we're pushing the envelope," Jennifer cooed in a bored voice. "We're going to visit the part of this barn that nobody's seen in years. Come on." She turned her flashlight to the stairs. "Dylan, lead the way!" Dylan nodded, and they filed down the cobwebbed, concrete stairs to the byre. Dylan crossed into the little room on the other side of the entry area, Jennifer at his side. They all turned to see a steel door on great hinges bolted shut and padlocked. The group fell silent as their flashlights scoured the edges of the door. A feeling of dread drowned the room as Stefan's shears grazed the padlock and scraped the steel.

"What's in there?" Samantha leaned into Matt.

"It's a surprise," Dylan said gruffly as Stefan's shears clamped down on the padlock, shattering it. Pieces of metal clattered to the floor. Stefan pulled the bolt from the floor and the other one from the ceiling and stepped back. They held their breath as the door swung open, its hinges singing.

Flashlight beams landed on a steel hatch, padlocked shut on the floor.

Matt squinted. "That's not—"

"The tunnel," Natalie whispered.

"I don't understand," Samantha breathed, "a tunnel under a barn? This is too far north for any Underground Railroad type deal."

"We never had subways," Natalie retorted. Samantha gave her a slanted look. "Oh, you mean like for slavery? Harriet Tubman? No, none of that either."

"The old Norwood was across Galvin Road, on the site of the Scrap Company," Matt elaborated. "The barn here was for the farm where the patients did labor for therapy. The tunnel kept them from finding the road and escaping. It had skylights, electricity, and pumps to keep it from flooding."

"Rumor has it that it was a terrible asylum. Like Guantanamo with a Frankenstein twist." Jennifer walked into the room with the hatch. "They used electroshock therapy on the patients, both children and adults, inducing bone-breaking seizures. They put patients in ice baths until they passed out from the cold, and delivered massive volts of electricity directly to their brains to try and rewire them to be normal. A little girl was fried," she whispered, "burned to death in the wing that stood on the other end of the tunnel."

"Ya, and that's not even the worst part," Dylan said, his voice almost giddy. "Two patients were sodomized to death in the tunnel with a wooden-handled flyswatter. They died from internal bleeding right where they were found. One intern fled to Chicago. Guess who the murderer was. Their spirits are still down there, right now, looking for revenge."

"So, two patients were sodomized and bled to death in this tunnel? This tunnel that we're unlocking?" Samantha turned to stare at Matt. "I wanna go home. Now. This is too much."

"Relax Sammy, it's just a scary story." Jennifer tucked the flashlight under her chin. "Remember how much you like scary stories?"

"Not anymore!" Samantha yelled. "I don't want to be here. Matt, Becca, please, take me home now."

"I'm scared too," Natalie's breath was shallow. "I don't want to anger any spirits."

"You guys are just a bucket of pollos." Laderia stepped closer as Stefan began clipping the padlocks off the hatch. "People used to swim through the tunnel all the time to get into the old hospital building, before they tore it down. It's not a big dealio."

Jennifer popped her gum, flipping her flashlight around. "Stefan, you got it?"

Stefan grunted. "This is harder than it looks." He swore in German as he struggled to clip the last lock. Finally it snapped. He sank to his knees, breathing hard, and pulled the pieces off the door.

"Open it." Jennifer shined her flashlight on the bland steel. Stefan and Dylan each grabbed a corner and lifted. The door shuddered open and fell back onto the brick wall, leaving a gaping hole in the floor. They gathered around on their hands and knees, leaning forward with their flashlights.

"I guess the pumps aren't working," Laderia said as the flashlight glinted off black water three feet down. "Where are the stairs?"

"The stairs were wood. They rotted away long ago," Dylan said.

Jennifer walked over to where Samantha was kneeling, looking down at the dark water. "So Sammy, you wanna go for a swim?"

"Are you kidding me right now?"

Samantha felt a push between her shoulder blades. The water suddenly seemed a lot closer, and for a split second she felt a pull into the hatch. She screamed and leapt back as Jennifer laughed and walked back around the hatch to Dylan.

"That was so mean!" she yelled.

Matt's brows furrowed. "This place is making me claustrophobic." He sat back on his haunches. Everyone else leaned back as well.

"Everything makes you claustrophobic these days," Dylan grumbled.

Samantha leaned onto Matt's shoulder, her heart racing. She felt him tense and frowned.

"You two are so cute." Natalie gushed from the other side of the gaping hole. "I want to get a picture." She pulled out her cell phone. The bright flash made them all flinch.

"Natalie," Matt growled, "now is not the time."

"Oh come on, we'll try this again." She leaned as far as she dared, stretching her phone hand out. "This is so going on Facebook—" The phone suddenly plunged from her hands into the water. Natalie shrieked and tumbled in after, her splash contained as the heavy metal of the hatch slammed down with a bang.

Laderia screamed. "Get her out of there! She'll freeze to death!"

"Matt, grab the corner!" Dylan was at the edge of the hatch. Matt grabbed the next corner, and Stefan hoisted in the middle.

"It von't budge!" Stefan's voice jumped an octave.

"Maybe we're on the wrong side! Shine some light on the hinges!" Matt ordered. Jennifer, Becca and Laderia aimed their flashlights at the hatch's edges.

"I can't find the hinges," Becca sobbed. "They're not on this side or this side!"

"They better be," Laderia said. "They're not over here either!"

"You guys must have the right side! Pull harder you pussies!" Jennifer roared, grabbing the corner Dylan had in his hands. "Sammy, get your ass in motion!" Samantha grabbed hold with Matt. The five of them yanked up as hard as they could, the sounds of splashing and Natalie's screams echoing dully through the hatch door.

"Natalie, stay above the water!" Laderia shouted into the metal.

The five heaved at the door again.

"It sounds like she's drowning," Becca sobbed.

"She's not!" Laderia yelled back.

"We should never have come here! Nothing's working!" Becca wailed from the corner.

Laderia rounded on her. "Pray we get her out!"

Becca nodded, and crossed herself. A high-pitched scratching sound filled the air, like metal ripping against metal.

"Those are claws!" Samantha shouted.

"You're wrong!" Matt heaved. "Stefan, where's the shears?!"

Stefan heaved. "They must have fallen in!"

"That's Natalie!" Jennifer yelled. "She's got 'em! She's scraping the underside."

"Oh God, please let us get her out," Samantha groaned. "Dear Lord, please, please help us get her out!"

"That's not going to help her," Matt snapped. "Stop it and heave!"

"Please God, please, please—" Samantha repeated through gritted teeth.

A long, echoing scream took the place of the scraping and scratching. The door suddenly gave; flying up and open, it crashed into the wall. Matt and Dylan scrambled to hold it there.

"Natalie!" Stefan reached his hand in, grabbing a handle of the shears. He pulled it, and Natalie emerged from the water, draped over the other handle.

Samantha grabbed Stefan around his middle and pulled. In a wet slump, Natalie was out of the tunnel and in Stefan's arms. Samantha panted and sat next to him as Dylan and Matt lowered the hatch door.

"She's not breathing," Stefan moved to begin CPR just as Natalie coughed up water and rolled onto her side.

"Oh Natalie, are you all right?" Becca sobbed, falling to Natalie's side as Stefan cradled her. She clutched the other girl's wet, trembling hand in hers. "She's so cold. Guys, she'll get hypothermia."

"Is that blood on her legs?" Samantha pointed.

"We gotta get her to the hospital," Laderia said.

"Are you serious? What do we tell them?" Dylan asked, eyes darting. "We can't tell them it happened here, right?"

"I SAW MOVEMENT." Levi pointed to the window above them from the bed of his truck. "Right there." The silhouette of a man.

"What is he doing?" Tim ran a hand through his spiky hair.

"Maybe he's looking for drugs." Levi looked at Tim. "Do you have any enemies or territory issues?"

"Are you kidding?" Tim scoffed. "This is Marshfield! We all respect each other and there is no territory."

"That sounded like sarcasm to me."

"Maybe it was."

"You're positive nobody from the drug world is in the apartment?"

"I didn't say that," Tim blinked. "It *could* be my supplier. But I always give him his cut, so it couldn't—" He suddenly gasped. "What if my supplier was usurped?"

"Then we better confront that dick-wad." Levi pulled the gun from the hem of his jeans. "Let's get up there."

Tim hopped out of the truck and bounced back and forth from one leg to the other. Levi jumped down as well. The door was unlocked, so they crept up the steps to the apartment's front door. Tim stopped them just outside.

"I open the door," he whispered to Levi.

"I got the gun," Levi retorted. "I open the door."

"But what if he has a gun too? Whoever it is, he's expecting me, not you," Tim whispered. "If I open the door, I can go in first, and you can jump in after me and save my ass. Sound fair?"

"It makes sense," Levi said reluctantly.

"Okay," Tim gulped, grasping the handle. "Here goes nothing." Levi pressed himself against the wall next to the doorframe and watched Tim push the door open and step inside.

"Look who's finally home," came a deep voice.

"What the hell are you doing here?" Tim's voice rang with anger. "Chicago not big enough for your ego?"

"Someone's followed you. Call him in."

Levi's heart leapt and he whirled into the doorframe, gun aimed. He was met by a matching gun aimed back at him, held by a tall man in a white dress shirt, green tie and gray slacks.

"Drop the weapon," the man said, his deep voice deadly calm. Levi didn't waver. The man cocked his gun.

"Felix, chill the fuck out!" Tim roared.

"This snot has your gun, Timothy." The man named Felix narrowed his pale green eyes. "The gun I gave to *you*."

"Ya, about that. I—" Tim began to reply.

"Why the fuck does he have it?" His voice was level and his face stoic, but Levi could feel the rage pouring off of him. "And why the fuck did I get a phone call from Barbara Bennett informing me you forged my signature on a work permit form?"

Tim met Levi's gaze, his face drained of color.

"Start talking."

"It was the only way," Tim forced the words. "You don't know—"

"Save the excuses," the man cut him off. "I can always tell when you're preparing your lies. Don't waste my time."

Levi was hit with realization, and lowered his gun. "Hey…you're—"

"Felix Kerner." The man didn't lower his weapon; his icy eyes burned with rage. "Timothy's older brother. Who the fuck are you?"

Chapter 5

Lies

"This place is packed." Samantha had to raise her voice to be heard over the noise of people thronging the snowflake-decked halls. The line of children at the face-painting stall was exceptionally long and chatty. "I don't understand the winter theme. It's only the first weekend of November."

"It's been very warm this year. We usually have a foot of snow by now." Becca mixed some colors together on her palette. "Maybe you brought some of the Mid-Atlantic heat with you when you moved here. We used to go trick-or-treating in snow pants."

"That's just gross." Samantha noticed the line getting longer. "Alpine must raise a lot of money."

"A lot of the alumni come back and bring their families. It's a really big deal for the school," Becca agreed as she worked on painting a little girl's face. "They need the charity."

"Is that why they require all the students to work Alpine hours? Slave labor to raise money?" Samantha concentrated hard as she dabbed the little brush of yellow paint on the boy's face. "I just don't see the point. People pay to attend the school, then work for free to support it. Where is all the money going?" The boy rubbed his nose and the paintbrush scraped across his cheek.

"Ow!" He put a hand to his face, smearing her work.

"Stop it! Now I have to start over." Samantha grabbed him and dabbed a bit of wet paper towel, wiping his face clean.

"What's going on?" Becca leaned over. "You smeared the smiley face."

"No," Samantha huffed, "he moved again!"

"Stop making excuses. I'm giving these kids dragons." Becca turned back to her work creating a dragon that wrapped across a little girl's face. "You're terrible with kids, Sammy. Get it together."

"We need to visit Natalie," Samantha changed the subject. Becca froze for a moment, then continued painting. "She's been checked into Norwood for days. She must be bored, or behind on homework, or—"

"I'd love to, but you gotta remember why she's there," Becca said crisply. "Us."

Samantha sighed. "It was a freak accident. We didn't try to lock her in that tunnel. The hatch slammed shut by itself."

"Ya, by itself," Becca scoffed. "I don't want her to blame me. She does that—blame other people for her mistakes."

"I don't think it was her fault either." Samantha dabbed some black paint on the boy's cheek. "There. Done. Don't touch it until it's dry. Go!" She shooed the kid away. "We should visit her, though. Next!"

"You just moved here." Becca pursed her lips as another kid sat in the chair in front of Samantha. "You don't know her like I do. One time, in the sixth grade, she knocked over an easel in art class and ruined some kid's painting. She blamed it on me, and I had to apologize in front of the class and clean the whole thing up."

"Aren't you a junior?"

"I skipped seventh grade."

"I can't believe you're so concerned about saving your hide." Samantha rolled her eyes.

"I don't like admitting this Sammy, but Dylan was right." Becca sent the little girl away and another sat down. "It's trespassing. That barn is on private property. If we get busted, we would be juvenile delinquents!"

"Technically we already *are* juvenile delinquents."

"Only if we're caught," Becca said. "And I don't plan on it."

LEVI AND TIM walked through the packed halls of Columbus with Felix looming behind them like a thunderhead. They passed beneath crudely-made paper snowflakes dangling from the ceiling and alongside random bits of winter-themed art taped to locker doors. His stoic expression didn't waver as his gaze swept over every decoration.

"This school is nothing like I remember."

"Not my fault," Tim grumbled.

Felix's pale eyes locked on the sad-looking Christmas trees that filled the lobby. "How lackluster. Whatever happened to the wood paneling?"

"They covered it with the white walls," Levi said. "I think it was done to make the building look more modern."

Felix didn't say anything, but he radiated disapproval.

"The one weekend a year this place goes all out to raise money, and look what happens," Tim murmured. "At least the crowds showed up anyway."

"Out of loyalty to their alma mater, not because they approve," Felix shook his head.

"What's the alternative? It's better than abandoning the place." A note of defensiveness slid into Levi's voice. "If they didn't have Alpine Holiday, the school would close."

"The school probably should close." Felix stopped and looked at the trophy cases filled with student artwork. "Where did the trophies go?"

"They moved them when they remodeled the lobby years ago."

"This is abhorrent," Felix muttered. "I'm going to find Barbara Bennett." He stalked off into the packed gymnasium.

"He's upset all his track records are gone." Tim grinned wickedly at Levi. "He was really good. My grandma always said how great he was—" The words stopped coming and he turned away.

"I'm really glad we did the set-up shifts yesterday." Levi looked into the gym, where the beer garden was filled with adults and the auction tables were crowded with old ladies examining craft items.

"Symanski's probably working right now." Tim pointed down the middle school hallway. "I heard she signed up for face-painting with Becca."

"So what?" Levi looked over his shoulder at the crowd of sophomores that pressed by. "I don't care."

"I do." Tim put an arm around Levi's shoulders and pushed him across the lobby to the middle school hallway. "We never found out what happened at Norwood on Halloween night."

"Why don't you ask Jennifer?"

"Because Moede is practically babysitting her. I can't get her alone."

"You mean she won't talk to you when he's around?" Levi tried not to laugh.

"Apparently he's worried she might turn him into the police for whatever happened on Halloween. If he's really that concerned, then he's dumber than he looks. There they are."

"I don't care. Let's go."

Tim smacked the back of Levi's head. "Hey Sammy-pie." He stopped by the painting booth where a blonde and a brunette were facing the opposite direction. Samantha turned around, her hair glinting under the fluorescent hallway lights. "We thought we'd drop by and find out how things are going."

"They're good," Samantha said flatly. "Can I help you?"

"Just wanted to check in with our periodic lunch buddy." Tim smiled. "You haven't sat with us in a while."

"We have the same complaint." Becca nodded to Samantha. "She's always ditching us to cut classes with Matt."

"And now we've got three weeks of detention together." Samantha's grin made Levi want to vomit. "It's like I can't lose."

"Speaking of losing, where's Natalie?" Tim asked. "Haven't seen her since Halloween night. The school's been abuzz with speculation."

"She got sick," Becca said. "If you'll excuse us, we've got painting to do." A little girl stood up, her face decorated with a dragon, and walked away.

"That is one sick dragon." Tim pointed at her face. "Levi, do you see that?"

"Ya, get in line to get one," Levi said. Tim marched to the back of the line. Samantha and Becca exchanged a glance.

"Is there something you want?" Samantha asked, not looking at Levi.

"Just information on Natalie's whereabouts," Levi ran a hand through his hair. "I'm in a couple of her classes. I can drop off notes to her." Samantha turned her head slightly, and Levi felt a little thrill of victory.

"You could give me the notes and I can get them to her," Samantha said.

"It's better if I do it in person," Levi replied, keeping cool.

"You remember what happened the last time you brought a girl notes?" Samantha asked. Levi couldn't decide which emotion was behind it—frustration, hate, anger—jealousy?

"You were the last girl I brought notes to," Levi said carefully. "Why would I bring you more notes after that incident?"

"Incident? You never told me about an incident," Becca shot a glare at Samantha. "Are you keeping secrets?"

"Aren't you supposed to be somewhere?" Samantha growled at Levi over her shoulder.

"Waiting for Tim," Levi matched her irate tone.

"Your boyfriend will be fine. I'll make sure he doesn't do anything stupid. Now go away so we can talk." Becca turned her scowl on Levi, and he rolled his eyes. He stalked past classrooms filled with crafts and through the loud crowds toward the lobby, where Felix stood with Barb, his steely gaze colliding with hers. He walked up to them, and neither turned to look at him.

"…by your reaction on the phone," Barb was saying, her eyes narrowed. "I don't buy that you forgot you signed the form. How would you forget that?"

"Miss Bennett, I'm a busy man, and it's a fact of life that people forget things. Especially when they juggle so many responsibilities at once."

"You're twenty-five, Felix. Perhaps you should consider turning over some of the responsibilities you're juggling to the state," her tone was menacing. "If Tim is such a hassle—"

"Hey Barb," Levi interrupted. Barb turned to him, surprised.

"Levi! Don't you usually have…nightly duties to perform?" she asked, her attempt at stealth in front of Felix failing. Levi concluded she was more effective at being menacing than stealthy.

"Nobody died today," Levi replied. "No nightly duties." Felix's eyes flashed, and Barb suddenly looked nervous.

"We're heading home after Miss Bennett and I finish our conversation," Felix informed Levi.

"Tim and I will go home after his face is painted, Felix."

"You're not staying for the band?" Barb asked.

"Not my scene," Levi shrugged. "Later Felix. Barb." He listened intently as he made his way to the crowded gymnasium.

"Levi is a good influence on Tim, I've noticed," Barb began to say. "He no longer acts so out of sorts. He's been in class, attentive—"

"While it's good to hear of progress, these are all problems you never informed me he had, Miss Bennett." Felix's monotone darkened. "Levi is a good boy, I'll agree. What nightly duties does he have that you are referring to with so much *familiarity*?" Barb didn't respond. "If you aren't going to be forth-coming, I'll get to the bottom of this on my own." Levi felt his stomach squirm as he headed for the gym door.

"I REALLY HOPE he didn't go through the armoire," Levi said to Tim in a low voice. "My lock picks, all my stakes and weapons are in there."

"Relax, he won't come to the right conclusion. My brother's the most uptight guy ever. It would never cross his mind that you're something as out-of-the-ordinary as a vampire slayer. He'll probably think you just have a sick fetish." Tim rummaged through the yellow cabinets in the tiny kitchen. "Where the hell is my weed?"

"Maybe you should be concerned about what he goes through, too." Levi eyed the many drawers and doors of the cabinets with distrust. "He did say he was going to get to the bottom of it."

"Don't fuck with me, Levi." Tim slammed the cabinet door.

"Why did your brother buy you a gun?" Levi asked. "I thought you got it to protect yourself while dealing."

"Like I'd ever have to use that thing in this town." Tim climbed on the counter. "You're gullible."

"And you're a coward," Levi shot back. "But if you've never used it before, that explains why you couldn't use it that day in McMillan Marsh." Tim was silent. "The next question is, why carry around something that the brother you hate gave you?"

"I don't hate him," Tim said. "I *despise* him."

"Because he's got the personality of a headstone?"

"Because he's only ten years older than me, and he treats me like I'm his kid." Tim jumped off the counter-top. "Just because he's my legal guardian. So what?! I'm his brother, I can do just as much as he can do!"

"You never told me why he has custody."

"We used to live with my grandma. She died when I was eight, and there was no one else who could take care of me. So Felix was appointed my legal guardian to keep me out of foster care."

"That doesn't sound like a bad brother."

"You know he's buying groceries for us right now because he thinks that I can't afford them?"

"He asked if you had any more of the money he sent, and you said no." Levi threw his hands up. "Tim, I've seen the money you make from dealing. It's substantial, but it's a bad source. If your brother's sending you the money you need to live, then why deal drugs? That's wrong."

"Fuck off, Levi."

"Tim, I'm not trying to judge you."

"Yes you are, man! It's stupid! I don't need your probing."

"Tim, I'm paying half the bills. I wanna know where this extra income we could be using is going."

"It's not your business, Levi. You're not on the lease. I let you live here. You pay half the bills, and I pay half. That's fair. The rest of my finances are confuckindential." Tim's eyes burned into Levi's.

"If that's how you feel, alright." They both exhaled.

"Seriously, I cannot find my marijuana." Tim paced the kitchen, circling like a shark. "I need something to take this edge off."

"He did play along that the work permit's signature was his," Levi puzzled. "That means he's in favor of you working."

"For a vampire, great." Tim let out a sarcastic laugh. "I have two jobs, go to school, *and* help you fight the forces of darkness. It's a wonder I'm any fun to be around at all."

"Not since your brother came," Levi confessed. "You're a nightmare."

"Hold off." Tim leaned on the avocado fridge. "I'm not a nightmare. He's the nightmare. Remember how he held you up at gunpoint the other day?"

"That must be a Kerner family trait. But it was funny seeing his face when he realized you had a roommate. He looked so sad that he wasn't going to get to sleep in a bed."

"On the plus side, he's staying at the Holiday Inn across the street. We get evenings without him."

"Am I really so bad?" came Felix's cold, disgruntled voice. He stood in the doorway with bags of food in his arms. "I was hoping we could spend a nice night here talking about all the—*interesting developments*—in your young life, Tim." He glowered at the dragon on Tim's face.

"Oh, ya." Tim's expression soured and he stalked over to the couch. "Interesting developments." Felix set the bags on the tiny counter and began putting the food away in various cabinets.

"You shouldn't let your resources dwindle," Felix muttered as he arranged cereal boxes, snacks and chips. "There are two of you paying bills. That means you should be able to afford groceries with the other half of your money, instead of wasting it."

"It's your money, not mine. And I don't waste it," Tim glowered. "The milk goes on the top shelf in the fridge, not the bottom."

"If you want something done your way, do it yourself," Felix replied, and continued putting items away. Tim launched into the kitchen and began taking out everything Felix put away, reorganizing it. "You don't live here anymore. You don't get to decide where things go."

Levi suddenly felt very uncomfortable being in the same room with Tim and Felix, and stood up.

"Where are you going?" Tim asked as he relocated the milk to the top shelf in the fridge.

"To chill in my room," Levi said.

Although feeling safer in the confines of his room, he regretted not leaving the apartment. The thin walls invited him to listen to the brothers' heated discussion.

"Tim, I know you're doing drugs."

"That's speculation."

"I found this bag of weed in the cabinet."

"Circumstantial. How do I know you didn't plant it there?"

"You're my brother, Tim. I can always tell when you're bullshitting me."

"It's Levi's."

"No it's not. He doesn't reek of pot when he walks through hallways."

"Even if it was mine, what business is it of yours?"

"I'm your legal guardian. If you get caught, you'll not only be put into the foster care system, but I could be charged with neglect."

"Would that charge really be unfounded, Felix?" There was a leak of satisfaction in his voice.

"I'm doing the best I can with you, Timothy. You know that. And it's not enough. I know that." Felix's voice was harsh in spite of his words. "I won't let you tear this family apart."

"This family's already in shambles, Felix. Grandma's dead. Grandpa's senile."

"And mother and father are dead." There was a long silence.

Levi stared at the ceiling, trying not to breathe.

"You'll never let me forget that I killed her, will you?" Tim's voice broke.

"Today Barb threatened to call the state regarding our situation," Felix pressed on. "I believe the only thing that's stopping her now is Levi's presence in your life. For some reason, she's okay with him living without his parents, but not you."

Levi's eyes grew wide. Did Felix somehow know his parents were dead?

"Barb's always been like that with Levi. She has her reasons."

"Levi's presence won't save us forever. You need to stop doing drugs, Timothy. You need to grow up and become the best student at that fucking school, or you'll wind up in foster care… and I'll wind up in prison." There was another long silence. "Do you understand me, Timothy? Whoever you wind up with in the system won't give you the freedom you have now."

"I don't have freedom. I'm stuck here." Tim's voice was bitter. "You're the one who's free."

"Youth is wasted on the young." Felix let out a dry chuckle. "I don't have freedom, Timothy, you do."

SAMANTHA RUMMAGED THROUGH HER NOTES, pulling together everything she had on the few classes she shared with Natalie. She stacked them on her bed before going downstairs to get breakfast.

"Hey sis." Brandon raised his spoon from the dining room table.

"Good morning Samantha." Her mother sat across from Brandon, her laptop in front of her next to a pile of papers on the table. Samantha walked past her and continued into the kitchen. Her mother came in after her. "You know it's rude not to reply when someone wishes you good morning."

Samantha pulled out a bowl, a box of cereal, and milk.

"Did you notice I rearranged the pictures in the dining room? You haven't mentioned them. I think I've finally got them the way I want them. It looks better, more balanced. You're certainly in a rush for a Saturday morning." Mrs. Symanski watched as Samantha poured the milk into her cereal. "Eager to work your second day at Alpine?"

"Umm, yeah," she nodded, moving to put the milk away. "Do we have orange juice?"

Mrs. Symanski gestured to the fridge. "Samantha, honey, we need to talk."

"Not really." Samantha pulled out the carton and grabbed a glass from the cabinet.

"Yes, really. You still haven't told me where you went Halloween night."

"Does it matter? You extended my grounding for leaving the house. I don't know why you need to know where I was." She poured the orange juice into the glass.

"I'm going to pretend you didn't say that for a moment. Samantha, when your brother and I came home from trick-or-treating, all the lights in the house were on and the television volume was cranked as high as it could go."

Samantha felt a hitch in her throat and looked at her mother. "I only left the porch light and the foyer light on. I was going to be home before you were back."

"I have a hard time believing that," Mrs. Symanski said. "Either you did it yourself or someone else did. Maybe one of your friends broke in while you were gone and did it."

"Doubt it," Samantha muttered, putting the orange juice back in the fridge.

Mrs. Symanski's phone vibrated on the counter. She grabbed it, looked at the screen and silenced it. "You've been skipping classes for weeks, even though you're grounded. I'm constantly negotiating with Barb to not suspend you, and the only reason she's letting it slide is your grades haven't fallen—yet."

"That's not a surprise. They don't teach anything." Samantha sighed. "I haven't done any real homework in weeks and my grades are terrific. You said that Columbus was the best school. It's not."

"Why are you acting like this? Are you mad at me because you don't have enough homework? Are you doing these things to embarrass me in front of Barb?"

"You think this is about you?" Samantha took her bowl and her glass of orange juice and walked to the dining room, her mother hot on her heels.

"I know Matt came and got you. Where did you two go?" Mrs. Symanski's voice grew louder as Samantha plopped down at her seat at the dining room table.

"It wasn't just Matt. It was a group of us." Samantha started to eat her cereal.

"And where did you go? What happened?" Samantha could feel her mother's intense gaze, waiting for a response.

"Nowhere special. And nothing happened."

"Then how come you came home in the middle of the night and cried in your room for an hour?" Samantha continued to eat her cereal, ignoring her mother. "I waited up for you, so don't pretend that nothing happened. Did you and Matt have sex?"

"Good gravy, no!" Samantha felt a furious heat in her chest. "What kind of girl do you think I am?!"

"I thought you were the good, responsible kind, but lately I've been proven wrong. I don't like being wrong, Samantha. Especially when it involves my children."

"Well that's unfortunate, because you're wrong all the time!" Samantha yelled. "You were wrong about this town being safe, you were wrong about the school being great, you were wrong about me being a cheerleader—"

"I don't let you go to practice because you skip class!" Mrs. Symanski roared. "The consequences are more than fair—in fact they're a bit generous—and you brought them on yourself."

"It's your fault I had to go out on Halloween! I missed so much practice that the other girls on the squad were going to throw me out of their group! I'd have no friends here at all!"

"You guys are too loud!" Brandon yelled, his hands clamped over his ears.

"You are going to have to do better than that to justify your extreme delinquency to me, young lady! No boy is worth it!"

"Dad was worth it!" Samantha huffed. "You did all the same stuff I did now! You ran away and got married right out of high school!"

"And look how it turned out!" Mrs. Symanski threw her hands up. "I'm divorced with two kids, living in a town where everyone else remembers all the supposedly awful things I did in high school—and I don't have a clue!" She paced back and forth. "Do you realize I haven't had any adult conversation in months?!"

"That's your fault for moving us here!"

Brandon got up from the table and ran to his room.

"See what you did now?" Samantha pointed at Brandon's empty seat. In a flurry of frames, all the pictures on the wall came crashing down at the same time, the glass shattering. "Ugh! Brandon!" Samantha yelled.

"Don't yell at your brother," Mrs. Symanski said quietly, looking at the frames shattered around the room.

"He must have done something upstairs to make everything fall off the walls like this. You don't discipline him like you should." Samantha shook her head. "Mom, I'm fed up. For serio. I'll grab the broom."

LEVI, TIM, AND FELIX sat in the pews farthest from the altar in Our Lady of Peace church. It was awkward for Levi as Tim insisted he sit between the brothers. He was on Levi's left, noticeably piqued. Felix was on his right, his icy green gaze not deviating from the altar where the priest went about conducting Sunday mass.

Usually Levi tried to get a better spot. From so far back, it was hard to see what was happening. He exhaled slowly, and looked at the backs of the heads of the laity. Jennifer and her father were a couple pews up, the Moedes sat across the aisle. Samantha's blonde hair was closer to the front, with her little brother sitting between her and her mother. He wondered why that was, when he felt a small nudge on his right elbow. He glanced over and Felix leaned closer, his face not turning from the altar. Felix's deep voice dropped to a barely audible whisper.

"After Mass, you and I need to have a talk."

"About what?" Levi whispered back.

"You'll find out." Felix straightened up.

Levi felt electricity course through his veins as his stomach tied in knots. What could he possibly want to talk about, other than what was in the armoire? Rent, maybe? Hopefully not Levi's living situation. For the remainder of mass, Levi squirmed.

After the final song, they genuflected and headed out the main doors to Fifth Street, where Felix had parked his nondescript sedan. They piled in. "Look at the cloud cover. It'll snow soon. Which funeral home do you work at, Tim?"

"The one on Palmetto, between Veterans and Roddis Manor," he murmured. The drive there was silent. They pulled under the porte-cochere of the symmetrical beige building to the double front doors. Tim got out, bundled his coat around his body, and gave Levi an accusing look through the windows before turning to head in the building.

"Levi," Felix began as he turned the car around. "I've got some pressing questions for you."

"What do you want to know?" Levi asked warily from the back seat.

"I'd like to know why you live with my brother. You're now highly aware of our family situation, and I think it's only fair that I understand yours." Felix met his eyes in the rearview mirror. "Explain."

Levi felt his mind go blank as he scrambled for a story that made sense.

"Whatever lie you're concocting, throw it out and give me the truth." They turned onto Central Avenue, heading back to the apartment.

"I...I moved in with Tim because it's an easier commute."

"So that beat-up truck in the lot *is* yours?" Felix's voice sounded thoughtful, but Levi didn't see his face move. "You don't have a license. Or a learner's permit."

"I know," Levi said in defeat. "Without the tutoring and an

instructor, I can't take the test until I turn eighteen."

"So, your parents won't enroll you in Drivers Ed or teach you."

"They can't," Levi admitted.

"Why not?"

"They're not around these days."

"You're alone." Felix's voice was unsurprised. Levi felt suspicion creep up his spine. "You've been alone for a while. And yet you've managed to avoid foster care."

"Yes."

"You must have been set up with a safety net of some sort," Felix pondered. "It would allow you to continue posing as a normal teenager, even though you're alone."

"My father was a good planner. He was always ready for the worst."

"He was a remarkable vampire slayer as well," Felix said casually. Levi's heart stopped beating in his chest.

"I don't know what you're talking abo—"

"Levi, if you can find a plausible explanation for having a dozen stakes in an armoire, I'll give you this car and walk back to Chicago." Levi was silent. "So, that settles it. You're a vampire slayer. Levi Mauer, son of Ethan William Mauer and Lorraine Maxine Mauer." He laughed a little, and Levi was perturbed.

"How do you know that?"

"I know a lot more than you think I do," Felix said. "As it turns out, you and I are quite a lot alike."

"Really." Levi couldn't believe what he was hearing.

"Let's grab some coffee and talk about it inside."

He parked in front of the Daily Grind. The coffee house was in a narrow building in the downtown historical district. Tiny wooden tables crammed against the long brick walls and a counter displayed coffee cakes at the back; a massive chalk menu hung on the brick wall to their right. The snow began falling outside, and no one was in line at the counter. They ordered two cups of coffee and sat down at a table close to the windows.

Levi wrapped his hands around the cup, letting the warmth seep into his fingers. "How do you know about slayers?"

"My father was…familiar…with the vampire slaying families in Central Wisconsin." Felix glanced out the windows at the swirls of white. "The Mauers were one of the last families left in the small towns. There used to be more families doing what you do. Over the past several decades they've flocked to the cities, following the shifting vampire populations."

"Vampires don't shift locations," Levi corrected as Felix drank his coffee. "They're static creatures, competing with each other for territory. They spend years arranging their next lives. It forces them to stay in an area they can monitor. Smaller communities serve them better. That's what my dad taught me."

"Exactly right," Felix agreed. "But that means there's something happening in the cities that is making it easier for them to survive. Probably a new, organized underground. With the internet, now they can connect and help each other arrange their new lives— vampires are taking on positions they've never held before."

"Go on." Levi sipped his coffee, waiting for Felix to continue.

"It makes sense if they fill roles that allow their kind to set up new lives easier—little mom and pop shops, butchers, retirement home administrators, funeral home directors—specialized family-run businesses directly related to their interests, so to speak. The kind that provide easy access to blood and the most control over the transition from one fake life to the next."

"I see," Levi murmured. "How do you know that?"

"The slayer families in the Chicago area are networking—working together," Felix looked down into his cup. "My father stays in contact with them. He and I talk about the developments when I visit him."

"But your father's dead—"

"Au contraire, Levi, he's very much alive."

Levi suddenly felt as if he had four shots of espresso. There was a ringing in his ears. "Where is he?"

"In prison, serving a life sentence for murder." Felix took a swig of his coffee.

Chapter 5

Levi held his breath for a moment, his mind racing as he processed the new information. He knew he would have to address the issue of Tim's father being alive eventually, but decided to focus on the vampires instead. "If what you're telling me is true, then why doesn't Tim know about vampires? When I told him I was a slayer, he laughed at me. He didn't believe vampires or vampire slayers were real."

"I never take Tim to visit our father." Felix continued to stare into his cup. "The man won't have it. It's better Tim thinks our father is dead."

"Why?"

"Father doesn't want us to live the hunter lifestyle. I was old enough to learn a lot about it, even began training, before he was arrested."

Levi looked out the window at the snow whirling and twirling between the old buildings, then met Felix's eyes. "Who did he kill?"

"A werewolf." Felix's voice was barely audible, his pale green eyes hard as ice.

"Bullshit." Levi leaned back in his chair. "I ask for a name and you give me a fairy tale creature. Your whole story is bullshit."

"That's incredible." Felix let out a low chuckle and rubbed his very short beard. "You kill vampires and don't believe in werewolves."

"Why should I? It's not like I've ever seen one. I'm surprised you believe it. Your family being slayers—"

"No Levi, I said *hunters*, not slayers." Felix narrowed his eyes. "As in werewolf hunters."

"Again, I call bullshit."

"Did you know wolf migration patterns and werewolf sightings in Wisconsin coincide along a stretch from the southern part of the state up through the Northwoods?" Felix drew a diagonal line across the table as if tracing a map. "That's a huge swath of land to cover. Larger than some countries."

"Ya, it is."

"Werewolf hunters have to constantly be on the move, watching reports and paying attention to rumors and stories. My family used Marshfield as a home base because it's in the center of the state. We traveled to sightings all over Wisconsin, from Bray Road in Elkhorn to Ashland and the Apostle Islands. Vampire slayers, on the other hand, stay in the same town and monitor deaths and burials."

"You say that like it's boring." Levi drank his coffee.

"You imply that it's not. You're limited to staying in the same place most of your life." Felix leaned back. "That's incredibly frustrating—especially in a place as small and unforgiving as Marshfield."

"It could be worse."

"You know what I used to call this place growing up?" Felix locked eyes with Levi. "Marstown. Because living here is like living on another planet. Nobody here cares about the outside world, everyone knows each other, everything you do is scrutinized, and nothing is forgotten. It's very different from the rest of the country."

"If you miss Chicago so badly, you can go back," Levi countered. "Tim won't mind if you cut your visit short."

"Nor would I." Felix's pale eyes seemed to grow distant.

"You don't seem like brothers at all," Levi murmured.

"We are, though."

"You're so intense and harsh. Tim is a bubblehead."

Felix's face somehow grew even more serious. "It's our father's desire that Timothy grow up and have a legitimate life, without the burdens of the werewolf hunter. He can never know what we just talked about. Nothing about his father or werewolves."

"I'm fifteen. You really think I can keep a secret that big?"

"You're a vampire slayer. If you couldn't keep a secret, you'd be dead."

"But I live with Tim. He's—he's my best friend." Levi's face pinched into a scowl. "I can't keep something about his own life from him."

"You have to," Felix said with expressionless eyes. "If you don't, he'll become a werewolf hunter just to spite our father. He's not trained, he's not informed, and he's not mature enough. For God's sake, he lets a stranger carry his gun. He can't handle the truth."

"I REALLY HATE SNOW." Samantha looked out the window of the English classroom at the parking lot, which was being blanketed with inches as they spoke. "The only thing I hate more than snow is that we don't have a snow day right now."

Students filed in, their shoes squeaking from the puddle-filled hallways.

"This fluffo isn't bad enough for a snow day in Wisconsin," Laderia informed from the seat behind her. "You need negative 76 degree wind chill before the buses stop running."

"You're not serious!" Samantha whirled around. "You'd be dead waiting for it to arrive!"

"That's why God gave us snow pants." Laderia pulled out a nail file and got to work. "So skinny bitches like you don't freeze to death."

"My mom almost killed me driving us to school today." Samantha pulled out her notebook. "We did a complete spin backing out of the driveway. If that doesn't warrant a snow day, I don't know what does."

"Oh wells." Laderia blew the dust off her fingernails. "Have you heard how Natalie's doing lately?"

"No, how is she?" Samantha asked.

Laderia glanced around, and Samantha noticed the students around her were silent, eavesdropping. "I want to visit her tonight. Dance team practice doesn't start until six anyway."

"I wanna drop some notes to her," Samantha said. "Can I come?"

"I was going to ask you for a ride." Laderia wrinkled her face. "Becca and Jennifer won't give me one. Chicken bitches."

"I have detention from three to four."

"Visiting hours end at four," Laderia whispered. "Do a lunch detention. Matt can give us a ride there."

"But I was going to go to lunch with him at El Mezcal."

"Not today." Laderia nodded to the window. "Work some negotiating magic."

"You're right…I'll talk to Barb about serving detention during lunch."

THEY STOMPED through the snowy parking lot to Matt's car.

"Thanks for giving us a lift. I miss your Cuda, Stauber." Laderia climbed in the backseat. "It was too coolio."

"I miss it more than you do," Matt said as Samantha got in the passenger seat next to him. "Off to Norwood, huh?"

"Off to Norwood." Samantha shivered, glancing over at Matt. "Where's your winter coat?"

"I'm not cold." Matt rolled up his sleeves. "This sweater's actually kinda hot." He started the car and they were on their way.

"Your arms are getting fuzzier." Samantha ran her cold hand up and down Matt's forearm. "No wonder you're warm."

"He's finally hit puberty." Laderia laughed from the backseat.

"Nah, boys are always warmer than girls." Matt grinned. "It's God's way of making sure they'll want to touch us." Samantha pulled her hand from Matt's arm, blushing.

"Like she needs a reason," Laderia cackled as Samantha shot her a dirty look.

"HOW WAS SCHOOL TODAY?" Felix asked as Tim and Levi climbed into his sedan.

"Frigid," Tim muttered. "They didn't turn the heat on until fourth period."

"Not surprised." Felix was stoic as he pulled away from the curb.

"There's a suitcase back here," Levi noted from his seat.

"I'm leaving for Chicago after I take you boys home." Felix adjusted the collar of his black wool coat with leather-gloved fingers.

"I thought you were leaving tomorrow." Tim's voice was guarded.

"I'm not taking any chances with this weather. The drive could take a lot longer if the snow keeps up."

Tim shook his head. "But it's supposed to stop."

"After how many more inches? The plows have been out today in town, but there's no guarantee the highways—"

"Wait it out here then," Tim crossed his arms. "It's stupid to drive in this."

"Timothy—"

"It is," Tim emphasized. "Drop the act. You're just using this as an excuse to ditch me a day sooner. You don't have to lie; I'm used to it by now."

Felix's gloved hands gripped the steering wheel hard. Levi was silent, waiting for the tension to blow over. Any sudden moves and they might remember he was there.

"Timothy, being around you for longer than a few days...is torture," Felix ground out. "I do my best, because it's my responsibility. But my best is not good enough."

"You always say that." Tim stared out the window. "You always tell me how horrible I am—"

"I've never once told you you're horrible."

"What other explanation do you have for me, brother?" Tim spat the last word. "Why is being around me torture for you?"

"You'll never understand." Felix shook his head. They pulled up to the apartment and Felix parked the car. "Timothy, go inside. Levi, I need to talk to you." Levi looked up in surprise. Tim grabbed his backpack and got out. He slammed the car door hard before storming into the building.

The new Norwood Mental Hospital was in a bland brick building with tinted windows, tucked behind Rose Bowl Lane and Culvers. They parked and walked up the snowy, sloping lot to the main entrance.

The gray sky and bitter wind had Laderia and Samantha bundled, but Matt walked through the harsh weather in nothing but a sweater. They passed through the glass doors, entered the carpeted lobby, and went to the receptionist's low wood desk.

"Welcome to Norwood." The receptionist glanced up from her

computer. "Checking someone in or visiting?"

"Wow, it's like a hotel," Laderia laughed a little.

"Once you're checked in, good luck convincing them you're sane enough to check out." Matt snorted. Laderia elbowed him.

"We're visiting." Samantha gave Matt and Laderia a stern look. "We're here to see Natalie Devereaux. She's our friend. We brought school notes and stuff." She held up her backpack.

"Just one moment." The receptionist typed something into her computer. "Oh my. It seems I cannot help you."

"What does that mean?" Matt asked, scratching his leg.

"I cannot help you." The receptionist smiled.

"Where is she? Did she check out?"

"I'm not able to tell you that." The lady raised her hands.

"But she *was* here, right? Why can't you tell me?"

"Legally, I can neither confirm nor deny that a Miss Devereaux stayed here," the receptionist replied.

"Then where is she?"

"You say this…Miss Devereaux…is a friend of yours? If I were looking for a friend, I'd start at their home. Have a nice day." The receptionist continued to type on her computer.

Samantha turned and they walked to the doors. "What now?"

Matt shrugged. "We go to Natalie's place."

"WHAT DO YOU WANT to talk to me about?" Levi asked.

Felix turned to look at him from the front seat. "Remember our last private discussion?"

"You mean the one that never happened?"

"Yes. Not a word to Timothy, alright? If you tell him about his father, the werewolves, any of it—I will alert child protective services to your situation."

"Why is everybody holding that over my head?!"

"You understand my terms?" Felix grabbed the suitcase from the back.

"I understand your terms," Levi said as Felix hauled the suitcase between the seats. "But there's one thing I don't understand. Why do you let him feel like shit? You don't really hate him, you're brothers. You needlessly let him think the whole situation is his fault—"

"Levi Mauer, I'm thrilled you give a damn about my brother's emotional well-being. I truly am." His pale green eyes met Levi's in the rearview mirror. "Because that is something I cannot bring myself to do."

Levi felt like he'd been slapped in the face. "Explain that bullshit."

"I often get told I'm very mature for my age, Levi. And there's a reason for that. I spent my youth playing father to my younger brother, at the behest of my own father." Felix adjusted his gloves. "I did the right thing and took on all the responsibilities. It's affected every aspect of my existence. I don't like my life, Levi. I don't enjoy myself at all. If I could do it all over...I'm not sure I'd make the same choices."

"What you did made a difference. His life is better than it could have been."

"Is it really? Certainly Timothy didn't wind up in foster care, but the trade-off is that he's all alone and doing drugs."

"He's not all alone," Levi said quietly.

A hint of a smile graced Felix's face. "Maybe not. He does have a friend now, someone who can really be there for him—companionship."

"All you have to do is talk to him. Call him, chat. Whatever. It's so little to do."

"Levi, I've given him so much, but I can't be a mother to him too. I'm spending my life maintaining this situation. Maintaining lies to the government, my employer, and my family. To be frank, I have no more fucks to give."

SAMANTHA THOUGHT IT IRONIC that Natalie lived in a house on Cherry Avenue—a redhead living on a street named after a red...berry? Or was it a fruit? She banished the mental debate as she stepped onto the house's porch with Laderia and Matt. They knocked. A red-headed woman answered the door, her pale face stricken.

"Can I help you?"

"Hey Mrs. D. We're here to see Natalie," Laderia said.

"I don't think that's such a good idea." Mrs. Devereaux narrowed her eyes and forced a smile. "She's not well yet."

"I understand she's still recovering, but Natalie's probably falling behind in school," Samantha prattled. "We brought notes from the classes she's missed. Can we drop them off to her?" The cold winter air was thick with tension as Mrs. Devereaux scrutinized them one by one.

"I'll allow you two in, but no boys in her room."

"It's alright." Matt pulled at the collar of his sweater. "I'm feeling a little warm. I'll go for a walk." He turned and paced down the snowy sidewalk.

"If he ditches us, I'm blaming you," Laderia muttered to Samantha. They went inside, and Mrs. Devereaux gestured upstairs.

"You know the way, Laderia."

They ascended the stairs to a closed door and Laderia turned the handle. They stepped into a small room so thoroughly covered with posters and magazine cutouts that the walls were completely hidden. A tall window, a dresser strewn with clothes and makeup, a nightstand with a pink lava lamp, and a rather uncomfortable-looking wrought-iron bed filled the small space. Natalie sat in the bed, reading, and glanced up when they came in.

"Oh-Em-Geeeee!" she squealed, a huge smile spreading across her face. Samantha and Laderia squealed back and ran to hug her where she sat.

"Oh guys, I've missed you soooo much!" Natalie wailed. "I'm so bored! They gave me an old copy of People magazine! I'm losing my mind!"

"If you say that any louder, they'll keep you home another week," Laderia scolded.

"You brought me school stuff!" Natalie beamed as she took the stack from Samantha. "I've missed it so much—did I just say that?

How was your first Alpine?"

"Good," Samantha smiled. "Very busy. But really, we're here to talk about you. How are you doing?" She tucked a lock of Natalie's hair behind her ear. Samantha noticed bold streaks of white throughout her red mane. "We thought you were at Norwood."

"I was there for three days. They can only keep teenagers for three days."

"How'd you wind up there in the first place?" Samantha asked.

"After my parents came home, they freaked because I was shaking so bad. They took me to the emergency room. The doctors said I was fine physically, but then they sent me to Norwood for a mental evaluation."

"What did the Norwood doctors say?"

"They're saying I suffered from some sort of episode. That I had hallucinations." Natalie was quiet, her blue eyes staring off into space. "They think it was a mental breakdown. They interviewed me a lot when I was there and said I seemed stable—not suicidal anyway—and sent me home. I feel a lot better, but my mom says I'm not well enough to leave the house yet. I don't know why."

Samantha and Laderia looked at each other, alarmed. "Natalie," Laderia began, "I want to know what happened in the tunnel Halloween night."

"I do too," Samantha agreed.

Natalie's face looked just as stricken as her mother's, then shifted to resignation. "Close the door," she murmured, "not all the way. My mom will freak if we're all in here with a closed door." Samantha pushed the door almost shut. A giant cutout of Robin Thicke was taped to the back. She grimaced at it.

"Well?" Laderia leaned close.

Natalie screwed up her face in concentration. "I remember all of it. Getting my costume. I looked so cute. Going down Fifth Street with you guys, getting Sammy, going to Norwood…the hatch…"

"You fell in," Samantha finished for her.

Natalie was quiet for a long moment, her eyes wide. Her lips trembled as she finally spoke. "When the lid shut, the first thought I had was 'I'm going to die in here.' I couldn't see. I couldn't breathe…and I was freezing. I've never been so cold before, or felt more alone." She completely zoned out as she continued to speak. "I remember the echoes my screams made in the tunnel. I was kicking so hard, trying to keep my head up. I could barely hear you guys above me, screaming for me, trying to open it. Then something happened…" Natalie paused, seeming to run out of words.

"What happened?" Laderia urged her on.

"The lights all came on." Natalie made eye contact with her.

"What lights?"

"The lights in the tunnel," Natalie said. "They ran down the side of it, bright yellow lights, going all the way to the other end. I could see the pipes on the ceiling." She flashed a nervous smile at Laderia, whose bronze skin went pallid.

"And then?" Samantha stared hard, watching Natalie's every move, waiting for a glimmer of mischief. Was she lying? Leading them on?

"The lights, um, began to flicker," Natalie opened and closed her hands. "Like they were about to blow up. I was all like, O-M-G, and I tried reaching up to grab the handles on the hatch. I could see Stefan's shears jammed up there, in the handles. I managed to grab the shears, and I hoisted myself up as high as I could. Then the shears pulled out of the hatch, and I fell under the water again, but I had the shears in my hands."

"Oh good gravy," Samantha whispered.

"I opened my eyes underwater. I could still see. And…" She stopped. "I can't tell you the next part."

"Why not?" Laderia moaned.

"Because the doctor said it's completely made-up and I should stop believing in that nonsense and start examining my conscience to determine what in my shallow little mind conjured that image."

"He did not," Samantha gasped.

"He did!" Natalie huffed. "Well, maybe not in exactly those words, but he still made me feel crazy and stupid at the same time! He couldn't let me be one or the other!"

"You told your doctor the whole story?" Laderia met Samantha's eyes. "Did you mention any names?"

"No!" Natalie was stunned. "How stupid do you think I am?"

"I'm so sorry Natalie," Samantha sighed. "If it wasn't for me and Matt, this wouldn't have happened."

"What do you mean?" Natalie eyed her.

"You fell in trying to take a picture of us," Samantha replied. "Because we were—"

"It has nothing to do with you at all," Natalie cut her off, her voice filled with gravity. "I didn't fall in."

"Yes you did, we saw it!"

"I was pulled in."

"What?"

"My cell phone was smacked out of my hand. I felt it. Then something grabbed my wrists hard and pulled me down." She held out her wrists—pale purple remnants of bruises remained.

"We saw those when we got her out," Laderia said to Samantha. "Remember?"

"Yeah," Samantha breathed. "What did you see underwater? The part the doctor said wasn't real?"

"Two men," Natalie whispered. "One had each of my legs. They were dragging me down with them." Natalie raised the legs of her pajamas and pulled back bandages. Scabs were healing on deep scratches on her calves. "The men who died in the tunnel."

The goosebumps on Samantha's arms were almost painful.

"Then all the lights went out again." Natalie bit her lip. "I gave up, then you guys pulled me out."

"That's it, I'm never going back there again," Laderia concluded.

"You believe me?" Natalie asked.

"When Jennifer and Dylan dragged you upstairs, Becca was bawling in the living room and said we should have taken you to the hospital," Laderia sighed. "She was right."

"I don't know," Natalie shook her head. "It could have been worse. My parents think I had a falling-out with one of you at a wild party and I'm over-reacting."

"They can't really think that." Samantha shook her head.

"They do. Trust me, I can tell." Natalie ran a hand through her hair. "I miss my social life…but as long as I believe what I saw, they won't let me go out."

"Easy fix," Laderia waved a hand. Natalie raised an eyebrow. "Just play to what they want to hear. Say you were having a lesbo romance and your girlfriend dumped you at a party, so you had a complete breakdown."

"I am not telling my parents that I'm a lesbian!"

"Pretend you were experimenting," Laderia shrugged. "Oh, get off your high horse! It's a perfect cover! The social pressure alone would be enough to cause a breakdown!"

"What will they think?"

"Once you're on the outside and dating boys again, your parentals will be thinking that gays can be cured."

"She has a point there," Samantha nodded.

"And which one of you is supposed to be my girlfriend?" Natalie blinked.

"Jennifer," Samantha and Laderia said in unison.

Natalie considered it and nodded. "It's not perfect, but I don't have a better idea. Oh, and just to clarify, I'm not okay with you guys dropping me at home in the wrong bed as a good party move after my polar-plunge."

"Okay," Samantha chuckled. "Sorry."

"Seriously, I'm calling the Chestnut Center and thanking them for hosting that Halloween Ball every year. If either of our parentals were home, we never would have gotten away with this." Laderia shook her head.

"I still have to fake being a lesbian to escape my house," Natalie glowered, "without my parents killing me. We can celebrate when I'm back in the real world, okay?"

"SO, WHAT DID YOU GUYS talk about?" Tim asked. Levi ignored him. "I know you heard me, man."

"We didn't talk about anything."

"Liar."

"I'm not lying," Levi said.

"Now you're lying about lying, Mauer."

"He bitched a lot. It was awkward." Levi pulled a plate out of the cabinet and grabbed two slices of bread and peanut butter.

"Worthless conversation. Sounds like Felix." Tim stretched out on the couch. "At least he bought us groceries while he was here. It's snowing pretty good out there. We still gonna head over to the library tonight?"

"I am. You gotta work again."

"I hate going to work." Tim sat up. "I'm still squeamish around—"

"Have you noticed anything strange?"

"While I've been working?"

"Yes. Anything out of the ordinary?"

"No."

"You're supposed to be looking for stuff like that." Levi put the peanut butter away and pulled the jelly out of the fridge. "That's the only reason you're there."

"Forgive me if I can't tell the difference between the normal and abnormal goings-on in a funeral parlor." Tim flopped back down. "He has me doing a lot of cleaning lately; keeps me out of the basement. I guess I should be grateful there are no mirrors in that building…outside of the restrooms, of course. I've always hated cleaning glass."

"Maybe we should stake it out overnight," Levi murmured. "I know he's got shit in that basement that he doesn't want anyone to know about."

"That'll be difficult with the snow now. We'll leave tracks wherever we go. Besides, when are we going to find a free night to do it?"

"We stake it out from a safe distance. It has to be a night when we don't have to be at the cemetery, when there's no deaths in the paper," Levi shrugged. "How long of a wait could that be?"

Chapter 6

Don't Let 'Em See You Sweat

"I'm not seeing any obituaries tonight." Levi flipped through the Marshfield News-Herald. "We can scope out the funeral home." He set the paper down and began to slip on his coat.

"Hold off! Listen to this." Tim leaned over the paper. "'Retired Marshfield Couple Vanishes From Home.'"

Levi paused as Tim spun the paper around and began to read. "Mr. and Mrs. Philip and Edna Noble of 662 Pecan Parkway led a quiet life, according to neighbors. 'They were private people. I've only been over there once,' said neighbor Marjorie Wilson. 'They were very nice whenever I saw them out.' Though their absence from public life was not suspicious, neighbors began to suspect something was wrong as newspapers piled up. 'It was unusual. Phil always kept the papers picked up,' Wilson stated. The Nobles' vehicle remained at the house, and Wilson went over to check on them. 'I knocked on the door,' she said. 'Usually Edna would come to the door. No one answered. I figured maybe they left on a long vacation, but forgot to ask someone to collect their papers.' Three weeks after her failed visit, Wilson called the police. 'Something was definitely wrong,' she said. 'I picked up so many newspapers from that yard. No one goes on vacation that long.' Officer Emma

Horace of the Marshfield Police Department confirmed the Nobles have been missing since early September. Speculation about a connection to the disappearance of Arthur Harris, which occurred in the same timeframe—"

"Tim, stop." Levi sighed, sitting back down in his chair. "Remember Arthur Harris?"

Tim shuddered. "The man I had to bury…thanks to you."

"No, thanks to *them*," Levi corrected, pointing at the headline. "They were a vampire couple. I staked both of them the same night I staked Arthur Harris."

"The night before the first day of school—in that house?" Tim squinted at the picture, then looked at him. "What were you doing there? I thought you always hung around the graveyard."

"I usually do." Levi shook his head. "There was an obituary for them in the newspaper. I went to the graveyard, searched everywhere for the headstones. They weren't there."

Tim was quiet. "The paper was wrong?"

"They issued an apology the next day. Said it was a misprint and that a wake would be happening there…at 662 Pecan Parkway. I had to scope it out."

"And nobody else noticed?" Tim scanned the story closely. "Not even this Marjorie Wilson chick?"

"I didn't go during the wake's scheduled time. I went late at night, to investigate the place. That misprint made me suspicious, as did the lack of a burial site at Hillside Cemetery. So I went into the house. The place seemed empty. But then I heard voices in the basement."

"It sounds like you were set up."

"I was."

"How many vampires were there?"

"The couple, Lancaster, and our favorite wannabe, Arthur Harris."

"And you killed the couple and Arthur Harris. You badass."

"Lancaster got away," Levi frowned. "I was stunned when I recognized him. I worked for him for months, and I never suspected he could be—"

"Did he know you were a slayer when you worked for him?"

"No, Tim."

"That makes sense. The set-up was for *any* vampire slayer in Marshfield."

"They were doing a conversion." Levi scanned the library. Nobody paid them attention. "That's a lengthy ritual, usually done somewhere safe. I'm still not sure why Lancaster would try to have a slayer show up. It makes *no* sense."

"Maybe he wanted to see if there was a slayer in Marshfield at all." Tim shrugged. "This is a small town in the middle of nowhere. You realize we're almost four hours away from the closest Cheesecake Factory?"

"Whenever I think about what qualifies a place as 'somewhere,' its proximity to the Cheesecake Factory is the first thing that comes to mind." Levi stared at Tim.

"My point is, who would guess there'd be a slayer here? No better way to check than create a set-up and have back-up. Just in case."

Levi's brow furrowed. "That's cunning."

"You're dealing with what Mr. Becker would call an undead sociopath, Levi. If he plans on living forever, he better be cunning."

"Sure. But he's been in town for years. Why is he scoping for slayers *now*?"

"RUMOR HAS IT there's a big sleepover at the Symanski abode tonight." Matt strode up to Samantha, bouncing a basketball against the gym floor, the hair gleaming on his muscled chest. "You weaseled your mom into letting you have a life again."

"Less weaseling and more like a deal with the devil. I had to clean the whole house first." Samantha pulled a scrunchie out of her hair and flipped it onto her wrist. Sweat poured off her face and she fluffed out her t-shirt to create a breeze. "And that was after not skipping class for a week. But now, I can go to Dance team practices."

"Cool. The basketball and dance practices line up a lot, so we'll see each other."

"It's been torture not spending time with you." Her eyes lingered on his torso. "What is this, shirts versus skins?"

"Shirt's too confining. You could join my team if you're up for it."

"Only if you join the Dance team."

"I'm tempted. You look hot dripping wet," Matt murmured, standing close to her.

"I look like a drowned rat and I smell like a boy," she grumbled. "I'm not used to working out, especially like this."

"It's just the dance team. How much worse can it be than cheerleading? You practice in the cafeteria, for crying out loud."

"I didn't think it would be that bad either! But we have a new routine for each home game, and now we're learning the huge routine for the Christmas game. We'll be practicing it for a month."

"Wait until they make you do it in a sweater with elf ears," he snickered.

She smacked his muscled arm. "You got so hairy."

"'Cuz I'm a beast."

"The only way your neck can hold up that big head is because it's full of hot air."

"Which big head are we talking about?"

"The only one I've seen on you." Samantha raised an eyebrow. "And it's staying that way...for now."

"You're a tease, Symanski."

"I'm fifteen. And you are—"

"Sixteen, going on seventeen." Matt dribbled the ball between his legs.

"Baby, it's time to think." Samantha tapped her temple. Matt looked confused. "Never mind." A cell phone vibrated. Matt tucked the ball under his arm and pulled his cell out of his pocket and began texting. "Matt, who's that?"

"Nobody."

"Since when did *nobody* have a phone?"

"What a stupid question," he murmured, a shadow of a smile on his face as he continued to look at his phone.

"Why won't you tell me who it is?" Samantha crossed her arms.

"It's just Kaeli. You know, the other junior class representative."

"Oh…what did she say?" His phone vibrated again as he held it in his hands.

"She just asked how practice went." He typed his response.

"And how did it go?"

"Oh, now you wanna know?" Matt met her eyes. She didn't recognize the expression on his face, and full-fledged alarm rose in her chest.

"Of course I do, you're my boyfriend, Facebook official and everything. My profile picture is of us in the movie theater."

"And mine is us at Homecoming." Matt took a deep breath. Samantha watched his chest rise and fall. "And you never asked before."

"Well, how was practice?"

"It was good. Long." His phone vibrated again. A wicked grin spread across his face.

"What did she say now?"

"She said 'that's what she said.'"

"Is she watching us?" Samantha glanced around the gym. A couple boys were sitting on the bleachers as the coach collected basketballs. The rest of the dance team had gone into the girls' locker room.

"No, I texted her the same thing I told you." Matt continued to stare at his phone.

Samantha felt a wave of anger. "Oh, so you think Kaeli and I are equal now?"

"What? Where the hell did that come from?"

"You must. You text her just as much as you talk to me. You even type out exactly what you say to me! I might as well be in the phone with her."

"Samantha, Kaeli and I are friends. I've known her since elementary school. I've known you since September. I don't know you that well yet."

"Maybe you'd know me better if you'd text me more often." Heat flushed across her face and she struggled to keep her voice down. The boys on the bleachers were eyeing them inquisitively.

"So you'd rather have me text than talk to you face to face?"

"This isn't face to face! You're facing your phone."

"You don't text me either. It goes both ways."

"That's because I want you to have your space." Samantha flipped her hair. "That doesn't mean you get to text Kaeli all the time instead!"

"What, we can't be friends?"

"You can be friends, you just have to talk to me more than her!"

"So now all the pressure is on me to figure out when you actually wanna talk and to make sure I talk to you more than her? How is that fair? I'm not a mind reader."

"You have no pressure on you, it's just common sense! I'm the one restraining myself."

"Restraining yourself from what?"

"From texting you!"

"Why? Because you don't wanna piss me off? What if I'd like you to text me out of the blue?" Matt paced back and forth dribbling the ball with one hand, his phone in the other. The boys on the bleachers were paying close attention now.

"You say that like it makes sense, but I can't possibly know how frequent 'out of the blue' is for you. At what point does 'out of the blue' become 'expected' or 'overbearing'? You'll get angry at me for seeming clingy."

"I'll let you know when enough is enough."

"And if I don't want you to train me like a pet? What if I wanna text you whenever the hell I feel like it?"

"Fine, then do it!" Matt roared. "I can always block your number!" The gym was silent. The coach stared. Samantha felt as small as an ant. It took all her strength to maintain eye contact with Matt's angry face before finally turning and walking, head held high, to the locker room.

"KAELI EDWARDS is texting your boyfriend." Natalie sat on the end of Samantha's bed. "Skeazy, sleazy girl."

"You could give her lessons." Jennifer popped her gum as she leaned forward to paint her toenails.

"You're not going to be able to wear anything open-toed for a while." Becca leaned over from her spot next to Samantha. "It's pointless. Why bother?"

"It's winter half the year, I'll paint them whenever I damn well feel like it." Jennifer shot her a look. "Hey Natalie, how come you haven't dyed your white streaks yet? I thought the B took you to the office about it."

"I had her call my mother and she explained that my hair really is white. The policy is no unnatural hair colors, and this color is unfortunately natural." Natalie held up a strand of her hair. "But it's kinda cool at the same time."

"How come your mom doesn't want me to be friends with you anymore?" Jennifer set the nail polish down and put her hair up.

Samantha and Natalie's eyes met. "I don't know," Natalie said evenly. "I still want to be friends. I had to lie and tell her you wouldn't be at this sleepover. Just so she'd let me come."

"Can we get back to me?" Samantha asked.

"Yes," Natalie gushed in relief. "Continue, Sammy."

"I think the worst part is that he didn't even want to tell me it was Kaeli. I mean, he said it was nobody at first. What does *that* mean?!" Samantha threw her hands up.

"I think it means he doesn't want you to know about what he and Kaeli talk about," Becca suggested. "Very suspicious to me."

"Or he means that Kaeli's not worth worrying about." Jennifer gave Samantha an exasperated look. "It's not that fucking complicated."

"Unlike the Christmas dance routine," Natalie butted in. "Doesn't it seem overly difficult this year? Who knew that *A Mad Russian's Christmas* was that long?" She laughed nervously.

"You know what's long? How much time has passed since I was allowed at Natalie's house," Jennifer glowered.

"Nice try, Jennifer, but we're still talking about Matt and me," Samantha's forehead wrinkled.

"Why?" Jennifer selected a different nail polish and shook the bottle. "The only problem I see is why the hell I can't hang out with Natalie at her house anymore."

"I told you, I don't know."

"You're lying, Natalie."

"Jennifer, how are you and Dylan doing?" Samantha tried to change the subject.

"We're doing well. Why?"

"Have you had any fights yet?"

Jennifer shrugged. "Not since Halloween. He was upset I called him out for being a pussy. Boys don't like that."

"How did you guys get past it?"

"He admitted he was a pussy."

"I got brownies bitches!" Laderia burst through the door in her jacket-covered neon polka-dotted nightgown, two pans of brownies under one arm, her sleeping bag and overnight bag on the other. "Hurry up and take them before I drop everything."

"What, no enchiladas?" Jennifer waddled over, keeping her toes off the floor, and took the pans. Laderia let her stuff drop to the floor.

"Why were you so late?" Samantha asked.

"I spent twenty minutes with my *madre* in the car outside, convincing her this place isn't haunted." Laderia rolled her eyes. "She's a hardcore Hispanic Catholic, and majorly superstisho."

"You're majorly superstisho." Jennifer plopped on the bed and took the lid off a pan of brownies.

"Why would she think my house is haunted?" Samantha remembered the mothers whispering on Halloween.

"Because it was a Masonic Temple for forty years or something," Laderia said. "She was babbling about how the Catholics and the Masons don't get along; something about witchcraft or devil worship—"

"Oh please. The Order of the Masons had nothing to do with

that at all. It was a power strategy by the Catholics to isolate the Masons and limit their influence." Jennifer pulled a brownie from the pan. "The Church was freaking out because Mason members were usually the most powerful people in a community, and they all got together and socialized at secret meetings and nobody outside of them knew what they were up to. The Church painted it as a conspiracy to rule the world."

"Like when Selena Gomez dumped Justin Bieber and now everyone likes her," Natalie chimed, pulling her red and white hair into pig tails.

"No, that was just common sense," Becca nodded. "Any boy that's prettier than me is a threat. They can be competition—going after the same boys I'm after."

"You worried they'd pick Justin Bieber over you?"

Becca painted a protective coat on her nails. "The only kind of boy I attract is the Tim Kerner kind—Skeazy Dealer Extraordinaire."

"I think you're mistaken. He's head over heels for Jennifer," Laderia popped a brownie in her mouth. "Just like every other toolio in the box."

"Dylan's my favorite toolio in the box." Jennifer cracked a grin and blew a bubble. "But Tim Kerner is useful to me. Cheaper prices, free samples every now and then…it's great. I got some joints in my bag if anybody's up for—"

"No!" Samantha was appalled. "Y'all will *not* smoke in here. I have asthma."

"Whatever." Jennifer pulled her gum out of her mouth. "You know, this house *is* really old…it was owned by a doctor before it became a mysterious, secretive Masonic temple. What if someone died in this room? In a bed in this same spot?"

"I hate you so much Jennifer." Natalie pulled her knees to her chest.

"I overheard some ladies talking about it on Halloween—so my house really is haunted?"

"No, it's not. There's no such thing as ghosts," Becca said

emphatically. Eyes shifted to Natalie. She twirled a lock of red and white hair before nodding in strained agreement with Becca. Samantha glanced at Laderia.

"Don't worry about it," Laderia said. "All old houses have creepy stories. And there's a lot of old houses in this town."

"Not one that was a Masonic temple," Natalie whispered. "What if they really did do devil worship in here—and we're spending the night?!"

"Ooh, I know a fun game we can play!" Samantha clapped her hands. "My mom said they used to do it at slumber parties in the eighties."

"Truth or dare?" asked Natalie.

"Spin the bottle?" Jennifer eyed Natalie and took a bite of a brownie.

"Umm, let's not, and, how awkward." Becca raised an eyebrow.

"Light as a feather, stiff as a board!" Samantha announced.

"Oh, I've heard of that!" Becca smiled.

"Ditto!" Laderia licked brownie off her fingers.

"Isn't that the levitation trick? We should try it!" Natalie bounced.

"Who first?" asked Laderia.

"What the hell, I'll go," Jennifer drawled. "Just to stop you hens from clucking." She popped the last bit of brownie in her mouth and wiped her hands together. "Okay, how does this work, Sammy?"

"Lie on the bed, in the middle, and you cross your arms over your chest like a mummy."

Jennifer flopped in the middle of the bed and crossed her arms. "Big deal. Now what?"

"No, you're laying the wrong way. Here." Samantha yanked the pillows and arranged them at the foot of her bed. "You need to lie here."

Jennifer rolled her eyes and switched positions.

Samantha stood at the foot of the bed, and placed her fingertips on Jennifer's temples, gently massaging. "I'm going to tell you about your own death. When it's over, we'll chant 'you're dead' over and over. Then we'll chant 'stiff as a board'. After that, we'll chant 'light as a feather' a bunch of times, then each of us will put two of our fingers under you and see how far we can lift you up. Back at River Hill, we raised Tiffany Sarasota almost to the ceiling once before she fell to the floor. So concentrate."

"Wasn't this in a movie?" Becca flipped off the light switch. She turned on the desk lamp for lower light. "It sounds familiar."

"Yeah, I think so, but we can do it too," Samantha agreed as the other girls gathered around the bed. "Are you ready Jennifer?"

"I'm a bored board right now. Get cracking."

"Now Jennifer Cromwell, close your eyes, and focus on my voice." Samantha massaged meticulously, in a slow, steady rhythm, and lowered her voice. "Your father bought you a new car, gleaming bright red. But you hate it so much, almost as much as you hate him. You grab the keys and drive away, to take your mind off of it. You drive in the country, windows down, flying down the endless straight roads, going as fast as you dare…you look in the rearview mirror, and there's police lights. You know you should pull over, but it's one of your father's officers. You decide to outrun him and press down on the gas as hard as you can. The car goes faster, faster. You hate the car, you hate your father, you hate the officer tailing you because he's just going to make you come back. You begin to outdistance him. You watch his lights disappear in the rearview mirror, and you're smiling. You're laughing on the inside, and then on the outside. You turn to look at the road, and it's blocked off ahead. You press on the brake, but nothing happens. The car doesn't slow down. You scream as the car busts through the sign. The windshield cracks, glass rains down on the dashboard, and you can't see. There's blood running in your eyes. You grab the wheel, you crank it hard to the left. The car doesn't turn. It's going too fast. Suddenly it flips, rolling over and over again. Your limp body is rebounding off the doors, the ceiling, the seats, and then your neck hits the steering wheel. You hear the crack, and all goes black. You're dead. You're dead. You're dead." The other girls' voices joined in. "You're dead, you're dead, you're dead."

Samantha looked around as she placed two fingers from each hand under Jennifer's body. The other girls did the same. "Stiff as a board, stiff as a board, stiff as a board, stiff as a board." They felt Jennifer's body stiffen underneath their fingers.

"Light as a feather, light as a feather, light as a feather," they began to chant. Slowly they lifted Jennifer up off the bed and into the air.

"Oh-Em-Gee! So cool!" Natalie gushed. Suddenly Jennifer slipped from their fingers and landed on the bed. "Oops!"

"How high did I get?" Jennifer rubbed the back of her neck.

"That's between you and Tim," Becca scoffed.

"Shoulder-level with me," Natalie pointed, "but I'm not very tall. Let's do me next!" She took Jennifer's spot on the bed and crossed her arms.

"Who's doing the story?" Samantha asked.

"You do it," Laderia said.

"I did the last one."

"It's always up to me, isn't it?" Jennifer took the position at the foot of the bed and began to massage Natalie's temples. "How did you start? Oh ya. Close your eyes, Natalie Devereaux, and listen to my voice or else."

"Say it like you're serious," Becca snapped. "You keep doing your sarcasm thing."

Jennifer rolled her eyes, sighed, and started over, going slower. "Listen to my voice, Natalie Devereaux. Relax. You're about to go to sleep. You're laying in your bed, in your room, in the dark. The covers are warm, cozy, like a hug all over. You turn to snuggle into your pillow, when you hear a noise. A creaking. You look over to the source, and your bedroom door is gliding open. No one is touching it. You know you can't sleep with the door open. It's not safe. You're exposed. You leave the warmth of the bed and walk to the door. You reach out to shut it when you hear another door creaking open downstairs. Your family's asleep. You know that the doors should not be opening. You step into the hallway, and look down the stairs. The front door is wide open, the wind blowing cold. You rush down the stairs to close it. Just as you get to the door, a hand clamps down over your mouth. You scream, but nobody hears you. A strong arm wraps you tight like a snake, and you can't even fight as the stranger carries you out of the house and throws you into an old van with benches in the back and chains attached to the floor. He puts you in chains with tape over your mouth and a bag over your head. You can't see. You can't move. You can barely breathe, but you listen as the van accelerates and slows down. You listen as the strange driver plays old songs that you've never heard before, talking with another strange man. You shudder in fear as they talk about normal things, like baseball games and World War II. It seems so old-fashioned. Suddenly the van stops. You hear them get out and come around to the back to get you. They unlock you from the chains in the van, and handcuff you. They set your bare feet on the cold, sharp gravel and remove the black bag. You look up at the brick barn towering over you in the night. You know this is all wrong. This is a bad place. They drag you through the gravel by your handcuffs as you scream into the tape for help. Your feet are bleeding and stinging as the tears stream hot down your face. The steel barn door thunders as it slides open, and they drag you into the dark, take you into a strange room, and point down a set of stairs that lead into the pitch black. 'You didn't really think we'd let you leave, now, Natalie,' says one. 'We've missed you so much,' says the other. 'We miss the cherry taste of your skin, the sweet strawberry mixture of pain and fear in your eyes.' You turn and run, but they push you back, laughing at your weakness. You feel shame coloring your fear. They step closer to you, backing you to the stairs, but you won't go down. With a sweet smile, they push you backwards and you fall down the steps, handcuffed. Your face hits the concrete first, blood pours from your nose and broken teeth. You wish it would have killed you as they laugh and come down the stairs, a wooden flyswatter in hand. Your fear overtakes you and everything goes black. That's when you realize you're dead. You're dead. You're dead." The girls placed their fingers under

Natalie's body as they chanted. "Stiff as a board, stiff as a board. Stiff as a board, stiff as a board. Light as a feather, light as a feather. Light as a feather." Natalie rose easily into the air on their fingers, until the girls had her over their heads. They stopped chanting and stared.

"She's not on my fingertips," Samantha whispered.

"She's not on mine either," Becca whispered back.

Laderia breathed out. "What the hell is going on?"

"Girls!" Samantha's mother burst into the room. Natalie fell and bounced on the bed. "Do you want anything else before I go to bed—what happened, Natalie? Was she jumping on the bed?"

"No," Samantha shook her head. "We were doing that 'light as a feather' thing."

Samantha's mother evaluated the group for several seconds before shutting the door. Her footsteps tapped down the stairs.

"That was odd," Samantha murmured.

"Jennifer, you are a sick, twisted bitch. You will not tell my story. I'm next." Laderia shoved Natalie off the bed. "And you bitches better heave."

"MATT, IT'S ALMOST Thanksgiving break. We need to talk. You know, before we're separated by our families and stuffed with food," Samantha said, uneasy. He shut his locker and turned to glare at her.

"So now you want to talk to me?"

"Yeah, that's why I'm here." Samantha gave him a confused look. "We keep missing each other and—"

"Don't make it sound like an accident. You've been avoiding me. I told you to text me whenever, and you didn't. You also didn't respond to any of my texts—"

"I'd rather have you call me." Samantha twirled a lock of hair.

"You never told me that. And that sucks because I hate talking on the phone."

"Even to me?"

"To anyone. It's awkward. I'd rather text." Matt stretched.

"Well, I'd rather talk to you. It's bad enough my friends have me texting all the time. Yet every now and then you text other people to tell me things instead of telling me yourself. You text Laderia more than me. I hate that too."

"We're talking now. What do you want to talk about?"

"The whole Kaeli thing," Samantha waved her hand.

"Are we really calling it that? The Kaeli thing?"

"It's a thing," Samantha replied curtly. "A very annoying thing."

"You find my friendship with Kaeli annoying." Matt gave her a strange look. "And you want me to do what about it?"

"I want to clear the air," Samantha said. "I've been avoiding you because of it."

"Because of what?"

"The Kaeli thing."

"What Kaeli thing?" came a female voice. Samantha practically jumped and turned to see Kaeli Edwards standing there, her eyes locked on Samantha. "Do you have a problem with me, New Girl?"

"To be honest, yes," Samantha replied.

"Well? Spit it out."

"I-I don't like how much you're texting my boyfriend."

"And I don't like how *little* you text my best friend," Kaeli countered. "It's been almost a month, and you've sent him ten messages. Ten. That's really low."

Samantha whirled around to glare at Matt. "You've been telling people about us?!"

"So have you," Matt retorted. "I heard Laderia and Jennifer talking in the hallway. If you can tell them, I can tell Kaeli."

"That's different, I was having girl talk!"

"And what do you call me talking to Kaeli?"

"FLIRTING!" Samantha was ready to tear her hair out. "You're flirting with another girl and you expect me to be okay with it! How is that supposed to—?"

"He is not flirting with me," Kaeli shook her head, as if pitying Samantha for suffering a delusion. "He's my best friend. And he's more like a brother—"

"Oh, drop the act. You're only his friend because you'd date him given half a chance!"

"Boys and girls can be friends without flirting." Kaeli crossed her arms. "We've always hung out a lot, told jokes and confided in each other—"

"That's the role of the girlfriend!" Samantha shot back. "You're *not* in that role, Kaeli, I am. He asked me out, not you!"

"Ladies, ladies," Matt grinned. "If you're going to fight over me, can we at least take this to a hot tub or mud pit or something?"

Kaeli wrinkled her nose at him.

Samantha glared at Matt and crossed her arms.

Kaeli looked her up and down and narrowed her eyes. "For your information, sophomore, if I was interested in Matt, he'd be mine. Because that's just how it is. Have a nice day, and try to feel a little more secure about yourself instead of blaming your ineptitude on me." Kaeli smiled pleasantly and walked down the hall.

"Oh snap," Matt said.

Samantha's face burned as she looked at Matt, his expression of shock about to be overcome with humor. "How could you let her humiliate me like that?"

"You're the one who raised your voice."

"I can't believe you. I saved your life, remember?"

"Sort of. Bits and pieces, mostly." Matt scratched the back of his leg.

Samantha remembered that was where the beast bit him and made a mental note before she continued. "You asked me out and said it was because we went through a lot—you said we went through hell together. Remember that?"

Matt leaned against his locker. "I also remember my parents freaking out, my dad's conniption fit about the car, the insurance and the medical bills, and the way my family used to treat me." He stared off down the hall. "Now they treat me like I'm...I dunno, different. Like I'm another person."

Samantha was quiet as he continued.

"They listen to everything I say, do anything I ask, and they're always watching me. Almost like they're afraid of what I'll do. But even with all that monitoring, no matter what I do, they don't try to restrict me now."

"You haven't been grounded? At all?"

"No groundings, no denying me privileges, nothing beyond the B's detentions. It's almost like they treat me like an adult now…or they're afraid of losing me…either way, I like it. But they don't like you one bit." He turned his gaze to her. "And they told me not to see you anymore, that it was bad for my mental health. But I like dating you. The forbidden thing makes it hot. So, this one time, can we just forget about this fight and move on? I don't like muddling through the drama."

"Oh…um…I suppose that's alright." Samantha felt very odd as Matt smiled at her, a hungry look in his eyes. "I'll see you at the basketball game Friday night."

"WHAT DO YOU WANT to do for Thanksgiving?" Tim opened and closed his lighter repeatedly as Levi scanned the day's newspaper in the library.

"You should put that away before they throw us out." Levi didn't take his eyes off the paper.

"Relax, it's not lit. I just like flipping the lid."

"Stop it or I'll flip your lid."

"You're a man bound by process and full of empty threats," Tim gestured grandly. "I was thinking we could try frying a turkey."

"Nah."

"Why not?"

"More people burn down garages doing stupid shit like that. It's bad enough you're playing with a lighter in a library." He flipped the page.

"You don't think I can cook."

"To be fair, you ruined the grilled cheese last time you tried to make it."

"I did not. I just forgot I was cooking. Besides, there's some awesome recipes in the cookbooks here." He pulled several loose pages from his pocket. "Well, there were."

"The fuck, Tim!" Levi hissed. "I come here all the time! You can't be doing shit like that! They might revoke my library card."

"Pfffft! They will not." Tim leaned back. "It's not like you read books anyway."

Levi scowled. "What do you think I do in the cemetery while you sleep in the truck?"

"Count the headstones? Masturbate? How the hell should I know."

"I read, dumb-ass."

"Oh really? What are you reading now?"

"*East of Eden.*"

"Never heard of it."

"Figures."

"Cut it with the judgment, Levi. Seriously. Are there any obituaries?"

"No."

"The library closes in a little bit. Let's go, man. We gotta get to the grocery store."

"DID YOU TWO TALK to your father?" Mrs. Symanski's voice echoed from the dining room.

Samantha walked down the stairs, feeling a hollow numbness inside. She wrote it off as being hungry. "We called, but he didn't answer."

"I'm sorry honey. Did you get his voicemail?"

"Yeah, we left a 'Happy Thanksgiving' message. Brandon's still up there with the phone." Samantha entered the dining room. "Wow, mom. This is incredible."

"I know." Mrs. Symanski beamed as she lit two candles in the center of the table. "I got some ideas from some magazines in the grocery store and thought, 'what the hell, I'm home this year.'" She scurried around the table, doing last-minute alignments to the place settings, and the huge glass serving plates laden with buns, turkey, ham, cranberry sauce, and vegetables.

"This is a lot of food for three people." Samantha orbited the table, the soft lighting of the twinkling chandelier and the candles giving the room a magical feel. "It looks like a real Thanksgiving meal."

"We'll have leftovers until Valentine's Day. Call your brother down." Mrs. Symanski gestured to the foyer. "I'll grab the potatoes out of the kitchen and we'll get started."

"Okay." Samantha walked to the foyer. "BRANDON!"

"Samantha, shut up!" Brandon appeared at the top of the landing, his little face wrinkled with frustration. "You're interrupting my conversation!"

"What did you say to me?! Who are you talking to?"

"Dad." He put the phone back to his ear. Samantha felt a little thrill in her stomach. "No, I didn't. She yelled first, dad." Brandon turned and went back to his room, slamming the door.

Samantha ran to the dining room. "Mom, he's on the phone with Dad."

"Oh?" Mrs. Symanski raised an eyebrow. "That's—"

"Not fair. I'm grabbing the extension!" She marched into the kitchen and grabbed the cordless.

"Hey dad!" She joined the conversation.

"Hey, Sammy." Her dad's voice came through the line.

"It's so good to hear from you! You sound tired."

"There's about a ten hour time difference here."

"Well, Happy Thanksgiving! How are you?" Her heart soared.

"Samantha, I'm talking now!" Brandon's voice cut in.

"Shut it Brandon, you got to talk to him longer than I did!"

"Samantha, don't yell at your brother." Her dad's voice was sharp. "That's not how we do it on Thanksgiving."

"But dad, I've missed you so much—"

"You're the oldest, you have to act like it."

"I do—I know. I'm not stupid."

"I know you're not, Sammy. You're temperamental. Like your mother."

Samantha's mouth twisted at the comparison. "When will we see you? Are you coming to visit any time soon?"

"We wanna see you dad!" Brandon shouted.

"Not sure kiddos. I can't get leave to come back to the States for another thirteen months. At that point I'm going to have to handle all my finances and house stuff in Arizona and—"

"You can still drop by and see us," Samantha urged, smiling despite her feelings of doubt. "Thirteen months is next Christmas." The silence made her heart skip. "Are you there?"

"Yeah, I'm here. Maybe, Sam. I'll give it a shot."

"I can't wait! We miss you a lot."

"We love you dad," Brandon said.

"I love you too. Tell your mom Happy Thanksgiving. Bye guys." The dial tone was hollow. Samantha felt her smile flicker and fade as she set the phone back on its stand.

"You guys have a nice talk?" Mrs. Symanski walked into the kitchen. Samantha stealthily wiped a couple tears from her face and turned to meet her mother's eyes. "It seemed so short."

Samantha forced a smile. "Yes, but he's so busy—protecting people and stuff."

"Did he mention any plans to visit?"

"He said he'd be back in the country in thirteen months. So maybe next Christmas we can see him."

"That's good…a long way out though."

"He's got plenty of time to plan and we can prepare. He can come visit and we can do real family stuff." She glared at her mother, daring her to object. "You could handle it?"

"Of course. I want you guys to see him as often as you can." Mrs. Symanski reached out and stroked Samantha's cheek. "I hope he can come this time."

THE FATHER HUGH DEENY AUDITORIUM could barely contain the crowd of the first white-out game of the basketball season. Bleachers threatened to buckle under the weight of students and parents of both teams, as well as Columbus alumni back in town for Thanksgiving. A line snaked from the lobby's snack counter across the glistening wet floor. Tim twisted his sneakers in the puddles of snowmelt with every step, admiring their squeaking and screeching.

"Stop it," Levi ordered as they shuffled through the crowd. "You're driving me nuts."

"Can't help it. I'm so pumped for this game." Tim patted his leather jacket. "Been starved for a big business opportunity."

It's better than using, Levi thought. "Get to it then."

"Will do, Biff. Where will you be sitting?"

"In the student section. What's with the incredulous look?"

"Nothing. I'll meet up with you later." Tim shrugged and disappeared into the crowd.

Levi looked around, scanning the faces of the students, parents and teachers that milled about. They passed without making eye contact, managing to walk around him like he was in a bubble.

A surge of nausea filled his chest. Clenching and unclenching his fists, he fought the urge to turn heel and walk out. Instead he forced one foot in front of the other on the way into the gymnasium. He walked to the far end of the wooden bleachers, where the Columbus student body was in full white-out regalia, boisterous and bustling as the band lined the front row.

The few classmates that met his eyes regarded him with barely-concealed contempt or indifference. Samantha Symanski sat with her gaggle of girls near the middle. She met his gaze, then looked away pointedly. He took a deep breath through his nose and started up the rows, searching for an empty spot. He found one near the top, and took off his coat.

"Hey Mauer, this is a white-out. Why are you wearing black?" Jacob Bauman turned to look at him in disbelief, his hair mussed up by a white bandana, his face streaked with blue and white paint. "That hoodie's gonna make us lose before the game even starts!"

"I got a white t-shirt on underneath. I'm being plenty supportive," Levi replied.

"No you're not." Samantha Symanski's blonde hair whipped around and she glared at him. Levi felt taken aback and happy at the same time. "Take that hoodie off."

Silently, Levi obeyed, and pulled the hoodie over his head.

Samantha blinked at him for a moment before nodding, her face tinged pink as she turned away. Levi felt self-conscious all of a sudden. He sat down on his coat and hoodie, the bumps on his arms firm as an icy breeze seeped through the closed windows near the ceiling.

THE GAME OPENED WITH Kaeli Edwards singing the Star-Spangled Banner—which irked Samantha to no end. *Columbus Away*, the school song, played by the band, followed. After the whistle, the ball was up, and the Greenwood Indians were on the offensive. The crowd in the gym was in constant uproar as the ball went back and forth, the air electric as Kaeli and Nikki Becker led the student section in cheer after cheer. Matt intercepted a pass and ran to the other end of the court. The crowd was on their feet as he sank the basketball in the net.

"He's doing awesome!" Natalie yelled to Samantha.

"What?" Samantha yelled back.

"This is the right way to start a game! Come on, we're gonna get changed for our halftime show."

"Already?" Samantha followed Natalie as they weaved down the bleachers. She glanced out at the court, and Matt winked at her as he ran, sweat pouring down his face. She glanced over at Kaeli, who undoubtedly saw the wink judging by the look of loathing wrinkling her features. Samantha let Natalie lead her down to the girls' locker room, taking her out of range of Kaeli's death-ray vision.

"LOOK AT YOU in your plain white T. How's the game so far?" Tim asked.

"It's been cold," Levi replied.

"I'm glad you decided to come with me, man." Tim stood next to him and pulled a wad of bills from his leather jacket. "I couldn't buy a better seat." He tucked the money back into his pocket.

"You made all that already?"

"Sales go up in winter. People get bored being stuck inside and buzzless."

"You're not smoking, are you?"

"Nah, I got no time to kill anymore, thanks to you. Gotta stay sharp."

"Glad I helped turn you into a productive citizen." Levi smirked.

"Speaking of productive citizens, how's the werewolf doing? Looks like we're winning—so far." Tim stood on the seat of the bleacher and squinted down at the court.

"He's not a werewolf, Tim." Levi pushed Felix's words from his mind.

"Then why does it look like he stole his arms from King Kong? He's got five o'clock shadow all the time. You see it, right?"

"That's just puberty. If you're lucky you'll be able to grow a beard one day too."

"I would look pretty cool with one, wouldn't I?" Tim massaged his jaw line. "My brother's got some scruff that goes all along here."

"I know, I met him."

"Ya, you never told me what you guys talked about."

"I did. You just don't remember." Levi knew Tim didn't believe him, but the other boy seemed to drop the idea as he continued to watch the game.

"Oh, did I tell you? I was cleaning the funeral home and I heard Lancaster on the phone."

"Anything interesting or suspicious?"

"I dunno, man. He sounded like he was arranging a meeting."

"A meeting? For what? When?"

"I'm guessing some sort of medical procedure. A lot of scheduling, bickering, and then he was going off about how 'you have to get here quickly or something-something will expire.'"

"Holy shit, Tim. That's out of the ordinary. Did you hear a specific day or time?!"

"This weekend."

"It's Friday night! Are you sure it's not just some old ladies arranging a funeral?"

"I'm positive. I think the meeting was for midnight tonight. That's not a normal time to meet with a client—at least, not a funeral home client. I mean, I've sold shit at that hour, but—"

"Tim, was that midnight tonight or midnight Saturday into Sunday?"

"I…uh…didn't get that part figured out exactly."

"You should have told me sooner."

"Aw, but then we would have missed the game. I wouldn't have made this." He tapped his leather jacket pocket. "You'd have had us sitting outside that home until the sun comes up. We got bills to pay. And a kitchen I want to paint."

"We should leave now." Levi grabbed his hoodie. "We wanna be there on time."

"After this free-throw." Tim pointed. "Come on, Stauber!"

The crowds hushed, and the student section all raised their hands and wiggled their fingers, waiting for the ball to pass through the net. Tim elbowed Levi in the ribs, forcing Levi to raise his hands as well.

Matt stood on the free-throw line, about to take his shot, sweat pouring off his body. The other players glanced at each other nervously as he visibly winced. He shook his head, resumed his stance, and winced again. Then clutching his stomach, he dropped the ball. The crowd leaned forward, murmurs of concern filling the air.

Matt fell to the ground on his side, curled up in the fetal position, and a scream of pain escaped him. The crowd filling the bleachers stood. The coaches ran to him, and the players backed away. Matt suddenly stood up, hiding his face with his forearms. Running, he stumbled out the gym doors, through the lobby, and out of the building. The gym was silent. People looked around and the coaches scratched their heads.

"Is he mental?" "He had a heart attack!" "He's got the flu." "It's heat stroke." "It must have been the pressure." "It was a cramp. What a pussy." The student section was instantly ablaze with rumors and speculation.

Tim turned to Levi. "Five hundred dollars says he's turning into a werewolf right now."

Levi smacked him, then looked over his shoulder out the gym window. He was unable to shake a feeling of apprehension as a full moon looked back at him.

"IT'S COLD IN HERE," Tim's breath fogged in front of his face. "Turn on the heat."

"I'd have to turn the truck on. The noise would give us away."

"So we have to sit in this rust bucket in the cold all night?" Tim shivered. "This is bullshit…"

"This is my life." Levi rubbed his hands together and peered through the windshield. "Welcome to the nightmare."

"Can you see anything?" Tim asked. They sat in a parking lot by the Marshfield Door factory, looking across Veterans Parkway at the Lancaster Funeral Home. The building was dark except for the decorative lights on the exterior, its parking lot completely empty.

"Nothing's happened. How long until midnight?" Levi asked.

Tim checked his phone. "About five minutes." He slid it back into his pocket. "I wonder where Matt is right now."

"He's probably at home, getting ready for bed."

"I doubt it." Tim ran a hand through his spiky hair. "The moon is still up."

"He is *not* a werewolf."

"Are you a moron? The moon rose and he started to change. He was sweating like, three times as much as all the other players."

"So what?"

"He's also been getting hairier. His body is undergoing the stress of the change and—"

"So he sprouts some body hair and has hot flashes and night sweats. Sounds more like menopause than the curse of a werewolf."

"The two phenomena are probably closely related," Tim said in a hushed voice.

"I should kill you."

"You just say that."

"Repeatedly," Levi emphasized. "You need to grow up and stop being so immature. You have some of the stupidest ideas—"

"They're not stupid, they save my ass. And they've saved your ass too, on numerous occasions. I shouldn't have to remind you of it all the freaking time." Tim shook his head. "Is anything happening yet?"

"No…hold on," Levi leaned forward. "You see that?" Two headlights swung up and into the lot.

Tim leaned forward as well. "That's a nice car. Cadillac. He's meeting up with some rich bastard right now."

The car parked near the entrance. They watched as a bald man got out, grabbed several briefcases from his backseat, and headed into the funeral home. The parking lot was still. A couple cars drove by on Veterans Parkway as they sat waiting for what felt like forever.

Tim glanced at Levi. "Should we get closer?"

"We're going to wait. Something tells me that man is not the only one who's supposed to be here tonight." Levi scanned Veterans Parkway. The high streetlights illuminated empty pavement stretching in both directions, traffic lights changed from green to red for nobody. The town looked deserted.

"I don't think anyone else is coming," Tim said. Just then another car came down Veterans Parkway, gleaming under the streetlights. It turned slowly onto Palmetto and pulled into the funeral home's parking lot. "That's a Bentley. That's a motherfucking *Bentley*."

"So what?"

"Levi Mauer, if you knew the price tag of that car, you'd be more suspicious." Tim squinted. "Who the hell is driving *that* in Marshfield?" The Bentley parked, and a chauffeur emerged. He walked to the back, pulled out a wheelchair, and helped a frail-looking woman into it, draping a blanket around her shoulders. He shut the door and wheeled her into the funeral home. The lot remained still.

"We need to get the license plate numbers." Levi opened the door. The icy wind gusted in. "Let's go."

"Aren't you worried about where Lancaster could be right now?"

"He's probably inside."

"But where's his car?"

"Why would he need it? He lives one block over. Follow me."

"We're walking across the parkway?"

"Yep."

"I've got a question," Tim announced as they shut the doors. "How come you park on a driveway and drive on a parkway?"

"You're turning into a burnout pretty fast."

"I don't smoke that much, man. It's recreational."

"Spell recreational."

"*You* spell recreational. Ass-wipe." They trudged across the open street, shivering every time the wind blew. The icy road was reflective as glass; patchy trails of rock salt saved Tim from a broken neck twice. When they reached the other side, Levi crouched low and began to trudge into the snow.

"No," Tim whispered.

Levi gestured emphatically.

"I'm not going in the snow, man!" Tim hissed. "We're going to freeze and leave footprints and shit! And you think I'm the stupid one!"

"Shove it," Levi hissed back. "Don't get pissed at me because you don't keep an extra set of boots handy!"

"That's because I'm normal and don't carry around blue duffle bags full of weapons and boots!" Tim grumbled and took some dainty steps into the snow, wincing as if in pain.

"What's wrong now?"

"My shoes are full of snow and it's melting into my socks." Tim's face was positively stricken. "Levi, I'm wet."

"Come on." They traipsed up the slope to the parking lot, crouching low and shuffling to the cars. They stopped at the Cadillac first. Tim pulled out his cell phone and snapped a picture of the license plate. They scuttled over to the Bentley and snapped another picture.

"Are we done?" asked Tim. They heard the door to the funeral home open and shut. Levi put his hand on Tim's shoulder and they ducked behind the Bentley. They listened as someone hurried across the parking lot to the cars, the footsteps growing louder. With baited breath, they waited as the door on the Cadillac opened and closed. The footsteps returned inside and the funeral home's door shut.

"Now we're leaving." Levi grabbed Tim's collar and dragged him to the snow. They slid down to Veterans Parkway and stepped carefully across the highway to get back to the truck. They climbed in and gasped, relief washing over them.

"Do you think he knew we were there?"

"No one knew," Levi murmured, looking at the funeral home. "How did the photos turn out?"

Blue light illuminated Tim's face as his finger slid across the screen. "They're good. I got both plates."

"Excellent. Is there a way we can get the names of the owners?"

Tim shrugged. "Maybe Jennifer will know a way."

Chapter 7

The King

Just as she was drifting off to sleep, Samantha's phone buzzed. She groaned and turned to her nightstand where her phone rotated around as it vibrated, its screen bright. She grabbed it and looked at the number.

"Sorry Natalie, it's late." She hit the 'ignore' button and set it back down, turning in her bed and snuggling into a comfortable position. She sighed as the warmth from the blankets wrapped around her.

The phone buzzed again. Positively irate, she sat up, grabbed it, and checked the number. "Sorry Laderia." She reached to set it back on the nightstand, but it vibrated in her hand. "Becca?" She ignored the call. It vibrated again. "Jennifer." She ignored it again. It vibrated again. She hit the ignore button on reflex. The phone vibrated again. Natalie's name flashed across the screen. Samantha rolled her eyes and answered it. "Okay Natalie, what the hell is going on?"

"Nikki Becker is missing!" The tinny voice wailed from the phone.

"Who?"

"Are you kidding me? Our Homecoming Queen! Mr. Becker's daughter—she led the cheers with Kaeli at the basketball game tonight!"

Samantha fought the urge to gag at the mere mention of Kaeli's name. "Okay, I'm listening. What happened?"

"Mr. Becker found her car at home, but all her stuff was in the snow—her purse, cell phone—"

"What if she just dropped it?"

"There was blood in the snow." Samantha blinked as she tried to piece the image together in her mind. "And by the way Samantha, what kind of teenager drops their phone and doesn't care?"

"A drunk one." The gasp of horror from Natalie's end of the line made Samantha feel ashamed in spite of herself. "What do you want me to do?"

"We're pulling together people to search her neighborhood!"

"At this hour?"

"Don't be so selfish! This is someone's life we're talking about!"

"I get it, but I don't really know her."

"That's ridiculous. You don't know me all that well and you saved me from the tunnel, and you said you saved Matt from the bear—you gotta help." Samantha didn't admit it, but even as Natalie scolded her she pulled off her covers and turned on her lamp to get dressed. "Mr. Becker's called the police, but I haven't heard anything else. Everyone's coming to look for her. What if some sicko at the game was watching her and decided to keep her for himself?!"

"Sounds like the kind of horror story Jennifer would tell."

"It does, doesn't it? Will I see you tonight?"

"If my mom will give me a ride. I have to ask her."

"Otherwise Becca can come get you."

"Okay, I'll see you soon."

THE TELEVISION PERCHED on its mobile metal stand at the front of the room as Mrs. Hansen fussed with its buttons and pondered over the remote. Students filed in, a somber mood hovering over the classroom.

"Mr. Becker's not here." Samantha slid into her seat next to Levi. He glanced at her and resumed leaning against the wall, eyes closed.

"I guess they didn't find Nikki yet. It's so weird, isn't it? You never think something like this can happen."

"What happened?" he asked without opening his eyes.

"She disappeared. We combed the neighborhood on Friday and Saturday, but there was no sign of her. Jennifer said the police issued an Amber Alert."

"That isn't weird. It's logical. Nikki's only seventeen. She's still a minor."

She could feel his irritation as he crossed his arms. "Seriously Stoner, are you ever going to get over it or am I doomed to be on your shit list for the remainder of my high school career?"

"What?" He cracked an eye open.

"Ever since that incident—you've been a jerkwad," she whispered, trying not to attract the attention of her fellow classmates.

Levi shrugged and closed his eyes again.

"You're so rude!" she charged.

"This from you," he whispered back.

"And you're a skeaze," she hissed, only to be shushed by Mrs. Hansen from the front of the room.

"Samantha Symanski, have some respect!" Mrs. Hansen adjusted her glasses and returned to fussing with the electronics.

"Do you see that?" "OMG." "Why are the cops here?" The students near the windows erupted with whispers.

Mrs. Hansen glared in that direction. Her face changed and she crossed to the windows. The whole class turned and looked outside. The sky was a solid mass of iron gray, still dark enough for the streetlights to be on. Headlights from several police cars pulling up were clearly visible.

"Good gravy, shouldn't they be out looking for Nikki?" "Surprise raid!" "Drug dogs maybe? They did that at the public high school." "Stoner better watch out."

Samantha turned back and met Levi's gaze. A thin veil of calm couldn't hide the panic on his face.

"It's about Nikki," Samantha said loudly. The room quieted

down.

The PA system crackled and Barb's voice filled the air. *"Good morning Columbus Dons. There are several announcements. First, the Marshfield Police Department is conducting an investigation into the weekend disappearance of one of our students. This is an incredibly serious matter. Interviews will be conducted throughout the day. We expect your complete cooperation. There is a possibility lockers will be searched. Second, basketball practice this evening has been cancelled. Thank you."*

"MR. BECKER ISN'T HERE TODAY. Did you hear what happened to his daughter?" Samantha crossed her legs as she sat by Matt on the floor.

"The whole school knows she disappeared Friday night." Matt's voice was mellow, almost sleepy.

"Yeah. She drove herself home from the game and they think she was snatched when she got out of her car."

"You don't sound upset," Matt commented.

"It's tragic, it really is. But I'm from the D.C. metro area. I know this sounds horrible to y'all, but crazy things like this happen all the time."

"To people you know? People you've grown up with?"

"Well, no one I ever knew personally."

"Then that explains why you're so flippant about it," he said.

Samantha chose to ignore his last statement. "Mrs. Hansen was subbing. She wouldn't answer any questions and made us watch this terrible movie on monkeys being taken from their mothers."

"Huh."

"Why are you out here? Shouldn't you be in the cafeteria, eating with Dylan and Stefan and the rest of the toolbox?"

"I'm not really hungry," Matt mumbled.

"Oh...you could've sat by me."

"I'm not up for being around people right now."

"Does that include me? What happened to you Friday night?" Samantha asked. "I heard you had some sort of fit and bolted out the front door." She leaned her head back against the lockers. "I missed it. I was changing for the halftime show."

"I...uhh. I forgot to take my medicine." Matt rubbed his leg. "It was just an accident. I took it today, though."

Samantha felt a bubble of insecurity in her chest. "Matt, I'm not an expert, but I am your girlfriend...and you looked, well, *off* that night. *Really* off. Almost unhealthy."

He gave her an unsurprised, blank stare.

She felt her speech speeding up. "You were cagey and sweating like a butcher. No one else on the court was sweating like that. It was like you were melting."

"I overheat a lot." Matt shrugged. Samantha nodded, giving herself a moment to mesh the explanation with what she saw.

"What exactly are your meds for?"

Matt tensed and spoke with a forced casualness. "My condition. The doctors warned me that something like that could happen, but I didn't want the meds to interfere with my ability to play the game."

"How would they interfere?"

"They practically knock me out," Matt replied. "I wouldn't have been able to play at all."

"As logical as that sounds, I feel like you're not telling me the whole truth." Samantha frowned. "What's going on, Matt? You've been acting so strange lately."

"I'm the one acting strange?" He scoffed.

"Yes, you are."

"You're the one prying into my medical history."

"I'm concerned."

He let out a bitter laugh, and Samantha got the distinct impression she somehow surprised him. "Don't be."

"Why not?"

"I don't want my business all over this fucking school, Samantha," he said.

She gaped, completely taken aback. "You think I'm looking for gossip? Like there's not enough to talk about already?"

"Your friends are fueling all those bullshit rumors about me. That I'm going crazy, had a breakdown, turn into a werewolf, the kind of bullshit sophomore girls make up all the time because they have nothing else to do."

"Tim Kerner's the one who started the werewolf thing. I'm not trying to dig up dirt, Matt. I just want to understand what's happening to you." Samantha set her hand on his shoulder. He bristled under her touch. "I want to be there for you. That's all, I promise." There was a heavy silence as she waited for his response.

"Right here, right now, you're with me. That's all I need." Matt pulled her into a forced embrace. She felt lighter in his arms, but his expression darkened as he stared off into space. "My business is my business. You don't need to worry about it."

"But—"

"My time with you is time I don't want to spend thinking about my problems."

"What should I do then?"

"Just...sit here with me. It's enough."

Samantha felt her voice catch in her throat as her mind twirled the possibilities. What should she say now? That denial is unhealthy? That talking is soothing? That bottling it up won't get rid of it? She resigned herself to silence and wrapped her arms around him. They sat on the floor leaning against the lockers, until a wide shadow loomed over them.

"Miss Symanski, Mr. Stauber." Barb's voice dripped with disdain. "While I'm delighted you're in the building during lunch hour, I'm appalled you're choosing to engage in such behavior under this roof. Especially considering the situation we're all dealing with. Break it up. Miss Symanski, you're needed in the office." Samantha pried herself from Matt. Barb turned heel and walked away, her short strides carrying her around the corner and out of sight.

"It's amazing we're not suspended." Samantha shook her head.

"If I wasn't on the team I would've been a long time ago." Matt stood up, helping Samantha to her feet. As she straightened her blouse, he roughly placed his warm hands on both sides of her face, tilted her head back, and pressed his lips to hers.

She felt electric as their skin grazed, the feel of his warm breath

216

on her face like a desert wind. She closed her eyes, melting into him, almost too late as he began to pull away.

"Thank you." His lips barely touched hers as he spoke.

"For what?"

He released her face, a heavy look in his eyes. The cold, dry winter air that filled the void of his hands left her with goose bumps as he walked away. The bell rang and Samantha made her way to the front office.

She walked in as Natalie was walking out.

"What did they ask you about?"

"About the search party," Natalie whispered.

"Why would they ask about that?"

"I don't know. They asked how many people were there, if anyone unexpected showed up or didn't show up, stuff like that."

"Samantha Symanski!" Samantha looked into the office where an officer was waving her over. She smiled weakly at Natalie as the officer escorted her through a back door in the main office that connected to Barb's office. A large bald man with a thick mustache squeezed behind the principal's desk, looking as uncomfortable as Samantha felt. He gestured for her to take a seat.

"Hello, Samantha," he said gruffly, his Wisconsin accent particularly thick. "I'm Officer Richmond, with the Marshfield Police Department. Are you aware of the reason we're here today?"

"Nikki Becker is missing," Samantha stated.

"Yes she is," Officer Richmond nodded. "What we're trying to do is find out what Nikki was doing before her disappearance. Who she was with, if anything unusual may have happened. We're especially interested in the observations of those that Nikki knew best—friends, family, fellow teammates. Does that make sense to you?"

"Yes, it does," Samantha nodded.

"Okay then, Samantha. It is my understanding that you and Nikki were both on the cheerleading squad for the Spencer-Columbus Rockets, as well as the Columbus dance team."

"We were, but I never really spoke to her. I'm new this year—I hang out with the other sophomore girls and she's a senior."

"Any particular reason you didn't want to speak to Nikki?"

"Not to be rude or anything. At my old school, it was weird for grade levels to associate with each other; you know, mix. The cliques were mostly with other kids in your grade. I'm still used to that, so everyone here thinks I'm stuck up or something."

"I've heard from other students that you're dating a junior boy." Officer Richmond's mustache twitched. "Matt Stauber."

"Yes I am." Samantha felt her face reddening. "He was the first boy to ask me out, and he's really cute, so I decided 'why not?'"

"Your mother approves?"

"I don't think so. She's says it won't work out a lot, but I know she's wrong."

"And how are things with Matt?"

"They're...they're good, I guess."

"You guess?"

"Well, it's a lot more complicated than I thought it would be," Samantha said. "He doesn't like calling, I don't like texting. He likes to talk about problems right away; I don't really like that at all. He likes country music, and I can't stand it. Things like that, you know?"

"You learn a lot in your first relationship." Officer Richmond nodded.

"I guess." Samantha twirled a lock of hair.

"I heard that Matt had an unusual episode during the basketball game on Friday night. Care to share your thoughts?"

"It happened when I was changing for the halftime show. I didn't see anything."

"Do you know what happened?"

"Not firsthand, but I heard people say he bolted from the gym during a free-throw shot—or was it a three-pointer?" Her eyebrows came together as she wracked her brain. "I don't know basketball very well. Come to think of it I don't know sports very well at all."

"It was a free-throw shot," Officer Richmond corrected her. "Have you spoken to him about it?"

"I have," Samantha said. "He said he didn't want to take his medication that night so he'd play better. He said it knocks him out."

"You helped in the search party on Friday night?"

"Yeah, the girls kept calling me."

"Did Matt join in the search party?"

"Maybe. I think he went home."

"But you don't know for sure?"

"No."

"What is his medication for?"

"I don't know. I think it has something to do with the animal attack."

"Animal attack?"

"On Homecoming Night."

"Ah. I heard about that. Highly unusual for a high school boy to try and take on a bear...Did he try to assault you that night?"

"What? No! He saved me, but he got badly wounded. I had to drive us to the hospital."

"Are you licensed?"

"No, but we talked to the police and the insurance companies about all that a long time ago." Samantha's brow furrowed.

"We'll double-check." Officer Richmond jotted down some notes. "Can you describe Matt's condition on Friday night? How was he before he ran out of the gym?"

"He...he was pouring sweat. A lot of it. It was really noticeable. I've never seen him sweat like that. He said he overheats easily."

"Possibly a medical side effect of whatever he should or shouldn't be taking?" Officer Richmond raised a bushy gray eyebrow.

"I'm fifteen, like I'd know." Samantha crossed her arms.

"Are you sure it was medication that Matt was taking? Not illegal substances?"

"No. I mean yes. At least I don't think any of it's illegal."

"He never mentioned it to you? Offered you some?"

"Never. I don't even know what his medication is called...Did he really take drugs?" Samantha clasped her hands in her lap as doubt crept up the back of her neck.

"If Matt Stauber were on illegal substances, where would he get them?"

"I…um…"

"Samantha, where would he get them?"

"Tim Kerner and Levi Mauer, *please report to the front office.*" Tim and Levi looked at each other across the table in the school library as the words made their way out of the PA system. "Oh shit, Levi." Tim whispered as they slowly stood in unison. "Oh shit, what if someone told them I'm a drug dealer?"

"I think you're underestimating the student body's ability to handle the police." Levi felt a smile tug at the corner of his lips.

"You think so?"

"Yep. There's enough people here who want what you've got and don't care if they have to lie to keep getting it." Levi slung his backpack over his shoulder. They walked down the hall to the front office in an unsettling silence. Levi felt his stomach drop as Samantha emerged, her face white. Their eyes met, then she averted his gaze and walked past him.

"Levi Mauer," the officer said, "you first." The officer gestured Tim to a seat and then led Levi through a door and into Barb's office. The officer sitting at the desk watched him from beneath bushy gray eyebrows. "Have a seat."

Levi sat in the warm chair as the officer's eyebrows shifted around on his forehead.

"You're Levi Mauer," the officer began.

"I am, and you are?" Levi stared down the officer.

"I'm Officer Richmond with the Marshfield Police—"

"I've seen you around town."

"Most likely. I think I've seen you too." Richmond's mustache twitched. "Driving."

Levi felt his heart pound but narrowed his eyes. "I can't drive."

"Not legally, according to the information I have on you,"

Richmond corrected. "How did you get to school this morning?"

"I don't see why that's your concern. I can't drive, so you must have seen me walking down the street."

Richmond gave him a long, penetrating stare, as if he were trying to bore holes in Levi's head. "Let's get to why you're here."

"Nikki Becker—"

"Is missing, yes. From what I've learned you're about as far removed from her social circle as it gets in a school this small."

"Exactly. So what do you want from me? Aren't most kidnappers close to their victims?"

"You're sharp," Richmond said, almost sulking. "You're not part of what the other kids would call 'the scene.' You don't attend the sporting events, you don't hang out with anyone, you barely speak in class. But you were at the game on Friday night. What was happening that night that brought you out?"

"Tim wanted me to go with him," Levi said. "We're friends, so I went."

"Tim's a good friend of yours?"

"He is."

"One might say you're dependent on him."

"As friends are."

"As a user might be on a dealer?"

"What are you implying?" Levi leaned forward, unblinking.

"I'm looking for relevant information."

"My friendship with Tim has nothing to do with Nikki Becker, Officer Richmond. Tim and I don't hang out with Nikki and her friends."

"I'll keep that in mind. What is Tim's relationship to Matt Stauber?"

"I'm not aware of a relationship between Tim and Matt Stauber. I thought Matt was dating Samantha Symanski." Levi fought to keep the smirk off his face. Officer Richmond was not amused.

"Is Tim a drug dealer?"

"No," Levi lied.

"Are you a drug dealer?"

"No."

"Are you aware of any drug dealings in the school?"

"I'm sure it's happening here, but it's none of my business. I like to stay out of all the drama and the bullshit."

"That's not a very Catholic choice of words." Officer Richmond scribbled down some notes.

"Judge not lest ye be judged." Levi leaned into his chair. "Are we back on track yet?"

"I don't appreciate your attitude, punk." Richmond slapped the desk. Levi jumped. "A girl is missing. And you're not helping her."

"I'm not involved in anything here, Officer Richmond. I'm not trying to be a pain in the ass, but I'm not part of the problem either." Richmond's mustache twitched violently as an eyebrow raised. "And you're not going to make me feel like I am. Do you have any other questions for me?"

"Where were you after the game on Friday night?"

"I was hanging out with Tim."

Officer Richmond stared at Levi again, then waved his hand in the air. "You can go now." Levi stood up and went through the door into the front office. Tim was pale as a ghost.

"I'm next," he trembled.

"You'll be fine," Levi said in the calmest tone he could muster. Tim walked in, shaking.

Levi sat in one of the chairs, deciding it best to wait. A policeman gave him a disapproving look. "He's my project partner. I can't work on it without him." The officer shook his head and looked away.

The office was uneasy with the whispers of the secretaries and officers mumbling to each other. Levi was hard-pressed to hear what was going on. He stood up and left the front office, looping around past the water fountain to the hallway entrance of the principal's office. The empty hallway was much quieter. He leaned on the brick wall next to the door, where he could make out the voices.

"—not a drug dealer!"

"Do you see what I have above my mustache?"

"A huge honker," Tim said.

"That's right. Let's not kid ourselves. What do you think you smell like?"

"Frankincense, myrrh, and the other stuff I buy from Avalon on Fourth."

"What's a Catholic boy doing at a magic shop?"

"They sell all types of weird stuff. I like to go in there."

"Often?"

"Sure, ya."

"You realize they sell bongs."

"And incense, don't forget the incense."

"So if I contact the owners, they would know you?"

"A lot of people remember me because of my hair. You'd have to take a picture along, but they would totally remember me. I could autograph it—"

"Don't be smart."

"That's not what the school is telling me."

"Listen to me, Timothy Kerner. Stay on subject or I'll be forced to think you're concealing evidence, and aiding and abetting a kidnapping."

"I'm trying to stay on subject, but you're not asking anything that makes sense!"

"You're aware Nikki disappeared from her car going home after the game that night."

"Ya, I got some texts."

"I've heard reports that at Friday night's game, a lot of people found it strange that Matt Stauber ran out of the gym during a free-throw shot."

"That was the highlight of my evening, man."

"Can you describe Matt's physical state around that time?"

"Sweat. Lots of it. Agitated."

"Abnormally so?"

"Sure."

"What do you suppose happened to Matt Stauber at the

basketball game?"

"Well, nobody else believes me, but I have a theory." There was silence.

"And? What is this theory?"

"You...you want to hear it? Wow. Someone usually cuts me off."

"Kerner, what is this theory?"

"You're not going to believe this—like I said, nobody ever does—but I know for a fact that Matt Stauber is a werewolf."

"A *werewolf.*"

"You heard me, officer."

"What would cause you to jump to this conclusion?"

"He was attacked by a howling creature on Homecoming Night—it was a full moon. Then on October's full moon, he wasn't in school, and some cows got ripped apart. This past full moon was Friday night. He was starting to transform and he had to leave! That's three weird full moons in a row."

"Do you take me for a fool?"

"No, seriously, man! The Clinic has him on all these meds that he has to take—and supposedly he didn't take them Friday so he could play. Stauber's been telling people how the pills knock him out and he wouldn't be able...balls! The Clinic must know! That's why they want to keep him doped up during full moons...oh ya, that makes sense! I am so *on* right now!"

"You're making a mockery of this. This isn't some sort of game Kerner. A girl is missing. You're wasting my time. Get the hell out of my office."

"This is Barb's office."

"GET OUT!"

Levi ran back around the corner to the main office and entered just as the door to interrogation central flew open and Tim emerged, his face flushed. "Can you believe that nut job? He didn't believe me—wouldn't even consider the possibility!"

"Unimaginable."

"You know, I'd at least look for a werewolf, just to rule it out."

"I'm sure you would," Levi said wearily.

"Seriously man. What if she was eaten?"

"ARE YOU SERIOUS RIGHT NOW?"

"Why not?" Tim scowled at Jennifer as she chewed her gum and played with her phone.

"Because introducing my police chief dad to my dealer is suicidal." She glared up at him for a moment. "What do I look like, a moron?"

"You did when you tried to go blonde in middle school," Natalie chimed. "You looked like a yellow crayon." Jennifer pinched her arm. "Ow! Why do you always do that?!"

"Come on Jennifer, I really need you to find out for me." Tim knelt down on one knee. "It's extremely important!"

Jennifer's eyes darted to the front office, where the police continued to mill around. She lowered her voice. "What makes you think I have any way of accessing information on people using only their license plate numbers?"

"Your dad's the police chief. You know all the police officers. Police officers look that stuff up all the time." Tim waved his hand. "When they pull you over, that's what they do, right? Access some sort of database with all your information in it?"

"I'm not the fucking NSA, Tim."

"No, but you're my client. A client who gets regular discounts. This information trumps our professional relationship, and if I have to jeopardize it then so—"

"Are you telling me you're going to mark up my goods if I don't do this for you?"

"Hey, you owe me and you know it."

"Tim, you're a fucking skeaze." Jennifer turned her attention to her phone. "I'll see what I can do."

"Thank you, babycakes." Tim strode to where Levi leaned against the white walls of the lobby, grinning proudly.

"That was impressive," Levi commented. "I didn't think you'd be able to stand your ground and get it done."

"Levi Mauer, I'm offended this little task impressed you. You act like I'm totally immature—all the time. Knock it off."

Levi smirked as they walked down the hall to the parking lot. "So tell me, how is this gonna roll? You think she'll be suspicious of why we want the information?"

"Jennifer's smart enough to not get involved in anything messy any more than she absolutely has to, believe me." Tim put his hands in his pockets. "She's been stringing me along for years."

"You learn something new every day," Levi mocked.

"Shut up. Let's get to the library." Tim's eyes locked on Matt Stauber, glaring at him from the corner.

"He has a problem with you," Levi narrowed his eyes at Stauber.

"Let's just go." Tim started walking. Levi shrugged and followed him.

THE CRACK IN HER CEILING was barely visible in the gloom. Samantha traced its path as she lay in bed, waiting for sleep to come. She couldn't stop mulling over the conversations of the day in her head. Matt's despondent and brooding mood, his words replaying over and over.

"He said it was an accident," Samantha whispered to the silence. "What if I'm dating a murderer?" She felt her stomach tie in knots as she thought about all the time they spent together, all the times he got her alone and could have killed her.

The wood floor creaking in the hall startled her out of her own terrifying thoughts. She stared at her door, eyes wide in the darkness. The door was shut, no light coming underneath it from the hall, the house silent. She allowed herself a breath before the floor in the hall creaked again, louder. Then came another creak, louder than the one before. She pulled the covers up to her eyes as a louder creak came. And another. It was coming closer.

Her blood ran cold as the creaking stopped in front of her door, her knuckles white as they gripped her covers. The doorknob began to rotate slowly, the old metal grazing and clacking on itself. She rolled over, pulled the pillow over her head and hid under the covers, pressing the front of her body as flat to the mattress as she could get it, hoping her bed would look empty and unmade.

The door slowly swung into the room; her heart pounded in her chest. She wanted to scream but her voice wasn't working. The creaking in her room moved closer to her bed one step at a time. She couldn't move. She couldn't bring herself to breathe.

"Samantha." It was the soft, tired voice of a little boy.

"Brandon." She felt a wave of relief, threw off the pillow and sat up. He wasn't there. She was in an empty room, the door open, gaping into the hallway. She looked around, searching for a hint of movement or life anywhere. The hair on her arms stood on end. Samantha lay back down, burying herself in the covers again, wishing whatever invisible thing she felt staring at her would leave and let her sleep.

"THEY STILL HAVEN'T FOUND HER, have they." Samantha sighed despondently after the announcements finished.

"I don't think so," Levi replied. They watched the police pulling up, the snow swirling. The psychology documentary they were supposed to be watching was blaring and Mrs. Hansen flipped the light switch, plunging the room into shadows.

"Matt's not speaking to me again," she whispered.

"So?" Levi raised an eyebrow at her.

"I know you don't think it's a big deal, but he's been so angry since the police interviewed everyone—"

"The police are paying a lot of attention to him. It would suck to be him right now."

"Levi, I don't know what to do."

"I don't think there's anything you can do," Levi murmured, suddenly feeling awkward. "You could just stand by him."

"But what if he did something wrong? Then I'm like all those politicians' wives. You know, the ones who should leave but don't, because they're too power-hungry—"

"Why are you telling me all this? I thought your opinion of me was less than positive."

"I don't want to be one of those people. And I don't want Matt to be a murderer."

"Nobody wants to find out someone they care about is evil." Arthur Harris's body flashed in Levi's mind, and he suddenly felt sick to his stomach. They sat in silence for the rest of the period. When the bell rang, Levi got out of there as fast as he could, and bumped into Tim by his locker.

"The cops are back," Tim exclaimed. "They pulled some juniors and seniors into the front office for questioning."

"That must mean they know *we* didn't do anything," Levi sighed in relief, then felt a pang of guilt for feeling relieved. "Have you talked to Jennifer about the—"

"Let's go find out."

"I HAVEN'T YET." Jennifer dropped her voice as a police officer walked past them in the lobby. "Let's talk in the middle school hallway." They made the short trip, stopping by the doors to the cafeteria. "I can't get into their system, Tim. I thought I could figure out my dad's password, but...I don't know what to tell you."

"It's alright—" Tim began, but Levi cut him off.

"We know you can do this. It makes no sense why you wouldn't help, when Tim's been more than generous in his dealings with you. You owe him."

"Now Stoner is speaking for Dealer?" Jennifer popped her gum, narrowing her eyes. "I don't owe you anything, Levi Mauer."

"You do," Tim came in on the defense. "Levi's with me. If you owe me, you owe him."

"So now you two are together?" she mocked.

"Just do as you're told," Levi replied, keeping his tone casual. "You have twenty-four hours or you're cut off." He grabbed the back of Tim's arm and led him to the high school hallway while Jennifer visibly simmered with rage.

SAMANTHA'S PHONE VIBRATED in her bag. She pulled it out, careful not to attract anyone's attention. Her biology class mulled away on worksheets while the teacher excused herself. She opened the text message from Jennifer. *'Bathroom now, bitch.'*

Samantha grabbed her bag and left the room. Some of the freshmen eyed her suspiciously. She slipped inside the girls' restroom where Jennifer, Natalie, Laderia, and Becca were having a meeting.

"Finally!" Jennifer tossed her hair. "Girls, I got a problem."

"What now?" Becca asked.

"You're all aware that I have an affinity for the dangerous."

"What else is new?" Natalie played with her striped hair in the mirror.

"I need some help procuring classified information."

"Those are surprisingly big words." Samantha said in genuine surprise, a bubble of humor in her chest.

"That's rich coming from a girl whose accent makes her sound retarded," Jennifer snapped.

"OMG, we don't use the R Word!" Natalie exclaimed.

"Fine, she sounds mentally handicapped!"

"Excuse me? Have you even listened to the Wisconsin accent? Y'all sound like Canadian hicks!" Samantha glowered.

"Now that's going too far," Becca warned. "Jennifer, what is this 'classified information' you need so desperately?"

"I need to find out who the owners are of the cars with these license plates." Jennifer pulled a piece of paper out of her pocket.

Laderia squinted at the paper. "Stalking someone?"

"I'm playing private investigator for Tim." Jennifer popped her gum.

"What you two do together is your business," Natalie said in horror. "I don't need to get involved with that."

"You told your parents we were lesbian girlfriends," Jennifer cut in. "Wipe that look of surprise off your face, Natalie. Your mom likes to rant. And I would never do anything as low as lying about sexuality. This is something else. Tim is looking for the owners of these vehicles."

"You're still aiding a drug lord." Natalie crossed her arms.

"Tim is hardly a drug lord, he has a boss," Becca corrected. "Why does he need this information?"

"I don't know. He said it was urgent. He's cutting me off if I don't come up with it in twenty-four hours."

"Oh grief, then you'll be even bitchier than usual," Becca moaned.

"Right. So help me find this information, or I'll be out of drugs."

The door swung open. The girls froze as a blonde policewoman walked in, her bland expression morphing into one of curiosity. The girls clustered behind Jennifer. The policewoman frowned.

"Jennifer, hello."

"Officer Horace." Jennifer stared her down. "What's up?"

"Shouldn't you girls be in class?"

"We had to pee," Jennifer replied curtly.

"It takes five of you to pee?"

"Girls always go together," Natalie said. "It's an unwritten rule."

"You're wasting valuable class time chatting away in here."

"Shouldn't you be off riding my dad like a pony?" Jennifer shot back. Officer Horace tensed.

"That's completely uncalled-for," she replied, her tone darkening. "Your father will not be happy to hear what you just said to me."

"Tell him. Like I care. I'm sure my mom would love to know what's going on. What do you want?"

"I came in to use the facilities. I'd like some privacy. If you could all leave—"

"What a sense of entitlement you have! This is a public restroom."

"This is a private school. And I'm in here to take care of some private business."

"If that's how it is, then same here. And we were here first. Get out."

"I will tell the principal, Jennifer Cromwell—"

"Don't you dare talk to me with that holier-than-thou attitude, Officer Ass-whore—oops, I mean Horace. We're almost done in here. A couple minutes of waiting isn't too much to ask of Marshfield's finest, is it?"

Officer Horace left, her rage trailing her like a comet tail.

"OMG Jennifer," Natalie whispered. "You just told off a cop."

"She deserves it. Slut."

"Hey, I think I've got a solution for you." Becca obviously wanted to change the topic. "My older brother works at the grocery store service desk. They do license plate sticker renewals, which means they have access to the DMV system. I bet he could look those up for you!"

"Becca, you're a genius," Jennifer tossed her hair.

"I know." Becca glanced at the door. "Now let's leave. It's suddenly incredibly awkward in here."

"WHAT IF SHE CAN'T get it, Levi?" Tim drummed his fingers on the table. "I'll lose a good customer with great connections."

"And your crush," Levi added. "Don't you have faith in her?"

"Yes, but to be honest, I'm kinda worried about putting her in that position."

"Why? She's tough. You said so yourself."

"She's going through some stuff. The last thing she needs is more insecurity in her life."

"If you think her having to find another dealer is too much, then you underestimate her connections. Jennifer's a girl. Girls love to talk, network and connect. Girls also have the most Facebook friends."

"You're not even on Facebook. How would you know?" Tim grumbled. "And all *that* means is she could *easily* replace me."

"She already has you in her clutches. Even if you're replaceable she would have to start over with another dealer. Her hard work schmoozing you would be wasted. I bet you a pizza she gets us exactly what we need." Levi slapped Tim's head. "I'll up your odds. I bet she has it before seven tonight."

Tim glanced at the clock hanging on the wall behind Levi. He cracked his knuckles nervously. "I'll take that bet. If I lose, it will be a celebration dinner."

"SAMANTHA, ARE YOU ALRIGHT? You look so pale."

"That's because the sun doesn't shine here, mom." Samantha pulled the blanket snug around her, grateful for the nap on the couch in the living room. "It's not like we're close to the beach anymore."

"Don't be like that."

"Sorry." Samantha forced her eyes open. "You got the tree up really fast. We're usually late on that."

"It took two hours. You've been sleeping the whole time." Mrs. Symanski adjusted a strand of lights on a branch. "When I was a little girl, we'd have it up on Thanksgiving and keep it up until New Year's. You get to enjoy it for a longer period of time. I thought we'd put it up earlier this year. Sound good?"

"It's better than putting it up the night before Christmas, I guess." Samantha watched as her mother plugged in the lights. The tree lit up brilliantly, and Mrs. Symanski fluffed out a few of the plastic branches.

"Are we ever going to get a real tree?"

"Sure. Whenever you find someone willing to clean up the needles as they fall to the floor and water the thing every day." Mrs. Symanski grabbed the stepladder. "Sound fair?"

Samantha shrugged.

"So what happened at school today? Did they find the missing girl yet? It's been a week."

"No they didn't. We're having another candlelight prayer vigil tonight at Mr. Becker's house."

"Did Jennifer mention any case details to you?"

"No. The police came back again, though. They had some boys in the front office."

"Did they interview Matt again?" Mrs. Symanski's demeanor darkened.

"I'm really scared for him, mom. The police are focusing on him a lot."

"He acted very strangely during the game, right?"

"You'd act strange too if you didn't take your medication."

"Skipping meds to play a basketball game. Sounds like the boy needs to get his priorities straight."

"He loves basketball."

"More than his health. That doesn't worry you?"

"I'm worrying about him a lot lately, mom."

"I bought all these new decorations. What do you think?" She grabbed a large cardboard box filled with ornament containers. "You need to have three main colors to work with when decorating a tree. I want this tree to be purple, white, and gold, like French royalty."

"Lovely," Samantha said monotonously.

"How's that boy Levi doing?"

"I don't know, and I don't care." The lights in the tree flickered. Mrs. Symanski paused and scrutinized the tree.

"That happens too much here. We must have really faulty wiring," Samantha shifted on the sofa.

"Are you suddenly an electrician?"

"Faulty wiring is better than the alternative."

"What alternative?" Mrs. Symanski unplugged the tree from the wall, stood back for a moment, and then plugged it back in.

"It's nothing."

"No Samantha, tell me."

"You'll think I'm stupid."

"Honey, just spill it. I guarantee you it'll help."

"Have you…um…ever felt like there was someone else in the room with you?"

"What do you mean?"

"Sometimes when I'm alone in my room, I feel like there's someone watching me."

"You're perfectly safe."

"I don't feel safe."

"What makes you say that? Did something happen?"

"It'll get really quiet, and suddenly I get this feeling like there's ice shooting up my spine. My heart races and I look around, because I know, I just know someone is watching me—staring at me. But there's no one there. The other night I heard a boy calling my name. I thought it was Brandon, but when I looked, no one was in my room."

"Samantha Rose Symanski, are you doing drugs?" Her mother didn't sound incredulous or stunned. It was more like the police interrogation.

"Of course not! It's just that…well, sometimes I think our house is haunted."

Mrs. Symanski's face fell and she left the room. Samantha rolled her eyes and pulled out her phone to check her messages as the Christmas tree flickered in the corner.

"SEVEN IS ROLLING AROUND." Tim shoved his phone back in his pocket. "You're gonna have to pony up for that pizza."

"We got an hour," Levi replied coolly. "Relax."

Tim's phone rang. "Hey," he answered quickly. There was a pause. "Don't say it on the phone. Meet us at Pizza Hut in thirty minutes." Tim shook his head. "What do you want on your pizza, Levi?"

"She got it." Levi smirked victoriously.

"Yes she did." Tim dialed. "I want hand-tossed, stuffed crust, everything on it. And what do you want, Levi?"

"Pepperoni and sausage. Why meet in person? Can't she just tell you their names on the phone?"

Tim regarded Levi disbelievingly and covered the phone with his hand. "Sometimes you're not paranoid enough." He put the phone back to his mouth. "Breadsticks please. The marinara dipping sauce…and the garlic."

"You worried the police are tapping your phone?"

"I never do business over the phone. Not with the NSA recording every phone call and text. I don't want to wind up on some list."

"WHEN DOES THE VIGIL START?" Samantha asked as she climbed into Becca's backseat with Matt and Jennifer. Natalie sat in the front, nervously playing with her hair.

"It started already." Jennifer popped a fresh piece of gum in her mouth. "We gotta stop at Pizza Hut first. I'm making a delivery." She glanced at Matt, who sat lost in thought between the two girls.

"Are you alright?" Samantha laid a hand on Matt's knee. His eyes darted to her hand, and then to her face, warning radiating from him. She took her hand from him. "Matt?"

"Stop asking me that question," he said, his jaw clenching.

"Okay," Samantha snapped. "I can't handle this side of you right now."

"What side?"

"This enraged and dark, brooding side, like you're tormented for doing something wrong even though you're not. Knock it off." Samantha tossed her hair and glared out the window.

"You two can keep your lovers' fit private, or you can walk." Becca pointed a finger from the driver's seat. "None of that in my vehicle."

"Where's Laderia?" Samantha asked.

"She's with Dylan and Stefan." Jennifer popped her gum. "They're going to meet us in the parking lot and then we'll head to Mr. Becker's house."

"I really hope they find her soon," Becca murmured from the front. "Wouldn't it be weird to have another death?"

"*Another* one? Does this happen a lot here?" Samantha asked.

"Every class has its tragedy. A huge horrible event that defines the grade forever." Becca flicked on a blinker. "Our class tragedy happened in the eighth grade. Remember, Matt?"

"Huh? Ya," he said.

"What happened?" Samantha blinked.

"A boy in our class got run over." Becca looked at Samantha in the rearview mirror.

"At least it's happened already. No more tragedies for your class." They all gave Natalie a strange look. "This is such a weird thing to be talking about."

"We thought the senior class would be the first to escape the curse," Jennifer popped her gum. "Every year since Columbus opened, each class has experienced something tragic and weird. At least until the senior class. But Nikki Becker's disappearance ended their lucky streak."

"You say that like she'll never be found." Natalie's eyes were wide and glassy in the passing streetlights.

"They'll find her dead, in pieces." Jennifer examined her nails. "If they find her at all. Mark my words, bitch."

"What is *our* class tragedy?" Samantha looked between Natalie and Jennifer.

"It hasn't happened yet." Natalie locked eyes with Jennifer. "Right?"

"Right." Jennifer blew a bubble. "Two and half years left to find out what it will be."

"We're here," Becca announced, pulling into the parking lot.

"CARRY-OUT MAKES GRAVE WATCHING so much more enjoyable." Tim did a little dance in the parking lot, stumbling on a patch of ice.

"If you crack your head open, I'll bury you with Arthur Harris." Levi scanned the passing cars on Central Avenue. "That's her. And her entourage."

"Great, Becca's car—and Moede's SUV—let's get this disaster over with." Tim sighed as the vehicles' headlights swung into the parking lot and cruised for empty spaces. Becca's car parked and Jennifer climbed out first, Samantha getting out on the opposite side.

"I'll pick up the pizza. You get the information from Jennifer," Levi murmured to Tim as he locked eyes with Samantha. "Give me the money."

"Okay man." Tim slipped the cash into his hand.

Levi walked into Pizza Hut as Tim headed over to the group. He pushed through the red doors to the register, where a waitress asked him about his order while drumming her nails on the counter.

"Two large pizzas, one with everything on it, the other pepperoni and sausage," Levi replied. "And breadsticks and shit."

"We don't serve shit here, kid," the waitress corrected blandly as she grabbed a stack of boxes. "Here you go." She rang him up, and Levi paid with Tim's cash. "Out of forty?"

Another waitress ran to the counter. "Allie, something's wrong." She gestured to the windows. A shuffling sound and muffled voices filtered through the glass from outside, louder than the noise of the diners. Several stopped and glanced out at the parking lot.

Levi turned around. Then he heard it. The sound of a girl shouting outside mingled with the unmistakable sound of flesh colliding with flesh.

"Someone's fighting in the parking lot! I'm getting the manager!" The waitress threw the change at Levi and ran into the kitchen. Levi's body tensed and he ran through the doors, leaving the pizza boxes on the counter.

"Tim!" Samantha shouted as Matt tackled the smaller boy to the pavement. Tim threw his arms over his head and face as fists rained down on him, the sound ricocheting in the icy air.

Samantha yanked Matt's shirt and pounded on his wide back. Jennifer and Dylan were trying to intercept the football player's arms, but he was ferocious, shoving them back with his elbows.

"You think I'm a monster?! I'll show you what the fuck I am!" Matt yelled at Tim between punches.

Levi charged, tackling Matt sideways off of Tim, the momentum bringing him down on top of Matt's back. He grabbed Matt's arm with one hand and twisted it, then used his other hand to shove Matt's face into the pavement. Matt roared, twisting under Levi's body.

Levi felt his stomach tie in knots as Matt wriggled out of his control with ease. Matt broke his arm free from Levi's grip, then struck Levi in the face twice before Levi released the back of his head. Matt flipped them over and put a hand on Levi's neck. Levi reached up and seized Matt's throat. They struggled, rolling across the cold pavement, the salt grinding beneath them.

Matt's strong hands were cutting off Levi's blood flow, his vision fading. The pressure in his head was building as he squinted up into

Matt's enraged, predatory eyes. Samantha yelled something in the background, but he could barely hear her.

Levi let go of Matt's throat and reached for the stake in his pocket, but his fingers started going numb before he could find it. Matt's mouth twisted into a heinous grin. Levi gave up and instead closed his numb hand into a fist and delivered an uppercut that sent Matt reeling backwards, clutching his jaw. Levi caught his breath and blinked, his sight clearing as he stumbled to stand up.

Laderia and Natalie were silent, taking in the situation. Becca and Jennifer hovered over Tim while Stefan and Dylan threw Matt up against the side of Dylan's Navigator and pinned him there, berating him.

"Levi, are you alright?" Samantha's eyes were wide as she wrapped her arms around herself and stepped toward Levi, her breath fog between them.

"Your boyfriend's a fucking monster," Levi growled, massaging his throat.

"I'm so sorry," she whispered. "I don't know what's happening, I tried to stop him—"

"You need to get away from him." Levi turned to Tim, leaving Samantha staring at the back of his head.

Becca handed Tim tissues as he sat up, trails of red pouring from his nose. He looked at Levi, completely dazed.

"Man, she got it." Tim grinned, his mouth full of blood. He handed Levi a piece of paper.

"I know." Levi crouched down by him.

"This better be worth it." Tim touched two fingers to his swollen lips. "Ow."

"Are you still in the mood for pizza?"

"You know I am."

"Not to interrupt this bro-mantic moment, but I wanna make sure you both are alright before we ditch. I don't wanna have to deal with my father about any of this," Jennifer raised her hands in the air. "Or either of your parents. We have to get to the prayer vigil for Nikki. We're cool, right?"

"Jennifer, how can you be like that?" Becca shouted. "Matt almost killed them!"

Samantha flew across the parking lot to Matt. Levi turned and watched as she slapped him across the face while Stefan and Dylan held him. "What is wrong with you?!"

"I didn't mean to—"

"You're losing it, man." Dylan slammed Matt against the Navigator again.

"You're not the Terminator," Stefan said in his thick accent.

"I'm not losing it, that fucking idiot is losing it!" Matt pointed at Tim. "The cops think it was me! They searched my house, they interviewed my family, they think I'm a werewolf! And it's *his* fault!"

"You're mental!" Samantha shrieked. "They wouldn't believe that! You got the cops' attention all by yourself!"

"*You* told me he did it!" Matt roared back. "This is *your* fault!"

"You obviously could have killed her." Samantha's hands were balled up into fists, shaking. "It would be in bad taste if you went to the prayer vigil."

"Bad taste? What the fuck does that mean? Why are you being this way?!" Matt tried to charge out of Dylan and Stefan's hold. They pushed him back into the side of the SUV with more than a little difficulty.

"For serio," Laderia spoke up. "Matt Stauber, you're having a Norwood-level breakdown. Dylan, let's take him home—now! For reallio."

"We'll talk about this later, Samantha," Matt warned. Samantha was silent, then turned to face Levi, Tim, Becca, and Jennifer. "Call me."

"Maybe I'll call you," Samantha said without facing Matt. "Maybe we'll talk about it."

"Samantha, I love you."

Levi felt his heart lurch at Matt's words, unable to tear his stinging eyes from Samantha's face. She blinked rapidly. "Go home."

"Alright," Matt nodded. "Anything." Dylan and Stefan

exchanged a glance, opened the back door to the Navigator, and ushered Matt inside.

Laderia trotted over to Samantha. "We're going to need a serio girl talk-o."

"I could go for tacos," Tim said. "Taco Bell's across the street."

"We just got pizza," Levi reminded him. "I'll get it off the counter."

"I'll help the nimrods take Matt to his casa. You guys enjoy your pizza." Laderia pulled her purse higher on her shoulder. "But I'm taking this opportunity to remind you I give you all food. Maybe someday soon you can return the favor. Dealio?"

"Dealio." Samantha's voice was quiet, her eyes not leaving Tim's bloody face.

Laderia waved as she walked back to the SUV. "Later bitches." She got in and they were gone, leaving Natalie, Becca, Jennifer, Samantha, Tim, and Levi in the parking lot.

"Is his nose broken?" Natalie knelt next to Tim.

"I don't think so." Becca searched Tim's face. "Lean forward, Tim."

"You're supposed to lean back with a nosebleed." Natalie shook her head.

Becca rolled her eyes. "Don't listen to her, Tim. The blood will run down your throat and pool in your lungs if you lean back."

"It's better than what is usually in my lungs." Tim laughed a little, the blood suddenly running faster. He leaned forward and drops of red spattered the parking lot.

"You guys have a ride home?" Samantha asked.

"We're getting picked up," Levi nodded. "You can head to the prayer vigil. I got him." The girls stood, looking at each other uneasily. Jennifer rolled her eyes and marched over to Becca's car, Natalie and Becca trailed behind her. Samantha lingered for a moment.

"You should go," Levi said.

"I'm not trying to be a bitch, Levi," Samantha's voice was shaking. "This shouldn't have happened. I didn't know we were coming here, I didn't put Matt up to this."

"I know."

"So why are you looking at me like that?" she challenged. "Like I did something wrong?"

"It's not about what you've done." Levi rubbed a hand on his throat. "It's about what you're doing."

"What am I doing?"

"Putting up with him," Levi replied.

"I'm not—"

"If you're as smart as you think you are, you'll leave him. You think his rage will only be directed at guys?" He watched with a sick sort of satisfaction as sparks of doubt lit in her eyes.

"He wasn't like this before." Samantha's face grew sadder. "Something's happening to him. He's changed."

"Are you sure he's changed? Or is he just showing you who he truly is?"

Samantha gave him an incredulous glare and retreated to Becca's car. The girls sped out of the parking lot. Levi helped Tim stand.

"He knocked the wind out of me," Tim gasped. "I need to be horizontal for a while."

"I'll get you in the truck," Levi said. "We'll skip the cemetery tonight."

"Are you sure you can?"

"We haven't had a vampire since the snow started. I'm starting to think they realize how stupid it is to dig out of a grave on a pristine, snowy night. It's too hard to hide the prints." Levi helped Tim into the truck and shut the door, then headed back into Pizza Hut.

"What happened out there? Friends of yours?" the waitress asked, her eyes round. "Your pizzas are still here. My manager will be back in five minutes. Can you stay and talk to him?"

"He'd have been here already if he really wanted to know what happened." Levi took the boxes and plopped the change back on the counter. "Thanks though." He turned to walk out the front door, only to be confronted by a short, thin, middle-aged woman in an oversized sunhat.

"Speak what we feel, not what we ought to say," she said in a girlish voice, peering at him from behind huge sunglasses.

"Excuse me." Levi tried to walk around her, but she hobbled in his way, causing him to nearly drop the pizzas.

"Fortune love you," she said.

"I wish it did." Levi rolled his eyes. "I gotta head home. Excuse me." He tried walking around her other side, but she blocked him with her walking stick. "Can I get through please?"

"Machinations, hollowness, treachery, and all ruinous disorders follow us disquietly to our graves." Her voice was low as Levi passed her. "Fare thee well, King."

Chapter 8

Changing Times

"This is the beginning of the apocalypse." Natalie sat stunned at the lunch table. "They cancelled winter formal."

"Nobody cares about that dance," Becca said without so much as a hint of concern.

"I care about that dance! Why doesn't anybody else like that dance?"

"They hold it in the elementary school gym in Our Lady of Peace. Can you believe it? The *elementary* school."

"Don't be such bimbos. They cancelled it because Nikki is still missing." Jennifer grabbed a hamburger from the enormous Hardee's bag Laderia plopped on the table. "The student council decided it's not right to have a dance without the Homecoming Queen there."

"Are they going to cancel Prom too?" Natalie's face warped with fear. "I'd just die. I'd literally die."

"Don't be ridiculous, Natalie. Hand me a burger please." Becca held out her hand. Laderia rolled her eyes and passed her one.

"You owe me for serio."

"Would you like to be repaid in burritos, Fritos, Doritos, Oreos or Cheerios?" Jennifer asked dryly before taking a bite.

"For serio, I'd like to shove that burger down your throat." Laderia tossed her dark hair. "Skinny bitch."

"Ooh, pass me mine." Natalie held out open palms. Laderia handed over two. "Give one to Samantha."

"I'm not hungry," Samantha sighed.

Natalie set the burger in front of Samantha. "You're on the manic depressive, self-punishing diet. You haven't eaten lunch for two weeks. That's not healthy."

"Neither is this." Samantha pushed the burger away as her stomach rumbled.

"I know what this is. The body is willing but the mind cannot follow." Laderia held up a hand. "I can read your auras Sammy, and my hellabitchin' senses tell me you have no energy. Protein will fix that. Eat up, girlio."

"I can't."

"Then whip out your purse and pay up the seven dollars for that burger."

Samantha frowned and pulled the burger closer. "Okay, okay. I'll eat it. Happy?"

"*Sí*, Sammy. So how's the haunted house treating you?"

"It's not haunted." Samantha shook her head and took a bite of the burger.

"Yes it is," Natalie nodded as Becca scoffed. "I know what the presence of ghosts feels like. Your house has a lot of them."

"Oh, so I guess you have hellabitchin' senses too, right?" Samantha rolled her eyes.

"No, but I would say I have the most experience. Remember Halloween? You know, just two months ago?"

"I do, and I'm choosing to believe my house is fine, regardless of what y'all say. Otherwise I'll get even less shuteye than I already do." Samantha pondered as she looked at her burger. "You know, I fell asleep in Psychology today. Mrs. Hansen slammed a textbook on my desk to wake me up. I slapped her out of reflex."

"Oh shiznit," Becca covered her mouth.

Laderia took a massive bite from her burger. "Are you getting detention again? Is that why you're sad?"

"No, I vomited apologies at her and she let me off the hook."

"That is the worst mental image to have while eating a burger." Natalie set hers down. "I need a moment."

"Now I want a Snickers," Laderia muttered.

"I'm upset about everything with Matt." Samantha lowered her voice and leaned forward. The girls leaned in to listen. "I'm starting to think he did kill Nikki." They exchanged apprehensive glances.

"I don't think she's dead," Natalie said matter-of-factly.

"It's been weeks, and she's a Homecoming Queen." Jennifer glared at Natalie. "Be realistic. She's probably in pieces somewhere near Baton Rouge."

"I am," Natalie replied. "They found those women in Ohio who were kidnapped way back when, when everyone thought they'd be dead. It happens. I think she's alive. I got a feeling about it." She picked up her burger.

"Do you have a feeling about Matt?" Samantha asked.

Natalie nodded. "I feel sorry for him."

"Why?"

"Because he's getting a lot of blame and suspicion thrown at him just because he has a medical condition."

"He's never told me what it is. Are you sure he's innocent? That he's really not—"

"I feel like he's got a real condition, and he doesn't know how to cope yet. But I also feel it doesn't have anything to do with Nikki Becker." Natalie took a small bite of her burger.

"So, it could simply be relationship problems caused by Blondie avoiding him again," Jennifer observed. "What's that all about, Sammy?"

"I'm scared of him now," Samantha said. "I'm scared to be alone with him. He beat up Tim. He would have killed him if we hadn't stopped it. Wouldn't you be scared too?"

TIM PLOPPED INTO THE CHAIR next to Levi, who was busy surfing the web. "I called Felix to find out his plans. He isn't coming up. We got the whole Christmas Vacation to ourselves. Just me, you, and the mystery of the strangers at the funeral home. Sounds like a Hardy Boys novel." The librarian walked by and gave Tim a scolding look, placing a finger over her pursed mouth.

"The swelling in your nose and lips hasn't gone away yet." Levi scanned Tim's features, carefully disguising his own concern with nonchalance.

"Really?"

"Felix should take you to the hospital."

"Yeah right. I feel pretty again," Tim grimaced, his swollen features almost comical. "Dig up anything new?"

"Not yet," Levi admitted. "I'm not finding any connection between Reinhart, Rothschild or Lancaster."

"Forget obvious connections. What do we have on them so far?"

"Dr. Reinhart is a surgeon specializing in organ transplants at the Clinic. He's been there for eleven years, has a great record, awesome patient reviews, blah, blah, blah. Avelina Rothschild was a New York socialite in the seventies and eighties. Never married, but released several clothing lines that were all failures. Moved to a Chicago penthouse in 1989, then retired in Milwaukee ten years ago because her family has some huge estate on the outskirts."

"Well, that explains the Bentley." Tim shook his head.

"Coasting on the family fortune. But what is her connection to Lancaster? Is she funding whatever evil he's concocting?"

"Maybe she's genuinely looking to find a nice place to host her funeral," Tim snickered. "She's old enough."

"That doesn't explain the surgeon," Levi glanced at him.

Tim rubbed his chin. "He must be in on it. Maybe she's a vampire."

"I don't think so."

"Google her. Does she have any pictures online?"

"Not from this century," Levi replied.

"What if they were turning her into a vampire while she was there?"

"She'd need a fresh kill right away, or it wouldn't work."

"Her chauffeur. She could have killed him."

"But that still doesn't explain the doctor." Levi tapped the table.

"Maybe he wanted to be a vampire too."

Levi shook his head. "Then why have all the briefcases?"

"Maybe she's unveiling a line of handbags! I don't know, it's your job to figure this shit out," Tim snapped. "I'm basically your cheerleader over here, ineffective, but nice to have around anyway."

"No, you're my trampoline. I bounce ideas off you. So just let me do that and stop getting irritated."

"Bounce ideas off me? Yeah, sure. I'm the one coming up with ideas, Levi. You're just rejecting them. Technically that makes you the trampoline." Levi could feel Tim's glare but ignored him as a long shadow fell across the glass doors of the library.

"Look who's here," he muttered, "running around in winter without a coat on like a moron."

"My nose is throbbing. Should I hide?" Tim asked.

"No." Levi didn't take his eyes off Matt as he walked into the library.

"Screw it, I'm hiding." Tim ducked under the computer station next to Levi's. Matt met Levi's eyes and looked away quickly. He walked to the reference desk computers and began typing. Levi watched him, unwavering. Matt pulled out a piece of paper, wrote some things down, then disappeared behind some bookshelves.

"What's happening?" Tim hissed from under the desk. Levi stood and crossed to the reference computer. He felt a chill run up his spine.

"What's he looking at?" Tim popped up next to him.

"Your area of expertise," Levi murmured. "Matt left his search results up."

"Drugs?"

"See for yourself." Levi walked back to his computer, surreptitiously scanning the library for Matt. Unsuccessful, he sat down wondering how such a tall jock could vanish so easily among some bookshelves. Tim came over and sat next to Levi.

"He's looking up werewolves," Tim said in a low voice.

"I know."

"You say that all the fucking time."

"I know."

"He's finally figuring out what's happening to him." Tim nodded with pity. "He must have realized he's transforming."

"He wasn't transforming," Levi said. "And he's not a werewolf."

"I don't know why you're denying the obvious. You're just like my brother." Tim made a face. "There he is, over there. By himself."

Levi looked over. Matt located a seat and set a stack of books on the chair next to him. He met Levi's eyes, barely nodded, and began to flip through pages.

"We should talk to him." Tim nudged Levi.

"He beat your ass in a parking lot. You'd be stupid to go over there and get involved."

"A big part of life is learning when to let go. It's been three weeks. My nose is almost back to normal and my face isn't as swollen."

"You said earlier your nose was throbbing. Take your own advice, Tim, and let go. He's not a werewolf; he's just a violent, possibly murderous nutcase who should be locked up."

"You're quick to condemn, vampire slayer. You killed a man and you're not so bad." Tim stood and walked over to Matt. Levi's mouth fell open in shock. Matt looked wary and tense as Tim took the seat on the other side of Matt's pile of books.

Levi watched Tim pick up a book, flip through it, and comment to Matt, who stared at him with a mixture of anger and horror. Matt's lips moved, and Tim nodded, muttering something back before glancing at Levi with a smirk.

Levi got up and walked over. He sat across from Matt. "What's going on?"

"Just talking about Matt's book selection." Tim held up one. *The Beast of Bray Road.* He held up another. *A History of Werewolves.* He grabbed another. *Werewolves in Lore and Legend.* I'm noticing a theme here."

"What the fuck do you guys want from me?" Matt's dark eyes

darted back and forth as he tried to stare them both down at the same time.

"You beat the shit out of me because of a rumor, Matt. I'd like an apology." Tim set the book down and narrowed his eyes.

"You first." Matt grabbed a book from his stack. Tim snatched it out of his hands.

"Why are you researching werewolves?"

"None of your business."

"You made it my business when you attacked me. You don't get to blow me off now. I'm too involved."

"Tim, give him a moment." Levi warned as Matt's nails dug into the arms of the chair.

"To do what? Comprehend what's happening to him? He already knows what it is."

"I don't know what it is," Matt grunted. "I'm just trying to rule things out. I have a feeling something's *really* wrong with me."

"You mean the more you thought about it, the werewolf rumor suddenly sounded plausible."

"What do you want?" Matt asked again, his voice strained. "You want me to tell you I'm a lycanthrope? Do you know how crazy that sounds?"

"We want to help you, man." Tim grabbed Matt's shoulder. The football player growled and the hand was promptly removed, but Tim continued with an easy voice. "In fact, I think we're the only ones in Marshfield who can even begin to help you."

"Doctors at the Clinic and St. Joe's Hospital are helping me. They're doing just fine."

"Oh really? Are you still having blackouts?" Tim met Levi's gaze and they both looked at Matt. He squirmed under their scrutiny.

"How did you know?"

"An educated guess," Tim's mouth quirked. "When do they happen?"

"Only around the end of the month," Matt said through gritted teeth. "When the—"

"Moon is full," Tim finished. "The next full moon's smack-dab between Christmas and New Year's Eve. This is going to be a very weird holiday season for you."

Levi fought the urge to punch Tim's smug, swollen face. "Do you remember what happened to you the night Nikki Becker disappeared?"

"Not much," Matt said. "I remember feeling a horrible pain, and the need to get outside. After that, there was nothing. I woke up hours later, with a hangover."

"You were drinking?" Levi frowned.

"I must have been. I felt like I had a hangover."

Tim glanced at Levi and raised his eyebrows meaningfully before turning back to Matt. "When you wake up after blacking out, do you find yourself in strange places?"

"Why am I getting the fourth degree here? I came to do some damn research!" Matt pounded the arm of his chair. A librarian shushed them from a distant desk. "I'm handling it myself. I don't need to put up with your shit, Kerner."

"You're not handling it well," Tim said. "See, I know a lot about werewolves, and that means I'm the proper person to talk to if you have any suspicions about yourself. I actually saw a werewolf once."

"Really?" Matt sounded skeptical.

"Totally man, you wanna hear my story?"

"No," Matt grabbed a book. Tim swiped it again. Matt leaned forward and grabbed Tim's collar forcefully.

"You ran out of the gym on a full moon, and have no memory of what happened," Tim said with complete calm, his nose practically touching Matt's. "Nobody knows where you went. There was a neighborhood search for Nikki Becker that night. You weren't passed out anywhere around the school or this part of town, or you'd have been found. Where did you wake up after that blackout session?"

Matt was silent, the conflicting thoughts he was having playing out on his face. "The hay loft—in my family's barn."

"Do you feel alright when you wake up? What state are you in?"

"I feel okay, I guess. It's always Wisconsin."

"Tim meant to ask what the situation is like." Levi exchanged a look of disbelief with the spiky-haired boy.

Matt looked around to make sure no one was nearby, then spoke in a barely audible whisper. "I always wake up...*naked*." He gripped both their arms firmly. "Don't tell anyone."

"Who would Levi tell? He's got no friends." Tim shrugged. "How do you handle that? Being naked?"

"I slip back into my house and get to my room before anyone sees me. I should keep a pair of clothes in the hay loft from now on, in case it happens again."

"Where was your car the night Nikki disappeared?"

"At the school. I had to get a ride to pick it up the next day."

"How did you get from the school to your barn with no car?"

"I don't know."

"What have the doctors told you about your condition?" Levi asked.

Matt gritted his teeth. "Dammit, stop. I've answered so many questions over the past week—I'm sick of it."

"We'll let you get back to your research," Levi said. "Just trying to help."

"If you want to talk or need someone to watch you the next full moon, let me know." Tim pulled out his phone and started scrolling. "Looks like I got your number. I'm sending you a text so you can add mine to your phone. Keep in contact."

A cell phone rang. Matt didn't move. The librarian stared at them malevolently.

Levi and Tim stood to leave. Tim cracked his knuckles. "What happens next is up to you, man."

"I'll keep that in mind," Matt said stiffly. Levi went back to his computer station, unable to shake the feeling of Matt's eyes boring angrily into his back. He logged off and let Tim lead the way to the truck.

"I LOVE CAROLERS." Mrs. Symanski slammed the front door. "Almost as much as I love these temperatures, and standing in the doorway letting the wind howl inside."

"You grew up here. Did you conveniently forget about the harsh winters?"

"You usually hold on to the nicer things in your memory. The rest fades. You'll see when you get older." Mrs. Symanski sat on the couch next to her kids. "Only a couple hours to kill before we leave for midnight mass."

"I never thought it could drop below zero outside." Samantha shivered under a blanket next to Brandon in the living room. "You hear about it but you never imagine what it feels like. Can we light a fire?"

"The heat is on and we've got candles going."

"Candles won't be enough." Brandon's teeth rattled. "I'll freeze to death."

"You underestimate the power of a single flame." Mrs. Symanski admired the Christmas tree in the corner. "Undoubtedly this is because you two were raised in a much warmer climate most of your lives. I can't wait to start driving lessons with you, Samantha. You'll get to learn how to drive on snow! Now that's something they don't teach you in D.C."

"Because you don't have to know how," Samantha shot back.

"Stop being so bitter and put on a Christmas movie. Maybe we'll light a fire tomorrow morning. How does that sound?"

"Not *It's a Wonderful Life*." Brandon kicked Samantha under the blanket.

"Fine, but I still get to pick," Samantha rolled her eyes. "Where's the remote?"

"Somewhere." Mrs. Symanski gestured at the room. Samantha got up and began to scan the furniture.

"Brandon, how's your Christmas break so far?" Mrs. Symanski ruffed the top of her son's head.

"Fun," Brandon smiled. "I wanna play outside in the snow more tomorrow. And build a fort, and have a snowball fight. Can I go over to Josh's?"

"On Christmas Day? We'll see. Ready for Santa to come?"

"I don't believe in Santa, mom. I'm not stupid. I know your handwriting."

Samantha leaned over to look behind the sofa. No remote. She checked the window sill. A silver device sat there, numbers changing on its little, unlit screen.

"What's this thing?" She held it up.

"Oh honey, put that back. I need it there." Mrs. Symanski stood and came over.

"Is this a recorder?"

"Yes, now don't touch it."

"What are you recording?" Samantha set it back down.

"Stuff for work."

"Why do you need recordings of our house for your job?"

"Just getting some sound effects for a presentation. It's no big deal, honey, and certainly nothing to be worried about. Here, let me help you find the remote."

TIM'S PHONE PLAYED Christmas songs as they sat in the living room of the apartment, playing Scrabble.

"This would be easier if I could spell," Tim frowned.

"I told you we needed a dictionary." Levi rearranged his letters.

"I can look anything up on my phone."

"Using the online Urban Dictionary is not helping you learn how to spell. Did you come up with a word yet? I've been waiting here for five minutes."

"I'm trying. I just need to figure out a word that uses a Q, an X, and a Y. I wanted to do 'queen' but I've only got two E's and a U."

"Ah. You're missing an N."

"Exactly. Would you like to trade?"

"No. Try exequy, e-x-e-q-u-y."

"What? That's not a real word," Tim moped.

"Look it up."

"I will." Tim typed on his phone. "Oh, come on."

"What did you learn?"

"It means burial rites."

253

"See? What did I tell you?"

"You *would* know that."

"Should we hit up Christmas mass tonight or tomorrow morning?" Levi watched as Tim put his letters on the board.

"Whatever works. Did you get me anything?" Tim asked.

"For Christmas? I give you my deepest gratitude for letting me live with you."

"Besides that."

"Oh…is your brother coming back for the holidays?" Levi changed the subject.

"I already told you," Tim replied with a grin. "It'll be nice having a Christmas without the awkward silences and accusatory glares…and the oversized ego. My first Christmas without him. How was your first Christmas without your parents?"

"It…it was quiet," Levi rearranged his letters. "I couldn't stay at home by myself in that empty house. I went to church. Sat there through mass after mass. I saw lots of people, sang songs. It got me through. How about you? What did you do?"

"After my grandma died, Felix and I sat around a lot on holidays. Didn't talk at all. It was horrible."

"You do love to talk," Levi said wryly, putting his letters down.

"Can you imagine me sitting silent?" Tim chuckled. "Fuck that. Is it your turn?"

"I went already."

"What?"

"I put down 'humble.'"

"I should be thinking about my next word then."

"Ya."

"So…how did your parents die?"

"We don't talk about this, Tim."

"Why not?"

"You don't tell me how *your* parents died, I don't need to tell you how *mine* died."

"Oh, you're gonna spin it that way? I'll call your bluff." Tim stretched. "My mom died right after I was born. Being in labor with me kind of killed her."

"That sucks man," Levi scratched the back of his head. "I'm sorry."

"It's okay. The trouble is getting Felix to believe that. There's nothing anyone can do about it now." Tim shrugged.

"And, uhh…what happened to your dad?" Levi asked, a sick feeling in his stomach.

"There was a car crash up near Ashland. He's buried there."

"Have you visited his grave?"

"No." Tim pushed his letters around. "I barely knew him anyway. He was always gone. Why dwell on it?"

"Don't you ever wonder what he's like?"

"Sure. Who wouldn't? But it doesn't matter, does it. He's dead."

"What if you could see him?"

"I can't, though. He's six feet under."

"I know, but what if you could? Would you? Like, if you could just go visit him somewhere, and he was there, and could talk to you, would you go?"

"I don't know. I don't think I would."

"Really? What if—"

"Levi, stop fucking with me. You're asking me to think about things I can't change. Do you know how much time gets wasted on 'what if'? Those two words are only good for insurance salesmen."

"That's not true," Levi said firmly. "If you don't consider alternate possibilities—"

"I've wasted enough time considering alternate possibilities," Tim said with a hint of warning in his voice.

"Bullshit."

"Fine Levi, I'll play along. If my father were still alive, my brother wouldn't hate me, or at least not as much. He'd be working at a job he liked and would be living his life the way he wants. I would live in a normal house with my dad, with normal problems, doing normal things. I'd be happy and I wouldn't concern myself with dealing drugs, working in a funeral parlor, or hunting vampires and werewolves."

"We don't hunt werewolves," Levi corrected.

"Yet," Tim shoved back. "But guess what? My father *is* dead. He's dead and my life consists of dealing with Felix's drama, your drama, stalking vampires, dealing drugs, working at a funeral home, and going to high school—and I *still* find time to be awesome."

Levi's frustration began to leak into his words. "What if your dad wasn't dead? What if he faked it—and just showed up one day—out of the blue?"

"I don't think I'd be able to face him and be civil," Tim said calmly. "Would you be able to forgive someone who disappeared on purpose and made your life and your brother's life a living hell?" He placed his letters: *d-e-c-e-i-t.*

Levi stared at the Scrabble board.

"What? I spelled it correctly. I before E except after C. So I told you my parental death story. What's yours?"

Levi's throat dried out, but he forced a slight grin. "A secret."

"Are you serious?!"

THE SKY ON CHRISTMAS MORNING remained the same flat shade of iron gray as the day before, and the day before that. Cold winds whistled as they blew past the windows. Samantha walked downstairs in a pair of flannel pajamas and slippers. The fire crackled and the Christmas tree was brilliant with its pile of presents glittering underneath. Brandon sorted through the heap, setting aside the gifts with his name on them.

"Where's mom?" Samantha looked around.

"In the dining room." Brandon gave her the most condescending look she'd ever seen grace his face. Samantha stuck out her tongue at him before heading into the dining room.

Mrs. Symanski sat at the table, laptop open, an enormous pair of headphones on as she rested her chin on her hand and squinted at the screen. An army of notebooks and silver devices littered the table.

"Merry Christmas, mom." Her mother didn't reply. She leaned toward the screen, and clicked away with the mouse. Samantha tapped her on the shoulder. Her mother screamed, then Samantha screamed. Mrs. Symanski slammed the laptop shut and pulled off her headphones.

"Samantha Rose Symanski, you scared the life out of me!"

"You scared me too."

"Don't sneak up on me like that. You'll give me gray hair." Mrs. Symanski put a hand over her chest. "What do you need, honey?"

"I wanted to wish you a Merry Christmas." Samantha looked from silver device to silver device. "What is all this stuff?"

"It's for work," Mrs. Symanski said quickly. "That presentation. Remember the little recorder in the living room?"

"It's right there on the table with a bunch of other ones." Samantha pointed. "I thought your job was just reviewing contracts from Washington or something. This looks like research equipment."

"Really? I wouldn't have thought so." Mrs. Symanski smiled, sickly sweet. "Why don't you go open your presents with your brother?"

"According to every Christmas movie ever made, that's supposed to be a family moment," Samantha countered. "Aren't you supposed to record it or take pictures or something?"

"Give me just a second." Mrs. Symanski walked into the kitchen and returned a moment later with a digital camera. "Here. Take video of your brother opening presents for me. We'll send it to your father. I'll be in there in a bit." She returned to her seat and put her headphones on. Samantha stood there. Mrs. Symanski watched her, a hand on her laptop, obviously not opening it until her daughter left the room.

Samantha rolled her eyes and went into the living room. The Christmas tree lights flickered. She turned on the camera and started recording Brandon.

"What are you doing?" he asked as he ripped the paper off a remote-controlled airplane.

"We're taking some video and sending it to dad. He'll want to see what Santa got us for Christmas."

"Santa isn't real." Brandon didn't look at her. "These are all from mom."

"We didn't get any from dad?"

"No."

"You positive?"

"Yes. What am I, four years old?" Brandon grabbed another present and began tearing the paper off. "I know how to read."

"Not even a card?"

Brandon shook his head.

"Maybe he'll call."

"MERRY CHRISTMAS," Tim announced as something large and flat smacked onto Levi's chest.

He sat up with a start, gasping for breath. "What the hell, Tim!" He grabbed the box roughly and threw it on the floor.

"Hey, hey, be gentle with that," Tim snapped. "It took me a long time to find!"

"What is this?"

"It's your present, motherfucker."

"Uh—" Levi blinked at Tim, who smirked and left the room.

"I'm expecting mine by New Year's Eve." Tim's voice came from down the hall.

Levi eyed the box on the floor. It was bland, wrapped in brown paper, and fairly heavy. He picked it up, shook it quizzically and tore the paper.

"You got me a leather jacket."

Tim reappeared in the doorway in his own leather jacket. "Now we match!"

"I'll look like a drug dealer."

"You'll look badass like me. And the best part is you can stop wearing all those damn hoodies." Tim's cell phone rang. He pulled it out. "Text from the furball. He wants to come over and talk tonight."

"On Christmas Day? Doesn't he have family?"

Tim shoved his phone back in his pocket. "Must be urgent."

SAMANTHA STARED AT HER CEILING as her new disco ball spun, a hundred little blue spots of light spiraling across the room. Tegan and Sara pumped out of her radio; while somewhere in the house, her brother crashed a remote control car. Her cell phone buzzed on the nightstand. She grabbed it without looking at it.

"Hello?"

"I have a chico problemo," said a hushed voice on the other end.

Samantha grimaced. "Laderia, what are you tal—"

"Stefan. He's over here. Right now."

"And?"

"He's been at my casa all day…meeting all my relatives. They think we're together. I want him gone with the wind-o."

"You're messing with me."

"Does this voice not sound serio to you?"

"Never. What the hell's going on? I thought y'all sort of had a thing—"

"He's not really my typo. I was gonna pull the whole 'we'll always have Paris' thing when he left—"

"Maybe he wants a green card."

"If he wants one, he should learn who he can legally marry, right? He invited himself over and has been suffocating me like a choker necklace."

"What's your family think of this?"

"My madre's thrilled. She wants us to get married. Like, tomorrow. I hope she's joking."

"That's, umm, well—"

"A nightmare. His last name is Willfahrt. Can you believe that's a real name? Willfahrt. W-I-L-L-F-A-H-R—"

"Laderia Willfahrt. Has a rumble to it—"

"Samantha, I don't think you comprehend."

"I heard parents can sign something and let you marry even if you're underage."

"Take this serio!" Laderia hissed. "That's why I called you and not Jennifer."

"You didn't tell Jennifer?"

"You think I want to be called Laderia Willfahrt for the rest of high school? Because that's what Jennifer will make happen."

"I know I wouldn't want that last name."

"Who would?! His mother was probably a mail-order bride." Laderia's voice was laced with disgust.

"If I were you I'd make him take my last name."

"Wait. Guys can do that?"

"It's possible." Samantha thought hard for a moment. "Stefan Valdez sounds so much more rugged than Stefan Willfahrt."

"You know, that does sound sexier." Laderia's voice changed, and Samantha couldn't stop herself from rolling her eyes.

"Considering giving this a shot?"

"I'll toy with the idea. I need to find out if he's man enough for me before I commit. So how was your Christmas, ho?"

"It was quiet. Yours?"

"You already know, Symanski."

"Ah yes. A date."

"And unlike your boy toy, he's only slightly loco. Go have yourself a Feliz Navidad," Laderia laughed wickedly. The call ended. Samantha sighed and put her phone back on the nightstand, wondering if she should she call Matt.

IT WAS DARK when they heard the knock on the door. Levi opened it, and Matt stood there in a black t-shirt with a coat slung over his shoulder, looking around nervously.

"Come in, man." Levi gestured into the apartment.

"Thanks." Matt stepped inside. He sat next to Tim on the couch, his fists clenching and unclenching. "You guys are roommates? Where's the adult supervision?"

"In Chicago, but he'll be back. So," Levi shut the door, "what brings you over here on Christmas Day?"

"The full moon is tomorrow night. I need your help."

"Does your family know you're here? Shouldn't you be with them?" Tim ran a hand through his spiked hair.

"They don't ask me many questions these days." Matt rolled his shoulders and stretched his collar. "It's hot in here. Can you open a window?"

Levi and Tim exchanged a glance. "What do you need us to do?" Tim asked.

"I need you guys to watch me," Matt swung his arms back and forth. "Babysit me, whatever. Tell me what's happening to me. Record it if you have to."

"I don't think we'll have to go that far." Tim looked at Levi. "That seems unnecessary, right?"

"Completely," Levi lied.

"Okay then, just watch me yourselves!" Matt wiped a bead of sweat from his brow. "It's so hot in here."

"Aren't you on medication?" Tim leaned closer.

"Yes, two kinds." Matt dug in his pocket. "I brought them along." He pulled out two amber plastic cylinders. "The doctors have me on these."

"Can I see them?"

"You can't have them." Matt's grip tightened on the cylinders.

"I just want to see them." Tim snatched them deftly from Matt's hands. "This one says aconitine. And this one is silver acetate."

"I've never heard of those," Levi commented.

"They're natural, and the doctors say they should work fine. I go in every two weeks for a check-up and a refill." Matt shrugged. "They're monitoring my dosage really close so I don't get argryria."

"Agryria, right. What are the pills supposed to do?" Tim's building enthusiasm colored his voice.

"The aconitine is supposed to keep me from overheating—"

"Hasn't helped." Levi couldn't hide the sardonic tone.

Matt furrowed his brow and continued. "The silver acetate is supposed to give me ataxia. But they only want me to take those pills on specific days of the months; the days around the full moon."

Levi crossed his arms. "What the fuck is ataxia and why do they want to give it to you?"

"Loss of muscle control," Tim said.

"The silver acetate is supposed to interrupt the message between the muscles and the brain. Makes everything uncoordinated, so deliberate movements are hindered." Matt ran a hand through his hair. "But even after I took it, I'd keep waking up in the barn after blacking out in different places."

"Effective," Levi said dryly.

Tim pressed on. "What's argryria?"

"Silver poisoning. It turns your skin blue-gray—like a dead person. It's disgusting."

Tim grabbed Levi's elbow and led him down the little hallway to their bedrooms. "Levi, they know—they *have* to know. The doctors *know* he's a werewolf."

"What, the silver acetate?" Levi knew he was grasping at straws. "It sounds like it's used for some legitimate medical conditions."

"You don't understand," Tim whispered urgently. "Aconitine is a neurotoxin. It's made from monkshood, otherwise known as *wolfsbane*."

"Uh-huh." Levi stared blankly at Tim.

"It's deadly for the average human to take, but they have him popping it in capsules *daily*."

"What are you implying? They're trying to poison Matt?"

"Think about it. His body recovers really quickly from injuries—remember how bad Symanski said he was injured after that animal attack? How she said Matt was holding his intestines? Then he comes back to school without so much as a scratch. A poison like aconitine in a regular person would destroy their mental functions. For a werewolf, it would just take the edge off—you know—damage him enough to mellow him out."

Levi scrounged around his mind for a change of subject. "How do you know about aconitine?"

"Are you kidding me right now?"

He rubbed the sweat from his hands off on his pants. "Oh of course…werewolves are your obsession. What about the silver acetate?"

"That's usually used to get smokers to quit. Makes the cigarettes taste awful," Tim squinted. "But Matt's not a smoker as far as I know."

"What are you guys whispering about?" Matt called loudly from the couch.

"Are you a smoker?" Tim and Levi went back into the living room.

"No," Matt replied.

"Silver acetate, Levi," Tim muttered, back turned to Matt. "They're testing to see if the silver in his body will mitigate the effects of the transformation. That's why they're monitoring him like he said. The ataxia should theoretically stop him from rampaging."

"That doesn't make sense, not with Nikki Becker's disappearance and all the cattle mutilations. I've even heard kids at school talking about missing dogs. How could he be responsible if he's knocked out by drugs? Matt," Levi said, "did you take the silver acetate on the night of the White Out game—the night Nikki disappeared?"

"No," Matt said. "I didn't take anything that night."

"So that means you'd still be free to run around and be a wolf. You're not planning on doing that tomorrow night, are you?"

"No," Matt shook his head. "No, I want to wake up in the same place that I fall asleep. That's all."

"That's not all, I can tell," Tim squinted accusingly at the jock.

"There is one other thing. I need a place to…to—"

"To change." Tim gave Levi a look that said 'I told you so.'

"No skin-changing in this apartment," Levi said coldly. "The last thing we need is a potential monster ruining the place. And we're in the middle of town."

"Levi, if it turns out that he's not a werewolf, the worst thing that will happen is we wind up hanging out with him for a night."

"I'm well aware this could turn out to be a crock of shit." Levi cracked his knuckles. "We don't have a place for him to change."

Tim sat up, as if a bolt of lightning hit him. "Yes we do, Levi." He cracked a grin.

Levi felt his heart plummet as he realized what Tim meant. "I know what you're thinking, and no. I won't allow it."

"Allow what?" Matt asked.

"Come on Levi, you're not using the place anyway."

"Shove it, Tim. That idea is not flying."

"What idea is not flying?" Matt glowered.

"Come on! It'll be just like the Shrieking Shack in Harry Potter! It's not like we have to worry about Lanc—" Levi clamped one hand over Tim's mouth, the other around his throat.

"Staple your big mouth shut and drop it, Tim! He is *never* going there!"

Matt lunged off the couch and snarled, shoving Levi and Tim apart. "Stop acting like a bunch of sophomores! One of you better spill. What's the plan?!"

LEVI BEGRUDGINGLY UNLOCKED the back door to the old brick house. It swung into an ice-cold interior. Matt and Tim followed him into the dark kitchen.

"What is this place?" Matt asked.

"It's been a long time since we've been here, huh, Levi?" Tim grinned as Levi stepped into the shadows and screwed some light bulbs into the ceiling fan in the dining room.

"Maybe for you, Tim." Levi walked over to the switch. The lights didn't come on. "That's right. I haven't been paying the electric bill."

"Hold up. This is the Mauer farm?" Matt shifted around. He turned to Levi. "Where are your parents?"

"None of your business, Stauber, so shut it." Levi turned the faucet on the kitchen sink. Nothing happened.

"Typical Wisconsin winter. Frozen pipes and all. No running water tonight, guys."

"And no heat," Tim frowned. "Good thing I brought some of my stash—"

"Not in this house, Tim," Levi warned.

"How else am I supposed to warm up? My body feels the cold, unlike wolfman over here."

"We should be able to get a fire going in the furnace. It's wood-burning." Levi rummaged through the lower cabinets. "I had some bundles of firewood around here somewhere—got 'em." He pulled out some wood and chucked it into the furnace. "Got any alcohol, Tim?"

"I have a little bottle of Everclear." Tim grabbed it out of his leather jacket. "Always ready to spike some punch." He handed it to Levi, who promptly emptied half of it into the furnace, struck a match, and threw it in. Flames roared to life. Levi grabbed an old poker and stoked the fire until it crackled away, the kitchen dimly illuminated with dancing orange light.

"Just like camping," Tim grimaced. "I'm not sure if I'm excited about that or disappointed."

"That fire's pretty warm already," Matt backed away. "Do we need it so hot?"

"I'm trying to warm up the pipes. Wouldn't want them to burst. We'll be hanging out here until the moon rises," Levi said. "Water would be nice."

"If I transform, what if I go into beast mode and try to kill you both?" Matt glanced back and forth between Tim and Levi.

"Do we want to keep him in the house and we can hang outside?" Tim looked at Levi. "Maybe lock him in the basement?"

"Alone? Fuck no," Matt interjected.

"Bad idea, it's a mess down there."

Tim rubbed his chin. "Then we hide out upstairs and keep him down here."

"Then we better move everything breakable," Levi sighed.

"There's nothing here," Matt looked around. "Some tables, chairs, and old sofas. That's it."

"Hey Levi, there's a bunch of water bottles in this closet," Tim shrugged. "We've got some time until the moon is full. What do you guys want to do until then?"

"Hang out," Matt said. Levi struggled to hide his anger and dragged some chairs from the dining room into the kitchen by the furnace. They each sat in a chair, and an awkward silence ensued. Levi studied Matt's face and demeanor. He noted the other boy's tense posture, his clenching jaw, and the sweat on his forehead.

"I don't do silence well," Tim commented with a smirk. "Just letting you two know."

Matt pulled out his phone.

"Who are you texting?" Levi asked.

Matt glared at Levi, who returned the look with equal ferocity and the addition of some cracking knuckles. "Don't threaten me, Mauer, I almost killed you at Pizza Hut."

"That was in public; but this is my house. I've got no reason to hold back here." Levi leaned forward, hoping his dominant act was enough to make Matt back down.

"I'm texting Kaeli," Matt glowered into the light from his phone. "Why do you care?"

"How are things with Symanski?"

"Since you told her to dump me, not very good." Matt didn't look at Levi. "That's right, I heard what you said to her that night. We're not officially broken up yet…but if it happens, it's your fault. I won't forget that, believe me."

"You're not well enough to be with her right now," Levi said. "I'm not wrong."

"What do you think you're trying to pull?" Matt roared.

"He's being stupid!" Tim yelled. "Relax, Matt. Levi, stop bringing up stupid things. We don't want Matt angry and a werewolf at the same time." He glared at both of them. "Dammit men, pull yourselves together."

"IT'S LATE. You should be in bed already. Anything good on?" Samantha sat on the couch next to Brandon, who was dripping with melted snow, ignoring her. "You must have been playing really hard outside. Look at you. You're like a drowned rat."

"Look at you. You're stupid," Brandon replied smoothly after taking a sip from his hot chocolate. He stared at the television.

"Be nice, runt." Samantha draped a blanket over her legs and pulled out her cell phone. "I should text Matt."

"Tell him how stupid you are." Brandon sipped his hot chocolate again.

"I'll ask how his Christmas went." She sent him a message. "Where's mom?"

"Doing work stuff."

"Upstairs?"

"Yup. She's setting up cameras."

"Cameras?"

"She said they're going to take pictures all night."

"What the hell is she up to now?"

"LOOK AT THIS, she finally sent me a message." Matt studied his phone screen.

"What did she say?" asked Levi.

"She wants to know how Christmas went." Matt's thumbs glided over the keypad. Levi had to consciously shove aside his revulsion as a grin spread across Matt's face.

"What time is it?" he asked.

"It's late," Matt replied without looking up.

"Take your pills again." Tim tossed a water bottle to Matt. He caught it without looking and continued to stare at his phone. Tim grabbed Levi and pulled him down the black hallway to the front door. "Remember the first dose he took? He's not showing any effects yet."

"He's supposed to have taxes, right? That'll put him to sleep?"

"*Ataxia*, Levi. He doesn't look very paralyzed to me."

"What does this mean? His dosage isn't high enough?"

"I don't know," Tim whispered. "We should be able to see an effect. If he's a werewolf, he's tied to the moon. Maybe when it's fuller, he gets stronger."

"Are you suggesting he should take a higher dosage?"

"I can hear you losers." Matt's voice echoed in the bare house. "Get back here and talk to me like I've got a brain."

"Matt, you should take another dose of the silver acetate," Tim said. "You're not experiencing any ataxia from what I can see."

"Okay, man." Matt popped another pill, swigged some water and made a face. "Those go down so bad...feel safer now?"

"A little," Tim frowned. "Do you ever feel paralyzed when taking those?"

Matt shook his head. "Just really slow and tired, like I'm in a fog. But I can still move everything."

"And how do you feel now?"

"I feel lazy."

"Then we'll see what happens man. Less than an hour to go until the moon is officially full." Levi's palms were sweating and his stomach tied itself in knots.

"HE'S WITH LEVI AND TIM," Samantha stared at her phone. "And he has to go."

"I don't care, stop telling me." Brandon kicked her under the blanket.

"That's so weird. They got in that huge fight. They've never been friends. Why would they be hanging out?"

THEY SAT IN SILENCE for what felt like forever. Levi forced himself to remain cool, but his sweating palms reminded him that, come the moon's zenith, he would have very little control over the situation. His mind raced back to his conversation with Felix in the Daily Grind. Did he say anything about werewolves? About their transformations? He wracked his brain until his head hurt, his stomach full of butterflies. He analyzed Matt, who continued to text away, staring at his phone from beneath half-lidded eyes. The football player's face glistened with sweat in the light from the furnace.

"H-how are you feeling?" Levi asked.

"I'm tired. And I'm overheated." Matt ran a hand across his forehead and flicked some sweat onto the floor. "I feel sick to my stomach, too."

"How are your reflexes?" Tim asked. He threw another water bottle at Matt. It slapped Matt's shoulder and rolled across the floor into a dark corner.

Matt glowered and put his phone away. "Don't surprise me."

"Okay. Catch this one." Tim chucked another one at Matt. It hit his hand, fell out of his grasp, and plopped into his lap.

"That was too fast again."

"I think it's just about time." Tim looked at his cell phone. "Two minutes, Levi. Let's head upstairs. You'll be alright, Matt?"

"Ya, whatever." Matt waved at them vaguely as they stood and went down the dark hall.

"I'm scared, Levi," Tim hissed when they reached the bottom of the stairs. "He's not doped enough. I don't know why the silver acetate isn't working. He shouldn't be able to talk."

"Relax Tim," Levi said, even as every hair on his body seemed to be standing on end. "It's nerves. You're a chicken."

A horrid scream of pain filled the house. Levi and Tim looked down the hall to the kitchen. "It's starting," Tim whispered. "Let's get upstairs."

Another horrible scream, along with a thud. Levi charged down the hall to the kitchen, while Tim yelled protests from the stairs.

"Get your dumb ass back here!"

"I gotta see this for myself," Levi said.

He entered the kitchen, the furnace casting everything in a hellish light. Matt writhed on the floor, struggling to get his shirt over his head. Levi gaped as the football player shredded the shirt, kicked off his shoes, and wrestled his pants off.

"It's so hot," he wailed. "Why is it so hot?!" His breath came in sharp gasps as sweat poured from his body. He crawled toward Levi, who backed up, staring at him in horrid fascination. Matt finally collapsed onto his side, and was still. The silence felt wrong.

"Tim!" Levi yelled. "Tim, what's wrong with him? He's not turning!" Tim's footsteps pounded down the hall and he ran into the room, looking down at Matt's limp body on the floor.

"He *is* turning, Levi," Tim whispered. "Look closer." He pointed to Matt's arms. "They're getting longer."

Levi got closer and squinted. As Matt's arms grew longer, his rib cage narrowed with each breath, the bones creaking as they shifted, looking more and more like a dog's. His face slowly pushed

269

outward, the skin stretching like a rubber sheet as a snout slowly formed. Blood seeped from his mouth onto the floor from gums that struggled to accommodate a second set of teeth.

"No—*fucking*—way." Levi walked around Matt's body. "Do you see this? He's growing a tail. A fucking *tail*." The appendage lengthened inches at a time, pushing and stretching the skin. Matt's backbone was clearly visible. His feet enlarged as his fingers shortened, their length replaced by claws growing from where his nails had been.

"He's almost done turning. Levi, we gotta get upstairs. Levi—Levi! Are you listening?" Tim backed down the hall.

Levi headed toward the hallway, keeping his eyes on the transformation. The ears grew to sharpened points as Matt's head finished remolding. Even from the stairs, Levi could see the dark fur that bloomed along its body, long, thin, and patchy. A low growl escaped the beast as it exhaled and slowly got to its feet, claws scraping on the floor.

Matt was gone.

Chapter 9

But Now, There's Nowhere to Hide

Levi's heart pounded as he raced up the stairs. The beast's growls filling the air. Tim stood in the doorway of the master bedroom. He gestured frantically and Levi finally reached him. They closed the door and locked it.

Tim was about to say something but Levi clamped a hand over his mouth. They listened as the clicking of the claws grew closer, louder. It was coming up the stairs. The moonlight spilling through the window illuminated Tim's wide, panicked eyes. They waited. Heavy panting and sniffing came from the gap at the bottom of the door. Another growl, accompanied by the sound of claws raking across the wood, sent chills up Levi's spine. There wasn't a door thick enough in the world to make him feel safe. He dragged Tim to the windows as the beast scratched at the door again and again.

He looked out to the roof of the porch below them. A pile of snow slumped under it, and from there it was only twenty feet to the truck. If they could get out the window and to the truck...they could think of a plan from there.

Levi released Tim from his grasp and unlocked the window. The click earned them a ferocious roar from the other side of the door. The claws scratched faster, the door cracking under the force.

"Hurry Levi!" Tim whispered. Levi yanked at the window, trying to pull it up. It wouldn't budge. He went to the window on the other side of the bed, unlocked it, and yanked. It stopped sliding after five inches.

"Help me, Tim," he hissed. Tim came over and together they forced the window up and open. The door started to splinter and bow. Claws were visible, scraping little lines of holes. The window was open about a foot.

"Can you fit?" Levi asked.

"I'll make it work." Tim stuck his head through the gap and managed to wiggle himself through, sliding onto the roof of the porch. "Come on, Levi!"

Levi glanced back at the door, which was in tatters. He could make out the shape of the beast as it whittled the remains and ripped bits off with its teeth. Levi forced his upper body through the window easily enough, but something ensnared him around the waist. "Oh fuck, Tim. This jacket."

Tim grabbed Levi and pulled his shoulders.

"It's caught!" Levi's voice betrayed his anger and panic. The snapping of the wood in the wolf's mouth rang in his ears and his adrenaline surged. Using his back, he pushed up on the window, giving himself an extra half-inch, and wiggled through. The door gave completely as Levi got his feet out the window.

The beast launched into the bedroom. Levi shoved the window back down behind them. Tim leapt from the roof and landed on his back in the snow. Levi leapt to his side, the pile cushioning his impact.

"To the truck. Now." He stood up. Tim didn't move. "Come on, Tim, let's go!" Tim didn't answer. He lay on his back, eyes closed. "Tim!" The wolf snarled through the glass. It wouldn't be long before it figured out the glass could break. Levi grabbed Tim's limp body around the waist, threw him over his shoulder, and huffed to the truck as fast as he could. He chucked Tim in the truck bed and hopped into the driver's seat. Sticking his keys into the ignition, the truck roared to life, its unmuffled noise making Levi feel strong. He whipped the truck around and pulled out of the driveway and onto the road. He looked in the rearview mirror. The wolf broke the window and leapt into the yard. Levi gunned it. The truck responded dutifully and they sped away.

A knock on the rear window made Levi yell. He glanced behind him. Tim's nose was pressed to the glass, brows drawn. Levi slid the window open and Tim forced his way into the cabin.

"You threw me into the truck bed?!" he yelled.

"You passed out on me," Levi responded. "Like a woman."

"Where's the wolf?"

"I don't care."

"What if he kills someone?!"

"What do you want me to do, Tim?! I have nothing! I cannot fight a werewolf—not without killing him!" Levi wiped his nose on his leather sleeve. "Fuck this jacket, man."

"What's your plan now, genius?"

Levi stared at the road. "We're going back to the apartment."

"That's a bad idea," Tim warned.

"Letting him change at my parents' house was a *bad* idea, Tim. And that bad idea was yours." Levi's knuckles were white as he gripped the steering wheel. "All the damage that thing caused!"

"So what? You don't live there now."

"Don't you understand?! It's where I grew up! It's where my parents are buried! It's where they—" Levi bit his lip to shut himself up.

"Where they died." Tim was so quiet the roar of the engine almost drowned out his words. "I wasn't trying to be disrespectful. It was the only place I could come up with."

"Do you think his parents know?" Levi changed the subject. "There's no way they could ignore his *condition*—"

Tim shrugged. "He got attacked in September. This is only his third transformation, so maybe not."

"They didn't wonder where the hell he was the other two full moons? Why the doctors have him on meds? What kind of parents don't ask those questions?!" Levi slammed a fist on the dashboard. Tim sat silently as they stopped at the four-way intersection of McMillan Street and St. Joseph Avenue. "Do you have any more water bottles, Tim?"

"No man, they're in the bag. I left that at the house. We'll have to get it tomorr—"

"Dammit, one more thing to do." Levi ran his hands over his face. "And we gotta get Matt's car back to him somehow. It's at our place—"

"Levi—have you looked behind us recently?" Tim's eyes were fixed on the rearview mirror.

Levi looked. Something huge and dark lumbered through the snowy ditch along the road.

"He's coming after the truck," Tim whispered.

Levi glanced down St. Joseph Avenue, the Security Health Plan building looming ahead, then in the rearview mirror. "How did he keep up with us? He can't be that fast!"

"He must have cut through the fields and woods." Tim said, turning in his seat to look out the back. "Creepy. He stopped and is just staring at us."

"What's creepy is that you're calling it 'he'," Levi muttered.

"He's Matt—just as a werewolf."

"Matt wouldn't try to ingest us." Levi looked around the intersection. "Fuck it, we gotta go through town now."

Tim turned on Levi. "No! We gotta wear him out driving down the country roads."

"I don't have enough gas in the tank," Levi pointed at the dashboard display. "I don't like this any more than you do." He stepped on the pedal, and the beast darted under the street light.

"He's going to follow us all the way home." Tim spun around.

They pulled up to the four-way stop at Upham Street and St. Joseph Avenue. The graveyard stretched out to the right, the hospital rising ahead on the left.

"Alright." Levi tried to shake the worry. He proceeded down St.

Joseph Avenue, watching for cops, other vehicles, and pedestrians. "No one's out."

"Good," Tim whispered. "Keep your eyes on the road."

At the intersection of St. Joseph Avenue and Veterans Parkway, they hit a red light. Despite every urge to do otherwise, Levi slowed to a stop. The wolf paused, ears flattened, and howled, long and low. Levi felt the hairs on his neck stand up. He looked left and right. No vehicles. He ran the red light, and the werewolf bounded after them. St. Joseph Avenue turned into Oak Avenue and they went through a series of icy curves. Levi took them carefully, and the truck bounced from the weight of the werewolf leaping into the back. "Holy fuck!"

"Shake him off!" Tim yelled. Levi fishtailed the truck, but the werewolf braced itself, claws clattering on the metal. Coming up to the Fourth Street intersection, Levi cranked the wheel hard, and the truck did a three-sixty. The werewolf leapt back onto the road, slipping on the ice. Levi corrected and had them going down Oak to Seventh Street. On the left turn the truck fishtailed again. They passed Veterans Park and came to a stop at the lights of Central Avenue, barely two blocks from the apartment. Levi turned to look over his shoulder. The werewolf limped into Veterans Park.

"Where's he going?" Levi whipped the truck around. They followed the limping beast from a distance as it moved through the empty park down West Park Street, where it finally collapsed on the snow-covered front lawn of number 311. "What the fuck? Is it dead?"

"We wore him out," Tim grinned. "Pull over."

They got out and ran through the snow to the beast laying on its side, panting for breath, eyes closed. "He's out cold."

Tim hit Levi's shoulder. "On Symanski's lawn!" They grabbed the beast's legs and pulled, but it didn't budge. "Is it just me or does he weight five hundred pounds?"

"We can't move him, and we can't leave him." Levi looked up at the brick house looming over them. "What do we do with him?"

Tim smacked a hand to his forehead. "Oh, this can't get worse.

He's going to get discovered."

"We'll…we'll bury him."

"In the snow? Overnight?!"

"Do we have a choice?" Levi looked at Tim, his expression hollow.

A FIERCE RAPPING on the door woke her. "Samantha, Matt's outside."

"Tell him I'm not here."

Her door swung open and lights flicked on. "No honey, he's passed out…and naked. Is this typical for him?"

Samantha sat up in bed, her eyes not wanting to open. "You're lying!"

"Look out the window." Mrs. Symanski turned and left.

Samantha's legs were still half-asleep as she stumbled to her window and looked out over the front yard. Sure enough, a limp, muscular body lay face down, almost completely buried in the snow. She watched as her mom went out there with a huge blanket, threw it over the body, and proceeded to shake it awake. Matt sat up and rubbed his eyes. Samantha felt her heart skip, and she threw on a pair of sweat pants and a shirt and ran downstairs. She reached the foyer as her mother helped Matt walk in the front door.

"Matt, what happened?!" she asked.

"I-I don't know," he said. "The last thing I remember I was at—" He shut up, suddenly looking very panicked. He pulled the blanket tight around himself.

"I got a text from you last night saying you were hanging out with Levi and Tim," Samantha said, suspicion brewing in her voice. "Did they have something to do with this?"

"I-I wanted to apologize," Matt said through gritted teeth.

"I'm more concerned with how you wound up naked on my front lawn," Mrs. Symanski said. "You certainly must be partying hard."

"It wasn't a—okay, it was a party," Matt said. "It was a party that got out of control. I lost control."

"I should call the police." Mrs. Symanski shook her head. "Your mother must be worried sick."

"No, no. Please don't," Matt pleaded. "It was stupid. It will never happen again."

"And what would you have me do instead?" Mrs. Symanski's lips pursed.

"I need a telephone," Matt said. "Please, ma'am. Let me just call for a ride. I know what it looks like—but calling my mom or the police won't make it better. I'm really sorry. I promise, this will *never* happen again."

Samantha held her breath as her mother leaned into Matt's face. She saw his eyes widen with frustration. "I want you to end whatever it is you have going on with my daughter. You do that, and I won't call the police."

"What?! No—mom, you can't!" Samantha grabbed her mother's arm.

"Watch me." Mrs. Symanski rounded on Matt. "From what I gather, you're a suspect in the disappearance of a classmate. You think this is the appropriate time in your life to be partying too hard? You drag my Samantha out of school every day for weeks on end skipping classes—who the hell do you think you are?! There is something very wrong with you, and that's your curse. I won't have that garbage inflicted on my daughter—"

"Mom, please—"

"Don't you dare drop your standards just to get back at me!" Mrs. Symanski wrested her arm from her daughter's grasp. "It's self-destructive and you're smarter than that! Go to your room! Now!"

"I hate you!" Samantha couldn't hold back the tears burning in her eyes. Her mother ignored her. She turned heel and ran to her room, slamming her door behind her. She flung herself on the bed, buried her face in a pillow, and screamed as loud as she could into the fabric. Struggling to get control of her emotions, she settled herself down by staring at her butterfly collection.

The sound of a loud truck pulling up drew her to the window. It looked like a rust bucket stopped in front of the house. Through the windshield, she could barely see the shape of the driver and a passenger. She watched as Matt, still bundled in the blanket, bolted down the icy walkway on bare feet and hopped in the passenger seat. She caught a glimpse of a leather jacket on the other passenger before Matt shut the door.

"Is that Tim?"

"WHAT A FUCKING NIGHTMARE." Matt pulled on his pants and scanned Levi's kitchen floor for the rest of his clothes and shoes. "Her mom chewed me out—I wanted to rip her babbling blonde head off."

Levi coughed. "You'd be on your own at that point."

"Have you taken your chill pill yet?" Tim asked.

"No I haven't. How the hell did I wind up at Samantha's?" Matt pulled his shirt on.

"Did you not see the broken window upstairs when we pulled up?" Tim ran his hands through his hair. "We drove off and you stalked us into town! Although we should have expected that; the Beast of Bray Road can keep up with vehicles. And Levi, I'm going to take this opportunity to say I told you so! I fucking told you so!"

"Ya ya, rub it in." Levi walked around the kitchen, looking at every claw scratch on the floor. He followed the claw scratches up the stairs. The hallway was full of shredded bits of the master bedroom door. Scratches covered the walls. He stepped through the tattered remains that somehow stayed on the hinges, and into the master bedroom. The gaping hole to the outside let in an inch of blowing snow.

"What a mess." Tim stood behind him. "Sorry about your house, man."

"Not as sorry as I am." Levi looked around.

"We had no other options—"

"Don't comfort me. Where's Matt?"

"Gathering the rest of his stuff from downstairs. We're just about ready to go."

"I can't leave it looking like this," Levi said. He pushed past Tim, bolted downstairs, and grabbed a toolkit from one of the kitchen cabinets, along with a couple trash bags. He ran back upstairs, covered the broken window with the trash bags, and nailed them to the window frame. He grabbed the comforter off the bed and nailed that up over the trash bags. "That should hold for now." He fought back the burning feeling in his eyes as he ran his hand over the musty fabric of the comforter.

MUSIC BLARED FROM HER SPEAKERS. Samantha hadn't left her room since her mother sent her there. She sighed, and pulled out her phone. *'Sorry about my mom. She doesn't respect me and she does NOT speak for me. Are we really broken up?'* She sent the text.

'Whatever you want,' came the response. *'But I want us to be together.'*

Samantha smiled. *'Me too.'*

The lights flickered. She looked around her room and rolled her eyes. The lights flickered again. She decided to ignore it and sent Matt another message. *'What are you doing for New Years?'*

'Party at the Studio,' came the response. *'Wanna come?'*

'Who's going?'

'Everyone. We do it every year.'

'I should be allowed out of here by then. What's the Studio?'

'Dance studio above the China Chef restaurant on Central Ave. Ask Laderia for directions and ride.'

'Will do. Cya there!'

LEVI HELD TIM'S CELL PHONE in his hands, feeling like he wanted to throw up. He listened as the shower began to run, and then took the phone into the kitchen. He unlocked the phone, scrolled through the contacts list, and hit the call button. It took one ring before he heard the familiar distasteful tone. "What do you want, Tim?"

"Felix, it's Levi."

There was a pause. "What do you want?"

"I—we need to talk."

"Alright. What is this about, Levi?"

"There's a werewolf in Marshfield."

Levi could feel Felix smirking through the phone. "Of course there is…so you're finally a believer? How did that happen?"

"I saw the transformation," Levi said. "But you can wait to rub it in. There's a problem."

"And what is that?"

"There's a good chance this particular werewolf is responsible for the disappearance of a girl at Columbus. She's been missing since the Thanksgiving basketball game."

Felix's silence on the other end of the line was deafening. "What are you going to do about it?"

"I know how to deal with vampires, Felix. Not werewolves. What should I do?"

"That's not my problem, Levi. If I were you, I'd kill the werewolf and get it over with."

"That's not an option."

"Why not? I thought this werewolf was an immediate danger."

"It's another student."

"That means nothing. The longer the curse is tolerated, the greater the chance it spreads."

"Isn't—isn't there a cure?"

"Yes. Death."

"There must be a way—"

"Get off that tangent, Levi. You'll waste your life looking for a cure. A lot of hunters have."

"Someone must have found a way."

"The curse is for life; the only thing you can do is put the sufferer out of their misery. Think of yourself as a veterinarian. Sometimes you gotta put them down."

"I'm not strong enough to kill a werewolf."

"Maybe not, but a werewolf is only a werewolf during a full moon. He's a man the rest of the month. Can you kill a man?"

Arthur Harris's face swam in Levi's mind. "I won't do that."

"You won't," Felix said. "But you could."

"I could, but it's not going to happen."

"Why not? It should be easy. You already know who it is—"

"Because he's a normal person—"

"If this really is another student, I'm sure you've seen other changes; angry outbursts, overheating, the need to be alpha—"

"He's just a football player. How is that different from be—?"

"You know what you have to do, Levi."

Levi brought his fist down on the countertop. "I won't do it!"

"Then why did you call me?"

"Isn't there another way?"

"I already told you, kid."

"But you have connections—you know the slayer families, the werewolf hunters. Maybe someone else figured something out. Please, Felix—"

"Breathe, kid. I'm going to recommend you to the best werewolf hunter I know. He once told me he found the cure."

"Are you—for real? That's great. You got his number?"

A sarcastic laugh. "Trust me, you're going to want to see him face-to-face."

"I can't drive to Chicago."

"Lucky for you, he's in Marshfield. You can find him at the Stony River Assisted Living Retirement Home."

"He's retired? Is he still any good?"

"He's the best. That's why he's still alive."

"Okay—what's his name?"

"Randolph. I gotta go. And remember, don't tell Tim about any of this. He can't know anything that might lead him to become a werewolf hunter. You haven't told him about this other student, have you?"

"No," Levi lied.

"Do not take him with you to see Randolph, either. I won't have it."

"Okay."

"Goodbye Levi." The call ended.

"WHAT ARE WE DOING HERE?" Tim asked as they pulled up to the Stony River Assisted Living Retirement Home. "You're not having me get another job, are you?"

"Of course not." Levi parked. "We're here to talk to someone."

"Who would want to talk to us? And about what? Is this about Lancaster?"

"He's a separate mess," Levi sighed. "There's a man here who knows about werewolves."

"Really?" Tim looked skeptical. "More than me?"

"Yes," Levi pulled the key from the ignition. "I need to talk to him."

"How'd you hear about him?"

"I got my sources."

Tim gave him a strange look.

"Let's go."

They got out of the truck, shut the doors, and walked into Stony River. The interior was painted in bright, sunny colors. The staff walked around in white, and the elderly meandered around with occasional assistance. Levi went up to a desk.

"I'm here to see Randolph."

"Are you a relative?"

"Grandson," Levi said evenly. He could feel Tim's dubious gaze intensifying.

The woman nodded. "You two can have a seat. We'll bring him out."

"Thank you." Levi picked up a magazine. They sat at a table and waited. He paged through photos and articles without seeing them, instead watching the clock. A nurse approached, escorting a dilapidated-looking man. He draped his arm on her for support and took tiny steps, as if moving hurt.

The nurse sat him down across the table and walked away.

The old man stared at them hard from behind his glasses. His large nose pointed first at Tim, then Levi. "Who'd you bring to visit me, Carson?" His voice was deep and raspy.

"Who?" Levi leaned forward.

"Not you, I'm talking to Carson." The old man smiled at Tim and reached a trembling hand across the table. "My son, I haven't seen you in so long."

Levi looked at Tim; his face was ashen. "Tim, are you okay?"

"What kind of joke is this?" Tim's jaw didn't move as he spoke.

"I don't know what you're talking about."

Tim punched Levi in the shoulder. "Why the fuck would you bring me here?!" The people around the room stopped and stared at them.

"I—I don't understand—"

"Felix put you up to this!" Tim stood up and punched Levi square in the face. Levi reeled, but Randolph leaned across the table with a surprising burst of agility and caught him before he fell out of his chair.

"Carson, get yourself under control," Randolph reprimanded Tim. "They're watching us." Sure enough, they managed to attract the attention of every staff member in the vicinity. "Nothing to see here, you nimrods! Get back to work, supervising the crazies!" He waved at the staff angrily, and they turned away with shrugs.

"What are you doing here, grandpa?!" Tim asked. "Felix told me you were in a mental institution!"

"I'm too old for that." Randolph tapped his spindly old fingers. "Years of good behavior will get you an upgrade like this. Why are you so shocked, Carson?"

"I'm not Carson, I'm Tim. I'm Carson's son. Your grandson."

Randolph waved it off. "Don't mess with your old man. I'll always see right through it." He pointed a crooked finger in Tim's direction.

"I-I missed you so much." Tim's eyes were shining. He went around the table and threw his arms around his grandfather. Randolph looked surprised, then hugged him back.

"Tell me, how's Harlow? Why isn't she here?"

"She's fine," Tim whispered. "She couldn't come."

"Ah, she owes me. My Harlow always was unstoppably busy." Randolph laughed. "So tell me, why are you here?"

"We're here for the werewolf cure." Levi glanced at Tim.

"Shut up, Mauer," Tim said darkly. "He doesn't know anything about werewolves."

"Ah! I thought I recognized you!" Randolph held his hand out. Levi took it, disquieted by Randolph's sudden reaction to him. The man's grip was strong despite how old and frail he looked. He had to be close to a hundred. "Little Ethan Mauer, you've gotten taller since the last time I saw you!"

"Um…" Levi felt his breath hitch in his throat. He looked at Tim, who stared at him with a mixture of hate and shock. "I'm Levi Mauer. Ethan was my father."

Randolph leaned close over the table and lowered his voice. "I'd ask you boys what year it is, but I don't want to have a heart attack this early in the morning." He cackled. "Did you marry Lorraine yet? Carson's been married to Jocelyn a couple years already. Harlow and I are expecting grandchildren."

"This is very important."

"Nothing's more important than family." Randolph tapped the table for emphasis. "So, when are you boys busting me out of here?"

"We're here because something very serious has happened." Tim refused to look at Levi. "And my friend here is convinced you know a lot about werewolves."

"Of course. I taught you everything you know." Randolph gripped Tim's shoulder. "Son, you're getting scrawny. Eat. It's good for you."

"Randolph—" Levi began.

"You want to know *what* about werewolves, vampire slayer?" Randolph fixed Levi with a wild, penetrating stare.

"I need to know the cure. How to remove the curse from a werewolf," Levi said evenly, forcing away his shock.

"Why would he know that?" Tim asked angrily.

"Because I'm the best werewolf hunter in Wisconsin." Randolph's chest puffed with pride. "I've killed two dozen werewolves."

"Have you ever cured one?" Levi asked.

Randolph scratched his chin, looking puzzled. "Who are you again? Not with the government, are you?"

"I'm...I'm Ethan Mauer." Hearing his father's name leave his lips left a tight knot in his chest.

"Then you already know." Randolph clapped his hands. "You don't need me, sir."

"I do—I need to know exactly what you know, and I need to know it now." Levi's frustration was beginning to show. "What's the cure?"

"I got it from you." Randolph squinted at Levi. "You look different somehow."

"I can't get through to him." Levi turned to Tim, who responded with a threatening glare. "Please. He knows a cure for Matt."

"We're talking after this," Tim snarled through his teeth. "You've got a lot of explaining to do."

"Fine. But help me get the cure from him."

"Grandf—I mean, dad." Tim forced a grin and Randolph looked at him and smiled back. "What's the cure for lycanthropy?"

"Aconite," Randolph nodded slowly. "The wolfsbane will ward off any werewolf. We planted it around the house to keep them away."

"Aconite," Tim breathed. "It doesn't cure a werewolf."

"No, it keeps them away." Randolph waved a hand and stared blankly at the ceiling for a moment. "What was it you needed to know?"

"The cure for lycanthropy!" Tim smacked a hand to his forehead.

"There's three things you need to cure a werewolf." Randolph held up his fingers. "Three things."

"Three things? What are they?" Levi gripped the table.

"You need them to ingest silver," nodded Randolph, "and wolfsbane. They don't like to down that at all, but if you can get them to do it in their human form, you got a shot."

"Okay, what's the third thing?" Tim asked.

"I don't really think it'll help you." Randolph shook his head. "So hard to find—"

"What is it?"

"It's the key," Randolph said. "But it doesn't—it's one of three things. The other two are silver and—"

"You covered that already," Tim seethed. "I need to know about the key."

Randolph squinted at him. "Are you talking about the saints again, Carson?"

"Saints? What saints? The New Orleans Saints? I'm talking about a key," Tim glowered. "Not about saints."

"It won't cure her," Randolph frowned. "I don't know why you didn't listen to me."

"Listen to you about—never mind. I need to know what this key is."

"It won't help your boys, Carson, now that their mother is gone." Randolph shook his head. "Poor Tim will grow up never knowing his mother. Are you going to remarry? You should remarry. Someone to help with the boys—"

"No," Tim shook his head. "What are you talking about?"

"You haven't heard about Jocelyn?" Randolph's eyes widened behind his glasses. "I'm very sorry, Carson, but…she's dead."

"What happened to Jocelyn?" Tim asked.

"Tim, who's Jocelyn —" Levi tried to interrupt, but Tim held up his hand.

Randolph's face grew grave. "It was a werewolf. She—she was put down. There was no other way."

"But I thought you knew the cure."

"I do. You need wolfsbane, silver, and St. Hubert's Key. Together. You use them for the ritual and the curse will be lifted."

"What is St. Hubert's Key?"

"It's the key to removing the curse," Randolph whispered. "But they vanished. No one knows where they are."

"There's more than one?"

"Yes, one for each hunter line, passed down across generations. There may be dozens. But, you know that already. Why are you asking me about it?" Randolph's voice grew louder. "You know they were stolen. All of them. A century ago."

"Who would want to steal them? Other werewolves?" Tim's hoarse whisper quieted the old man.

Randolph gazed at Levi. "The vampires." His face contorted with confusion before turning to Tim. "Carson? What are you doing here?"

"We're done here." Tim rose and stormed out.

THE STRANGLED RATTLING of Levi's truck filled the silence, emphasizing the widening divide between them. Tim didn't look at Levi and Levi didn't dare to speak. When they got inside the apartment, Levi felt a punch to the back of the head. Stars exploded in front of his eyes and he fell forward onto the kitchen floor.

"What the fuck was that about?" Tim yelled as he circled Levi. "You've been playing me!" He kicked Levi in the stomach as hard as he could. Levi gasped, but didn't retaliate. Tim dragged Levi up by the collar of his leather jacket and marched him backwards into the living room, threw him down on the floor, and straddled him. He punched Levi across one side of the face, then the other. He alternated back and forth a few times. Levi let Tim vent his fury, the unending series of stars in front of his eyes oddly comforting. Eventually he tasted copper in his mouth. He heard Tim pant for breath, then stand and pace.

Levi sat up. His dizzy vision found Tim in the kitchen marching back and forth.

"Tim," he said, almost choking at a clot of blood in his mouth. "Tim, calm down."

"How the fuck did you know he was there?!" Tim demanded. "There's absolutely no way—someone told you!"

"Felix," Levi massaged his jaw. "He told me."

"You've been speaking with him?!"

"I had to."

"Why?!"

"He knows a lot about werewolves—"

"So do I!"

"No you don't. Not compared to Felix. I asked him if there's a cure. He said a guy named Randolph would know, and that he's in Marshfield. He was the best werewolf hunter he knew—"

"Bullshit, Levi. This is bullshit. Felix wouldn't keep that from me—"

"Yes he would, Tim." Levi breathed. The stinging pain in his face made every word hurt. "He thought you were better off not knowing."

"How does lying to me make me better off, Levi?! Explain that!"

"He thought you couldn't handle—"

"Oh, so you could handle the truth, but I can't? Who gets to make those judgment calls?!"

"I had no idea Randolph was your grandfather! Felix told me not to take you along. I did anyway."

"Why wouldn't he want me to see my family?"

"Felix thinks you don't know anything about werewolves. He wanted to protect you—"

"From what? My family's suddenly obvious history of dealing with the supernatural? Dammit, Levi! You're from a vampire slayer family. I'm from a *werewolf hunting family*. This is—this is destiny."

"Felix said the family business was over."

"He doesn't get to decide that. And neither do you!"

"It wasn't my decision, Tim. I only wanted to respect his wishes."

"There's something else you're not telling me," Tim paced. "I can feel it."

"No there isn't," Levi lied.

"What's the real story of my mother and father? You must know."

"I don't know."

"Come clean. What happened to my father?"

"I don't know," Levi lied again.

"What's Felix holding over you? He must—"

"There's nothing."

"So you were just an asshole to me for the fun of it."

Levi kept quiet as Tim passed judgment.

"Play it that way. Conspiring with my asshole brother, making calls about me and my life that were never yours to make." Tim stormed away from him. He came back and threw a pile of clothes at Levi's feet. "I wasted valuable time helping you. I risked my life for you. And now I can't even look at you. I want you out of my apartment. This friendship—this bullshit is over."

SAMANTHA, LADERIA, AND BECCA arrived in the parking lot behind the China Chef restaurant. Even from there, they could spot the party as lights flashed in the windows on the upper floor. A block away stood Tower Hall, a rising brick lady far more elegant than the surrounding buildings. The clock gleamed in the floodlights.

"Another year is about to end." Becca said.

"Big dealio." Laderia adjusted herself. "Let's get inside. I gotta turn Stefan Willfahrt into Stefan Valdez. That's my Spanish mission for this *noche*."

"You gonna give him a New Year's kiss?" Samantha grinned.

"If I gotta hold him down." Laderia smiled hungrily.

They marched up the icy flight of stairs leading to the entrance, and slipped inside. Blacklights occupied every light socket. The crowd wore glow sticks and neon. The entire senior class was there, and most of the juniors and sophomores. A couple freshmen milled through the crowd.

"Let's find Natalie and Jennifer," Becca shouted over the music, and pulled them through the crowd of students. They found the largest room in the old dance studio. Mirrors lined one wall with a ballet bar, the other wall covered in neon-painted cardboard. Strands of Christmas lights stretched across the ceiling, along with rolls of toilet paper. Dylan stood by the DJ, who turned out to be Stefan.

"This house is on fire!" Stefan hollered in his thick German accent. The crowd cheered and resumed bumping and grinding.

"Hey Dylan!" Samantha popped up next to him. He was shirtless with neon hand prints running down his body and a pink neon fedora on his head. "Have you seen Jennifer?"

"She's over there," he gestured into the dancing mob with his cup. Samantha turned and saw Jennifer and Natalie grinding on each other in matching neon boots and vests.

"What are they doing?!"

"Don't stop them," he yelled. "This beat is sick!"

"This is why they make us go to confession twice a year." Samantha made her way through the crowd and pulled Natalie aside. The redhead's eyes were as wide as her smile.

"Oh, Sammy, you made it! I love your outfit! You look like a Jetson! Do you like my hair extensions? They glow in the blacklight!"

Samantha brushed it aside. "Did you hear what happened?"

"About you and Matt? I'm so sorry you broke up!" Her neon makeup made her frown rather clownish.

"What? No, we're still together." Samantha was puzzled. "My mom just *thinks* we broke up. Why do you think we broke up?"

"Oh, nothing," Natalie said quickly, leaping back into the mob with Jennifer. Samantha tapped Jennifer on the shoulder.

"What do you want?" she yelled over the music.

"Where's Matt?"

"With Kaeli. They were over here for a while—"

"Then disappeared!" Natalie interrupted.

"Kaeli's probably eating his face right now!" Jennifer wiggled two glow-painted fingers at Dylan.

"Don't tell her that! We don't know if anything's really going on!" Natalie protested.

"She can't stay naive forever. Keep a better tab on your boyfriend, Symanski!" Jennifer ran over and pulled Dylan onto the dance floor. Becca and Laderia flanked Stefan as he monitored the computers and makeshift lighting system.

Samantha meandered through the crowd, searching for a shape that could be Matt. She asked several people where he was and found her way to a side room off the main party, where a lone blacklight bulb barely illuminated a boy and girl making out. "Matt!" she yelled with uncertainty.

"Shit!" The boy leapt away from the girl.

"Oh come off it," Kaeli's annoyed voice said. "You two are done. Get over it."

"No, we're not!" Matt turned to Samantha.

"We are now." Samantha was breathless as she stared into Matt's horrified face. Smeared neon lipstick glowed on his mouth and neck. She walked out of the room.

"Wait! Samantha!" He reached out and snagged her wrist, effortlessly pulling her back to him. "Let me explain—"

"You told me you wanted us to be together!" Samantha slapped him across the face with all of her might. Matt released her. "Why are you so predictable?! And why do I keep putting up with this?"

She made her way back to the dance floor, where Laderia was grinding on Stefan while the onlookers were frozen in shock. Natalie wouldn't meet Samantha's eyes, and for some reason, that made Samantha angry. She ran out of the party and stood on the landing outside, looking over the parking lot. She inhaled the cold air and blew it out slowly, letting the fog float away. She liked how it formed vague shapes before vanishing into the night. Maybe she should take up smoking? Oh wait. Asthma. She stared at the clock gracing the top of Tower Hall. A little woman stood there in the lights, looking out over the town, her large hat and sunglasses unmistakable.

"King Lear," Samantha whispered, a sardonic smile twisting onto her face. "What should I do?"

The gnarled little woman turned in her direction, and even though she shouldn't have been able to, Samantha could have sworn King Lear heard her.

291

CHRISTMAS BREAK ENDED and the school year resumed. Nikki Becker was still missing, her father wasn't teaching, and the student body was still discussing their holiday. Samantha felt empty as she sat in psychology. She looked at Levi, in the seat next to her like usual, slouched over, chin resting on crossed arms—but he wasn't sleeping. He stared off into space, looking completely detached from reality.

"Hey. Are you alright?"

"Huh?" He blinked.

She lowered her voice. "You're not high right now, are you?"

"No," he replied with a shadow of a smile. "Are *you* alright? I heard the news about Matt."

"I should have seen that coming a mile off," Samantha said. "My mom was…right. He turned out to be a real animal, just like you said."

"Matt's not all bad." Levi's voice was muffled by his arms. "He's going through some crazy shit."

"There's no excuse for anybody to act the way he did."

"I think this time there is."

Samantha clenched her pen. "You're not serious."

"It's his issue to deal with, not yours. If he gets it cured, then you two could—well, you know."

"A little over a month ago, you told me to leave him. Remember that?"

"Things change…people make mistakes."

"You don't sound like Levi right now. What's going on with you?"

"You don't know me, Samantha. But know I'll get through it. Just like you'll get through it." Levi's demeanor was gentle, almost beaten down, even as his eyes hinted at some inner strength.

Samantha tilted her head. "You're oddly reassuring today."

"It's a day to be oddly reassuring."

"What happened to you? You're not angry at me."

"I don't wanna talk about it."

"Ever the mystery, aren't you?" She ran her fingers through her hair, sending it rippling in the fluorescent lights. "Sometimes Stoner, I think you'd be fun to hang out with…sometimes. In very fleeting instances."

"I don't know if I could hang out with a girl who lives in a haunted house," Levi let out a humorless chuckle.

Samantha's eyes widened. "You really think my house is haunted?"

"You don't?"

"I'M TELLING YOU, it's been weeks since they've talked." Jennifer leaned against the locker next to Samantha's. "See? Watch this. Here comes Stoner." She nodded to Levi coming from one end of the hallway. "And here comes Dealer." She pointed with her thumb to Tim on the other end. "They walk towards each other, then BAM! They look away, and each continue onward, forlorn and alone."

"That's so sad," Natalie droned as she checked her phone.

"I think this is the perfect time to go work on some lower prices from Tim." Jennifer fluffed out her wavy brown hair and adjusted her cleavage. "Lonely boys need company."

"You're despicable." Becca made a face. "They must have had a fight. Leave Timmy alone."

"Best time to get something from a man is when they're distracted." Jennifer tugged her shirt down. "Works with my father." She sauntered off after Tim.

"There's something wrong with her," Becca said to no one in particular.

"What happened between them?" Natalie asked. "Not that I really care, but Stoner and Dealer had such a nice bromance going on."

"I don't think that qualifies as a bromance." Becca narrowed her eyes. "But then again I'm not *that* familiar with the definition."

"I'm sure it has something to do with Matt," Samantha said with more than a little conviction.

"Not everything is about you and Matt!" Becca snapped her

fingers in Samantha's face.

"I'm serious, Becca. He texted me over the break. Said he was hanging out with Levi and Tim."

"That's really, really odd," Natalie looked up from her phone. "They're, like, not even in the same social circle…is Matt buying drugs from Tim?"

"Unlikely." Samantha pulled a book from her locker. "His doctors would have noticed something during his checkups, so I don't think he's buying drugs. He's on whatever the Clinic wants him to be on."

"That's, um, okay, right? They want to make him better." Natalie smiled.

"It's not working yet." Samantha tossed her hair. "Can you believe February's almost here and he still hasn't sent me an apology for New Year's Eve?"

"Maybe he's not sorry." A subtle note of satisfaction reverberated in Becca's voice.

"Well, at least one good thing came of that party." Natalie's eyes pointed down the hall. "Laderia and Stefan are now an item."

"And that is the most unusual item I've seen in my years at this school." Becca raised her eyebrows as Laderia approached on Stefan's arm, beaming madly.

"Hey chicas," she chirped. "Stefan and I were just on our way to the cafeteria. I ordered us a romantic bucket for two from KFC."

"No—no chicken for us?" Natalie asked.

"Not while I got a man to feed," Laderia replied. "He gets one, I get three. There's gotta be some balance. Unfortunately this means no more sharing lunch food with you. Sorry chicas."

"There goes our gravy train," Becca sighed.

"Wow. She's totally blowing us off." Natalie waved her hand as Laderia and Stefan made their way to the cafeteria. "It's like Samantha and Matt all over again. No offense, Sammy, but you were a grade-A bitch."

"I wish I could say none taken, but that's a little—"

"I should have dated Jacob Bauman when he asked me," Natalie pouted. "Then I could guilt him into feeding me."

"You could pack yourself a lunch." Samantha shut her locker.

"Whose side are you on, anyway?" Natalie rolled her eyes.

LEVI SAT at the lunch table, alone again. The occasional glances of his fellow classmates did little to cheer him up. He'd been sitting alone for almost a month now, and was used to moping about his current situation at the table. He let his mind wander to how he was going to pay for the many repairs his house needed, especially the window in the master bedroom. It made the place so much colder. He resorted to flipping the mattress from the bed up and blocking off the room to help keep the heat in, but knew he needed to fix it.

A shadow on the table interrupted his thoughts and he looked up at Tim. He felt a thrill of hope and squashed it back to some invisible place. "What do you want, man?"

"Matt texted me," Tim said through lips that barely moved, looking straight ahead instead of at Levi. "I told him you and I aren't speaking. He told me to get over it, lives are at stake. So I'm here to relay that message as you're such a tightwad you don't even have a phone. In short, Matt needs a place to transform this full moon or he's liable to rip a head off."

"It didn't work out so well last time," Levi replied. "What makes you think it could work this time?"

"I have a theory." Tim's carefully neutral face couldn't conceal the light in his eyes.

"Do I get to hear it?"

"Give me a ride home. Then I'll tell you."

LEVI WAITED IN THE LOBBY for Tim. He walked over with Jennifer at his side.

"Oh come on, Tim, it'll make you feel better." She was practically purring. "You and I watching movies, hanging out, getting high—"

"I got shit to do." Tim waved her off. Jennifer's jaw dropped, her gum falling out of her mouth onto the floor.

"I don't believe you." Her face reverted to its usual look of disdain. "Here I am, going out of my way to be sympathetic, to be there for you—"

"This is the part of the conversation where bullshit *stops* spewing." Tim turned to her. "I'd love to hang out with you, Jennifer. Genuinely, I would. I would also love it if you wanted me for more than my—my business."

"Fuck you," she said, smooth as glass.

"Maybe one day soon." Tim looked her up and down before walked down the hallway like a runway model, flashing the bird over her shoulder.

"She's amazing." Tim cracked a smile at Levi.

"I never understood that thing you have for her, and I never will."

"When you fess up to why you like Symanski, then I'll explain it to you." They walked silently down the senior hallway to the parking lot entrance.

After they got in the truck, Levi turned to Tim. "So, what is your theory?"

Tim dug in his backpack, and pulled out a bag of wet leaves.

"Your weed is in terrible shape." They pulled out of the parking lot.

"This isn't weed. It's aconite. You know, wolfsbane. What I have in this bag is the real deal, not ground-up twigs in capsules."

"And you want Matt to…"

"Eat it."

"Something tells me he'd prefer to smoke it."

"It would take too long to dry out. Besides, if you eat it, the effect lasts longer."

"Then how come his pills don't work?"

"Same reason pills don't work for a lot of people. You need a meal with those pills to absorb them properly. Cut the doubt. This will look a lot more appetizing when presented in the right way."

"When's the full moon?"

"Tomorrow night." Tim sat in the passenger seat, waiting for the reply.

Levi felt his throat constricting and took a breath. "Come over whenever."

Levi pulled up to Tim's apartment. They sat in the truck for a moment. "Any developments in the vampire world that I should be aware of?" Tim asked.

"No," Levi murmured. "Unless you got news for me from inside the funeral home."

"I haven't showed up there since, uh, you know." Tim stared out the windshield at the bland brick of the building. "Thanks for the ride."

Levi nodded. Tim got out and disappeared into the apartment.

"YOU'RE SO...pissed," Samantha said.

"Yes," Jennifer grabbed Samantha's arm. "I need someone sane to help me keep a level head."

"Why? Isn't it just dinner?"

"No, my father's staging an intervention. I need you to vouch for my good behavior," Jennifer snapped. "So be prepared to lie your ass off. Got it?"

"Why couldn't Natalie or Becca—"

"You're the only friend I have that the police like," Jennifer replied. "Your TP job on Barb's house is still the talk of the precinct—when they're not talking about Nikki."

"But I wasn't even the one who—you're joking with me."

"I wish I was," Jennifer sighed. "Go ask your mom. Now." She shoved Samantha out the front doors of the school as Mrs. Symanski pulled up in her black SUV.

Samantha gestured for the window to be rolled down. "Hey mom. Jennifer wants me to eat dinner at her house tonight. Can I?"

"Will Matt be there?"

Samantha's cheeks flushed. "No, she's the police chief's

daughter."

"Do you need a ride?"

"No."

"Have fun! Love you!" Mrs. Symanski smiled and waved. Samantha waved back as her mother pulled away.

Jennifer joined her at the curb as Dylan pulled around in his Navigator. It was a short ride to Jennifer's house, a split-level on Shawano Drive.

Dylan let them out at the end of the driveway after Jennifer gave him an absurdly passionate kiss. "Come on, bitch." Jennifer stormed up to the front door of the house and flung it open. "I'm home!"

"Already?" A woman came around the corner with a wine glass in her hand. She was a brunette, thin, with watery, puffy blue eyes. "Nice to see you, baby. Oh, you brought a little friend home."

"Maybe little compared to Laderia."

Samantha contented herself with a mental image that involved her stomping on Jennifer's face.

"You girls will always be little to me." The woman smiled and held out her hand. "I'm Mrs. Cromwell."

"Samantha Symanski." She barely shook the woman's hand before it was snatched away.

"Jennifer never mentioned she had a friend named Samantha."

"Thank you?" Samantha suddenly felt uncomfortable.

"You're an odd one, aren't you?" Mrs. Cromwell tilted her head and studied Samantha. "At least you're pretty. Jennifer, dinner will be served when your father gets home." She turned and headed around the corner.

"What was that about? You think I'm fat?" Samantha whispered to Jennifer.

Jennifer rolled her eyes. "Follow me." She led Samantha upstairs to her room.

"Ooh, I get to see Satan's lair," Samantha grimaced. "So exciting."

Jennifer ushered her into the bedroom.

"This can't be your room." Samantha looked around as she walked in. The walls were a pale pink, the bed white wrought iron with a desaturated purple and white comforter and lacy pillows. The furniture looked antique, frilly. Pictures of flowers adorned the walls. "Where are the fire pits and tortured souls?"

"What is that supposed to mean?" Jennifer promptly began checking under her bed and behind her pillows.

"Where's all the stuff that you like?" Samantha stared at Jennifer's bored face. "Flower pictures? You're not eighty years old. This looks like a guest room."

"I'm not here very often." Jennifer began going through drawer after drawer. "It's a place to sleep and it holds my clothes."

"Weird." Samantha shook her head. "My room has things in it."

"Ya, butterflies." Jennifer snorted. "At least you're not the girl who has tons of horse stuff. That's Becca."

"Butterflies are the only bug I like. My dad used to catch them for me when I was a little girl."

"My dad catches criminals. You don't see me lining shelves with them." Jennifer hunted through her closet.

"What are you looking for?"

"The nanny cam. My parents like to spy on me when I'm in here too long. It's usually in a teddy bear—"

"Are you serious?"

"It's not here."

"We should get some homework done—"

"Let's not." Jennifer turned on her radio and flopped on her perfectly-made bed. "We're going over our strategy."

"We have a strategy?"

"For dinner. You have to help me get through this. If they ask if I do any drugs, say no. If they ask if I'm sexually active, say no—"

"Are you?"

"None of your business, brat. Did I ever ask *you* that question?"

THE SOLE OBITUARY in the Marshfield News-Herald was for a burial in Pittsville, so Levi was okay with staying home. Stretching out on his bed, he stared at the ceiling, a light bulb in the hallway his only illumination. He heard Matt's car pull up. He went downstairs and met Tim and Matt as they walked up to the door.

"Welcome back." Levi addressed Matt, who nodded and ducked inside. Tim came in after him, holding a pan.

"What's this?"

"Aconite brownies," he whispered. "Don't eat them, there's enough aconite in there to kill a man."

"What?" Matt looked pallid.

"Relax, it won't kill *you*." Tim set the tray on the counter. "He ate about half the pan already. I should open a bakery."

"That would interrupt your werewolf hunting," Levi said before he could stop himself.

Tim's face was stone. "Don't talk about that," he said. "It pisses me off."

"Okay." Levi ran a hand through his hair. "Do you think this will work?"

"It should."

"My house can't take any more of this," Levi said. "I'll freeze to death."

"Maybe you should just pay your bills and live a comfortable life." Tim walked around the room, looking at the empty light bulb sockets.

"I do pay my bills. I got my electricity back on, and my water is running now that I've had the furnace going." It was Levi's turn to get pissed. "It's a lot more expensive with a gaping hole in the house."

"Alright, don't be testy, I didn't mean anything by it." Tim moved the pan from the counter to the table.

"When's the moon's zenith?"

"Thankfully it's soon." Tim turned to Matt, who was shoveling in brownies. "Rumor has it you're seeing Kaeli."

"No I'm not," Matt mumbled with a full mouth. "I got drunk. We were talking and I don't know what happened. We're just friends."

"You need to tame your inner beast," Tim smirked.

"That's why I got you guys," Matt swallowed.

"Take your pills." Levi handed him a bottle of water, Samantha's face floating in the front of his mind.

"SO WHAT'S THE STORY ABOUT New Years' Eve?" Jennifer quizzed Samantha.

"You were at my house. We watched the ball drop on television. My mom gave you a ride home."

"Perfect," Jennifer nodded. There was a knock at the door.

"Girls, dinner's ready," Mrs. Cromwell's voice called.

"Whatever!" Jennifer yelled. "Let's give it a minute. She takes forever going down the stairs with that wine glass in her hand…and I don't want to walk with her."

They joined the Cromwells at the dining room table, Mr. and Mrs. Cromwell at opposite ends. The air felt electric, like they were intruding on a private battle. Samantha and Jennifer sat next to each other, Jennifer taking the spot closer to her father.

"Who's your friend?" Mr. Cromwell addressed Jennifer.

"Sarah," said Mrs. Cromwell.

"Samantha," Jennifer corrected without looking at her father.

"Oh. Welcome Samantha. Everybody dig in." Mr. Cromwell was a husky man with a handlebar mustache and a worn-out face. He passed several dishes around until everyone had chicken, mashed potatoes and corn on their plates. "Jennifer," he began, "how's school?"

"Fine." Jennifer concentrated on ladling gravy onto her potatoes.

"How are the students coping?"

"Fine," Jennifer repeated.

"Are you sure—"

"For Heaven's sake, Bill, she said it was fine. Don't interrogate your own daughter in front of company." Mrs. Cromwell took a healthy swig from her wine glass.

"Slow down on the wine, Hilary." Mr. Cromwell scowled. "Like you said, we have company."

Mrs. Cromwell looked him dead in the eye and drank down the rest of her glass. "Excuse me girls." She stood and walked into the kitchen. Mr. Cromwell's scowl somehow grew more severe as he watched his wife leave.

"You still seeing that Dylan kid?" he asked, turning to his daughter.

"Am I, Samantha?" Jennifer stared at Samantha as she cut her chicken.

"You are—not," Samantha covered. "It was over a long time ago."

"Yes it was." Jennifer ate her chicken.

"So...um...how's the Nikki Becker search going?" Samantha turned to Mr. Cromwell. He looked at her, surprised.

"Stalled for now," he said. "Got a lot of leads to sort through."

"Like Matt Stauber?" Samantha couldn't believe she asked.

"He's not a suspect for now." Mr. Cromwell narrowed his eyes.

"Oh, that's a relief," Samantha forced a weak smile. "He was my boyfriend for a while."

"How did you know he was a suspect?"

"He was the only student who got a lot of police attention," Samantha set her fork down. "The whole school knew."

"I should have sent you to public school." Mr. Cromwell said to Jennifer.

"Do you have any theories on what happened to her?"

"Nothing I can reveal, Samantha. Eat some chicken."

"But this is your house, can't you tell—"

"That's not how my job works."

Samantha shrugged. "Sorry. No one has a clue where she went. I remember there were no tracks from the site where she was taken. Nothing was found in the snow except the blood and—"

"Oh yes, you were in the search party," Mr. Cromwell nodded, jumping to a new topic. "Jennifer, you did that too, didn't you?"

"Did you forget?" Jennifer glowered.

"Any strange leads?" Samantha pressed. "I've watched crime

shows on TV and they always say the police get a lot of strange leads when people go missing."

"They do indeed," Mr. Cromwell agreed, his mustache twitching in appreciation of Samantha's interest. Jennifer rolled her eyes.

"Tell her about the crazy lady." Jennifer gestured to her father with her fork. "About what she said."

"What crazy lady?" asked Samantha.

"You know who," Jennifer hinted.

"King Lear? I saw her on the clock tower on New Years' Eve!"

"No, you were at home on New Years' Eve, and I came over." Jennifer emphasized every syllable.

"Oh, yeah. Must have been another night." Samantha took a gulp of water.

"Anyway, father, you told me the story, you can tell her."

Mr. Cromwell gave them a look. "She called us up and claimed she saw a girl flying through the air in a swarm of bats."

"For real?"

"That woman's a loon. She makes several crazy calls a year. Claims she's psychic. She's a real train wreck." Mr. Cromwell shook his head. "Speaking of train wrecks..." His wife entered with two bottles of wine.

"I couldn't decide between red and white." Mrs. Cromwell set the open bottles on the table and slipped into her chair.

"That's a lot of wine for one meal." The words slipped out before Samantha could stop herself.

"Mind your own business, sweetie." Mrs. Cromwell poured herself a glass of the red.

"Hilary, that's enough," Mr. Cromwell said. Samantha's eyes widened as the dread of an impending storm filled the room.

"What are you going to do, Bill? Go to your whore? Complain about your wretched, unsympathetic wife?" Mrs. Cromwell drank her glass down and poured another.

"Not in front of company," Mr. Cromwell grunted. "Get a hold of yourself."

"Don't avoid the truth," Jennifer snapped at her father. He slapped her across the face, the sound reverberating through the house. Jennifer held a hand over her cheek and met Samantha's eyes. "I'll be in my room." She stood to leave.

"You'll sit your ass back down," Mr. Cromwell replied. Jennifer sank into her chair, raising her chin. "Tonight we're staging an intervention."

"Jennifer doesn't have a problem—" Samantha began, but Mr. Cromwell's expression shut her up.

"You shouldn't even be here." He turned to his daughter. "Jennifer, you know better than to drag someone from outside into our family's business. It won't stop what needs to happen from happening, no matter how much you don't like it."

"Nothing needs to happen." Jennifer glared at him.

"Yes it does. All the women in this family have problems." Mr. Cromwell threw his knife and fork at his plate. "And it's about time we address the root cause."

"Your libido," Mrs. Cromwell said.

"Your alcoholism," Mr. Cromwell glared.

"She wouldn't drink so much if you weren't cheating," Jennifer started, the tears rolling down her cheeks.

"If you don't shut your mouth, I'll shut it for you!" Mr. Cromwell pounded the table. Samantha jumped. Jennifer was remarkably composed even as her makeup began to run.

"She's right, Bill." Mrs. Cromwell swirled the wine around in her glass. "You know you're the reason I drink."

"Hilary, your drinking is the reason we no longer have a relationship," Mr. Cromwell countered. "Emma's helped me to realize—"

Mrs. Cromwell yelled and threw her glass at the wall. It shattered, the red wine running down the wallpaper like blood at a crime scene. "I don't want to hear about your bimbos and sluts!"

Mr. Cromwell stood swiftly and his wife ran into the kitchen. "Get your drunk ass back here!" He went after her, and they started screaming at each other. The crash of dishes filled the air.

"You can't make me!"

"I'll divorce you, you trash!"

"I'm not going! You just want to get rid of me! You've always wanted to—"

Samantha reached out to Jennifer, her hand unsteady. "We have to leave."

Jennifer looked bored even as tears streamed down her face. "I was wrong. He's going to take *her* to rehab, not me." The handprint on her face was bright red.

"I can't stay here. This is too much for me."

"You'd rather chill at that haunted house you constantly bitch about?" Jennifer chuckled.

"Yes." Samantha stood up and ran from the table, her heart pounding. She bolted up the stairs to Jennifer's room, grabbed her things, and ran back down the stairs and out the door. She gasped for breath and looked around. The street was dead. She pulled out her phone.

"Hello Samantha!"

"Mom, I need a ride home." The words flew out of Samantha's mouth as tears filled her eyes. "They're fighting and I can't stay here, Jennifer's just sitting there like it's nothing. These people are crazy, they're yelling about divorce—"

"Slow down, slow down. Where are you?"

"I'm on Shawano Drive. Please come get me."

"I'm on my way, honey." Mrs. Symanski hung up.

LEVI FELT THE SAME NERVOUS build-up to the event as he did last time; sweaty palms and nausea hit him with full force as he glanced at the claw marks on the floor between them.

At the scheduled time for the moon's zenith, Matt lurched to the floor as if on cue.

"Oh God! It's starting," he whined as sweat dripped from his face. "Help me—I'm dying. I'm dying, I can feel it. Please!"

"You're okay." Levi kept his distance as Tim retreated down the hallway. "I'll take you to the basement. Tim! Come help me!"

They grabbed Matt as he gasped and cried. Tim helped put Matt over Levi's shoulder. "Open the basement door!"

"Which one is—"

"The one under the stairs." Levi struggled to keep Matt on his shoulders. The door was opened. "Thanks." Levi rushed Matt down the stairs as fast as he could without tripping. The rough stone walls and uneven floor were swimming in shadows. Levi set Matt at the base of the stairs and ran back up.

"Wait! Don't leave me!" Matt's face contorted. "I'm scared!" He doubled over where he sat and groaned.

"You'll be fine!" Levi said. He closed the door.

"NO!" Matt screamed as Levi locked it. He could hear him sobbing as he dragged over a chair from the dining room and braced the door.

"Is he alright?" Tim asked.

"I don't know, he's still screaming. Give it a couple minutes, he'll get quiet and transform."

"Okay," Tim nodded. "You're right. He should pass out."

They waited. Matt's screams and cries continued. Levi stood, frozen, staring at Tim who paced the hall. He glanced at the door repeatedly. "He hasn't stopped."

"I know," Levi whispered back.

"We should check on him."

"I don't want to open the door and meet a werewolf on the other side."

"Right. Better play it safe." Another five minutes passed as Matt begged and pleaded from the basement.

"Please help me! I don't know what's happening," he choked out the words between sobs.

"It really scares me to hear a guy as tough as him cry like that." Tim checked his phone. "Levi, it's fifteen minutes after the zenith. He hasn't changed."

"Maybe—maybe the moon's not high enough yet." Levi rushed to the windows and scoured the sky for the full moon. A solid ceiling of clouds destroyed any chance of seeing it.

"Levi, this isn't right." Tim slipped his phone back into his pocket, looking stricken. "Let's check on him."

Levi took down the barricade, unlocked and opened the basement door.

Tim turned on a bright light on his pone and aimed it down the stairs. Matt's body was halfway up the stairs, face-down, his clothes drenched. He was still sobbing. Levi approached him cautiously as Tim illuminated the stairs. Gingerly, Levi set a hand on Matt's shoulder. He let out a horrible, sad noise. Levi rolled him over. He almost toppled over when he saw Matt's face.

"Tim! Tim, something went wrong!"

"What do you mean?" Tim came down the steps. "Holy shit, Levi."

"We gotta get him into the kitchen." Levi maneuvered around Matt and hoisted his slumped body up the stairs. Tim cleared the way and Levi dragged him, whimpering, up onto the kitchen floor.

"What happened to him?" Tim asked in a voice that was barely a whisper.

"I don't know." Levi's panic threatened to override his system.

Matt's face had stopped in mid-transformation, the snout half the length it should have been. His mouth was crowded with a collection of half-grown teeth. Blood seeped from his gums. His ears were pointed, his skull almost soft.

"He's bleeding all over the floor." Tim grimaced. He grabbed Matt's arm and lifted it up. Matt's hand looked deformed, the fingertips bearing bloody claws that pushed the human nails up. Tim and Levi looked down the length of Matt's body, the arches of his feet now twice their former length.

"This must be the aconite." Levi looked at Tim, horror-struck. "This is why werewolves avoid it."

Matt's eyes fluttered open. The irises were gold, contrasting sharply with the bloodshot veins. "I'm dying," he gasped, blood spattering his contorted lips.

"You're not," Levi said as coolly as he could. "This is perfectly normal."

"I want you to kill me," Matt said, his voice warped, tears rolling out of his bloodshot eyes and into the thin patches of hair forming on his cheeks. "I can't fit my tongue in my mouth. Kill me. Please."

Tim shook his head.

Levi rested a hand on Matt's misshapen shoulder. "I won't. You'll get through it. Breathe."

Matt sobbed and coughed. "I don't want to." He gasped and coughed again. "I don't want to…every month. I can't."

"You won't have to. There's a cure," Tim said quickly.

Levi wasn't sure Matt even understood what Tim said. He looked up at Tim. "There's no way we can cure him."

"We need St. Hubert's Key—whatever that is," Tim blurted. "It's the last part of the cure. We have everything else."

"But the keys are gone—"

"Stolen. By vampires, Grandpa Randolph said. What do you think the chances are that Lancaster has one? Or—or maybe he knows a vampire who has one?"

Levi shook his head. "That would mean he's connected to an entire network of vampires. This is Marshfield. Vampires are few and far between."

"Levi, there is something called the internet that's used to connect billions of people across oceans. Chances are Lancaster's aware of it and is using it."

"Fair point," Levi murmured. "The implications aren't fun to consider though."

"I agree. But at least there's a possibility we can find the key."

"This really sucks."

"On the bright side, your house isn't getting damaged tonight." Tim turned his attention to Matt's panting form. "I hope he makes it. I couldn't live with a death on my hands."

Levi's mind raced to Arthur Harris's body in McMillan Marsh, and then to Lancaster.

"YOU'VE BEEN STARING AT YOUR ceiling for hours." Mrs.

Symanski sat next to her daughter on her bed.

"I'm stunned." Samantha took a deep breath. "They were so loud, and they threw things. They *need* to divorce. You and dad never did that. Why did you—?" Samantha had to stop before the tears came. "Why did it happen?"

Her mother sighed and set a hand on her daughter's shoulder. "Samantha, your father left us long before I left him. We did all the same things you saw tonight. We shouted, we threw things—we were a mess. We were also very lucky you guys weren't around for most of our fights. A lot of babysitters made good money off of our failing marriage."

"I didn't know," Samantha said. "Everything seemed fine and then you guys just decided to split."

"Nobody divorces lightly." Mrs. Symanski put a strand of Samantha's hair behind her ear. "At least, we didn't. He wasn't happy and I wasn't happy. But it wasn't your fault and it wasn't Brandon's fault."

"What went wrong?"

"I don't know," Mrs. Symanski frowned. "We were fine for years, and then one day, he wasn't satisfied with what we had. He met a woman at work and decided that was more worthwhile than sticking with me and working out whatever he didn't like. He was a grown man, even if he didn't act like it. I couldn't stop him, but I tried."

"He didn't—"

"They had their affair, it ended, and he came back to me." Mrs. Symanski forced a smile. "But it destroyed me. I couldn't take looking at his face as he shared my bed, knowing what he did with someone else. My options were divorce or murder. I knew how much it would hurt you and Brandon to not have him around anymore, so I went with the option that gave you a chance to see him again." Her mother's smile grew but Samantha saw the sadness in her eyes.

"But we haven't seen him in years."

"I can't *make* him visit, Samantha. I also can't keep him from visiting you. But if I had the power, I'd have him in town just for you guys…the other end of town. And we'd shop at different stores…and eat at different restaurants—I think you get the picture."

Samantha nodded. "He still hasn't visited us."

"I know. I hope that changes one day." She patted her daughter on the back. "Until then, you're stuck with me. I hoped this move would give the three of us a fresh start. I wanted you and Brandon to look at this as the beginning of a new life." Mrs. Symanski stood.

"Mom," Samantha said as her mother reached the door. "What do you do?"

"What do I do?" Mrs. Symanski was surprised by the question.

"What's your job, exactly? I know dad worked for the NSA for a while, and then he got into defense contracting work—but you have the same story. How can you work for a defense contractor in D.C. from Marshfield?"

"Oh Samantha, you know I can't tell you that," Mrs. Symanski smiled. "When I'm retired, maybe then I'll tell you."

"Is our house haunted?"

"You keep saying that." Mrs. Symanski shook her head. "You're perfectly safe Sam. Otherwise I wouldn't have bought this house." She walked down the hall.

Chapter 10

The Meaning of Life

When Samantha got to school, everyone was milling in the hallways, including the staff. The front office was closed, and no lights were on in any of the classrooms. Students relaxed by their lockers as Barb stormed the halls in full fury.

Samantha went to Natalie's locker. "What's going on?"

"It's the senior prank," Natalie whispered. "Try not to talk about it. The teachers are having a meltdown." She went back to perusing her locker, adorned with pictures of dresses.

"Are you…are you planning your outfit for Prom?" Samantha studied the pictures.

"Yes," Natalie chirped. "Nathan asked me to go with him."

"I thought it was only for the junior class."

"And their dates," Natalie nodded. "Laderia won't be there. Neither will Jennifer. Speaking of, you've been avoiding her since that dinner. What happened?"

"I…I got ringside seats to the Cromwell family throwdown."

"Her mom's a lush," Natalie agreed. "And her dad's, well, a—"

"Skeaze," Samantha finished. "A complete skeaze who runs our police department. Way to inspire confidence in our civil protectors."

"It's not as terrible as it sounds," Natalie replied. "On the plus side, we have more cops per capita in Marshfield than any other city in the state."

"And they still haven't found Nikki Becker," Samantha fumed. "They had cops patrolling left, right, and sideways during Homecoming."

"That's because the doctors don't want their houses toilet-papered."

Barb jingled down the hallway, an enormous set of keys in hand, followed by Father Declan.

"Be quiet, it's starting." Natalie shut her locker. Becca slid next to Samantha.

"They're about to figure it out." Becca's voice was low behind her hand.

"I don't know what's happening," Samantha whispered. "What's the prank?"

"Ask Dylan," Becca nodded to her left.

"This is too funny." Natalie pulled out her phone and started recording. They watched as Barb went to Father Declan's office and tried a key. She turned red and tried another key. And another. And another. And another. Finally Barb handed the keys to Father Declan and stormed back into the lobby. Natalie snickered as the befuddled priest kept trying keys. The first bell rang. The teachers wandered around scratching their heads as the students burst into conversation.

Samantha searched the senior hallway and found Dylan standing with Jennifer, talking to Stefan and a bunch of senior boys.

"Dylan, what did you guys do?"

Dylan beamed like an idiot as he leaned down to whisper to her. "We switched all the doors."

"What?"

"We switched all the doors in the school. Took them off the hinges and put them on different frames."

"When did this happen?!"

"Last night. Stefan's been making copies of the keys all year, and we finally had a complete set. So we broke in and switched the doors. I bet you noticed all the room numbers are wrong now."

"He's brilliant," Jennifer said, popping her gum. "They put the middle school doors in the high school and vice versa. Then they switched the doorknobs on top of it."

"How long did that take?" Samantha raised an eyebrow, avoiding Jennifer's eyes.

"Hours. Which will be how long it takes before they sort which doorknob is which." Dylan winked. "Did I mention we stole the skeleton keys?"

"You really are brilliant," Samantha whispered. "How are they going to teach us today?"

"Who cares," Dylan snickered. "I'm not sure anyone can top this."

"Challenge accepted." Matt walked up to them. "Next year, we'll blow you out of the water. Hey Samantha."

Samantha didn't acknowledge him. She turned and walked back to her locker, forcing herself to take confident, well-paced strides instead of running away like she wanted to.

"I CAN'T BELIEVE Nathan asked you to go with him." Becca made a face at Natalie as they sat in the cafeteria. "Now I gotta put up with you at Prom."

"Just because you skipped a grade doesn't mean you get to do everything first." Natalie smiled.

Samantha tuned them out as she ate her sandwich. Every now and then she glanced over at Levi, who continued to sit alone. At least he was sleeping through lunch again, instead of staring off into space. Could that be a sign things were returning to normal?

"Samantha, what do you think?" Natalie asked.

"What do I think about what?"

"I was going to go in green," Natalie said. "A sleeveless emerald green."

"A sea green would go better with your eyes," Samantha replied.

"Screw it, go in turquoise," Jennifer chimed in, surprising the other girls. She hadn't spoken much at the lunch table lately. Jennifer glanced at Laderia who sat with Stefan by the senior guys.

"Why don't you sit with Dylan?" Natalie gestured to the far table.

Jennifer scoffed. "You can't get rid of me that easily. Why don't you sit with Nathan?"

"I'm not dating Nathan," Natalie shook her red and white pigtails. "We'd be Nathan and Natalie—that's too cutesy for me."

"Nothing's too cutesy for you," Samantha rolled her eyes. "You don't like Nathan?"

"To be honest, I'm just going with him to scope out how this year's juniors will do prom so we can one-up them next year." Natalie made a face.

Becca laughed. "That's silly. Being competitive over a dance—can you believe it?"

"It's not about competition, it's about legacy," Natalie huffed. "The past two prom themes were Fairy Tale Endings and Evening of Elegance. Both were pretty classy."

"They were in a gym. You're overestimating the level of class." Becca pulled her PBJ out of a brown bag. "This year's theme is Come Sail Away, for goodness sake."

"Turquoise." Natalie looked thoughtful for a moment. "It *is* an ocean color. It could work."

"You're a speed bump." Jennifer put a piece of gum in her mouth. "A mental speed bump."

LEVI STARED AT THE MONITOR in the Marshfield Public Library. He thought back to the night Matt semi-transformed, and the promise Tim made to him about finding the cure.

He searched for images of St. Hubert's Key. Lots of pictures of oversized nails with elaborately-shaped heads popped up. "None of this is helpful," he muttered out loud. The air was devoid of a witty response. He ran his hands over his face and leaned back, staring at the ceiling. He couldn't think. Why couldn't he think?

He reverted to his normal posture and searched for Avelina Rothschild. "What have you been up to lately?" He clicked on the news tab and scanned the headlines.

"Rothschild Recovers." He clicked the article from a socialite magazine, and began to read. "Avelina Rothschild, daughter of tycoon Aaron Rothschild, was spotted walking unaided while shopping on Chicago's Magnificent Mile after months of recovery from extensive surgery. She previously suffered from a debilitating condition. It was said by one Rothschild insider to particularly affect Mrs. Rothschild's tendons and knees. Since 2003, Rothschild used wheelchairs and canes, often accompanied by a manservant or escort. We are thrilled to see her walking on her own for the first time in over a decade. Unfortunately, it was in a pair of canary-yellow Versace trousers."

Levi leaned back in his chair again, puzzled. Avelina Rothschild had to be carried into the funeral home. Levi clicked to enlarge the photo next to the article. Rothschild was striding down the Magnificent Mile, her legs long and strong in a pair of pants. A large pair of sunglasses shrouded her face. She definitely looked a lot healthier…younger even. Levi suddenly felt sick to his stomach. She couldn't be…could she?

He decided to delve a little deeper into Avelina Rothschild's history. She had to have a connection to Lancaster. How else would she know to get in contact with him? A couple searches pulled up a more detailed history.

"Avelina Rothschild was born to Aaron Rothschild and his wife Loretta in 1953. She grew up in New York—who the hell was Aaron Rothschild?!"

The librarian shushed him from her round desk. Levi waved back, barely concealing his resentment. He clicked the link to Aaron Rothschild's biography.

"Aaron Rothschild was an oil and banking tycoon in the 1920s and 30s. He had numerous ties to the mob, Al Capone, and was responsible for the construction of—whatever. Bullshit, more bullshit. Avelina Rothschild is the sole heir to his oil and banking empire." He felt like this was important. This was massively important. But he couldn't be certain. He needed a second pair of eyes. Or a trampoline.

LEVI KNOCKED ON THE DOOR, feeling very awkward. It opened and Tim appeared, looking wary. "What is it man?"

"I need to talk to you," Levi murmured. "Can I come in?"

"No." Tim stood in the doorway.

"But I gave you a ride home that time—"

"You also fed me bullshit for months while I let you live here," Tim replied. "I'm not making the mistake of having you in my commode."

"I think you mean abode."

"I probably do."

"You're smoking pot right now."

"Maybe I am." Tim blew a cloud of smoke in Levi's face. "What's it to you?"

"I need your opinion on some information. A sober opinion. But right now I don't think that's possible."

"You need to open up your mind," Tim made a grand gesture. "Or you'll continue to make the mistake of thinking possible things are impossible."

"Is that an invitation to come in?" Levi's mouth twitched.

Tim knocked on the door and looked at him. "Are you a vampire? Do you need permission?"

"Obviously today, yes I do," Levi stepped in.

"Stop trying to sound clever. You came here for my help. What's the problem?" Tim shut the door.

The living room was an absolute haze as Levi took a seat on the couch and tried not to breathe. "I've hit a dead end."

"A dead end on what?"

"Lancaster. I no longer have any eyes or ears on the inside of the funeral home." Levi gestured at Tim. "I've drained my brain trying to find Avelina Rothschild's connection to him."

"Who the hell is Avelina Rothschild?"

"That old woman we saw getting taken into the funeral home that night."

"I can barely recall." Tim shrugged. "What about Avelina Rothschild confuses you?"

"She's the daughter of a huge tycoon, and the heiress of his massive fortune. She's single—"

"Ooh, a rich single girl. Sounds fine to me," Tim chuckled, his voice muffled by smoke.

"Focus, Tim. For a long time she was in poor health—but all of a sudden, newspapers are reporting that she's healthy, glowing—"

"Plastic surgery will make anyone look good."

"It's not plastic surgery. She was suffering from some disease that was killing her tendons and knees or something. She couldn't walk. Now she can."

"Good for her."

"Tim, we saw her the Friday after Thanksgiving. It's February. Could she really have gotten her knees and tendons replaced and been completely rehabilitated in less than three months?"

"I'm not a doctor, Levi."

"I know. Just speculate with me. Wouldn't surgery that massive take a lot longer to heal? I mean, she's walking down Chicago streets like it's nothing, when before she had to be carried to her wheelchair. Something's very odd about that."

Tim responded with a blank stare. "What about the doctor? There was a doctor too, wasn't there?"

"Reinhart. He's a surgeon."

"You think he performed surgery on her that night in the funeral home?"

"Maybe. Either that or she's a vampire. If she's a vampire, it doesn't explain the doc. If it was surgery, that would mean there's an operating room in the funeral home. And that's ridiculous. Who wouldn't notice that?"

"There were doors to rooms I wasn't allowed in." Tim shrugged. "It's possible, man."

"But what on earth does Lancaster need with an operating room? And why couldn't this wealthy woman get her surgery at some legitimate hospital? We have a world-class medical facility right here in Marshfield for crying out loud—"

"They're experimenting on werewolves," Tim replied in a hoarse whisper. "Not exactly reputable."

"They are *not* experimenting on werewolves. You're the one who was experimenting and mixing other stuff with Matt's medications."

"I'm going to ignore that last bit." Tim took a drag. "So Lancaster is secretly a doctor to the socialites of decades past. Dun, dun, DUN!"

"Shut up, Tim."

"You will not tell me to shut up in my own apartment." Tim got right in Levi's face. "Show me some damn respect. And stop being an asshole." He stood up and almost fell back down.

"I'm not being an asshole."

"Yes you are."

"I'm not."

"You are. You come up into my apartment, asking for my help. But the whole time you're here, you're looking at me sideways like I'm garbage, and why? Because I smoke pot? Big deal. I sell most of it. I could pay my own tuition if I felt like it. You don't see me judging you for killing Arthur Harris, do you?"

"Tim—"

"Do you?!"

"No, you dropped that a long time ago."

"Yes I did. Follow my example. And keep your judgment to yourself." Tim stormed into his tiny kitchen.

"Tim, I think Avelina Rothschild is a vampire."

"Don't try to change the—what?"

"Look, I printed off the picture from the article. She looks good, right?" He held out the paper. Tim walked over and took a look.

"She's not my type." He wrinkled his nose.

"She looks healthy."

"Healthy, but old."

"Better than when we saw her."

"Ya, I'll give you that. What's your point?"

"A two-month recovery time for a surgery that probably replaced knees and tendons is a little short, right?"

"I don't know."

"You're one of the most qualified people I know to answer health questions."

"You really need to get out more, Levi." Tim gave him a look.

"Give me your best guess."

"I'd guess two to three months. But so what? It's not outside the realm of possibility; no supernatural explanation required."

"You cannot tell me you're not the least bit suspicious about how fast she healed."

"So what if I am? What do you want me to do about it, go ask her if she's been craving blood lately?"

"No, but that's not a horrible idea." Levi raised an eyebrow. "I want you to get your job at the funeral home back."

Tim gave Levi a long, cold sneer. "No. *You* get a job at the funeral home."

"I can't, remember?"

"You're not making me do it. Fuck you."

"Tim, I don't want to do this, but I will if I have to."

"Do what?"

"Turn you in for drug use. I could report you to Barb, to the Marshfield Police, to Social Services—"

Tim laughed out loud. "Are you kidding me?! I can report you for *murder!* To all the same people. Face it Levi, you don't have my dirt, my resources, or my trust. You have no power over me."

"You're right, I don't," Levi rubbed his knees. "It was stupid to resort to those measures. I just need you to be inside the funeral home. I would do it myself if I could."

"Well I won't," Tim shook his head. "Here's an idea. Why don't you just ask Lancaster if Adelaide is a vampire?"

"Avelina," Levi corrected him.

"Whatever."

"I can't ask him because then he'd know I've been watching the place. That'll piss him off. The goal is to do this without his knowledge."

Tim shook his head. "I still don't know what you're expecting me to find. Why would he keep information on Avelina in the funeral home?"

"I think you're just chicken."

"I think she may be a werewolf," Tim said, smoke rolling out of his mouth.

"You think everyone's a werewolf."

"So far I've been right," Tim replied. "Matt healed really fast from that botched transformation. He was ready to go home by seven in the morning. Lycanthropy could explain her speedy recovery."

"That's a possibility I haven't considered," Levi rubbed his jaw. "But that just gets us back to the whole vampires and werewolves thing. If Rothschild is a werewolf, why would she get surgery at a funeral home? If she healed like that, she'd be in perfect health and wouldn't need it."

"Maybe she didn't get surgery. What did Grandpa Randolph say? Something about St. Hubert's Key. And the vampires."

"He said the vampires took the keys." Levi rubbed his forehead with his hands.

"Well, that's just mean-spirited. Levi, maybe you're going about this all wrong. Maybe you should focus more on Reinhart and drop Avelina Rothschild."

"But she's prominent. It's really a mystery—"

"It's a mystery what a Marshfield surgeon would be doing late at night at a funeral home," Tim countered. "Focus on what you can do, man."

Levi leaned back into the sofa and thought a moment. "You're right. I've been looking at this wrong."

"I'm always right." Tim took another puff.

"Your ego is deceptively enormous," Levi grunted.

"That's not the only thing on me that's deceptively enormous." Tim blew smoke out his nostrils.

"What am I allowed to say besides 'shut up' that conveys the same meaning?"

"AREN'T YOU DOING ANYTHING for Valentine's Day?" Mrs. Symanski asked Samantha as she got ready for school.

"No, I didn't even get Valentines for my friends." Samantha put her hair in a ponytail. "Maybe I should braid it. I haven't done that in forever."

"You're making a mistake." Mrs. Symanski crossed her arms. "This is a small town. You have to participate in holidays. And remember to treat everyone the same. Otherwise they notice who you play favorites with—don't burn your bridges."

"I am treating everyone the same. Nobody gets anything from me." Samantha pulled her hair out of the ponytail.

"Then you put people who would give you a Valentine in the awkward position of a one-way exchange."

"So?"

"It means they thought enough of you to give you something, but you don't think enough of them. That's just cruel."

"And what about kids who can't afford Valentines?" Samantha flipped her hair first over one shoulder, then the other.

"Right now, we're blessed to not be in that position," Mrs. Symanski replied. "And I'm sure your friends know it. They've been over here. This isn't a cheap house."

"What a surprise." Samantha put her hair back with a headband. "Oh, I don't like this either."

"Dammit Samantha, just pick a hairstyle! You're making me frustrated just watching! What's the big deal?"

"I have to look extra awesome today, mom. Matt's with Kaeli and I'm single, thanks to you," she glowered. Her mother looked very proud of herself. "But I'm still going to look amazing."

"At least you're funneling your anger into self-improvement." Mrs. Symanski smiled. "That's not a horrible thing." She turned and walked down the hallway.

Samantha stared at herself in the mirror, pouting. For a split second, she thought she saw her reflection lean forward and kiss the mirror. She blinked and hurried downstairs.

CARNATIONS WERE DELIVERED IN EVERY classroom, every period. The girls wore pink in some way, shape, or form, and were particularly giggly. Half the boys looked on edge, the other half bored. Levi fell into the bored category. He was ready to pass out in study hall when Tim sat at his table, a goofy grin on his face.

"I thought you didn't want to talk to me," Levi muttered.

"I just came to tell you Samantha Symanski got seven carnations today."

"So what."

"That's more than any other girl in school so far," Tim said. "And I know who's sending them."

"And I don't care," Levi replied, burying his head in his arms.

"You do." Tim slapped his hands on the table to wake Levi up. "I know you do."

"If you have nothing else to say, you should go away."

"I do have something else to say," Tim replied.

"Well? Spit it out."

"You need to stop moping and do your damn research," Tim scolded. "Have you learned anything else about Doc Reinhart?"

"He's not in the phone book. No address listed," Levi replied.

"You have to find it."

"Maybe. I just feel out of it."

"This is urgent, Levi. Lives are at stake."

"I don't see how. What if all that's happening is Lancaster somehow arranged to have surgeries performed on his premises?"

"That's illegal. It's gotta be," Tim shook his head. "Look, you're the one who told me vampires spend their existence arranging fake lives, faking deaths, yada yada yada. That's why you hang out in the cemetery."

"I do that a lot more in the months without snow." Levi looked at Tim. "What's your point?"

"My point is, they have to be financing this endless set of lives somehow. They have to keep their various identities solid for lifetimes. This type of deal requires money—an awful lot of money."

"Which he has," Levi replied.

"He doesn't," Tim insisted. "Lancaster's a recent convert. You told me Homecoming night."

Levi picked dirt from under his nails. "I only know what he spilled, and that may or may not be true."

"I have a feeling it *is* true. He's involved in something illegal and highly profitable. He's doing it to build up his resources. He'll need a lot more money than an undertaker makes to live forever."

"He can't enter the cemetery. He's hardly an undertaker."

"Don't scrutinize my words—you know what I mean." Tim squinted at Levi. "He's gotta earn enough income for multiple lifetimes and he's gotta start fleshing out his next life."

"I know. All vampires have to do that."

"To find out exactly what he's doing, you need Reinhart. He's the link between Lancaster and Rothschild."

"I know. I get it."

"And you're still doing nothing?!"

"Tim, I don't know what to say. I'm out of steam. I need a break. I think I've earned that."

"Levi, the wicked don't rest. You can't afford to slow down."

"You're really bad at pep talks."

SAMANTHA'S JAW DROPPED as another carnation was delivered to her in class. "Eight?"

"You're popular today." An unmistakable tone of resentment permeated Natalie's voice. "Someone's going to ask you out."

"They won't get a yes," Samantha replied. "I have nowhere to pin this without looking like a hippie or a hula girl." She had two in her hair, two on her shirt, and three in her locker. "You want it, Natalie?"

"Don't you dare re-gift a carnation." Natalie's eyes flashed. "That's not intended for me."

"No need to be testy." Samantha rolled her eyes.

"Did you send them to yourself?" Natalie asked.

"Of course not. You know I don't care about this holiday."

"I noticed," Natalie sniffed.

"People who send these things are just too pathetic to tell people to their face how they really feel. It's insulting to me."

"You realize one of those flowers was from me."

"…No." Samantha felt her face turning colors. "No, wow, I put my foot so far down my throat."

"You should keep it there." Natalie stared at the chalkboard. "Then I don't have to listen to you bitch about being liked. Ooh, poor Samantha. Whatever."

"OMG Natalie, tell me how you really feel." Samantha was thunderstruck.

"You know what? I *will* take that carnation. You didn't send me one. You obviously don't think of me as a friend. I want it back."

"No Natalie. I do consider you my friend. I'm just not used to these customs." Samantha sighed. "I wasn't very involved with friends and other people at River Hill. To be honest, I was a loner. It's going to take me a while to come around to the idea of maintaining friendships properly and stuff. I'm sorry."

"You should be." Natalie played with her hair. "But I forgive you. It's not your fault you're uncivilized."

The bell rang, and the day ended. Samantha and Natalie were walking to their lockers when Samantha noticed Matt leaning on the locker next to hers. His eyes met hers. She felt her stomach drop.

"It looks like he wants to talk to you," Natalie said under her breath. "Good luck, see ya!"

"I don't want to talk to him," Samantha whispered, but Natalie had already abandoned her. Matt's face changed, as if he heard the comment. She felt a pang of guilt. He remained by her locker nonetheless. She began to spin the dial when he spoke.

"Hey."

"Hey," she said as uncaringly as she could muster.

"You've been avoiding me again."

"I have no reason to talk to you, and you have no reason to talk to me." Samantha opened her locker.

"I see you're wearing the carnations I got you."

Samantha looked Matt dead in the eye and pulled the carnations from her hair. "I shouldn't have worn them." She held them out to him in her hand. "You should have given them to Kaeli. I noticed she wasn't wearing any."

"I didn't want to give them to her, I wanted to give them to you," Matt closed Samantha's fingers over the flowers.

"Matt, what are you trying to do?" Samantha searched his face, a burning sensation filling her chest. His brown eyes were filled with sorrow, his lips turned in a frown. She looked away to hide the sudden surge of emotions threatening to erupt. "You cheated on me on New Year's Eve. That's not the best way to start the rest of the year."

"I'm sorry Samantha. It was my mistake. I got drunk and lost control of myself."

"You have very little control of yourself," Samantha retorted. "And it's getting worse."

"Samantha, I can't lose you." Matt rested a hand on her shoulder. Samantha pulled back out of his grasp.

"Will you let me get my things so I can go home?"

"Look, I've been scared to death of this conversation for weeks. There's a lot going on with me that I can't tell you about. It's affecting everything. But I want you—I want you in my life."

"Do you really?" Samantha narrowed her eyes, but inside she felt her resolve against him cracking.

"Yes I do."

"What if I don't want you?"

"I'll work harder until you do want me," Matt said. "We belong together. I still think about how you saved me on Homecoming night."

"I thought you barely remembered Homecoming." Samantha pulled her coat out of her locker and slipped into it. "Now suddenly you're feeling all gushy inside?"

"Don't mock me," Matt said through gritted teeth. "I want to prove to you that we work well together, that we're made for each other."

"You want me to take you back?"

"I do. I want us to go back to the way things were." Matt grasped her arm. "Let me take you to prom. We'll have a great time. We'll dance, hang out, get back to what made all those times skipping out during lunch so exhilarating."

"You have been much better about being in school the past few weeks." Samantha hesitated. "It's nice…seeing you across the cafeteria, looking normal."

"I'm taking my medication every day. I'm much better."

"I…I'm sure you are."

"Is that a yes?"

"I don't know," Samantha replied. "I have to think about it."

"Come on, it'll be fun."

"Matt, don't pressure me, okay? You really hurt me—"

"I'm sorry."

"I know you are, but if you can transgress that easily—you weren't even that drunk. I don't want to be involved with a guy who can't—"

"I won't drink on prom. I'll be sober. We'll have a nice dinner. We'll dance. It'll be respectful. I can drop you back at your house at the end of the night."

"My mom won't approve."

"So? I haven't done anything my parents have approved of since September."

"Your parents aren't like my mom. She does this horrible guilt thing that makes you wanna kill yourself. I'd have to go with the girls and meet you."

"I'll wear a black tuxedo this time. Just in case it gets stained."

Samantha bit her lip to keep herself from laughing. "I'll be sure to match you. But Matt, won't Kaeli be there?"

"Yes, she's a junior."

"How will she take this news?"

"She'll have to deal with it," Matt replied, grabbing Samantha around the waist and pulling her in for a quick kiss. He pressed his lips to hers and released her. "I'm looking forward to dancing with you again."

"This is back to a first date deal," Samantha warned. "You'll have to impress me all over again. Can you handle that?"

"You got it, Princess Samantha." He leaned in close and smiled.

LEVI PULLED HIS TRUCK into the parking lot of the Marshfield Clinic, within sight of a black Cadillac. He looped it several times before parking to make sure it was the right one.

As he waited, his mind wandered to the image of Samantha, sitting on her bed, her face tinted pink with a light blush, her eyes wide in surprise. It was an image his mind wandered to frequently; it made him feel better about everything somehow.

Then he remembered her anger, her shock at his kiss. He felt the hot grip of shame in his chest, and he threw it aside. Bandana covering his face, he pulled *East of Eden* out of the backpack on the passenger seat and began to read.

Hours passed. The sun set and the streetlights came on. The Clinic closed, the cars filling its many parking lots dwindling to a handful. The Cadillac sat there, its owner nowhere in sight. Was he coming? Levi put his book away. It was far too cold and dark to get any more reading done.

Flashing lights made him sit up straight. The Cadillac's parking lights were on. A bald man in a long coat with a briefcase was walking to the vehicle. Levi noted the man's hurried motions as he got in. The car started, headlights flashing. Levi turned his truck on. The Cadillac pulled out of the lot. Levi followed.

The car traveled down St. Joseph Avenue, turned on McMillan and went under the viaduct. Levi followed him down Lincoln Avenue, picking up speed. He felt the urge to gun it and keep up, but fought it, instead going the speed limit. The less obvious, the better. The Cadillac turned left on Adler, right on Hickory Lane, and then took another left into a tiny cul-de-sac, pulling up to a large, modern-looking house that dominated the street. Levi drove by, his heart pounding as the bald man got out of his car and the garage door closed, leaving the cul-de-sac in darkness.

Levi clenched his fingers on the steering wheel. Reinhart's house was just blocks from Columbus. His mind raced as he considered the possibilities.

THE SOUND OF GENTLE FOOTSTEPS creaking across her floor made Samantha's eyes open wide. She could feel someone staring at her, and she held her breath, waiting for whoever—or whatever—it was to go away. It didn't.

"Samantha, I had a nightmare," Brandon said, hovering over her.

Relief flooded her. "Go away, I'm trying to sleep."

"But I did. It was awful."

"Go back to bed." She pulled her covers tighter over her body and shut her eyes.

"I'm too scared to sleep alone. Can I sleep in your bed?"

"I'm too scared you'll pee in my bed."

"I won't. I haven't wet the bed since I was nine."

"That's not that long ago, Brandon. Go back to bed."

"I tried, but I can't."

"Why not?"

"Someone else is in my bed."

Samantha sat up. "Who?" She stared at the dark shape of her little brother, standing there in his nightshirt, pressing his fingers together.

"A lady," he said finally.

"What lady?"

"I don't want to sleep in that bed with her."

"What lady, Brandon?"

"She didn't tell me who she was. She was just there, under my covers." He gestured to the hallway.

"It was your nightmare." Samantha flopped back into her bed. "If you're so scared, go to mom's room."

"I can't."

"Why not?"

"There's a man in the hallway by her door."

SAMANTHA DIDN'T SLEEP at all after Brandon woke her. Instead, she spent the entire night lying awake, staring at the door, while her little brother eventually nodded off next to her. When the sky began to lighten, she worked up the nerve to turn on her bedroom lights, then flipped the switch in the hallway. No tall, dark, broad-shouldered figure. She flipped the switch in her brother's room and ripped the blankets from his bed. It was empty. She worked her way from room to room, turning lights on and looking in corners, nearly giving herself a heart attack as she pulled back the shower curtain. She checked the front door, back door, and side door. All were locked. All the windows were closed and locked. She was in the kitchen, turning on the outside lights to peer into the yard, when a voice behind her made her scream.

"What are you doing up?"

Samantha gasped for air, turning to see her mother looking at her with an annoyed expression under her face mask.

"Brandon saw a man in the hallway upstairs."

"Excuse me?"

"A big, tall, shadowy man. He said he was standing in front of your door."

"There's no one here."

"I know that."

"He must have had a nightmare, sweetie."

"That's what I said. He came into my room because he was afraid of the lady in his bed under the covers with him and couldn't get to your room because of the man in the hallway in front of your bedroom!"

"What have you told him?"

"What?"

"He's young and impressionable. He probably saw whatever he heard you describe. You've been telling him scary stories again."

"I didn't tell him anything! He came into my room and told *me* about it! He said there was a woman in his bed, so he slept in mine!"

"He's too old to be doing this." Mrs. Symanski threw up her hands. "We'll discuss this over breakfast. Go put your brother in his own bed."

"YOU'RE DOING THAT more and more," Levi commented. Samantha stirred in her desk and cracked open an eye to peer at him. "Sooner or later Mrs. Hansen is going to come over and slam a book on your desk to wake you up. Of course, you might slap her a second time…"

"I'm not sleeping very well lately."

"We've had this conversation before." He watched as Mrs. Hansen stood and left to visit the restroom.

"It's going to keep happening, I'm afraid." Samantha shut her eyes and buried her head in her arms, sighing a little. "I told my mother the house is haunted. Again."

"What did she say?"

"She said the house is fine, that everybody's getting worked up over nothing. I can't believe she doesn't believe us."

"Us?"

"My little brother and me. We've seen some strange things. Sometimes I think I'm going crazy, but how often do two people go crazy at the same time?"

"We're in psychology. Maybe you should ask Mr. Becker." Levi watched as a shadow of realization passed over her face and vanished.

"But he's not here."

"He's probably at his house. You could visit him."

"I can't." Samantha met his eyes. "His daughter's missing. He's probably a wreck. He doesn't need to have my problems on his shoulders."

Levi nodded. "Actually, he might be grateful for something to take his mind off of his missing daughter. I know I would, if it were me."

"I wouldn't presume to think my haunted house trumps his missing child, Levi. That's unrealistic."

"Samantha, it's not about trumping his missing daughter, it's about finding a solution to your problem."

"How would he be able to help me?"

"I don't know. But what if it *is* just you and your brother

330

imagining things?"

"BECCA, I HAVE A FAVOR to ask you."

"Shoot."

"Can you give me a ride to Mr. Becker's house?"

Becca stared at her, incredulous. "Why would you wanna go there? His daughter's missing. People shouldn't bother him."

"I—I just need to ask him some things. I don't want to deal with my mom or trying to get her to drive me. Please?"

"Come on, Samantha, who's going to drive you home?"

"You could pick me up."

"We all have dance practice tonight. Getting ready for the St. Patrick's Day game halftime show. You have to be there, too."

"I know, I know," Samantha frowned. "But before we do that, can we go to Mr. Becker's? It shouldn't take long."

"Now you want me to stay there with you?"

"It would be awkward if I went by myself."

"Good gravy." Becca rolled her eyes. "Fine."

BECCA AND SAMANTHA WALKED to the front door of Mr. Becker's house. The pathway hadn't been shoveled in a while; their footsteps sank through inches of snow.

"I don't want to be here," Becca muttered.

"I need you with me." Samantha took a breath and rang the doorbell. They could hear it ringing inside the house from outside. Footsteps slowly approached the door. It sounded like four different locks turned before it opened.

Mr. Becker's gray-tinted face appeared in the gap. "Students from Columbus." He stared like a wounded animal. "What do you two want?"

"Mr. Becker, hi," Samantha began, sounding too cheery for her own good. She cleared her throat, trying to find a more appropriate tone. "I know this may be a bad time, but I was hoping I could ask you some questions—"

"Get out of here." The door slammed, the locks turning again.

Samantha rapped on the door.

"Please sir, it's not about Nikki! I need your help!" She pressed her ear to the door. The wind rustled through the icy trees. The locks clicked again and the door opened.

"What do you want, Miss Symanski?"

"Oh, good, you remember me!"

"Of course I do. I remember all my students."

"The way you slammed the door I thought—"

"Would you two like to come in?"

"Samantha," Becca whispered, setting a hand on Samantha's arm.

"Yes." Samantha grabbed Becca's arm and they walked into Mr. Becker's house. He led them to the living room, which was very small and cluttered. He sat in an armchair. Samantha and Becca sat on the sofa.

"You said you needed my help." Mr. Becker adjusted the tie around his waist.

Samantha nodded, realizing Mr. Becker was in his pajamas, wrapped in a robe with slippers on. "Yes, um—how do I say this? What sort of psychological stuff makes people see ghosts?"

Mr. Becker's mouth turned. "Why do you ask?"

"My little brother thinks our house is haunted," Samantha admitted. "Sometimes I think it is, too." She heard Becca's "ugh!" of disbelief.

"A lot of people think they're being haunted because of physical conditions in a given location. Often, it's not necessarily anything psychological." Mr. Becker's face contorted with curiosity. "You and your brother seeing things?"

"Yes, and hearing things too," Samantha replied. "You're saying there's nothing wrong with us mentally?"

"I can't make any promises." The hint of a smile graced a corner of Mr. Becker's mouth. "But you seem sane to me."

"Okay," Samantha nodded, feeling better. "So it's the house."

"Usually people think they're hearing strange noises in a house when the noises they're hearing are actually not strange. Houses age, and are subject to all sorts of weather conditions. The air pressure outside pushing on the walls can make a house creak. They settle onto their foundations, and pictures will slant. Things will fall. Wiring goes faulty and lights will flicker. All very common things that people tend to think of as spooky or evidence of a haunting. Have you experienced much of that?"

"Oh yes. The lights flicker every time my mom and I fight." Samantha shrugged. "All the pictures in the dining room fell off the wall at the same time once, so that makes a lot of sense."

"If that's it, then you're fine," Mr. Becker replied.

"The thing is, Mr. Becker, that isn't all there is," Samantha twirled her thumbs. "I've seen my reflection do things that I'm not doing—maybe it's just a trick of the light—but it scares me. A few nights ago, my brother woke me up and told me there was a man standing in the hallway. I looked and I couldn't find him, but I believe he did see someone."

"Did you call the police?" Becca exclaimed.

Samantha shook her head. "My mom thought maybe he was just imagining it."

"What if it was a home invader?! Someone could have kidnapped or killed you!"

"You really should call the police if he sees that man again." Mr. Becker nodded. "Protect your family." His eyes glazed over, and he looked away for a while. Samantha and Becca looked at each other, helpless, then back at Mr. Becker. He took several deep breaths to compose himself.

Samantha spoke after the lengthy pause. "I just don't know what I'm protecting us against and what I can do about it."

"Tell your mother."

"She doesn't believe me."

"Indulge me for a moment. Which supposedly haunted house do you live in?"

"She lives in the Doege House," Becca cut in.

"Now that raises some interesting questions." Mr. Becker stroked his chin.

"Like what?" Samantha asked, practically breathless.

"There have been rumors surrounding that place for decades. With that history, it's entirely possible there could be ghosts in your house."

"Why? Because it was a Masonic Temple?"

"This is starting to sound like a conspiracy." Becca's words dripped with disapproval.

"Don't get me wrong, I'm not saying Masons are evil," Mr. Becker chose his words carefully. "From what I understand, one of the membership requirements was being a religious person. The danger with the Masons is that they didn't care which god a person believed in, as long as they believed in something. This of course left them open to more—shall we say—possibilities. Buddhism, Sikhism, Satanism…" His droning voice trailed off.

"The Masons are not Satanists," Becca said. "That's just defamatory."

"They don't promote any one religion, but they require members to have religiosity of one sort or another. In short, they're not *against* Satanism," Mr. Becker corrected. "All it would take is one ritual, for *any* religion. Done incorrectly, it could invite all kinds of spirits."

"You can't honestly believe all that garbage," Becca was flabbergasted. "You teach psychology for Heaven's sake!"

"Becca, you weren't there," Samantha shot back. "You didn't see what I saw. If you did, you wouldn't be so quick to dismiss possibilities."

"I don't believe in ghosts," Becca replied. "I don't believe in demons either. Or magic. Or any supernatural anything."

"Why not?" Mr. Becker asked.

"Because it's ridiculous, that's why!" Becca snapped. "Why the hell would people be worried about paying bills and getting promotions if there are demons and ghosts alongside us? How would anything on earth retain its importance when the other side is possibly spilling into this one?"

"Yet you believe in God, and angels?"

"I guess so." Becca sounded reluctant to agree.

"It is logical to think they'd have counterparts. Your attitude implies that paying bills and getting promotions is all that matters. Maybe everything we experience here on Earth—maybe none of it is really important." Mr. Becker sighed. "Have you read Ecclesiastes?"

"No," Becca shook her head.

"I've been reading the Bible a lot lately…for all the reasons you might suspect. In Ecclesiastes, it is written that everything is meaningless." Mr. Becker waved his hands in the air. "Wisdom, foolishness, getting rich, pressing onward through life day after day until death inevitably swallows us all up." He stared out the window. "What's the use?"

"That's a hopeless point of view," Samantha said.

"But I see the truth in it," Becca conceded. "Seems the only reason society exists is because we need companionship and drama to keep us from getting bored as we get old and die. If we didn't have that, we'd probably check-out a lot sooner."

"There's more to it than that." Samantha couldn't believe her ears.

"Come on, Samantha. Have you even thought about it?" Becca tossed her dark hair. "My life will probably consist of going to college, getting a degree, getting a job I won't like, friends I barely talk to, a husband I'm only half-satisfied with, children I can't relate to, and on top of it, I'll slowly morph into my grandmother. Then I'll die."

Samantha felt an inexplicable urge to laugh. Becca glared at her and she felt the smile slide off her face.

"All our days have passed away in your indignation; we have spent our years like a sigh. Seventy is the sum of our years, or eighty, if we are strong. And most of them are fruitless toil, for they pass quickly and we drift away." Mr. Becker rubbed his chin again.

"Life really can be satisfying," Samantha interjected. "People don't live to get *stuff*. Stuff breaks. It's replaceable. I don't know one person whose favorite memory was of an object. People live for love, and joy, and family."

They were all very quiet again. Becca shifted uncomfortably. Samantha looked around at the clutter in the living room. She noticed a lot of cards lying around and several vases of dying flowers. She wondered how long it had been since anyone visited.

Mr. Becker considered her for a moment. "I think it's entirely possible your house is haunted. There's nothing wrong with you." He stood up. "It's time for you girls to leave now."

"Are you sure?" Samantha stood slowly as Becca jumped to her feet. "We could stay and talk some more."

"If I'm not mistaken, dance practice starts soon. Have a good night." Mr. Becker led them to the door.

Chapter 11

Collide

"Not another one," Levi groaned as Matt glared at him. They were standing in the senior hallway, close to the parking lot doors, during lunch.

"It's not my fault, man. I thought you were trying to help me."

"I was. But I've cleaned more of your blood off of my kitchen floor than I can take. I don't want to host the transformation again."

"B-but where will I go?"

"Rampage like you did before we helped you."

"I can't do that. I could kill someone."

"Chances are you already did."

Matt's fist missed Levi's face by inches and dented a locker. "Don't fuck with me."

"You didn't take your pills today," Levi narrowed his eyes. Matt brought his fist to his side and huffed. "I won't help you if you skip your meds."

"Fine man, fine, I'll take my pills. Just don't make me eat any wolfsbane brownies."

"Tell it to Tim. Is he helping?"

"I can't find him," Matt shrugged. "He's not in the cafeteria."

"Can't you sniff him out or something? He has an easily

identifiable aroma."

"If you're talking about his pot stink, you're right. I can smell him coming down a hallway," Matt nodded, eyes growing wide. "Wow."

"So can everyone else. You're a pretty useless werewolf, you know that?"

"Lower your damn voice!" Matt growled, glancing down the empty hallway.

"Why don't you just transform in your barn? You said you wound up there a few times."

"I did." Matt ran a hand through his dark hair. "Okay, maybe I could transform there. But I broke down a door and escaped your house that one time, remember?"

"Boy, do I remember."

"What's to stop me from busting out of the barn and wreaking havoc?"

"My first inclination is to shoot you with silver bullets." Levi smirked. Felix's words played in his mind for a moment. "But lucky for you I don't have those."

"You don't, huh?"

"Do I look like I can afford silver bullets?"

Matt's face scrunched up in judgment. "I'm happy about that. I don't wanna be shot."

"Great. Now find Tim and let's see if he'll help us figure out what to do with you."

"I'M SO EXCITED for the St. Patrick's Day game!"

"Hoo-hah," Jennifer rolled her eyes. "You'll get to dress in green again. Like we didn't do that for Homecoming."

"Now the whole school has to do it," Natalie bounced. "And we don't have to buy new stuff."

"I'll need more fake green hair."

"And of course we need to get ready for prom." Becca opened her milk carton and placed it on her tray. "Samantha, you wanna come with Natalie and me to go dress shopping?"

Samantha beamed. "You had to ask?"

Jennifer popped her gum. "You bitches have fun at prom. Laderia and I will be hanging out with our boyfriends that night."

"You've planned that night out already? It's not until April." Natalie twirled a lock of her hair.

"You've been planning our Prom since the eighth grade," Jennifer said. She glanced at the group of senior boys one table over. Laderia's raucous laughter rang across the cafeteria. "Fuck this, I'm going over there." She stood and walked to the other table, forcing Dylan to slide down so she could sit next to him.

"It'll be nice to have a dance without her negative attitude bringing it down," Natalie huffed.

"So are we going shopping after school?" Samantha turned to Becca.

"In a few days," Becca said. "Before dance practice."

HEAT FROM THE HAY in the loft kept the Stauber barn a decent temperature even in the middle of winter. Levi and Tim sat on the top of a tower of bales, watching the werewolf beneath them roll around in the loose hay.

"Pot brownies have done the trick," Levi said.

"I still can't believe it worked," Tim stared. "It's a lot more effective than the aconite brownies."

"You should have more faith in yourself."

"I have plenty of faith in myself," Tim snapped back.

"I wasn't trying to dig at you, man." The werewolf growled almost playfully as it meandered around the floor, then laid down and licked its claws.

Tim squinted at Levi in the darkness. "I don't know what your deal is. You lied to me like it was nothing, I kick you out for two months, and now you're all supportive. What do you want from me?"

"I just want to be on the right side," Levi murmured as the werewolf rolled on its back and panted.

Tim looked down at the scene. "They really *are* ugly."

Levi's shoulders shook as he laughed. "Those long arms and

claws are like a sloth's."

"The semi-hairless thing is what freaks me out," Tim shuddered. "That balding look. With skin like a corpse's scrotum."

"Disgustingly accurate," Levi concurred. "He's like a puppy down there. A big, disgusting, man-eating puppy. With scrotum skin."

"Let's just hope his high lasts through the night," Tim said. "We're saving lives."

"And depleting your stash," Levi smirked. "I feel good about that. Keeping you out of drugs and clean."

"Don't parent me, man. How's your investigation into Reinhart going?"

"I know where he lives."

"Cool, when did you find that out?"

"Sometime around Valentine's Day."

"And?"

"And what?"

"That's all you learned?"

"Yup."

"Levi, even I know you need to do more digging."

Levi rolled his eyes. "I'm going to break into his house soon."

"Really? It's already March. That's like two weeks of doing nothing about it."

"I wasn't doing nothing, I was doing homework. And there were a couple burials at the cemetery that needed my attention. It's been snowing less and less lately. I have a lot to do. But I will get around to Reinhart. The problem is he comes home at different times. His schedule isn't fixed. I need a second pair of eyes to warn me when he's coming so I can get out of the house."

"Oh no, you're not roping me into that again," Tim glared.

"Tim, come on. You're the only one who knows I'm a vampire slayer. You're the only one who can help me."

"I won't, man. You can find another way."

"There is no other way."

Tim looked at the werewolf again. He didn't speak for a long time. "Okay, I'll help you. But I'm not doing it for you. I told Matt we'd find the cure, and that requires having St. Hubert's Key. My grandfather believes the vampires stole them. Chances are Lancaster has heard of it." He turned to Levi. "We have to find out what he knows."

SAMANTHA PERUSED THE DRESSES on the racks at Circle the Date Dress Shop. The chandeliers throughout the store sparkled and threw light onto shimmering fabrics, sequins and glittering silks. Becca stood next to her.

"What's the prom theme again?"

"Black Tie Affair? I don't care," Becca sifted through hangers. "Natalie would know."

"She's in the changing room."

"It doesn't matter, Samantha. You said Matt's going to wear a black tux. Anything you put on would go with that."

"You think I should do a black dress?"

"Maybe not totally black. You don't wanna look Goth."

"Do you even know what Goth is? I haven't seen one Goth person in this town."

"We have Goth people," Becca retorted.

"It takes a lot more than wearing black to make a person Goth. And if the theme is Black Tie Affair, I could go Goth for the night if I wanted and show y'all a thing or two."

"I don't think so. The pictures will be on Facebook and in the yearbook forever. You know how damaging that could be to your reputation? Employers look at all that stuff these days."

"You worry way too much about being an adult," Samantha shook her head.

"I've got one more year left of high school after this. That's it. Then, I technically am an adult. I have to be ready." Becca pulled out a shimmering red dress. "How about this?"

"Too restricting," Samantha said. "It should have a slit or something. You won't be able to dance."

"I really want something red," Becca ran her fingers over the shimmering fabric. "Natalie always gets to wear red."

"She's a redhead. I think I want this purple one," Samantha pulled it from the rack. "Spaghetti straps, just a hint of sparkle—look at the way it catches the light!"

"You're selling it to yourself," Becca sighed. "How are you going to pay for it?"

"I borrowed my mom's credit card." Samantha pulled it out of her pocket. "She said to keep it under two hundred dollars."

"Does she know you're going with Matt yet?" Becca pulled out a black dress and held it to her frame.

"No, and she won't find out, either."

"What if she wants to see pictures of you with your date? You have to be on the arm of a junior to go. She's an alumna, she'll know that." Becca put the black dress back and pulled out a white one. "Does this look too much like a wedding dress to you?"

"I was hoping to borrow your date for some photos. And that dress screams 'divorce pending.'"

"Message received." Becca put it back on the rack. "Why did you say yes to him?"

Samantha pulled a lavender dress from the rack. "He begged me to go."

"Kaeli's not very happy about it."

"Who cares?"

"You should care. He's two-timing both of you." Becca walked to the next rack. "Haven't you heard the saying 'players gonna play'?"

"I heard Dylan was the player, not Matt," Samantha responded with tacit fury. "OMG, look at this one." She held the dress up. Becca made a face and Samantha put it back.

"Girls, how about this one?!" Natalie's voice rang through the store. Samantha and Becca went over to one of the dressing room sitting areas. Natalie came out in a turquoise mermaid tail dress with silver detailing. "Does this say 'Come Sail Away' or what?!"

"*That's* the theme! I totally forgot!" Becca put a hand to the side of her face.

"How can you forget? It's for your class!" Natalie spun around. "Now give me your honest opinion!"

"I like it," Samantha said. "Keep your hair down and you could be Ariel from *The Little Mermaid*."

Natalie squealed in delight and scurried back into the dressing room.

"I'll get a black strapless and go as Anorexic Ursula." Samantha grinned at Becca.

"And what kind of look should I go for?" Becca asked, her brow wrinkled in frustration.

"You could get that white dress you liked and be the Sea Witch in Disguise." Samantha grabbed it off the rack and handed it to Becca. "We'll all be properly themed out."

"I didn't *like* it," Becca sighed. "I just didn't hate it."

"Get a pair of awesome shoes, do your hair right, and you'll love it."

"You called it a divorce dress."

LEVI SPREAD THE Marshfield News-Herald out before him on a table in the library. He scanned the obituary column. Nothing. He flipped from page to page, casually taking in the headlines. *How to Cure Winter Blues, New Bakery Opens on Cleveland Street, More Animals Attacked, Hotel Remodeling*—wait, what?

"The remains of six deer were found brutally ripped apart just east of Marshfield," he read, barely a whisper. *'The number of carcasses found in that small area is staggering,' said Officer Emma Horace. 'Our friends at the DNR say this is highly unusual.' Wisconsin's deer population supports a billon-dollar hunting industry that caters to over 600,000 hunters annually. The Marshfield Police Department has consulted the Wisconsin Department of Natural Resources about the attacks around the city, which seem to be escalating in ferocity with each passing month. 'The DNR is very interested in what is happening in our area,' Horace added. 'They advised us there may be another pack of wolves moving into our region, or more likely, a rabid bear. We urge residents to keep a close eye on their pets and be watchful while outside, especially at night.'*

"Boo!" A hand clamped down on Levi's shoulder. He winced in pain and grabbed the hand, twisting it. Levi turned to glare at the owner of the hand, and his face fell, eyes wide with dread. He composed himself the best he could and said, "Go away."

"I don't think so." Lancaster pulled up a chair and sat next to Levi. "It's a public place. I pay my taxes."

"Not all your taxes." Levi hoped Lancaster couldn't tell his heart was pounding as his muscles clenched and unclenched. "What do you want?"

"I wanted to see how my favorite slayer is doing." Lancaster folded his hands on the table, his goatee emphasizing his twisted smile. "So how are you doing?"

"I'm fine," Levi said, narrowing his eyes. "Why do you care?"

"I was wondering how that truck of yours is holding up." Lancaster leaned closer to Levi, and dropped his voice. "You know it's illegal for a boy your age to be driving without a learner's permit and an adult in the vehicle. But don't worry, I won't report you. Our deal still stands."

Levi's face wrinkled in a disgusted scowl. "What do you want?"

"There's something you have to keep in mind about me, Levi. I'm a businessman." Lancaster adjusted his glasses. "As a businessman, I have a lot on my mind. Maintaining a funeral home, financing my endeavors—"

"Of course."

"And as you are probably aware, the business world is…cutthroat." He chuckled a little. "I daresay it's a bit more than that sometimes."

"Where are you going with this?" Levi studied Lancaster's face, wondering how he was here, in a library with security cameras everywhere.

"It's make-up," Lancaster informed him. "Try to be less obvious, Levi Mauer. How can you be an effective slayer with a poker face as pitiful as that?"

"So you got yourself all prettied up just to visit me? I can't begin to imagine what you want right now," Levi said. Lancaster slammed his hand down on the newspaper. Several people in the library looked over. He leaned in close to Levi.

"I want you to stop spying on my business," he uttered evenly. "I've seen that ugly truck lurking around for months now. Across the Parkway, in the cemetery—you're interfering. I warned you to stay away from my business."

"I warned you to stay away from *me*," Levi countered. "I know you had that Tim kid working at the funeral home since October. You had him doing double-duty, keeping tabs on me in school—I'm not stupid. He was spying on me long before I was spying on you. You broke the agreement, not me."

"He no longer works for me."

"That's supposed to make up for the stalking?" Levi crossed his arms.

"Consider us even, slayer," Lancaster growled. "I don't want to see your truck anywhere around my property again. If I do, I'll kill a child each time. Let me remind you the middle school is behind my house."

The library mulled, people whispered along walls, footsteps came from behind shelves.

"If you spy on *me* one more time, I'll end you." Levi sat taller and leaned closer to Lancaster, pushing back. "I'll end whatever con was pulled over on the real Lancaster to get you into his body. Because I know the truth. You're not Thomas Lancaster. You're a monster—a demon. You and all your parasitic kind need to be eliminated from this earth."

Lancaster watched him, not breaking eye contact for a moment. Eventually he stood up, held out his hand and smiled. "You're not a very smart kid, Levi Mauer."

"You're not very smart either. We're gridlocked with these threats again." Levi ignored his hand.

Lancaster's face soured and he walked out of the library.

SAMANTHA WALKED UP THE STAIRS to her bedroom, her prom dress safe in its black bag. She set it in her closet, and walked into the hallway. At the end of the hall, a new bookcase stood, loaded with framed photographs. She spotted one she recognized.

The frame was white. She picked it up and ran her fingers over the glass. It was from so long ago. She stood on the Mall next to Brandon, the Washington Monument rising in the background. Closing her eyes, she remembered the feel of the wind pushing the humid air, and the brightness of the sidewalks as the sun beat down on them. She remembered the elephant in the Natural History museum, and the huge spacecraft in the Air and Space museum. And Dorothy's ruby-encrusted slippers in a glass case in the Museum of American History. She set the picture back on the shelf and looked at some others.

Her and Brandon at Six Flags. Her and Brandon at Kings Dominion. Her and Brandon at the National Aquarium in Baltimore. She could see the long shadows of both of her parents standing next to each other creeping into a picture of them at the beach in Ocean City. She blinked back a tear. Then she noticed something small tucked between two frames on the second shelf. After returning the picture to its place, she peered at the silver thing and noticed its glass lens. Picking it up, she realized it was a tiny camera. She put it back, her heart pounding, and whirled around to look behind her. The camera was aimed down the hall at the doorway to the master bedroom.

"Mom!" She rushed downstairs.

"Yes, honey?" came her mother's voice from the kitchen. Samantha walked in.

"What's with the new bookcase in the upstairs hallway?"

"Oh, we needed more space to put up pictures. I don't want to hammer anymore holes into this house's old walls. It's been there for awhile. I can't believe you haven't noticed. Do you like it?" She smiled at her daughter, but it didn't reach her eyes.

"I…I think it's nice," Samantha said with caution.

"Do you want to show me the dress you picked out?" Mrs. Symanski asked as she kneaded bread dough.

"No, flour might get on it. Maybe later."

"Sounds reasonable. You can show it to me after I get done baking."

"Mom, can I ask you something?"

"Sure thing, honey."

"What do you *do*?"

"You flip the dough over, then press your knuckles in—"

"I mean, I know you work for some defense contractor thing, but I have no idea what you do. You're always on your computer—"

"Samantha, you know I work for Aegis Dynamics." Mrs. Symanski shook her head and smiled at the bread dough. "I've been doing that for years."

"Okay, yeah, but what do you *do*?"

"I review papers and make corrections. Think of it as reading essay after essay of five-syllable words and searching for flaws."

"Ew." Samantha tried to seem light, but knew she was struggling.

"Exactly. It's incredibly tedious and oftentimes boring, but it pays the bills." She flipped the dough over and wiped her brow. "Why this interest?"

"You're always home," Samantha shrugged. "People ask me why they never see you out and about, and I don't know what to say." She felt the seriousness of her tone betraying her words.

"I work from home," Mrs. Symanski replied. "And I catch your brother's games and sometimes I watch a Dons game at the school and see your dance routines. I get out plenty."

Samantha drummed her fingers on the counter. "If you say so."

"I admit I miss adult conversation," Mrs. Symanski continued. "It's been a long time since I've hung out with anyone my own age. But work before play."

Samantha plucked a grape and popped it into her mouth. "You probably wouldn't be able to talk to anyone anyway…with your job being like it is. Other people won't understand you keeping secrets."

SAMANTHA STARED at the illuminated face of her digital alarm clock. It was just past midnight when her mother finally came up the stairs. She listened hard as her footsteps went first to Brandon's room. Then she rolled over quickly and pretended to be asleep. Her mother opened her door. It creaked on its old hinges as she shut it again. The footsteps went back down the hall, and finally the light from under the door went dark.

She waited until her mother's door shut before she opened her own as quietly as she could. She glanced down the dark hallway, and tiptoed alongside the walls so the floor wouldn't creak as much. She made her way downstairs, holding her breath as she entered the dining room, the dim yellow light of a nearby streetlamp falling against the crystals on the chandelier.

Her mother's laptop sat on the table, a little blue light blinking. She slid into her mother's seat and flipped it open, pressed the space bar, and the screen loaded to a password request.

She slowly typed in her name. Denied. She typed in her brother's name. Denied. Her father's. Denied. Birthdays, anniversaries, favorite animals, holidays, maiden name. Nothing worked.

Samantha fumed, running a hand through her hair. She closed the laptop to head up to bed, and the room was plunged into darkness. She sat and waited for her eyes to adjust.

"Samantha," a soft voice breathed.

Samantha launched out of the chair with a gasp and turned to look for the source of the voice. The dining room was empty. She stepped around the table, holding her breath, eyes wide, heart beating so hard it hurt. She walked into the foyer, found the railing for the stairs, and made her way up as quietly as she could, glancing over her shoulder often.

No one was there.

Tiptoeing down the dark hall to her room, she noted a tiny light on the bookshelf. She mentally kicked herself for getting caught on camera. She stepped into her dark room, and turned to take one last look down the hall. The figure of a tall man leaned against the wall by her mother's bedroom door. His head slowly turned in her direction. She slammed the door shut and locked it.

"THEY'RE PUTTING UP POSTERS for the musical." Levi watched Samantha as she slumped over her desk onto her backpack.

"Uh-huh..." She adjusted her arms.

"It's *Grease*."

"Good gravy," Samantha groaned into her backpack. "I can't escape it."

"You must have gotten less sleep last night than I did."

"Leave me alone." Samantha buried her face as the class murmured. Levi leaned against the wall, closing his eyes.

"Good morning, Columbus Dons." Barb's voice echoed over the PA system. *"There are several announcements. Our Dons played fabulous basketball this season, but unfortunately lost over the weekend and won't make it to the playoffs. Congratulate them on their excellent season and all their hard work. I'm pleased to announce that advanced tickets for 'Grease', the spring musical are going on sale today. Ten dollars for adults, six dollars for students. The show isn't until May, but please mark your calendars and tell your parents."*

There was a long pause and the speakers buzzed. Levi opened his eyes, curious. The room seemed to freeze.

"We have one final announcement. Last night, our beloved faculty member, Mr. Donald Becker, tragically passed away. We ask for your prayers for his soul and for the well-being of his family; pray especially for Nikki Becker, who is still missing. Keep them both in your hearts and minds. Grief counseling will be available in the Father Hugh Deeny auditorium."

The speakers crackled off. Everyone looked around the room, silent. Several students' eyes were shining and wet. Mrs. Hansen sniffled. Samantha sat up straight, her face ashen as she stared at the ceiling.

"What happened?" Levi whispered. Samantha shook her head and bit her lip. Levi could tell she was fighting the urge to sob with each breath. Mrs. Hansen rubbed her eyes behind her glasses and coughed. They stood for the Pledge of Allegiance.

"Do any of you girlios know what happened?" Laderia asked as she applied lip gloss.

"I don't know a thing," Natalie said. "Oh gosh, I'm gonna cry." She wiped at her eyes. "I hate crying in bathrooms. My eyes get all puffy and I look like Raggedy Ann."

Samantha watched as Becca exhaled and looked at the floor, trying to control her emotions.

"It's okay." Samantha's words sounded as empty and meaningless as she knew they were. Becca shook her head.

"Did he have a heart attack?" Natalie asked. "A stroke?"

Becca covered her face with her hands. "Where's Jennifer? She should have been able to get here by now." Samantha felt her mouth water as if she was about to vomit.

The door swung open and Jennifer walked in.

"Where were you?" Becca asked.

"Mrs. Black didn't believe I had to pee. So I said I wanted counseling and she *escorted* me there. Then I asked them if I could pee. Can you believe that? Symanski can dodge class for half the year and I'm the one they're worried about."

"Do you know what happened?" Samantha asked.

Jennifer nodded. "You don't want to know."

"I want to know," Becca said. "How did this happen? He didn't have any health problems that I'm aware of."

"You're right. He didn't," Jennifer muttered. "He killed himself."

Natalie gasped. Samantha put a hand over her mouth, and held her breath.

"Stop doing that, Samantha. You'll pass out." Jennifer popped her gum.

"How did he do it?" Natalie whispered, her voice somehow squeaking despite its softness.

Jennifer pulled out a cigarette and a lighter.

Laderia slapped them out of her hands. "Not now."

"I want a smoke. This shit's affecting me too." Jennifer grabbed the cigarette off the floor and threw it away.

"You know what happened. Just tell us." Laderia crossed her arms.

"It's grisly." Jennifer rubbed her temples. "My dad had to—I don't even want—" She tossed her hair. "I'll be surprised if the casket's open. Happy?"

"Are you pussying out right now?!" Laderia snapped. "We *know* he killed himself. How did he do it? Hanging? Gunshot?"

"It was a train, wasn't it," Becca said.

Jennifer nodded. "How'd you know?"

"It's always a train in this town." Becca crossed her arms and stroked her own neck. "There was some girl who killed herself back in the eighties. She parked her car, got down on the tracks and was beheaded."

"Becker drank at least a bottle of wine, took some pills...passed out in his car on the train tracks by the Hume Road crossing," Jennifer said.

Other than Natalie's sniffles and squeaking sobs, the bathroom was silent.

"I barely knew him," Samantha said finally. "But when we went to visit him, I could tell...some part of me just knew this was coming."

"You could tell by his speech." Becca nodded, her voice trembling.

"I've never seen someone so hopeless." Samantha felt tears stinging her eyes. "Oh gosh..." She stared at Becca. "What if we killed him?"

"I was thinking the same thing." Becca's tears broke free and she sobbed.

"Shut up," Natalie whined. "You guys didn't do anything. You couldn't have killed him!" She wrapped her arms around Becca and they cried together.

"I'll take you two to counseling." Laderia put her hands on their shoulders, her eyes just as empty as Samantha's as she led Natalie and Becca out of the bathroom.

Jennifer leaned against the sink, her face colorless. "I feel nothing. That makes me a freak, doesn't it?" She tilted her face to the ceiling and closed her eyes. "I need a joint."

"We should go," Samantha said.

"Sammy, it's a really shitty day."

"Yes," Samantha whispered. "It's a shitty day."

LEVI FOUND TIM SITTING ALONE in the small chapel off the school's lobby during lunch. He leaned against the wall as he sat. Levi couldn't tell if Tim was conscious, so he sat in the same row, two seats down from him.

"Hey man."

"Becker's dead," Tim said.

"Is that why you're in here?"

"I needed time to think."

"What's your conclusion?" Levi asked.

"I think everything is falling apart," Tim groaned without moving.

"What do you mean?"

"I'm behind on sales, Jennifer's constantly giving me hell, Mr. Becker's dead, Nikki's still missing, and Felix is coming back for Easter Break."

"What are you going to do about it?" Levi asked.

"I don't want to sell Jennifer anything for a while. Turns out I like seeing her going nuts and squirming without me. As far as sales, I'm either going to double my prices or charge Matt for the weed it takes to knock him out." Tim turned his head to look at Levi out of the corner of his eye. "What's wrong with you?"

"We need to move on Doctor Reinhart's house as soon as possible. Lancaster confronted me in the public library."

"Oh shit." Tim sat up straight. "He must have been wearing a ton of makeup to get in there with the security cameras."

"I couldn't even tell he had it on. He probably watches tons of tutorials on Youtube."

"He sought you out, Levi. What does that mean? What did he say?"

"He knows I've been watching him." Levi rubbed the back of his head. "He also threatened murder if I keep it up."

"He's panicking because he thinks you really do know as much as you pretend you know." Tim grinned wickedly. "That's excellent."

"He might actually kill someone. Middle school kids. He was dead serious. I don't know what to do."

"You already said you had to raid Reinhart. Technically that's not spying on Lancaster or getting in his space. Wait to think about your next move until after that. You don't even know what Lancaster's up to yet."

"What if I'm waiting too long? People could be dying."

"People always die. Some people even kill themselves." Tim stared at the altar surrounded by shimmering candles. "You can't save everyone, and moving rashly will get *you* killed. Then you won't be saving anyone." He ran his hands over his face and rubbed his temples.

"What are you going to do about Felix?" Levi asked.

"Same thing I do every time I see him. Try not to kill him."

"Are you going to confront him about…?"

"About my grandfather being in town? Hell yes I will. My brother's keeping my family from me. I'll also demand the truth about our parents…the werewolf hunters, my father's death, everything." Tim rolled his shoulders and cracked his neck. "This is going to be one hell of a fight. I'm going to get it all out of him."

"You deserve to know." Levi nodded, ignoring the horrible twisting in his guts.

"TALK TO ME, SAMANTHA ROSE. What's wrong? Why won't you say anything? You're obviously distraught, just tell me what happened."

Samantha entered the house and dropped her backpack in the dining room. She moved into the living room and threw herself down on the couch. Her mother was hot on her heels.

"Speak to me. That was the most awkward ride home I've given you—and there have been some bad ones this year!"

Samantha felt a hot, horrid pressure in her chest, and she wanted to scream into the pillow, but all that came out was a long, low sob. The tears burned her eyes and soaked into the fabric. She pulled in a raspy breath, and sobbed again in spite of herself. She could feel her mother's eyes on her, but it didn't matter as she twisted her fingers into the sides of the pillow.

"Oh honey, come on. Everything's alright." Mrs. Symanski

kneeled down next to the couch and Samantha felt her mother's hand caressing the back of her head. "Take some breaths, it's okay. See, you're sounding better already." Samantha shuddered as she sat up and wiped the tears from her cheeks with her thumbs.

"What happened? Can you tell me?"

Samantha tried to speak again, but another sob was looming. She closed her eyes and clenched her fists, regulating her breathing.

"It's not boy trouble, is it?"

"No!" Samantha burst, outraged as she blinked another onslaught of tears away. "I'm not that kind of girl."

"Uh-huh," Mrs. Symanski said with no confidence. "What happened? You make me repeat myself so much."

"…I think I killed a man."

"Colonel Mustard in the ballroom with the candlestick?"

"Be serious!" Samantha wailed. "My teacher is dead!"

"Barb?"

"She's the principal, mom. She doesn't teach any classes."

"Oh, that's sad. Which teacher?"

Samantha bit her lip. "Mr. Becker."

Mrs. Symanski was quiet, her lips pursed. "What makes you think you're a murderer? Did you really kill this man?"

"I didn't physically hurt him," Samantha said. "He committed suicide. He's been so depressed since Nikki went missing."

"Oh, he's her father," Mrs. Symanski nodded.

"Yes…" Samantha folded her hands in her lap. Her mother sat next to her on the couch and put an arm around her shoulders. "I went to visit him with a friend."

"You visited a teacher outside of class?"

"I had to! I needed someone to confirm that I'm not crazy."

"You should never visit teachers outside of class. Suppose one of them is a psychopath, or tries something inappropriate?"

"I went with Becca," Samantha retorted. "I asked him if it's normal to think your house is haunted."

"Don't be silly," Mrs. Symanski said. "We're perfectly safe—"

"Is that why there's a camera in the upstairs hall? Because we're perfectly safe?" Samantha narrowed her eyes.

Mrs. Symanski ignored her comment. "Tell me what happened next."

"He was all depressed, and we got to talking about the meaning of life."

"The meaning of life?"

"Yeah."

"What's the meaning of life, Samantha?"

"I said it was about family. Nothing's worth living for without family. And his daughter is missing. I should have thought about that before I said anything! And his wife's not in the picture…she's dead too. So I basically told him he had no reason to live."

"You think you were the straw that broke the camel's back? It sounds like he was looking for any excuse…a way out."

"And what are you looking for?" Samantha's eyes flashed. "Microphones, cameras, long projects on the computer, never leaving the house—you're keeping something from me."

"You're keeping lots of things from *me*. You visited a strange man's house without bothering to let me know where you were," Mrs. Symanski replied. "I don't know what's happening. Suddenly you have this attitude of entitlement, like you just get to go wherever you want and do whatever you want. Well guess what? You don't. You're grounded. No prom. Let your date know you won't make it."

"I can't believe you!" Samantha screamed, the tears flowing again. The lights flickered and Mrs. Symanski glanced around. "This is the worst day of my life *before* I get home, and then you manage to top it! You hate me! You must hate me! But that's fine! Because I hate you! I hate you for making me leave my old life. I hate you for moving us to this stupid town in the middle of nowhere, into this stupid house! And I hate you for making me into someone I don't like!" Samantha bolted to the stairs.

"You don't get to decide when this conversation is done!" Mrs. Symanski yelled and pursued her. "Samantha Rose! Get back here and listen to me!"

Samantha was in her room and slammed the door before her

mother got up the stairs. She locked it and leaned on the door. The doorknob jiggled.

"Go away!" she yelled.

"Samantha Rose Symanski, I am your mother, and this conversation is not over! Open this door right now!"

"No! I don't wanna see you!" Samantha's shoulders shook as she held in a sob. "None of this would have happened if it wasn't for you!" The lights in her room flickered. Her alarm clock radio went off and began playing *Hopelessly Devoted to You*. Samantha screamed and ran to unplug it. The room was silent other than her gasps and her mother's fist pounding on the door.

"Open this door or I'm throwing you out of my house!"

"That's fine with me!"

The sound of rattling glass filled the air. Samantha's butterflies began to fall from the bookcases one by one, and shatter on the floor. She backed away from the walls and stood in the middle of the room. The bed seemed to be shaking, vibrating the floor. Her alarm clock radio began to play again. Samantha stared at the plug, lying on the floor, a foot from the nearest outlet.

She felt her knees wobbling as she turned to her mirror. The dark figure of a man looked back, an arm draped around her reflection. She ran to the door, unlocked it, and flung it open. She slammed into her mother and they toppled over in the hallway.

"Samantha, what is wrong with you?!"

She shook her head in reply and got up, ran down the stairs, snatched her coat and disappeared out the front door.

LEVI AND TIM SPRAWLED across the floor of Tim's living room, homework scattered around them.

"I'm still not sure why he did it," Tim shook his head.

"Jennifer didn't hear about a motive?"

"No. What do you think?"

"I guess he thought he had nothing else to live for," Levi shrugged. "His daughter's been missing for months. What are the chances she's actually alive?"

Tim nodded, taking a drag from his joint. "What about his wife?"

"Dead. Brain tumor years ago."

"That is mondo fucked up." Tim exhaled a billow of gray.

"Then he's all alone."

"I know how that feels."

Levi shook his head. "You still have Felix. And your grandfather's alive. You're not as alone as you think."

"My brother hates me for God knows what reason and my grandfather is senile." Tim took another puff. "I really am alone."

"You're wallowing."

"You wallow a lot more than I do."

"I don't think so." Levi went to the window and surveyed the street. Central Avenue's lights were on as the sky faded from twilight into night. A few cars were driving, but traffic was sparse. "You're all emotionally wounded and shit."

"I'm just dealing with the massive betrayal of my brother and someone I thought was my best friend." Tim shuffled some papers.

"I was your best friend?" Levi smirked a little.

"Shove it, asshole."

"I'll let you cool off." Levi stood and left the apartment. He walked down the stairs and onto Central Avenue's sidewalk. Leaning against the building, he let the cold air sting his face. Cars passed. One slowed down. He watched it. The blinker was on. It turned into the parking lot and Levi felt a wave of dread as it parked.

"Levi," Felix said as he got out of the car. "I heard you and my brother had a falling out. What are you doing here?"

"Homework. I thought you weren't coming back until spring break."

"I am."

"You're a few days early, man."

"I know." Felix opened the trunk of the car and pulled out a suitcase.

"Why?"

"Because I have business to handle in town." Felix shut the trunk and locked the car. "It's going to take a few days."

"Does that business have anything to do with Randolph Kerner?" Levi raised an eyebrow as Felix turned his cold eyes on him.

"I have a lot of family issues to sort out this time around, Levi. The least of which is my brother's sudden relapse into drug abuse. Which, I understand, is your fault."

"You certainly like to blame other people for the consequences of your actions." Levi shook his head. Felix flexed a leather-gloved hand.

"Sounds like you're projecting your bullshit onto me, Levi Mauer. Take a walk and clear your head, before you say something you'll regret." He turned and entered the building.

THE BENCH IN VETERANS PARK chilled Samantha's body. A military helicopter mounted on a pole in the center of the park slanted forward, threatening to escape. City Hall rose in the background behind the chopper, a bland, blocky mass of brick that was easily tuned out. An occasional car went by. She closed her eyes and tilted her head back. The wind chilled her cheeks, and for a moment she was numb. She imagined she was floating. Footsteps crunching on the snowy sidewalk took her out of her reverie. She listened as the footsteps grew louder. She hoped they would walk by the little park. The footsteps stopped, as if whoever was walking had paused and looked around. Then they got louder still, coming down the path toward her. She opened her eyes to see a leather-jacketed boy standing over her.

"Hey," Levi said.

"Hey."

"You should scoot over." His breath was carried away on the wind.

Samantha obliged, and Levi sat next to her. "What do you want?"

"A place to sit," Levi replied. "What do you want?"

"A place to sleep." Samantha pulled her coat close to her body.

"On a park bench? You live a block away."

"Easy commute to breakfast in the morning." Samantha closed her eyes again.

"It's too cold to sleep outside."

"I know that."

"Then why are you—"

"Can you just shut up and let me relax?"

"Fine, I'm just—"

"Pointing out the obvious. Thanks. Your words are so profound." Samantha snuggled into her coat a little more, but a simple gust of wind shattered her illusion of gained warmth. Her teeth chattered. "Of all the places in North America, why did anyone move to Wisconsin?"

Levi was silent. Samantha furrowed her brow at him.

"Oh. That wasn't rhetorical?"

"I don't know what I expect from boys, honestly." Samantha shook her head.

"We're supposed to see some snow melting over the next few weeks." Levi looked at the icy trees. "Winter's almost over."

"It feels like it's been here since October."

"And it goes through April. Pretty normal here."

"I'll never get used to it. Good gravy, I hate talking about the weather."

"What do you want to talk about?"

"I just want to sleep, Levi."

"You have a bed."

"In a haunted house."

Levi was quiet again. Samantha waited for his response, uncertain.

"I'd sleep in your bed. Regardless if the house is haunted."

Samantha blushed in spite of herself. "You phrased that very strangely."

"I'm not that articulate."

"You know how to use 'articulate' in a sentence. That means you're articulate."

"I read that book." Levi cleared his throat. "*East of Eden.*"

"Really."

"It's not about a man who falls in love with the wrong woman."

"It is so."

"No. It's about brothers fighting. Like Cain and Abel. The older brother gets the younger brother killed and then has to deal with it. Three generations of a family reliving the Cain and Abel story over and over again."

Samantha thought for a moment. "I suppose that's true too."

"You should go home," Levi said. "It's late."

"My mom's not worried," Samantha scoffed. "She's not concerned about me at all."

"You're wrong about that."

"She's lying to me, keeping secrets from me—"

"Sometimes you have to lie to people you care about to protect them." Levi stared at the silent military helicopter. "Lying isn't a sin."

"Let's avoid whatever drama is on your mind," Samantha said. "I gotta worry about my own."

"Ya. You're right." Levi stood up. "I'm glad I ran into you tonight, Samantha. I'll see you at school."

"Yeah," Samantha nodded, unable to suppress the feeling of curiosity. "You look like you had an epiphany."

"I feel like I've had an epiphany." Levi bent over her. For the briefest moment, his icy lips grazed her numb cheek, and she felt a bolt of electricity course through her. "Later."

"I'M GLAD YOU CAME BACK." Mrs. Symanski sat up on the couch, wincing a little as she grabbed the arm. "Where were you?"

"Nowhere." Samantha shivered as she put her coat in the closet.

"You were gone for a while."

"Just went to Veterans Park."

"Oh honey, you might get sick."

"I'm going to bed." Samantha headed up the stairs.

"Samantha." Mrs. Symanski followed her daughter up the stairs. "You need to talk to your brother. He was devastated when he found out you left."

"Fine. Where is he?"

"He's in your bed."

"What?!"

"He was scared, and it had to do with you, so I let him sleep in your bed. I'm warning you fair and square."

"I can't deal with you right now." Samantha walked down the hallway into her bedroom where she saw the boy-shaped lumps in her comforter. She slipped into a pair of pajamas before crawling under the covers. Brandon lay on a pillow next to her.

"Samantha," he whispered as she fluffed her pillow.

"What is it, runt?"

"Why did you leave me?"

"I didn't."

"You did so. You ran outside—"

"Go to sleep or I *will* leave."

"Please don't." She felt his little hands seize her sleeve. She looked into his round eyes, shining in the darkness. "You're not like dad."

Samantha was torn between wanting to slap him and comfort him. She sighed.

"There's nothing wrong with being like dad. I'm a lot like him," Samantha said. "I got all his good sides. So did you. Don't forget that."

"I won't," Brandon murmured.

The room was silent save for the sound of Brandon's rhythmic breathing.

"Brandon, I need your help," Samantha whispered.

"Why?" Brandon wiggled next to her.

"We need to find out what mom's up to."

"Nuh-uh."

"Yeah-huh. Do you know what mom does for her job?"

Brandon's eyes opened and he frowned. "No."

"Isn't that a little weird?"

"I don't know what anybody else's parents do for a job either. So I don't care."

"Still, we should find out. I got a plan. It's going to be just like in those spy movies."

"And I get to help?"

"Yes," Samantha nodded. "Here's what I want you to do."

NO ONE SPOKE DURING BREAKFAST. Samantha chewed her cereal while Brandon munched on his toast. Their mother had her laptop out, and squinted at the screen, typing sporadically. Samantha finally worked up the nerve to speak.

"I wish you'd tell me what's going on."

"There's nothing going on," Mrs. Symanski replied, not looking up from her laptop.

"You're lying. I've lived with you my whole life. I know when you're lying."

Mrs. Symanski met her daughter's eyes. "My job is nothing you need to concern yourself with. Now eat your cereal."

"What about career day?" Brandon asked. "You wouldn't be able to tell anyone about what you do. That'll make me look bad."

"No one looks good on Career Day," Mrs. Symanski snipped. "Besides, my job is boring."

"But—"

"Brandon, don't you start off on this nonsense like your sister. My job is important, so important that only people in my company get to know what's happening. Understand?"

"Yes," Brandon simmered. Mrs. Symanski returned her attention to the screen.

Samantha drummed her fingers on the table and huffed. Brandon went into the kitchen. The sound of pattering keys kept the silence at bay. Samantha glanced at the kitchen door. The sound of the microwave shutting made her heart race. She looked at her mother, who stared, unwavering, at the laptop screen as her fingertips pecked away at the keyboard. It took almost five minutes before the smoke detector started beeping.

"MOM!" Brandon yelled.

Mrs. Symanski bolted into the kitchen, leaving the laptop open and unattended. Samantha slid into her mother's seat, whipped out her cell phone and snapped a picture of the screen.

"Brandon, what did you do?" Mrs. Symanski's voice echoed from the other side of the kitchen door.

"I'm sorry, I didn't mean it! I wanted something else to eat!"

"It's okay. Get a cup of water, we gotta put this out."

Samantha clicked on tab after tab and snapped picture after picture. Palms sweating, she returned the screen to its original tab and slid back into her seat. She shoved her phone into her pocket as her mother burst back into the dining room.

"What happened?" Samantha asked, her voice shaking.

"He put pancakes in the microwave for ten minutes instead of one. They caught fire." Mrs. Symanski looked at the laptop screen, grabbed the mouse and began clicking away. Samantha knew she was shutting the tabs. "He's never touching that microwave again." She shut her laptop screen. "Come see how bad these are burnt. It's hilarious."

"Okay." Samantha felt a wave of elation as she entered the smoke-filled kitchen and Brandon subtly gave her a thumbs-up.

"WHY ARE YOU TWO always at each other's throats?"

"I thought I explained that months ago." Tim shot Levi a look.

"Ya, you did. The situation is different now. I figured, you know, things must have changed..." Levi sat with Tim in the apartment, popcorn bursting in the microwave.

"Have you ever noticed that popcorn sort of smells like urine?" Tim winced as he sniffed the air.

"You've ruined it for me forever. Thanks."

"Any time, my man."

"Where's Felix?"

"I imagine he's off to the old folks home to visit the grandfather he's pretending doesn't live around here anymore."

"You haven't confronted him yet?"

"Not yet. When you bailed, he came in. Thanks for the warning, by the way."

Levi brushed off the guilt. "Anyway—"

"Yes, back to my story. He laid into me about my habit. Started rummaging through my cupboards, looking for my stash. He hasn't found anything yet."

"But don't you usually keep it in the—"

"I move it around the apartment," Tim snapped. "And I'm not disclosing the location to you. You'll probably just turn on me and tell him. Then he'll take it all and destroy it."

"No I wouldn't."

"History proves otherwise."

"I wouldn't," Levi maintained. "Matt needs it to transform safely."

Tim nodded, but didn't look convinced. "When Felix comes back, I'm letting him know that I know."

"Okay."

"Popcorn's done," Tim announced as the microwave beeped.

"I think I should go." Levi stood up. "Need to get the furnace fire started at home."

"Not sticking around for the fireworks?"

Levi couldn't hide the dread in his words. "I'm sure I'll hear all about the fight."

SAMANTHA LAY IN HER BED, her door shut. Sweaters and dresses were draped over the mirrors, her alarm clock providing the only light besides her phone. The screen cast a powerful beam as she aimed it around the room like a flashlight. Satisfied she was alone, she hid under the covers with her phone and pulled up one of the pictures of her mother's computer screen. She squinted and zoomed in on the picture. It was blurred, but she could still make out some words.

"'*Aegis Dynamics*...*Symanski. Report number*' something something '...*in cooperation with HSARPA*...*Project Runway*...'" She blinked. "Project Runway?" She kept reading. "*Evidence is scattered*...*subject to tricks of*...' tricks of what? *Devices to monitor locations in place*...*No activity observed. Audiovisual recording devices imply activity overall is sparse. Activity stronger on second*...' second what? '*See footage to observe several instances of...'* of what? *'Sound activity more...'* more what?" She flipped to the next picture.

"'*...into the supernatural with Project Doorways.'* Oh, so it's not Project Runway. '*...It is in the best interest of the United States Federal Government and its people...alternate forms of warfare, defense, and covert operations are sufficiently explored. In part, HSARPA...partner with former Aegis Dynamics members via the implementation of Project Doorways to investigate alternate forms of...'* Forms of what?"

The next picture was a still from footage of the hallway. It was empty. There were several bar graphs that looked like sound recordings.

"What the hell are you researching, mom?" Samantha whispered. She turned her phone off and tried to close her eyes, but her mind raced with questions.

LEVI STOKED THE FIRE in the furnace. It glowed as he put in a half-log of wood and shut the grate. The house was hard to keep warm despite his best efforts. He shoveled the snow out of the master bedroom and insulated the shattered window with tape, garbage bags, and a mattress, but without more heat, the floor would ice over. At least the days were getting longer again, promising an eventual end to the typically wicked Wisconsin winter.

The sound of a car door slamming made Levi tense up. He went to the kitchen window and looked out. A bland sedan was parked at the side of the road, and Felix stalked down the snowy driveway toward the house. Levi felt his stomach drop and ducked from view. He heard Felix stomp onto the porch and pound his fist on the door.

"Levi!" he screamed. "Levi, you little shit, open the damn door!"

Levi held his breath and stood in the kitchen, a wave of panic overcoming him. Felix continued to pound on the door.

"Don't hide from me! I see your goddamn truck parked out here, you motherfucker! Open the damn door or I'm blasting my way in!" The door boomed, making the house shake. It boomed again. Was he kicking it? There was a pause. Levi looked down the hall from the kitchen to the front door. The wood above the door handle exploded as the sound of a gunshot ripped through the air. Levi's ears were ringing as Felix's foot pounded the little hole larger. His gloved fist came through, and unlocked the door from the inside. It swung in on creaking hinges, the cold outside air whistling in around Felix's menacing frame.

"You broke your promise," he fumed, shutting the door behind him.

Levi couldn't help but back away as he saw Felix's gun glinting in his hand. "I did," he admitted. "But not all of it."

"You're a filthy liar," Felix snarled. "You know what the next step is. I call social services on your ass."

"And I'll turn them onto you and Tim," Levi replied as calm as he could manage, backing down the hall.

"I could just kill you now," Felix said with a half-smile. "Bury you under that collapsed barn, maybe. I bet that's where you buried your parents. You could all be reunited."

"Felix, don't." Levi felt his voice crack as Felix raised his gun to eye level. "I kept your promise the best I could."

"Then explain why Tim is cross-examining me with questions I answered years ago."

"He realized the answers you've been giving him are wrong."

"I told you not to take Tim to the retirement home. I told you not to let him find out about the family." Felix cocked his gun.

"I didn't know Randolph was your grandfather," Levi countered. "If *you* would have been straight with me, I wouldn't have had Tim along."

"I told you not to take him *at all*, and you did anyway. You're blaming others again for your inability to follow directions, Levi. Randolph doesn't even remember Tim."

"He called him Carson," Levi said. "He called him Carson and started going on about Jocelyn...your mother."

"Shut up," Felix growled, his cold eyes on fire.

"Randolph's the one who let out the truth. I wouldn't have taken Tim if I had known, Felix. I swear."

"Shut up!" He let off a shot into the ceiling. Levi jumped. Tiny pieces of plaster rained down on the floor. Felix breathed deep, closing his eyes and rubbing his temples.

"You're paying for that," Levi said. "That and my front door." The wind whistled through the hole in the door as if to emphasize the point.

Felix sighed. He strode over to the lone couch in Levi's living room and sat down, a bit of dust flying up. He looked around in revulsion. "Now Tim thinks he wants to hunt werewolves and he's hounding me. I can't have him doing that. Father will kill me if he ever finds out Tim knows."

"He's in jail. He only knows what you tell him."

"You don't know anything about this whole set-up. See, I'm not his only visitor," Felix chuckled. "He still has his friends in the hunting community. If Tim starts down that path…he *will* find out."

"You couldn't just lie?"

"To my father? I've had to put up that charade for at least a decade, to my own brother. I can't do it to my father as well." He scratched his forehead with his thumb.

East of Eden flashed in front of his eyes, and he swallowed hard. "I have sympathy for you, man," Levi mumbled. "I know what you've been going through."

"You don't know shit, Levi Mauer, and if you value your life you'll stop talking."

"I do know," Levi continued. "Your father pitted you against your brother by making you his caretaker and father. At the expense of your pain and frustration, he saved Tim from a lifestyle he didn't bother to save you from."

"There's nothing to save me from. I'm *not* a werewolf hunter," Felix said.

"You're still around it," Levi replied. "Surrounded by the remnants of your father's life. His friends, his contacts, you've been handling his responsibilities while he's been—"

"In jail," Felix huffed.

"And you don't feel like *you're* in prison?" Levi shook his head.

"I don't."

"Deny it if you want, Felix. You're the brother who doesn't want to hunt, but Tim does. You want a normal life. It's written all over you. Look at that boring sedan you take up here. You have all the normal, boring shit. Except for that damned gun you have at all times."

"I live in Chicago."

"Isn't it illegal to have guns there?"

"That's why more Americans die in Chicago than Iraq." Pale eyes narrowed at Levi. "I'm no fool."

"You're willing to live in a dangerous city to be as far from Tim and your father as you can possibly be."

"Yes I am," Felix said. "I prefer it. And here you are, surrounded by *your* father's empty house, carrying on *your* father's work, and you seem to be just fine with plodding away, wasting your life in Marshfield."

"I'm not wasting my life," Levi said. "I'm a sophomore in high school. I don't have a life to waste yet."

"Believe me, Levi, you have a life. And you're wasting it." Felix stood up. "Handling your father's responsibilities."

"We're a lot alike," Levi surmised.

"Indeed."

"Felix, stop trying to be Tim's dad. It's not your place."

"It's not *your* place to tell me what my place is, kid."

"Double standard right there, but I'll let it slide for now," Levi murmured. "You're Tim's brother, not his father. Be an older brother to him."

"And what would you know about being an older brother?"

Levi threw up his hands. "Tell him the truth and look out for him! Stop trying to raise him to fit the mold your father wants! That's your father's job, and when he decides to take a role in Tim's life, he'll get to have a say. But not until then. It's not fair to Tim, and it's not fair to you."

"There's a lot about life that is unfair, Levi. You of all people should know that."

"You feel like Tim owes you for all your efforts, and he doesn't appreciate what you've done."

"He couldn't possibly. He doesn't understand what I'm doing and why," Felix shot back. "Of course I feel that way. And it's true; he'll never be able to make it up to me. Everything I've sacrificed."

"I think, if you give him a chance, he'll pay you back. It'll be worth it."

Felix seemed to ponder Levi's words for a minute, his face somehow a myriad of expressions yet devoid of emotion. "You seem so full of..."

"Wisdom."

"Bullshit," Felix corrected. "To be fair...you make more sense than most kids your age."

"Thanks. Are you going to pay for the damage to my house?"

Felix stood and looked at the hole in the ceiling, then walked to the front door and looked at the hole over the handle. "I'll buy you a new door and have someone come out and plaster that ceiling back up. But you gotta make this place look less...abandoned. The repair guy will just drive by."

"I'm not here much," Levi said.

"I noticed you moved out of the apartment."

"Tim and I had a fight."

"About me."

"About what you asked me to do," Levi grunted.

Felix blinked, his cold eyes flashing a glint of warmth. "It's my fault you two are no longer friends."

"We're still friends."

"Are you?"

Levi nodded. "He still helps me out when I ask, and I've been over a few times."

"But it's not the same," Felix concluded.

Levi glanced down.

"That's a shame. It's rare when friends click so well they can live together." Felix put the safety back on his gun and pocketed it. He strode to the front door. "You should think about trying to live in town again. A new front door won't make up for the lack of companionship." He shut the door behind him. Levi stared at the hole above the handle, listening as Felix's steps crunched through the snow to his car.

"H...S...A...R...P...A," Samantha murmured as she pulled out her phone and stared at it. She sat in the hallway by her locker. She pulled up DuckDuckGo and typed in the letters. The results page popped up. "Homeland Security Advanced Research Projects Agency." She frowned. "Research projects?" She decided to head to the library during study hall to gather more information.

"How are you holding up?"

Samantha jumped up in shock. "Hey Matt."

"You look like you've seen a ghost." He peered into her eyes.

She blinked and pushed at him. "I'm just tired."

"You're always tired these days." His eyebrows came together.

"Life's exhausting."

"That's what sleep is for," he replied. "And you're not getting any."

She blinked at him, her thoughts fuzzy. "Do I look that bad?"

"Oh come on, Samantha. You look like hell."

"Thank you for your sensitivity," she spat. "You don't look so great yourself. One day you look like you're on speed, the next day depressants."

"Hey now, there's no reason for that," he raised his hands.

"It must be depressants today," Samantha concluded as Matt's face fell. "I'm...I'm sorry. Did you want to talk about something?"

"We haven't spoken since Becker died. I thought I'd see how you are."

"I'm fine," Samantha lied.

Matt tilted his head in disapproval.

"You don't want to hear it," Samantha sighed. The concern in his eyes made her go on. "I can feel the blood pulsing through the back of my neck, and it's sore. My brain feels heavy, and my eyes ache. How am I supposed to get through this day?"

"Go sleep in the school chapel. It's always warm in there. And quiet. Nobody will bother you."

Samantha shut her locker and leaned against it, closing her eyes, imagining the chapel's cushy seats, the altar bathed in warm candlelight and the air thick and drowsy with frankincense. "Maybe I'll do that…"

"We're still on for prom, right?"

Samantha cracked open her eyes and forced a smile. "I got the dress and everything."

"Cool." Matt drummed his fingers on the locker next to hers. Samantha could feel his hot breath on her face as he leaned closer to her.

"Can you answer a question for me?" Samantha slid away from him.

"Shoot."

"Mr. Becker's funeral…when is it?"

"Friday at OLP, right after school. The wake's on Wednesday at the funeral home down by Beell Stadium. You need a ride?"

"That would be nice."

"Hey Matt, Samantha." Kaeli strode up to them. "Matt, you'll never guess who's taking me to prom."

"Who?" Matt asked.

"Micah Schuh," she said, obviously searching his face for a reaction. "Be jealous."

"He graduated two years ago, Kaeli. He's too old for you."

"You just wish you could go with him."

"We still get one dance together, right?"

Samantha huffed. "Excuse me." She shoved past them and headed for the chapel.

SAMANTHA STARED AT HER mother's face as she drove on their way home from school, waiting for the excuses to begin, mentally preparing how to get around them.

"What would make you ask that question Samantha?" Her mother pretended to be absorbed with traffic, which consisted of three minivans tailgating an old sedan driving under the speed limit.

"It stands for Homeland Security Advanced Research Projects Agency." Samantha watched as her mother's face crinkled into a scowl, her lips pursed in anger. They turned onto Eighth Street.

"Will's mother picked up your brother today. Brandon's going over to their place until five. He's making more friends. Isn't that nice?"

"I know that Aegis Dynamics works with HSARPA on some projects. Are you on one of those projects?"

"Did you also know that if you ever get into my computer again I'll glue your fingers together?"

"I saw it on Wikipedia," Samantha pressed. "HSARPA is common knowledge, and so is their partnership with Aegis Dynamics...your employer."

"And?" Samantha's mother was practically steaming. "What's your point Sam?" They turned onto Oak Avenue.

"I think your company partnered with HSARPA and you're running some sort of experiment on our house."

They turned onto Park Street. "You and Brandon already know that I cannot and will not talk about my work—ever—with either of you. Do you have any idea what you have done? Do you realize I could lose my job over your little stunt? Then where would we be?"

"You moved us into that specific house for a reason. You knew it was haunted. It would explain the cameras and other monitoring devices you have stashed all over the place. You put us in danger, mom!"

Her mother turned off the engine and screamed. "I have never put you kids in danger! We are fine!"

"Fine?! I haven't slept in weeks! Brandon sees things, I see and hear things. Stop avoiding me! Just tell me what the heck is going on!"

"Nothing's going on! I'm working from home for Aegis—that's it. Why can't you accept that?" She got out of the SUV and slammed the door.

"You're studying something! Something in this house! In *our* house!"

"Samantha, don't be ridiculous. Go to your room before I say something I'll regret. You had no business snooping in my computer."

Samantha decided to change her approach. "Fine. But if anything ever does happen to me or Brandon and it was connected to your research, you'd never be able to live with yourself."

Samantha's mother pursed her lips as she opened the trunk and pulled out a bag of groceries. "Take this inside for me."

"I know you recorded something."

"It's not what you think, Samantha."

"Then tell me what it is!" Samantha's mother stared her in the eyes and shrugged. "I can't believe you're being this way! No wonder dad left!" Samantha stormed into the house. Mrs. Symanski followed her daughter, slamming the back door behind her.

"Samantha, you have to stop using our divorce as a weapon against me. Haven't you noticed your father hasn't been to see you or Brandon since?"

"Shut up." Samantha threw her backpack on the floor and hung up her coat.

"Don't talk to me that way Sam. I'm your mother, I'm always here and I don't deserve that kind of treatment. You wouldn't want to live with your dad. He's not the type of man to plant roots and tend to them."

"I'm not listening—"

"Yes you are."

Samantha crossed her arms. A chill ran down her body like a splayed hand, the hair rising on the back of her neck. "Did you feel that?"

"He'd have dropped you off to me one way or another, so be grateful that I love you enough to come back to this horrid town to give you and your brother a normal childhood! I've sacrificed a lot because you guys are my life on four legs. I love you both very much. I hope you know that."

Samantha felt her hair yank straight up. She clutched at her scalp and screamed.

"Samantha!" Her mother's face was pale, her eyes wide, as she watched her daughter's hair stand straight up in the air and then cascade down her shoulders.

"You know what?! I'm done! I'm calling Natalie, Laderia, Jennifer, I don't care. I'm not sleeping here tonight." Samantha pulled her phone out of her pocket and went into the kitchen. She couldn't stop the tears flowing down her cheeks.

"Samantha, I'm so sorry!"

"No you're not! Laderia said this place was a Masonic temple. Her parents didn't even want her to spend the night. The moms on Halloween were talking about it. Matt told me it had a dark past. And you're *from* this town! How could you not know?! You brought us here on purpose for your research! How stupid do you think I am?!"

Her mother stood in the kitchen while Samantha dialed Natalie's number.

"Hey girl!" Natalie's bubbly voice overwhelmed the speaker.

"Hey, Nat. Can I stay with you tonight?"

"As long as you don't call me Nat. That's a bloodsucking insect."

"Okay *Natalie*. Your parents are cool?"

"Oh, they're not. But if you're willing to climb a wall to reach my window—"

"I'll call Becca."

"Sorry! Bye."

Mrs. Symanski hugged her daughter's shoulders as Samantha dialed Becca.

"Hello!"

"Hey Becca, can I spend the night at your house?"

"Sure. You can help me brush my horse and we can carpool to school tomorrow morning. Need a ride? I can be there in an hour."

"That would be nice. Is it okay if I spend a few nights at your place?"

"My parents are gone for the week on a business trip, remember? I could use the company." Becca hung up.

Samantha looked into her mother's sorrowful eyes. "I'm leaving in an hour."

"We need to talk, Samantha." She tucked a lock of Samantha's hair behind her ear and wiped a tear off her cheek with her thumb.

"It's too late, mom." Samantha walked out of the kitchen. Her mother followed her to the base of the stairs.

"You're fifteen. You can't spend multiple nights away from home. I forbid it."

Samantha stopped and turned around. "This place is not home, mom. You can call it that all you want, but it's not going to make it true. I'm packing a bag."

"Your brother's going to take this very hard."

"Tell him I'll be back in a few days."

"I DON'T WANT TO be here right now," Becca hissed.

"Too bad. We're paying our respects, like everyone else," Samantha hissed back.

"Why do you care? You weren't even here a whole year yet."

"It's courteous, and I liked his class," Samantha replied. "Besides, he was helpful when we visited him."

"Father Declan's services are terrible." Becca sighed. "We should skip it. Coming to the wake is enough."

"Will you guys be quiet? This is really traumatic for me." Natalie choked as she dabbed her eyes with tissues.

"You didn't even have a class with him!" Becca whispered in exasperation.

"But I wanted to," Natalie sobbed. "I'll never get to fall asleep in his psychology class! That's a rite of passage to graduate here!"

"The end of an era, truly." Jennifer groaned as she twirled her hair and chewed her gum.

"Ladies!" Mrs. Hansen turned around in her seat and glared at them. "This is a funeral parlor! Be quiet."

"Pay attention, grandma." Jennifer kicked the back of Mrs. Hansen's chair. "Show some damn respect for the dead."

Mrs. Hansen turned fifty shades of red as she stared Jennifer down, who looked completely unfazed. Samantha felt her palms sweating and stood.

"Where are you going?" Natalie asked.

"To get some air," Samantha mouthed as Mrs. Hansen continued to fume. She slid to the aisle, then walked through the doors of the viewing room to the lobby.

A large, high-ceilinged space lined by doors, the lobby was almost empty. Samantha noticed a spiky-haired boy in a leather jacket leaning over the guest book.

"Hey Tim," she waved. He jumped a little before he looked up at her.

"Hey Symanski," he nodded. "What brings you out here to no-man's land? Everyone else is inside."

"Jennifer's pissing off Mrs. Hansen and I don't want to be around for the fallout." Samantha crossed her arms and stepped closer to him.

"What did she do?"

"She's kicking chairs, chomping her gum, the whole bit. The entire school's here. You'd think she'd be on her best behavior."

"She is," Tim said.

Samantha shrugged in defeat. "Why are you out here?"

"I'm trying to find Mr. Lancaster."

"Mr. Lancaster?"

"You know, the guy who runs the place. I used to work here." He ran a hand over his spiked hair. It didn't move. "Need some extra income, so I'm looking to get back in."

"You have a job?"

"I have two jobs," Tim grinned. "But the whole school knows about my other one. Well, three, if you count Levi."

"Is Levi here?" Samantha asked, too quickly for her own comfort.

"He declined," Tim said. "But he's coming to the funeral at OLP."

"So I'll see him—"

"There you are!" Becca hissed as she closed the French doors behind her. "How could you leave me in there?! Hansen was about to go all Robocop!"

"Hey Becca," Tim lifted his chin at her.

"Skeaze," Becca snipped.

Samantha looked around the empty lobby. The chandelier twinkled overhead as soft music floated from a nearby room. "I'm bored. Tim, can you give me a tour of this place?"

Becca's eyes grew large. "Samantha, stop getting me in trouble."

"I won't take responsibility for you, Becca. You get yourself in your own trouble." Samantha tossed her hair. "So how about it, Tim? I don't want to go back in there with the school in meltdown mode."

Tim scratched the back of his head. "Follow me." He walked across the lobby to the open doorway. "This is where they showcase various types of coffins. Didn't know there were so many choices, did you?"

"Wow..." Samantha followed him in, Becca reluctantly on her heels. Casket cutouts lined three of the walls; the fourth displayed a huge glass case filled with what appeared to be vases.

"Those are urns," Becca pointed.

"Very good, babycakes," Tim said. "And those weird crystal sculptures in there are made from people's ashes."

"Good gravy, they can make jewelry out of your ashes," Becca gasped. "Samantha, read this description. I could turn my grandma into the Heart of the Ocean."

"'I want you to draw me like one of your French girls, wearing grandma. Only grandma.'" Tim cackled at his own joke.

"I want to see something else." Samantha moved toward the door.

Tim led them back into the lobby and crossed to a set of double doors. "Here's another room for funerals. And there's another over there. The offices are through that door." He pointed down a short hallway.

"What about *those* doors?" Samantha pointed to a set of double doors near the casket display room.

"Oh, that's where they prep the bodies," Tim said. "Clothes, makeup, the works."

"Can we go in?" Samantha asked.

"No."

"Have you ever been in there, Tim?" Becca looked over her shoulder.

"I have, but not when a body's in it. Most of the time the bodies are stored in the basement and moved up here closer to the day of the funeral."

"There's a basement?" Samantha grinned. Tim shrugged and pushed one of the double doors open. The red glow from the letters of a distant exit sign provided the only light in the yawning darkness.

Becca took a step back. "I've got a bad feeling about this."

"Stay here and be the lookout. We're going in." Tim grabbed Samantha's hand. He pulled her into the dark. The door almost shut, but a thin crack allowed a ray of light from the lobby to run across the floor. Tim led Samantha along a wall. She could hear his hand sliding along the surface until suddenly the lights clicked on. They were in a large room, with doors on both sides and a staircase in the middle.

"Where do the doors go?" Samantha asked.

"Storage spaces and the garage. Those two are elevator doors. You almost can't tell, right?" He led her to the stairs. "Let's go down here."

"Won't we get caught?" Samantha asked. "You won't get your job back if you're caught breaking the rules."

"If we get busted, pretend I found you wandering around. Lancaster will hire me back for stopping dumb blondes from intruding on the bodies."

Samantha sighed. "I hate playing the dumb blonde stereotype."

Tim grinned as they walked down the stairs. "As a fellow blonde, I've used it many times before. You shouldn't be afraid of using what you got, Samantha."

"You're a boy, so hair color doesn't mean anything."

"Sexist Sammy Symanski is at it again." He put a finger to his lips when they reached a hallway at the bottom of the stairs. Several doors led off on either side. Samantha recognized a pair as elevator doors.

"Which room is for embalming?" she whispered.

Tim pointed to a door at the end of the hallway. When they reached it, Tim held up a hand and Samantha froze. She watched him lean down and press his ear to the door. Heart racing, she glanced back down the hall to the stairs, half-expecting to see the dark silhouette of a man leaning there. It was empty. She turned around to see the door open, and Tim standing in a bland white room, with white cabinets and a metal bed in the middle. A strange-looking machine sat on the counter nearest the table.

"Is that a blender with a speedometer on the front?"

"They drain the body of blood with that machine," Tim pointed. "It also pumps in the embalming fluids. At least that's what Lancaster told me."

"Creepy." Samantha looked at the hoses snaking from the embalming machine. "So this is where it happens."

"Ya," Tim nodded.

"They can do it all with one machine. Right here."

"Ya."

"So why is this place so big?" Samantha's brow furrowed.

"What?"

"Haven't you thought about it? There's too many rooms here. They have an elevator. Lots of storage. But one embalming room. Just one."

"Right."

"Isn't that weird?"

Tim raised an eyebrow.

"What's behind that door? With the padlock?" Samantha pointed.

"I've never been in there," Tim said. "Closet, maybe."

"I don't think so." Samantha stepped up to it and grabbed the padlock. "Why have this?"

"Valuable chemicals stored inside, most likely."

"You haven't broken into it yet?" Samantha looked at Tim.

"What kind of guy do you take me for?"

"You're not more suspicious?"

"It's locked, Samantha."

"Not for long." She pulled a bobby pin out of her hair and shoved it into the lock.

"Symanski, what the fuck!" Tim hissed.

"Keep a lookout. I need a moment." She adjusted the pressure on the bobby pin as she wiggled it, and after a minute of her heart pounding in her ears it clicked and released. She pulled the padlock off the door and swung it open. A pale white light came on automatically, revealing a gleaming metal table, metal stands, and several enormous, disc-shaped lights on large robotic-looking arms. Blocky machines lined the wall with a black television monitor.

"Is that…is that an operating room?"

Tim peered into the room. "Looks like it."

"Do they do autopsies here?"

"Shut it, Samantha. We gotta get out of here. It sounds like the wake is ending." Tim pushed Samantha out of the way and put the padlock back on the closed door. She felt his hands digging into her back as he pushed her out into the hall, where she slammed into the chest of someone very tall.

"Oh! I'm so sorry!" she gasped, rubbing her nose. She looked up into the face of a pale man with dark hair and a goatee. There was something incredibly menacing about the unblinking way he stared at her, a hint of amusement pulling at his lips. "This area is off-limits."

"I'm sorry! I was looking for a bathroom and Tim found me—"

"Tim?"

Tim stepped next to Samantha. "Hi Mr. Lancaster."

"Why, Timothy Kerner. What are you doing back here? Haven't seen you in months."

"Ya," Tim shrugged. "Mr. Becker's wake is today."

"I know," Lancaster smiled. "But what I'd like to know is what you're doing in the basement, which is clearly off-limits to the public. You should remember that."

"I do," Tim replied. "I was looking for you, actually. I was wondering if I could get my old job back, sir."

"And you just happened to bring this young lady with you to restricted areas?"

"No. She thought the bathroom was this way."

"Yes." Samantha nodded. She could feel her voice getting higher as her throat constricted. "I thought the bathrooms were through the double doors, but it was the stairs, and then I came down here, and thought it was the door on the end, because no others had a sign, and—"

"I was looking for you, and saw her," Tim said. "I was just going to show her the bathroom's off the lobby."

"You realize it's against the law to be in an embalming room without a license to practice mortuary." Mr. Lancaster's eyes almost glowed behind his glasses.

"Thank goodness there were no bodies in there!" Samantha forced a laugh. "I'm so ditzy sometimes. Must be why I'm failing English." She laughed again. "Like, for serio!"

"Take her out of here." Lancaster said.

"Will do," Tim nodded. "Sir, would you consider giving me my job back?"

"No," Lancaster snarled. "You were always late, you did a sloppy job, and you didn't have the courtesy to let me know when you quit. Don't expect a reference from me, you little burnout."

Samantha felt the color drain from her face.

"As for you, girl," Lancaster rounded on her. "The next time you're down here will be when I'm draining the last drop of your blood and pumping your dead veins full of formaldehyde. Understand?" She nodded. "Good. Now get out."

She ran up the stairs, Tim right behind her. They went out the double doors into the lobby, where Becca stood trembling as people filtered out of the viewing room.

"WHERE'D YOU AND BECCA disappear to?" Matt asked as the waitress set a large plate in front of him. "You missed Hansen's conniption."

"I don't like having angry old women glare at me." Samantha stared at Matt's plate. "Bacon, sausage, eggs, and ham?"

"Need my protein. Perkins is pretty healthy." Matt grabbed his fork.

Samantha looked at her own plate, a club sandwich and a large pickle with fries. She picked up her fork and stabbed her fries. "Have you ever met Mr. Lancaster?"

"Who?"

"The guy who owns the funeral home. Really tall. Dark hair, glasses, goatee."

"I've seen him around town," Matt replied with a mouthful of ham. "Why are you forking your fries?"

She ignored his question. "What do you think of him?"

"He's weird. But that's par for the course for most undertakers."

"You know a lot of undertakers?"

"We're in a restaurant. You're supposed to eat, not talk."

"Am I talking too much for you?"

Matt wrinkled his nose at her. Samantha huffed and stabbed her fries so hard the table rattled. People looked over and Matt met their gazes. They returned to their meals.

"There's something off about him," Samantha said, Matt glaring at her as he chewed. "Becca and I were looking around the funeral home."

"Becca's not the type to snoop. We had to drag her into Norwood."

"Well, she snooped with me. Tim was there too. He worked there for a while so he gave us a tour." Samantha watched Matt's eyebrows rise.

"I didn't think he was at the wake."

"He was in the lobby."

"Huh." Matt leaned away from his plate. "I don't want you hanging out with him."

Samantha blinked. "We don't hang out. And even if we did, you don't get to tell me who to hang out with."

"I do so. It's fair."

"It's not."

"So you're telling me you get to hang out with Tim and I don't get to hang out with Kaeli. And that's fair to you."

Samantha felt her face flush. "You can't compare me and Levi to you and Kaeli. You kissed her New Year's Eve."

"We're talking about Tim, not Levi," Matt's brow furrowed. "Or *should* we be talking about Levi?"

Samantha's mind went blank. "I have to—excuse me." She stood and walked to the bathroom, Matt's eyes burning into the back of her head.

The white tiles and fluorescent lighting were a reprieve as she shut the door behind her. A toilet flushed in one of the stalls. Samantha went to the sink, where a gnarled wooden walking stick occupied the counter space behind the faucets.

She looked in the mirror and ran her fingers through her hair. "What's wrong with me?" she murmured to herself. "I shouldn't be upset. I don't love Matt. He doesn't love me. I can't possibly love Levi—"

"Love's not love when it is mingled with regards that stand aloof from the entire point," said a high, girlish voice.

"Are you talking to me?" Samantha looked in the mirror as a stall door opened and a woman in sunglasses and an oversized sunhat emerged. She hobbled over to the sink and loaded her hands with soap. "King Lear?"

"Who is it that can tell me who I am?" She turned her face to Samantha as her hands scrubbed.

Samantha felt herself tense up. "Who are you?"

Her mouth trembled. "Ursula." She shut off the sink and ripped paper towels from the dispenser.

"I've heard stories about you around town. That you, um, were a dancer—"

"I am a man more sinned against than sinning," her girlish voice reprimanded.

"Sorry," Samantha said.

"Her voice was ever soft." Ursula's gnarled hand gripped Samantha's wrist. She winced as the wiry woman pulled her close, her voice darkening. "He's mad that trusts the tameness of a wolf…a boy's love…or a whore's oath."

Samantha's eyes widened as Ursula released her. She backed up to the door, felt for the handle, and slipped away, practically running to her seat.

Matt looked up at her. "You're pissed at me."

"No," Samantha sat down. "I ran into King Lear."

"What?" Matt leaned to the left to see past her. "She's coming out of the bathroom now. Walking stick and all. Holy crap. Did she talk to you?"

"Yes."

"What did she say?"

"Nothing. Just gibberish."

"HOW WAS THE WAKE?" Levi asked as Tim and Felix came in the front door of the apartment.

"So boring my little brother decided to hang out in the lobby," Felix droned. "Very disrespectful."

"You want to talk about respect?" Tim glowered, an edge in his voice. "How about hiding my grandfather from me? And our family business?"

"We spoke about this already," Felix's icy eyes flashed.

"No we didn't. Before you bolted you said you'd tell me about it when I was ready. I'm goddamn ready!" Tim yelled.

"Give me a moment, Timothy." Felix ran his hands through his dark hair. He turned and walked down the hall to the bathroom.

"I've got to tell you something important," Tim whispered.

"Your brother's here," Levi muttered.

"Don't worry. He'll be in there for a while. He needs to plan out his lies."

Levi glanced down the hall toward the bathroom. "What did you need to tell me?"

"Symanski was at the wake."

Levi scowled. "So? She was probably sitting with Stauber."

"No man, you gotta listen. I was just standing in the lobby, working up the nerve to search the place. She showed up and we talked a little, and she asked if I could give her a tour. So we went down to the embalming room, and she broke into that locked room for me."

Levi blinked. "Are you serious?"

"Completely. And guess what was in there. A surgeon's table. And surgical lights. And medical equipment. I'm telling you man, there is a fully-equipped O-R in the basement of the Lancaster Funeral Home. You know what this means, right?"

Levi nodded. "Avelina Rothschild is somehow funding Lancaster."

"Irrelevant."

"Lancaster's raking in the dough competing with the Marshfield Clinic?"

"Dammit, man. It means we have to get cracking about Doctor Reinhart. Immediately."

The door to the bathroom opened and Felix came out, rubbing his temples.

"Alright Tim, let's get down to it. I'll answer your questions."

"I should go," Levi stood up.

"You should hear this too." Felix gestured for them all to sit down. "Now Tim, start asking questions." Tim stared at Felix, and they sat in silence.

"Anything you want to know?" Felix asked.

"I'm debating the odds of every answer being fiction."

"First I'd have to give answers, wouldn't I?"

Tim visibly seethed. "How did mom die?"

"She was mauled," Felix murmured. "She was a hunter along with dad. They were a team."

"And dad?" Tim glanced briefly at Levi, but it was enough to send a wave of nausea that threatened to overpower him.

Felix looked at Tim without blinking. "He tracked down the werewolf who killed mom—a store owner or something. Dad killed him while he was still human."

"So how did dad die?"

"He…" Felix looked Levi in the eyes. Levi couldn't move. "He was fatally wounded in the struggle and bled to death."

"That's the truth?" Tim narrowed his eyes. "He could kill werewolves but he couldn't kill a man? Even Levi—Levi could kill a man."

"That's the truth," Felix said. Unease settled in Levi's chest as Tim digested Felix's words.

"Why would you hide all this from me? What entitled you to keep me out of my birthright?"

"It's not a birthright, Tim. It's a choice. Dad didn't want you to be a werewolf hunter. He always said he wanted us to have normal lives, but after mom's death, he needed to know you'd be protected. He trained me for it, all the way up to his death. But he never wanted you to do it. He wanted you to have a normal life; to grow up a normal kid."

"It sure didn't turn out that way." Tim crossed his arms.

"I did my best," Felix said through gritted teeth. "I'm twenty-five, Tim. People often think I'm a lot older than that. I had to grow up fast to make your life the way dad wanted it. I tried to fulfill his wishes. And you've been very hard on me for it."

"You never told me any of this."

"He didn't want you to know." Felix looked at the floor. "If he knew I told you this right now, he'd probably kill me."

"If he knew what I do for a living instead, he'd probably kill *me*." Tim chuckled a little bit. Felix cracked a shadow of a grin. "What is St. Hubert's Key?"

Felix squinted at Tim. "I don't know."

"*That* I believe." Tim rubbed his hands together.

"Anything else you want to know?" Felix asked.

"You know Levi's a vampire slayer."

"Yes."

"Why would you make him lie to me?" Tim asked.

"He's a vampire slayer. I knew he could keep a secret. And I'd been keeping mine for far too long."

SAMANTHA WOKE TO THE SOUND of her cell phone ringing. She reached over to her nightstand and her hand hit a horse-shaped lamp. She spastically caught it and set it back in place. She realized she was in Becca's room as she answered her phone.

"Hello," she yawned.

"You left me," a little voice said.

"I'm spending a few days with a friend, Brandon. I didn't leave."

"You left me." The call ended. Samantha set her phone to vibrate and laid it facedown. She pulled up the covers and closed her eyes. The phone rang again, almost vibrating right off the edge of the nightstand. She answered.

"Brandon—"

"He's in the hallway again. He's waiting by mom's bedroom door."

"Is there a lady in your bed?"

"No."

"Brandon, are you in your bed?"

"I'm under the covers."

"Try to sleep."

"I'm scared."

"Okay," Samantha stretched. "Stay under the covers. Lay down flat. Close your eyes and keep the phone by your ear. I'm going to tell you a story."

"I'm eleven."

"You're never too old for a story."

"…what kind of story?"

"A happy one. Once upon a time, in a faraway kingdom under the sea, there lived an ugly barnacle. He was so ugly that everyone died. The end."

Brandon snickered on the other end. "You stole that one."

Samantha felt a smile tug at her lips. "Okay, a real story. Let's see. Once upon a time, there was a man and a lady, and they had a daughter. She was a lonely girl because her parents were so busy. So she prayed she would be given a little sister to keep her company. After a year or two of praying really hard, her parents brought home a little boy. She was upset they didn't give her the sister she wanted. So instead, she dressed her little brother up in pink whenever she wanted, and she realized he was perfect the way he was, because God gave her the brother she needed, not the sister she wanted."

"I hate pink. That story stinks."

"Really? Tell me a better one."

"Once upon a time, in a galaxy far, far away, there lived a... samurai ninja... who battled... aliens... in space... camp... fire... they were nasty... he killed them all..." She listened as his breathing steadied over the phone and she lay down in the covers, triumphant. She set her phone next to her on the pillow.

"Good night, Brandon," she breathed into the phone.

"Good night Samantha," a man's voice breathed back.

RED AND BLUE FLASHING LIGHTS cast long shadows across the front of 311 West Park Street as Becca and Samantha pulled up.

"They beat us here," Becca stopped her car.

"Good. Do you want to come in?"

"I'll wait here."

Samantha jumped out of the car before Becca shut it off and ran up the front porch. She burst into the foyer, where several police officers stood whispering to each other. A blonde female police officer nodded to her. "Samantha."

"Officer Horace," Samantha replied with an awkward nod. "Where's my mother?"

"In the living room, with the chief. Your brother's in the kitchen getting interviewed. I want to speak to you as well." She pulled out a pad of paper and waved for Samantha to follow her. They went to the landing on the stairs and sat down. They could still hear the officers muttering to each other in the foyer.

"Did you guys catch him?" Samantha asked, knowing the answer already.

"We haven't found any evidence of a break-in," Officer Horace said. "What prompted you to call 911? You weren't even home."

"My little brother called me," Samantha explained. "He was scared. He said there was a man in the hallway outside mom's room. At first I thought it was just his imagination."

"And why would you change your mind about that?"

"I'm sorry about Jennifer," Samantha gushed.

Officer Horace blinked. "Excuse me?"

"I-I...I'm sorry about how she talked to you in the bathroom at school that day."

The policewoman pursed her lips. "When the Becker girl disappeared."

"Yes. I remember how mean she was, and I'm sorry. Jennifer's just Jennifer."

"Getting back on track." Officer Horace huffed. "What prompted you to call 911 on what you thought to be a figment of your brother's imagination?"

Samantha bit her lip, wondering how she should phrase hearing a ghost's voice. "Brandon fell asleep on the phone...we left the phone on for a bit, he didn't hang up, and I was listening. Then a man's voice wished me goodnight. No men live here. So I called 911."

"Are you certain it wasn't your brother?" Officer Horace's insipid tone carried in the stairwell.

Samantha frowned. "He's eleven."

"When people sleep, their vocal cords relax and their voices deepen." Officer Horace gestured to her throat. "You'll learn that in biology."

Samantha felt a pressure in her chest. "He wouldn't sound like a grown man."

"Can you be certain? You were probably tired as well."

"I know what I heard. Why won't you believe me?"

"Calling 911 is no joke, young lady. We take prank calling seriously. You cannot do that. It wastes valuable resources."

"I wasn't prank calling you!"

"You were picked up for toilet-papering Ms. Bennett's house."

"During Homecoming—what does that have to do with

anything?"

Officer Horace shut her notebook. "I think I have all the information you have to give."

"That attitude is why Nikki Becker is still missing," Samantha shot back. Officer Horace glared at her. "And why her father killed himself."

"Don't disrespect an officer." She put her hands on her hips. "It's not wise."

"What are you gonna do, sleep with my father too?" The officers in the foyer hushed and stared at them. Officer Horace reddened.

"You're out of line." She stormed down the stairs and out the front door, slamming it behind her. Several of the policemen chuckled. Samantha walked down the stairs and into the kitchen, where Brandon sat with a policeman talking to him.

"He's here every night?"

"I see him a lot. And a lady. There's a lady too—"

Samantha left the kitchen and went to the living room, where Police Chief Cromwell sat with her mother.

"No one else lives here. Just me and my children."

"We found no sign of a break-in."

"Because there wasn't one."

"Ma'am, are you aware of this house's history?"

"I grew up in Marshfield, Bill, same as you. The rumors were swirling when it was still the Masonic Temple."

"You know it's possible this place is haunted."

"Chief, don't tell me you believe in ghosts."

Cromwell cleared his throat and shifted positions. "It's possible."

"It's absurd." Mrs. Symanski glanced at her daughter. Samantha felt her throat tighten up. A hand slipped into hers. She glanced down at Brandon and a wave of relief washed over her.

"Then I have nothing to tell you." Cromwell closed his notepad and stood up. "We'll compile the reports we took tonight and give you a call back with some recommendations for actions you can take. Maybe install an alarm system, that kind of thing. Something more substantial than that camera in the hall."

"I'll be sure to lock all the doors and windows." Mrs. Symanski stood and shook Cromwell's hand. "Thank you for coming so quickly. It makes me feel very safe knowing Marshfield's finest are always ready to respond."

"You're...you're welcome." Officer Cromwell nodded. He walked past Samantha to the foyer, and the police filed out. He paused at the front door. "Sandra, call someone tomorrow about installing that alarm." He shut the door on his way out.

Mrs. Symanski stood with her arms crossed, staring at her children. Samantha had to use all of her willpower to keep herself from looking down.

"Samantha, come with me." Mrs. Symanski walked to the closet and put a coat on. The front door opened and Becca came in.

"The police are gone," she said. "Hi, Mrs. Symanski."

"Becca, can you sit with Brandon in the living room? Samantha and I need to have a chat."

"Okay." Becca's eyes were wide.

The air was cold as Samantha followed her mother out the door and down the front walk to the street. "Mom—"

"You dragged the police into this...Samantha, I don't know what you want me to do." Mrs. Symanski looked up at the house. "This is impossible for me."

"I don't know what you're talking about," Samantha shivered.

"I know you were on my computer. That's how you figured out Aegis and HSARPA are working together."

"It was on Wikipedia—"

"Your curiosity about that came from snooping in my work. Don't deny it. You understand my job is compromised if you know about my work. I cannot risk that, honey. I need this job. *We* need this job. If I lose my clearance..." Samantha's mother shook her head as she kicked at the snow.

"You're researching the house—because it's haunted," Samantha said.

"Because that is what they need me to do."

"For Project Doorways."

Mrs. Symanski looked her daughter dead in the eyes. "That is not public information, Samantha. I can and will lose my job. Do you understand?"

"I understand. But I can't live here, mom. I can't function in that house. Brandon can't either. We're not safe here."

"We're safer here than we would be back east, believe me."

"I don't think so. Can't you just change careers?"

"I can't. We have no choice, Sammy."

MASSIVE ARRANGEMENTS OF WHITE LILIES surrounded the black marble altar in Our Lady of Peace. Candles on brass poles twinkled, a hint of warmth in the somber space. Sunlight filtered through the skylight over the transept, illuminating Mr. Becker's glossy casket. As Levi approached, he could see it was open. A node of discomfort filled him. Tim stood next to him as he leaned over it, viewing the lifeless body.

"He looks peaceful," Tim murmured.

"He looks horrible." Levi took in every detail of Mr. Becker's face. The expressionless way gravity pulled on the dead flesh. The color that didn't sink any deeper than the powder on his skin. The thin lips and over-manicured eyebrows. Hair that looked like it would be more at home on a mannequin than a person. "Lancaster's work is getting sloppy."

"I'd say it's fantastic, considering he was hit by a train." Levi jumped as Felix's deep voice chimed in. "His lower half is probably nothing but chunks of flesh and bone bits shoved in a plastic bag. This coffin is a little short for him. I noticed." Levi shoved his hands in his pockets.

"Acceptable given the circumstances," Tim muttered. "A sudden death, a missing daughter, with a poor Catholic school footing the bill...why spring for the full casket? It's not like you care when you're dead."

"Are you kidding? Just look at this travesty." Several freshman girls sniffled two feet away.

Felix scowled. "Levi, you're making people cry."

"It's a funeral. They'll be crying no matter what."

Tim nudged him with an elbow. "Let's sit down." They left Felix by the altar as Barb strode up to them. Tim followed Levi into the furthest pew in back, giving them about two rows of distance from the rest of the congregation.

Levi looked over his shoulder out the glass doors to the circular drive in front of the church. "I see him. He's standing on the sidewalk, being evil, reveling in his evilness. He needs to die."

"He can't come any closer than the plotline, Levi. Hallowed ground, remember?"

Lancaster checked his watch with a wicked smirk pulling his goatee. "Do you think he can see us?"

"Samantha's up front," Tim whispered before ducking down into the pew. Levi looked at the back of Samantha's blonde head next to Matt's. She leaned on his shoulder, her hair shimmering.

"Sit properly, Tim. I'm heading out this afternoon." Felix slid into the pew next to them.

Tim sat up and looked straight ahead. "Have fun in the city."

"I'll be back on Memorial Day, Fourth of July, and Labor Day," Felix said. "I'm sorry you'll be alone again."

"You'll be alone too," Tim replied. "But we're used to this thing, aren't we?"

Felix nodded. Barb walked by, heading to the narthex. She scanned them as she passed. Felix looked over at Tim and Levi. "You two should repair your friendship. It was never my intention to sabotage it."

"HOW DO YOU KNOW that nobody's home?"

"He lives alone. No pets. I've been scoping him out for a while."

"Does he have a security system? I see a couple signs over there—"

"No, he doesn't, thankfully."

"Did you bring your lock picks?" Tim asked.

"Got them in the duffle bag," Levi replied as they walked down Hickory Lane. The road was slushy, and Tim let out a noise of frustration. *"Shut up, Tim."*

"I really need to get some boots." Tim shook his foot out, letting the slush fly off.

"Sorry about that, man. Thanks for being here when I need you. I'm glad you came."

"Stop buttering me up and making me feel guilty. You're the one who should feel guilty."

"There it is." Levi's breath fogged and drifted away on the wind. They looked up at the shape of a dark house dominating the little cul-de-sac. The streetlight somehow failed to illuminate it at all.

Tim shuddered. "Charming."

"Watch the cul-de-sac." Levi pulled out a walkie-talkie and handed it to Tim.

"You're always making me hang out in the snow," Tim complained through gritted teeth.

"We had to hide the truck. Can't have Reinhart getting a description and turning it over to Lancaster. He'd know it was mine."

"I understand the logic, it just sucks. This whole night sucks."

"It's the wet shoes, isn't it?" Levi hoped the darkness hid the smirk tugging at his lips.

"It really brings down the whole evening. Nothing is worth doing in wet socks."

"Not even saving lives?"

Tim cast a baleful glance at the snow bank by the ditch. "Honestly, how many people are suffering from Lancaster? Maybe we should drop the whole thing."

"Arthur Harris is dead, and that's the best thing that could have happened to him. Otherwise he'd have become a vampire and killed someone else. Lancaster's proven he's not above turning people into monsters. It's only a matter of time before he tries again."

Tim sighed in resignation and stalked into the snow bank, hunkering down. "Ready," his voice crackled over the walkie-talkie.

Levi nodded and walked up to the front door. The lack of light made his other senses heighten. He pulled the lock picks out of his duffle bag and in a couple seconds had the door swinging open. He stepped inside, and shut it behind him. Tim's muffled voice came out of the duffle bag. Levi grabbed the walkie-talkie.

"Can you hear me? What do you see? Over." Tim's voice asked.

"Don't say over."

"Don't say what? Over."

"This must be the obligatory walkie-talkie joke that comes with using walkie-talkies." Levi crept into the foyer, assessing the darkness.

"Yes it is. Over."

"This joke is over."

"Let me know when you find anything interesting, Levi."

"Will do. Over."

"You said it!"

"I slipped." Levi set the walkie-talkie back in the duffle bag. The house was dark despite the walls of glass and large windows. The furniture was modern as well. As Levi meandered through the living room and dining room, he pulled out the walkie-talkie again. "Tim, this man has no storage."

"What are you saying?"

"There's nothing here. No tables with drawers, no desks, no bookcases. Nothing I can rummage through. Just couches and lamps and bare surfaces."

"He must have a home office then."

"Good idea." Levi wandered from shadowy room to shadowy room. A pair of wooden double doors almost blended into the wall. He turned the handle and saw the shapes of a large desk, file cabinets, bookshelves, and a chair. He could barely see the outline of a lamp sitting on the desk. Levi turned it on, and began scanning the files strewn across its surface.

"Levi? Are you there?"

"I found his office." Levi glanced at the names on several files. "These look like medical records. Are doctors allowed to have patient files at their homes?"

"I don't know. Anything interesting?"

"Just a minute. There's a mini-fridge." He walked over to the wall and opened the little fridge. Its white light spilled into the room. "Wonder what he's got in here."

"Get back to the papers! I'm freezing my ass off!"

Levi shut the fridge, the clinging of little glass phials making him cringe before he headed back to the desk. He pulled open a drawer and nearly dropped his walkie-talkie. "I think I found something."

"What is it?"

Levi pulled out a thick stack of papers and laid them on the table. "It's a pile of lists. A bunch of words are highlighted."

"Any you recognize?"

"They're in Latin. I think they're medical terms."

"He's a surgeon. That isn't unusual."

"This doesn't look right."

"What do you mean? What's on those lists?"

"There's one name on each page—name, age, blood type. Then a list of terms. The first one is Carol Newman, age 86—that name is so familiar...Then it goes *tendo Achillis, ligamentum patellae*...these are tendons."

"Maybe she has tendonitis."

"*Had*. She died yesterday. I read her name in the obituaries. That's why I remember it."

"Okay, well, that's not a big deal, is it?"

"Next page is Harold Green. Seventy-five. Died last week. *Femora, fibula, ulna*—"

"Those are bones, Levi. Arm and leg bones."

"There's no way he's performing surgery on these people." Levi looked at the next page.

"Donald Becker, forty-six." He fell silent and stared at the name. His eyes traced it again and again, not even bothering with the list of parts. "Mr. Becker..." After a silence, Levi jumped when Tim's voice finally crackled its response.

"Levi, there's a car coming. A black Cadillac."

Chapter 12

You Are Dust, and to Dust You Shall Return

Samantha rubbed her burning eyes, then resumed staring at the computer screen. The library's other computers buzzed around her as students whispered. Mrs. Hansen glared occasionally from the desk. After minimizing her English essay, Samantha pulled up Google and typed in 'ghosts.'

"In traditional belief and fiction, a ghost, or specter, is the soul or spirit of a dead person or animal that can appear, in visible form or manifestation, to the living…duh."

She frowned and typed in 'ghost research.' "Ghost research society…ghost hunting, paranormal investigators…" She rested her head in her hands. "This is insane."

"Talking to yourself is insane." Natalie slid into the chair next to Samantha, who hastily opened up her essay again. "It's so much nicer working on that stuff in here than writing it by hand in the classroom, isn't it?"

Samantha nodded, heart pounding. Did Natalie see what she looked up? Wait, why would Natalie care?

"You look flushed. How far have you gotten?"

"Not very far."

"Me either," Natalie sighed. "I mean, I got an outline, so the structure is fine, but I'm not feeling up to typing this out. You can open up whatever you were looking at again. I don't judge."

Samantha opened the page. Natalie leaned over and squinted at her screen. Samantha prepared herself for ridicule.

"Ghost stuff. Oh. My dad loves those ghost hunting shows too. You never told me you were a fan."

"I'm not a fan."

"So why are you Googling it? Oh! Are you going to have them come to your house? You should totally register for a paranormal investigation. I hear if the case is big enough, they'll come out and film it. Your house would be perfect! With all the history—" Mrs. Hansen shushed them so loudly the whole library stared. Natalie bit her lip. "But let's not bring that up here."

"I don't know much about its history, just that it was a Masonic Temple." Samantha ran a hand through her hair, messing it up. "I can't find anything about it online. But everyone around town seems to know something... What do you know?"

"Only what they say around town." Natalie played with her red and white tresses. "Doctor Doege had it built before he founded the Marshfield Clinic. He used to see patients there sometimes. Rumor has it he was sleeping with one of his nurses, and her husband killed her in that house, then blew his brains out. Doctor Doege had to dispose of the bodies, so he buried them in the back yard and built a patio on top of the graves. No one ever found out."

Samantha processed the story. "How would people know it happened if no one found out?"

"Oh, it's not true! Most likely just a rumor. Probably completely fake. But still...it's a creepy story."

"You're not helping me, Natalie. My house *is really haunted*, and I don't care whose ghost it is or how they died. I just want them gone and no one to think I'm crazy. Do you understand?!" Mrs. Hansen shushed them again from her perch.

"I understand," Natalie whispered. "More than you think. See this?" She grabbed a fistful of her hair. "White stripes. Like a zebra. Norwood barn."

"Oh yeah, I almost forgot about that," Samantha murmured.

"I haven't," Natalie said. "I haven't told anyone this, Samantha, not my parents, not my therapist, no one…but sometimes I see them."

"Who?"

"The dead men from the tunnel. Sometimes when I close my eyes or turn my head too fast, I see them for just a split second. It makes dancing a lot more stressful…I like to think it's just trauma from the incident that makes me see them. PSTD or something. It's a lot better than thinking ghosts follow me around everywhere I go."

"Natalie…I had no idea."

Natalie's lips curled into a cynical smile and she rested her hand on Samantha's. "We're sisters in arms, battling the forces of the undead."

"Why don't *you* talk to the ghost hunters?"

"Because I don't want to get into trouble for breaking into the barn! But you could call about your house. You live there, it's your property."

"Technically it's my mom's—"

"Still. You gotta do what gets you through life." Natalie shrugged.

"What do you do when you see them? To get your mind off of them?"

"I think about how awesome prom is going to be."

"That can't work."

"Oh, it does. You'd be surprised. I also enjoy blaring music, pulling together playlists, and planning out things for our class. After all, next year it's our turn to host prom."

"Great." Samantha rolled her eyes again.

"Well, I'm going to let you get back to typing your essay." Natalie stood. "When you're free, maybe you can tell me what was going on with all the police at your house. Keep your sister in arms in the loop." She left the library.

Samantha looked at the screen again, and typed in 'how to get rid of ghosts.'

"Exorcism…of course. I should have known…" She clicked the

top result and began reading.

"BODY PARTS, LEVI. He trades body parts."

"Yup," Levi said.

"He takes dead people apart, takes out all the good stuff to sell, reassembles them sans good stuff, and dresses them up for funerals." Tim shook his head.

"I get it, man."

"Like a used-car salesman creating a showroom."

"Stop it, Tim. I get it."

"Levi, when I get my license, I'm opting out of the organ donor thing. I don't want to be sold for parts."

"You'd be dead, and you wouldn't care."

"I certainly wouldn't want my parts harvested by a vampire. What he's doing has gotta be illegal. Black market stuff. That's why he's got his own O-R. He needs a skilled surgeon who can keep up with it."

"Lancaster recruits Reinhart, who keeps all the files and instruments, and Lancaster hides the operating table. I wonder where he hides the organs." Levi stretched his arms above his head.

"Do we really have to pursue this? I mean, he's stealing organs from dead people. Nobody's noticed yet. Looks like he's selling them to rich people. That means more legit donated organs for poor people, right?"

"He's taking organs from non-donors, Tim. That means he's desecrating corpses and breaking the law. He has to be stopped."

"We can't turn him over to the cops. He'll just turn you over. He said so."

"I know. That means I gotta slay him somehow."

"He hasn't killed anyone doing this, Levi. I think it's safer to let sleeping dogs lie."

"He's not a dog, Tim. He's a monster. And being a vampire automatically means he's killed at least one person. He's probably killed more. We can't let him do that."

"With all due respect Levi, you killed a person too. I shouldn't let you do that again either."

"Lancaster is *not* a person, Tim. Sociopaths don't meet the definition of human."

"Do…do you even feel remorse for Arthur Harris at all?"

Levi nodded. "I see him all the time. It isn't easy to forget someone you killed. The fact is…I'm more upset about not being able to forget him, than actually killing him…what does that say about me as person?"

"Have you gone to confession about it?"

"I don't want to be turned over to the police."

"The priest *can't* turn you in, moron. That's the beauty of it."

"I don't want to confess to Father Declan. He's a dope."

SAMANTHA STOOD IN THE HALLWAY behind the gym. She looked around, satisfied she was alone, and pulled a scrap of folded paper and her cell phone from her pocket. She dialed. For an instant she hoped the phone wouldn't ring, but it did. She held it to her ear, waiting for an answer. It rang. And rang. Finally she got his voicemail. "You have reached Ken Shepherd, Demonologist. If you are calling regarding a television appearance, conference or speech, please contact my agent Larry Jones. If you're calling regarding an ongoing case, I can be reached by text. If you are calling regarding a new case, please leave a brief message after the tone with your name and number. Regards." The phone beeped. Samantha hung up, exhaling the breath she didn't realize she was holding.

"Why are you not in the cafeteria?" boomed a voice behind her. Samantha whirled around to see Barb's scrunched face glowering at her. "Give me that phone. You will not use it during school hours."

Samantha shoved it in her pocket. "I'm sorry. I was expecting a call from my mom."

"I doubt it."

"For real. I was checking my voicemail."

"Hand it over or I'll suspend you."

"This isn't that big of a deal!"

"Then dial your mother right now." Barb stared her down.

Samantha pulled out her phone and Barb pried it from her hand. "You need to learn to submit to authority." She pocketed it. "That's something your mother is incapable of teaching you. Get to the cafeteria. You'll get this back after school." Barb stormed down the hall, Samantha in tow.

"Mr. Shepherd, my name is Samantha Symanski. I live in Marshfield, Wisconsin, and my house is haunted. We have at least three ghosts. I was hoping you could tell me what I can do to get rid of them."

"How did you get this number?"

"The internet."

"Listen, sweetheart," came a raspy, deep voice, "if you want to get your house on television, first you need to pick one of the supernatural investigator shows, and pitch them your situation. If they accept your case, you can ask them to involve me. They'll call my agent. There's a process for this sort of thing—"

"Mr. Shepherd, I don't want my house on television." Samantha couldn't hide the terror in her voice. "We...I actually need your help."

"Relax. How old are you, honey? You sound cute. Twenty-two? Twenty-three?"

"I'm fifteen." The line was silent for a while. "Hello?"

"Look, sweetie, I will not go to Marshall—"

"Marshfield."

"—middle-of-nowhere-Wisconsin, just because a fifteen year old girl hears her heater rattling and thinks her house is haunted."

"It's not just me! The whole town knows—"

"Have you had your home evaluated by a group specializing in the paranormal?"

"Like who?"

"Pulling up your zip code...the nearest paranormal experts for you are in Stevens Point. Why don't you schedule an appointment with them and they can determine if your house really is haunted...or if it's just a drafty old house."

"They're not drafts—"

"Sweetie, I only take cases from adults. Grown-ups, who can legally drink. And right now, to be frank, I'm not currently accepting new cases, so don't take it personally. Regar—"

"Mr. Shepherd, you're making a big mistake!"

"Honey, I'm not—"

"You don't understand how serious this is! I can hear them walking in the halls at night. When I look out of my room, there's a man standing at my mother's door. My brother says a woman lies in bed next to him and disappears. I've seen faces in the mirrors, pictures have fallen off walls, radios and televisions play with no power—"

"Calm down—"

"I don't know what to do! My mom *knows* the house is haunted, but she won't fix it because she's afraid she'll lose her job—"

"Now that's an exaggeration, sweetie. No one is going to fire your mom for getting rid of spirits."

"She works for Homeland Security Advanced Research! Of course they will! But that's not even the worst of it! I've felt hands touch me, had my hair pulled, they say my—"

"Hold on. Did I hear you say your mother works for HSARPA?"

Her breath hitched in her throat.

"Sweetie, did you say HSARPA?"

"I shouldn't—sorry." Samantha hung up and threw her phone on her bed, her face flushed. She wanted to slap herself as tears of remorse streaked down her cheeks. What if her mom did lose her job? It would be Samantha's fault. The phone rang. An unknown number. She absently answered it. "Hello?" She wiped a hand down her face.

"Sweetie, does your mother really—" Samantha hung up again. Her heart pounded as the phone rang again. She waited for it to stop and turned her phone off.

SAMANTHA FINALLY TURNED her phone back on during lunch the next day. She checked her text messages. *I did not intend to insult you.*

Call me back. She checked her voicemail.

"Listen, um, sweetie, if you were serious about your haunting, I'd appreciate a call back. I'll also need your mother's consent—or your father's—to perform an exorcism at your home. Regards." Samantha drummed her fingers on the side of her phone as a debate raged in her mind. Should she call him back? Maybe text him? Maybe he could help. Maybe he couldn't.

She stepped out of the bathroom and into the empty hallway.

"Hey Samantha, how's it hanging?" She looked over at the tiny bench outside of Barb's office. Tim sat, completely relaxed, feet as far apart as they could be. "You looked stressed, my break-in beauty."

"I am stressed," she sat next to him on the bench.

"What's bothering you?"

"Personal ghosts."

"Been there. You need a visit from Sister Mary Jane?" He reached in a pocket.

"No," Samantha sighed and leaned back, resting her head on the brick wall. She glanced over at Tim. "What are you doing out here?"

He looked at her out of the corner of his eye. "I'm debating whether or not to resume my business ties with our fair daughter of the law."

"Jennifer's in the B's office right now?"

"You mean the B's coffin? Of course."

"What did she do this time?"

"Busted for wearing too much makeup. I figured I'd catch her on the way back to English. Teacher thinks I'm in the john."

"I don't think you should sell to her anymore," Samantha said. "If her parents find out she smokes pot, she'll wear twice as much makeup."

"I don't follow."

"Her father hits her. I saw him do it at their house, over dinner. That's why she cakes the makeup on. She's hiding bruises…she should tell Babs."

Tim was quiet. Samantha searched his face for some sign of

shock, but it contained only acknowledgment. "You know, cannabis relieves pain and promotes relaxation…healing."

"This isn't the time in her life to be giving her drugs, Tim. Her dad just put her mom into rehab and she's being watched like a hawk. To be honest I don't understand how she gets away with what she does."

"It helps having a powerful father who cares enough to try to knock some sense into you," Tim murmured. "Not that I'm advocating abuse—"

"Don't deny it Tim, you are." Samantha rolled her eyes.

"You don't get to call the shots for her life," Tim replied. "She can make the decision not to buy it if she wants. As for me, I like to make money."

"You're going to get her hurt. Sure her dad refuses to do anything about her—it doesn't mean he won't have the same reservations when it comes to you."

"Jennifer won't hand me over to him. She keeps her dad off my trail and I keep her prices low. There. Now you see my strategy. It was never in me to hold her off like I've been doing, it was cruel."

"Why would you cut her off in the first place?"

"The logical answer would be for greater financial gain elsewhere. The real answer…I've had to redirect supply to less profitable causes. No, that's not it either. I wanted to see her need me. As it turns out, she doesn't need me as much as the drug. I was being selfish. That's bad in relationships…business or otherwise." They enjoyed a moment of silence before Tim shifted gears. "How are your personal ghosts?"

"They're all over the place," Samantha shook her head. "Thoughts that haunt me…"

"Like what?"

Samantha bit her lip. She wanted to tell him something. Any burden she could cast aside would be a relief. "I ran into Ursula."

"Who?"

"King Lear. In Perkins, after our little tour of the funeral home."

"Right. What did she say?"

"A lot of things. I could barely understand her. I think she told me my fortune, though. It was odd, because it sounded more like a warning. 'Beware the tameness of the wolf, a boy's love, or a whore's oath'...what could that mean?"

"You better not make promises to hookers."

Samantha laughed in spite of herself. "She's such a weird lady...but part of me thinks there is some truth in it. The tameness of the wolf...she might mean Matt."

"A boy's love could also refer to Matt. Come to think of it, so could a whore's oath." Tim gave her a sly grin.

"I'm probably thinking about this too much. She comes off with the craziest things. Jennifer's dad, Police Chief Douche, said King Lear called the police station the night Nikki Becker disappeared and said she saw some girl being kidnapped by a cloud of bats. I mean, how much more ludicrous can she get?" She turned to Tim. His eyes were wide.

"I have to find Levi." He stood and ran down the hall.

Samantha shrugged, and began typing a response on her phone. *'My mom is okay with using your services. What do you charge? We don't have much money.'*

'Let's worry about cost later. Do you have a specific date in mind?'

'ASAP.'

'The soonest I can do is the last Saturday in April.'

'That's my Prom Night.'

'You don't need to be there. Just your mother.'

'That will be fine.'

TOWER HALL LEERED OVER LEVI, daring him to come closer. He mustered some resolve and marched up to the door. It was locked. Next to the door he noticed a panel of buttons with names listed by them.

"Aw hell, Tim, what is King Lear's real name?"

"I think Samantha said Ursula."

He hit the button next to the name Ursula Smith. A moment later, a loud buzz echoed from the speaker. He pulled the door and

Tim followed him in. The walls were a pale beige color with very dark wood trim. They moved up the stairs and stood in the hallway.

"I don't know which apartment is hers..." Levi muttered.

"Let's wait. Maybe she'll pop her head out and we'll find her."

Levi nodded. Sure enough, a door at the end of the hall opened, and a sunglass-wearing face peered out. "Where's the king?" she asked.

"I'm here," Levi walked up to her. She cowered behind the door as she opened it. "We need to ask you some questions."

"Reason not the need," she said as Tim filed in. She shut the door behind them.

"We want to know what happened to Nikki Becker."

"She lives!" King Lear raised her hands at their faces, as if grasping at invisible handholds. "This villain of mine comes under the prediction..."

"What prediction?" Levi grabbed and held the old woman's hand.

"All dark and comfortless," she whispered.

"What took Nikki?"

"Things that love night..."

"Bats?"

"I will say nothing," King Lear's voice trembled. Levi released her hand. She slid her sunglasses off and looked at him with watery pale blue eyes.

"Lancaster," Levi breathed. "You know what he is?"

"I fear I am not in my perfect mind." She brought shaking hands to cover her face. "I stumbled when I saw..."

"Where? The funeral home? Roddis Manor?! You know where he took her!"

"She's lost her mind." Tim spoke low as he glanced back and forth from King Lear to Levi. "I'm amazed the police were able to figure out her bat story at all. Even they understand she isn't quite there."

"I have to be certain, Tim. If Lancaster has Nikki and she's alive...we have to rescue her immediately. You heard her. It sounds like she's talking about Lancaster, right? Or am I going mad like

King Lear here?"

"Oh! Let me not be mad, not mad, sweet heaven!" King Lear clutched Levi, her eyes wild. "Keep me in temper; I would not be mad!" She dragged him over to her window, and pointed to the middle school astronomy tower. "Oh, that way madness lies."

"We're going to have to search Lancaster's house again." Levi stared at the eaves of Roddis Manor through the trees. He startled as King Lear pressed a gnarled hand to his chest.

"Have more than thou showest, speak less than thou knowest." Her words were solemn.

SAMANTHA RAN HER HANDS OVER her black dress, smoothing it out and adjusting everything one last time in the mirror. Her makeup was on and her hair about as good as it was going to get. She went downstairs.

"So, you're getting a ride with Becca to prom," Mrs. Symanski said from the living room. "That's unusual."

"Natalie's going with us too," Samantha lied. "We're picking her up."

"Natalie's date isn't giving her a ride?"

"No."

"And what's your date's name?"

"I don't...um..."

"Samantha—"

"I'll ask Becca. She'll remember."

The doorbell rang its long, creepy gong. Samantha's heart pounded. She walked to the door.

"Becca must be here." Mrs. Symanski said, turning away. "I'll be in the kitchen."

Samantha pulled open the door. A middle-aged man filled the doorway, his ruddy hair almost brushing the top of the frame. His mustache twitched as he looked down at her.

"Samantha?"

"Mr. Shepherd," she gasped. "You're...you're actually here."

"Of course I am. May I come in?"

"My mom doesn't know who you are or why you're here," Samantha whispered. "Can you fix this place from the outside?"

"Little girl, I think you've deceived me."

"I have."

"I have to do my job from the inside of the house. That's how exorcisms work."

"I don't know *how* this is going to work."

"Let me talk to your mother."

"Mom!" Samantha yelled, her voice wavering. "We have a visitor."

"Who?" Mrs. Symanski walked into the foyer. Mr. Shepherd waved at her. She practically fell over. "Oh my God, Ken! What the hell are you doing here?"

"Sandra." Mr. Shepherd nodded. "May I come in?"

"Of course," she breathed, her face lighting up. "You know you're always welcome. You don't even have to ask."

"Old habits die hard." He stepped past a gaping Samantha and into the house.

"What brings you up here, Ken? Never knew you to be a fan of the cold." Mrs. Symanski had to crane her neck to look into his face. "It's been too long." They hugged.

"It has," he nodded.

"I hear you've been on television. How on earth did you ever pull that off?"

"Sunglasses and a makeup artist do wonders," he chuckled. "I dye my hair as well."

"Umm, you two know each other?" Samantha felt like she was balancing on a wire, waiting for a gust of wind.

"Oh, how rude of me! Ken, this is my daughter Samantha. Ken and I used to work together on various projects out east, many, many years ago." Mrs. Symanski smiled. "He's a good friend of mine."

"You never told me about him." Samantha met Mr. Shepherd's eyes. He smirked at her and she realized she was played.

"Nor could I, not with the work we had to do." Mrs. Symanski shook her head, her face radiating incredulity. "How did you find me, Ken? What brings you to Marshfield?"

"To be honest, this house." He gestured all around him. "I hear it's haunted."

"A town rumor," Mrs. Symanski laughed.

"No, this rumor is true. Very true," he said humorlessly. "I can feel them, moving through the space around us."

Mrs. Symanski's eyes flashed. "My new job—"

"Depends on this place. I understand…"

"And you know this how?" Mrs. Symanski's smile didn't waver, but Samantha saw her mother's posture shift.

"After Project Revenant was shut down, Homeland Security offered me a position with their Advanced Research Projects division. Said they were going to recycle trusted agents from Aegis Dynamics. I turned them down and got this ghost-consulting gig. Apparently I'm quite charming on television."

"Oh, you're charming everywhere," Mrs. Symanski waved.

"Anyway," Ken's smile was genuine, "we were solicited by people in the community who told us this house is haunted. They asked us to give it a look. I expected to greet an elderly couple at the door…until I checked the public records and found you bought it. And here you are, looking younger than the last time I saw you."

"Oh, you expect me to believe that?" Mrs. Symanski ran a hand through her hair. She looked at Samantha out of the corner of her eye.

"I gather because you're here, you took the project offer. I'm amazed you're into the supernatural side now. Remember when you told me years ago you wanted out? Yet here you are, going forward full throttle."

Mrs. Symanski met Samantha's accusatory stare. "It's difficult to untangle yourself from your past…but this is a step in the right direction."

"I'm happy for you."

A red car pulled up out front and honked. Samantha grabbed her coat. "I'm going to prom, I'll be back later." She kissed her mom lightly on the cheek before ducking out, an intense disturbance writhing within her. More and more questions plagued her mind, but answers would have to wait.

SAMANTHA STEPPED INTO THE GYM on Matt's arm, Becca and her date behind them. Round tables were everywhere with names on folded papers by every place setting. Matt pointed to a table near the center. "My name's over there." He walked her over, pulled out the chair next to his, and pushed it in as she sat.

"You're very polished tonight," Samantha commented.

"You make me better." Matt sat next to her. "I'm excited for tonight."

Samantha watched Becca and her date move to another table and sit down. She could feel Matt watching her.

"Are you alright? You seem…out of it."

"That's a common theme this year," she quipped.

Matt opened his mouth like he wanted to say something, but seemed to think better of it. He pulled out his phone.

"I'm looking forward to dancing with you." Samantha tried to fill the void.

"Me too." Matt looked past her to the gym doors. Kaeli walked in on the arm of a tall guy with slicked-back blonde hair. Matt's nostrils flared.

"Matt Stauber!" Kaeli waved and hurried to their table, her salmon dress pressed to the tall boy's side, her face smug.

"I can't believe you're here." Matt leaned back in his chair and sneered at the guy. "How much was the babysitter?"

"Not my turn to watch him," he nodded.

"Ooh look, we're at the same table!" Kaeli grinned as she took the labeled seat on the other side of Matt. The tall guy plopped in the chair on the other side of Kaeli. "It's been a while since we've hung out together, hasn't it, boys? Seven months?"

"Who is this?" Samantha asked in Matt's ear.

"Micah Schuh." Matt was fixated on him. "An old…friend."

"Enjoy catching up." Samantha, feeling abandoned, looked

around the room as other couples took their seats. Becca waved from a nearby table, looking lovely in her white dress. Samantha waved back, desperately wishing the seats weren't assigned.

"This is Samantha." A hand rested on her shoulder. She jumped and glared at Matt. "I was just introducing you." Matt looked at her like she had three heads. Samantha felt her face getting warm and nodded at Micah, who nodded back with a smile of complete vapidity.

"I was zoning out, sorry. How do you two know each other?" Samantha asked.

"We hung out a lot as kids. I grew up on the farm down the road," Micah said. "Matt and I are five years apart—"

"Four," Matt said. "You're bad with dates."

Micah reached around and slapped Matt on the back. He tensed. "This boy here used to bug me all the time. I hung out on their farm a lot, helped his dad with the vehicles."

"Micah's very mechanically inclined." Kaeli rubbed Micah's forearm, her eyes on Matt. "He helped Mr. Stauber build that Barracuda. You know, the one you totaled on Homecoming."

Samantha's jaw dropped. "I did not total the car!"

"She was driving because Matt was drunk and of course, could not handle a stick shift. She totaled it." Kaeli flipped her hair over her shoulder.

"We were attacked by a—you know what? I cannot believe I am still being grilled about this." Samantha shook with fury.

"I'm just joking! New Girl, you need to lighten up." Kaeli chuckled the phoniest chuckle imaginable. Samantha watched Matt cast Kaeli an amused smile.

"I didn't think it was funny when I heard about what happened." Micah put his elbows on the table and rested his face on his hands. "I put a lot into that car. So did Mr. Stauber."

"So did I," Matt said. "It was almost a perfect Homecoming Night."

"A perfect Homecoming would have been getting laid in the backseat." Micah leaned into Kaeli's ear, but the words were loud enough for the table to hear.

"Almost perfect," Matt bumped his elbow into Samantha's.

Her twisted into her dress under the table. Samantha spotted Natalie standing by Becca, blissfully chatting away. Two seats were left at the round table. She wracked her brain for the name of Natalie's date, hoping his name was on one of the place settings. Finally, a buff boy sat down next to Samantha and waved the redhead over. She sat down and flashed an award-winning smile at Samantha. "I look so cute in my dress. We have to get Becca and pose for the yearbook once photos start."

"Any excuse to get away from this table! I—I'm dying to dance," Samantha covered.

"First we have a three-course meal," Natalie clapped. "Served by the teachers!"

"You have *got* to be kidding me." Samantha frowned as metal trolleys squeaked into the gym, pushed by several tuxedo-clad servers—one of which looked suspiciously like Barb. "We're going to be poisoned tonight."

"NO TIM, you put the stakes in your sleeves."

"I don't want to ruin my leather jacket."

"You'll be fine." Levi handed Tim two more stakes.

"Levi, you've never trained me for this." Tim's eyes widened.

"I never thought I'd need your help to kill a vampire," Levi muttered. "But here we are, going to assault a manor. Just you and me."

"You've slain a bunch of vampires. Are you scared?" Tim asked. "You sound scared."

"I'm not scared."

"That's a lie. You're pale as a ghost."

"I'm pale because I live in Wisconsin. We need holy water."

"Remember what King Lear told you? You have more than you show and to speak less than you know." Tim stuffed the stakes in his sleeves. "Whatever happens, watch your mouth."

They parked the truck in the lot at the middle school. Levi left

Tim in the cab and snuck through the evergreen hedge separating Roddis Manor from the middle school. The ground was soft and muddy from snowmelt; he was hard-pressed to not leave shoeprints. He made it to the back of the garage, and peered in the window. No vehicle. He took a breath and moved to the side door again. It was locked. A cocky smile played on his lips as he thought about Lancaster changing his habits to keep out Big Bad Levi. He picked the lock, opened the door and slid inside. With the sun just setting, the house was easier to navigate. Orange light cascaded through the windows. The ticking of the grandfather clock was soothing.

He pulled out the walkie-talkie and spoke. "The house is clear, Tim. Come in through the side-door under the porte-cochere."

The walkie-talkie crackled. "On my way."

Levi locked the windows as he waited for Tim, keeping his eyes and ears peeled for any pitter-patter or meowing. There was no sign of Buttons. He heard the door open and shut. Tim came in lugging the navy-blue gym bag, its sides bulging with far more than its usual contents. Tim set it on the floor with a *thud*, and wiped his forehead. "This is a nice house."

"Sell your soul and it could be yours." Levi unzipped the gym bag and pulled out two hammers and a box of nails. He nodded to Tim, who pulled out a handheld steam cleaner, and plugged it into the nearest outlet. Levi began nailing the windows shut. "How long can we expect Lancaster to stay at the funeral home?" He pulled out a small cross and taped it to the mullions, careful to make sure it wouldn't be seen from the outside.

"Not much later than eight. He might have changed his routine to mess with you. Prevent you from doing something like this. It's incredibly risky."

"If he wanted to prevent this, he'd have a chain across the side-door." Levi took the hammer into the kitchen and nailed its window shut. "Grab the other hammer and get to work."

"Do you really believe Nikki is somewhere in this house?" Tim asked.

"There's only one way to find out. We'll search for her as we seal up escape routes. As I recall, Lancaster prefers escaping to actually fighting. This vampire will not get away from me again."

"Check the kitchen cabinets," Tim said. Levi raised an eyebrow at him. "It's possible to fit a high-school girl under the kitchen sink. Trust me."

"You do it."

"Fine."

Levi nailed the dining room windows shut, listening as Tim rummaged.

"Nothing here!" He joined Tim in the kitchen.

"Be sure to check the fridge as well." Levi walked past him to grab more nails.

The sound of the fridge opening was accompanied by a gasp. "Levi, come here!"

Levi was at Tim's side in a moment, looking over his shoulder into the fridge. Pale light gleamed on shelves packed with clear glass bottles, filled with a viscous, deep crimson liquid.

"Tell me that's Coca-Cola," Tim whispered.

"You know what it is," Levi said. His palms began to sweat even in the cold air from the fridge, the stagnant coppery smell lingering in his nostrils.

"That's more blood than one human body can hold. If that's all from Nikki, she's dead for sure." Tim's face grew pale.

Levi shut the fridge, breaking the other boy's gaze. "King Lear said she's alive."

"Do you think he's drinking from those bottles? Blood makes vampires stronger, and younger. Has Lancaster looked particularly youthful lately?"

"He has to kill her to gain her years, Tim. And he's not looking younger. She's alive."

"Then explain the bottles." Tim's voice cracked.

Levi grasped for an explanation to placate the swelling disturbance in his mind. He decided after a moment of silence to stifle it. "The downstairs is sealed. Crosses in every window. Front door, everything. The upper floors are next. Especially the balcony."

They sealed off the second floor, scouring the sparsely-furnished bedrooms for any sign of a teenaged girl. Nothing. They made it to the third floor, the entire space a large master suite. A massive vanity with shelves of makeup took up the far wall. An oversized four-poster bed lay opposite the balcony doors.

"Levi, do you see that?"

"I do." Levi's eyes couldn't leave the large areas of scratched wood on the bedposts. He touched the exposed, unstained wood with a ghost of a caress. "There were chains here."

"Someone definitely struggled. The wood's been rubbed raw." Tim looked under the bed and searched the room. "Levi, there's no chains. We haven't found chains in any room."

Levi nailed the door to its frame and hung a rosary from the handle. He had the sinking feeling that, wherever the chains were, Nikki would be in them.

Tim's yell made Levi jump. "What the hell, Tim?!"

"A cat! That fucking cat!" Tim sputtered and pointed. "Jumped out of the closet and tore down the stairs. Must have been locked in there."

"Ah shit. Find it." Levi ran down the stairs, Tim close behind, trying to step lightly to avoid scaring the animal any more. They made it to the second floor. All the doors were shut. Only the hallway was accessible, and there was no sign of a black cat. They went down to the first floor.

"He could be anywhere!" Tim threw his hands up.

A yowling sound filled the air. Levi felt Tim's fingers clutch his back. "Get off me." Tim relented and Levi slid from room to room, looking for the source of the noise. He got to the side door. The sound floated up from the basement. "Tim—stay here." With a shudder, Levi stepped into the darkness.

The stairs creaked under his weight. At the bottom, he found a switch on the rough wall. He flicked it and the basement glowed with a dull yellow light from bare bulbs. Narrowly-packed shelves lined with boxes filled the space. He moved at a careful, controlled pace, peering down the rows of shelves as he passed. The cat kept howling, wherever it was. He bumped into a steel wall on the other end of the basement. To his right, a large steel door with a simple lever handle taunted him.

Pulling it, the door popped open and a gush of frigid air escaped. A fluorescent bulb flickered beyond the door, casting light on a large freezer. Jars lined the shelves, filled with what appeared to be organs floating in questionable fluids. As quick as he opened the door, he shut it, his stomach churning. The yowling continued. It was louder, he was close. Just beyond the door, the steel ended and a stone wall began again. An archway in the stone led him into a small room with big iron bolts in the walls. Chained to two bolts in the corner was a figure curled in the fetal position. Her nightgown must have been white at one point. The cat sat next to the figure, its green eyes staring at Levi.

"Nikki Becker?" he whispered.

THE WELL-DRESSED JUNIORS and their dates bumped to censored versions of the hottest songs as teachers supervised the refreshment table in the stark white lobby. Kaeli laughed with Becca in the corner and Natalie was somewhere in the gym with her date. Samantha pulled out her phone and checked her messages as Matt waited in line for punch with Micah. Two texts from Laderia.

'*Oh bitch, you're missing my anti-prom!*'

'*Stefan has major alcohol tolerance. German boys be clinkin ale.*'

She shoved her phone into her purse as Matt returned with two glasses of punch, Micah next to him.

"…didn't know she was pregnant," Micah was saying. "It was such a shock."

"It's alright man," Matt replied. "You're old enough to be a dad. Just don't let her know you're here with Kaeli. Girls get stupid about that stuff."

"I was planning on that, but I forgot about Facebook," Micah smacked a hand to his forehead. "Marissa will see I was here. Can't wait for *that* conversation…"

"You're Marissa's baby daddy?" Samantha asked.

Micah turned three different colors. "I didn't think you knew who Marissa was."

"I don't," Samantha smiled, "but I've heard people say I look like her."

"A little," Micah turned his head to the side. "I'd do you."

"No you wouldn't," Matt growled.

"Relax, it was a compliment," Micah said. "Look at her face turning red. She liked hearing it. You gotta tell people what you think. That's another part of being an adult you have to learn."

"Oh, you're really mature," Samantha couldn't restrain the sarcasm. "You seem like the kind of guy who would be vandalizing property well into his thirties."

"Maybe," Micah whispered with a grin. "A bunch of us grads got together and hit up Barb's house. We were always too chicken-shit to do it in high school, but now that she has no power over us…" He let out a derpy laugh.

Her jaw dropped; Samantha slapped his arms. "I took the blame for that!"

"Yeah, Matt told me," Micah grinned, unfazed by her reaction. "Visited him at football practice on cleanup day. We hung out. Kaeli and some buddies joined us. Good times."

"Is that why you didn't help me?" Samantha rounded on Matt, who looked horrorstruck. "You were too busy hanging out with your friend while I cleaned up his mess?!"

"It wasn't just you, it was the whole school. You didn't need me."

"I cannot believe you didn't tell me!" Samantha wanted to pull her hair out. "You ditched me to hang out with this—this idiot and Kaeli!"

"Excuse me, Miss Prima Donna," Kaeli huffed, grabbing Samantha by the shoulder and turning her around. "You weren't dating Matt then. And you're not dating him now."

Samantha looked Kaeli up and down with contempt. "He's beneath me. And so are you."

"Nobody talks to me like that." Kaeli put a hand on her hip.

Samantha rolled her eyes and turned to find Becca in the gym.

She suddenly froze and gasped as a cold liquid splashed on her back and ran down her dress. The lobby burst into laughter. Samantha turned her glare on Kaeli, who looked rather pleased with herself as she crumpled the empty cup in her hand.

"You had that coming," she sneered.

Samantha took a moment to compose herself. She walked up to Kaeli, deadly calm, sipping the punch in her cup, not breaking eye contact. Kaeli crossed her arms and scowled.

"What do you think you're going to do—" She didn't get to finish the sentence. Cup in hand, Samantha decked her squarely in the cheek, splashing punch all over Kaeli's face. Kaeli reeled back, almost falling. Another student shoved Kaeli forward and, regaining her balance, she came at Samantha.

The gloves were off.

"NIKKI, CAN YOU HEAR ME?"

The thin, bald figure stirred, the chains clinking on her wrists and feet. She barely opened her eyes. "You're here to kill me," she said, her voice hoarse. "Just do it." Levi ducked out of Nikki's line of sight. There was so much he hadn't considered. She saw him without a bandana. She'd ask questions if he saved her, questions he couldn't answer. Now what? Why didn't he think of this earlier?

He fumbled for the walkie-talkie. "I found her," he said.

"Is she alive?" Tim's cautious words were barely audible.

"We forgot the bandanas. She's going to know who we are. She's going to know what we do."

"Bring her up."

"I...I don't—" Levi felt a sudden flood of shame as he realized he was considering leaving her chained in a vampire's basement. He took a ragged breath. "By myself?"

"Yes Levi, by yourself."

Levi's brows came together. "Don't chicken out on me."

"I'm sort of busy right now. Trust me Levi, I got your back."

Levi slid the walkie-talkie into his pocket and pulled out his lock picks. Heading back into the alcove, he quickly unfastened the chains around her wrists and ankles. Nikki sat up and the shackles fell to the ground. Buttons jumped away and paced the perimeter of the room. Levi knelt beside the girl and slid an arm under her legs and another behind her back. Standing up, he was surprised to find how light she was, though the smell coming off of her was wretched.

"Where are we going?" she asked.

"Outside," Levi whispered as he sidled along the stone wall, then the steel wall with the freezer door. Buttons streaked past his feet and waited for him at the stairs. Levi took them one at a time, his forearms and biceps warm. He made it to the top.

"Tim, bring the truck around. I got her." He hurried to the main floor. "Tim? Can you hear me?"

"He can't hear you, I'm afraid," a deep voice rang with amusement. Levi turned and noticed Lancaster sitting in an armchair in the living room, his feet resting on Tim's limp body. The vampire smiled. "Where do you think you're taking that, my boy?" He set his feet on the floor and stood tall. "I hope you don't think you're going to save her." His dress shoes clicked on the wood floor as he stepped over Tim toward Levi.

"What did you do to Tim?" Levi's voice was weaker than he wanted it to sound.

"I know you don't think I'm...very smart," Lancaster's goatee twitched, "but even someone as *stupid* as me can outsmart two teenage boys."

Say less than thou knowest, Levi bit his lip.

Lancaster cracked his neck and took a step toward him. Levi took a step back. "You've wasted so much of my time. And now you're stealing my supper."

"Do you really need to eat her?" Levi asked slowly. *Say less...*

"Of course not." Lancaster almost chuckled, looking at Levi with a mixture of disgust and amusement. "I don't need to kill her for...many, many years. No, I've just grown accustomed to...to the taste." His dark eyes danced. "I feel so recharged...powerful...dare I say, alive. I'm making blood a regular staple of my diet. All I needed was someone delicious."

"I don't understand." Levi's mind raced. *Less than thou knowest, less than thou knowest—*

"You should see what I got in my fridge," Lancaster remarked. "I've become a bit of a home brewer. I'm curious, though. What on earth made you think to look for a missing high school girl here?"

"I…" *Less than thou knowest…*"I didn't know she'd be here. It was a fluke."

"Then what brings you here? I thought we had a truce." Lancaster had Levi backed against the wall. Nikki felt heavier in his arms. He had to set her down if he was going to fight. He hadn't planned for this. Why didn't he plan for this?

"Are you worried about that burden?" Lancaster extended his hands toward Nikki. "I can take her for you."

Levi kicked him in the groin and turned, almost running, to the exit. Somehow, he tripped over himself and fell to the floor. Nikki hit with a thud and slid forward out of his arms. Levi looked behind him. Lancaster's hand clenched Levi's ankle. He smiled as he winced and writhed on the floor behind Levi.

"Run, Nikki!" He kicked at Lancaster's hand. The girl scrambled to her feet like a newborn deer. In a moment, the hall filled with a swarm of bats. Nikki screamed and covered her face, dropping to the floor.

The bats disappeared and Lancaster stood at the opposite end of the hall, his face a mask of fury. Nikki lay at his feet, cowering. Coughing made Levi look to his left, and he noticed Tim on his hands and knees, massaging his neck.

"Levi," his voice was hoarse. "Levi, he's here. He saw our muddy footprints in the driveway. He knew—"

"Shut up, you fucking burnout," snarled the vampire. "This tender morsel—you want to free her from this wicked life?!" Lancaster's large hands locked around the girl's small throat. He dragged her to her feet as she gagged. "You want to liberate her?" He hoisted her off the ground. Her little hands grasped at the vampire's fingers. Levi clambered to his feet, but with one shake of those hands, a crack filled the room and the girl went limp. Lancaster released his grip and she fell to the floor, absolutely still. Levi thought he saw Lancaster's mouth make words, but sound wouldn't come to him. He couldn't take his eyes off of that small bald person in the stained nightgown, once a girl with a home and a future, crumpled on the floor like a pile of refuse. He was in shock. He was numb. And he was furious.

SAMANTHA DIDN'T KNOW how she wound up straddling Kaeli, but she was glad she had the upper hand. The older girl shrieked under her as Samantha wrapped her fingers in that spray-saturated hair, and using her free hand, she slapped the girl's face back and forth. A hose-clad leg clocked her in the side of the head, and suddenly Kaeli rolled them over. Samantha was on the bottom, holding up her arms to defend herself as Kaeli clawed at her. As quickly as it started, it was over. Ten teachers surrounded them, shouting for the lobby to clear and hauling Kaeli off of Samantha.

"I don't need rescuing! I can take her!" Samantha yelled as Kaeli glared at her from Mrs. Black's grip, pulling up her shoulder strap.

"You will do no such thing!" shouted the gray-haired woman in the tuxedo. Barb's iron claws held her arm and dragged her into the gym. "Where are your things? You're going home right this instant."

"Over there." Samantha pointed meekly as Barb led her through the crowd of students who stood motionless in the gym as the music raged on. She could practically hear their shocked minds absorbing the scene and committing it to permanent memory. Barb gathered Samantha's coat and purse and shoved them into her arms.

The principal led her out the back doors to a small blue car in the corner of the parking lot. She opened the passenger door and Samantha took the seat, stunned as Barb got in and turned the ignition.

"This is your car?" Samantha asked.

"Yes, I own a car. Don't get punch on my seats." She pursed her lips, not looking at Samantha but focusing on the road as she pulled out of the lot. It was silent for a block or two. "I apologize."

Samantha looked at her, incredulous. "What for?"

"For accusing you of toilet-papering my home. I overheard you and Micah, as did half the school."

"It's okay," Samantha said. "I probably would have done it anyway."

"You should not have engaged Kaeli. It wasn't wise." Barb's voice was somehow both haughty and understanding. "And you should never fight like that."

"She threw punch on me. So I threw a punch back. An eye for an eye."

Barb looked at Samantha, her sour face scorching disapproval beneath her straight-cut bangs. "Don't argue with fools. Turn the other cheek. Never give pearls to swine, or the swine will trample the pearls and turn and attack you." Samantha looked at Barb, confusion stopping her from making a response. "We're in the New Testament now, Miss Symanski. Old Testament vengeance is out of style."

Samantha wiped the tears from under her eyes on the back of her hand. She nodded. "No pearls for swine. Got it."

They pulled in front of 311 West Park Street. A nice sedan was parked just down the street. Samantha took a breath as she realized Ken Shepherd was still there. She unbuckled, but Barb cleared her throat. Samantha knew what was coming and she paused, forcing herself to bear Barb's scrutinizing gaze.

"I'm going to have to call your mother when I get back to the school. And Kaeli's parents. It's very possible someone's going to take legal action. What you did was serious."

"I know, I'm sorry." Samantha felt her eyes burning as more tears threatened to come. "But it felt good to crush my cup on her fugly face." She hiccupped as tears escaped down her cheeks.

"Tell your mother what happened. She's a smart woman. She'll know what to do. Find other students who'll testify on your behalf," Barb said. "Columbus will not take sides. Do you understand?"

"I understand."

"Good. Now get out of my car, Miss Symanski."

LEVI SLIPPED A STAKE OUT of his pocket and lunged down the hall at Lancaster, who grimaced as he caught Levi's forearm. He squeezed Levi's wrist. Levi felt his grip on the stake weakening. Lancaster leaned closer, his fanged smile accompanied by a low throaty noise akin to the sound of a growling tiger. The air in front of his face clouded with steam and Lancaster roared, releasing him. Levi slid out of the way as Tim unleashed the spray of holy water in the handheld steam cleaner.

"How do you like that?" he asked with a wicked grin as Lancaster dove past them, his face peeling with blisters. The water ran down his cheeks, collecting thick makeup and traces of blood.

Tim went after him with the spray. Lancaster ran to the window and flung open the drapes. He hissed at the cross, and awkwardly tugged at the window while leaning as far away from it as possible. It wouldn't budge. Tim turned the spray on the glass, and Lancaster backed away from the window entirely, turning his gaze on the side door. Levi shut the interior door leading to the side door entrance, revealing another cross, and leaned against it, stake in hand. Lancaster looked at each of them in kind.

"Clever boys, setting a trap for me in my own home," he snarled.

"Who's panicking now?" Levi pointed the stake at the vampire. "I daresay I overestimated you."

"You're out of your minds if you think I'm alone in this," Lancaster growled. "If you kill me, another will come who is worse than me."

"I'll take that chance," Levi twirled the stake on his fingers, enjoying the way it reflected in Lancaster's eyes.

"Everything *will* get worse for you once I'm gone," Lancaster warned as Tim stepped closer with the steam cleaner.

"It can't get worse for Nikki," Levi said with deadly calm. "Let him have it, Tim."

The vampire shrieked as Tim unleashed another cloud of steam. "Stop! It burns!"

"You're not as good at taking it as you are at dishing it out." Levi crossed his arms. "You can't change to escape this time."

"The upstairs is entirely sealed off," Tim nodded. "Crosses on every door and window. I can easily make a cloud of holy water for your bats to fly through if you want this over faster."

"Stay away. I'll kill you," Lancaster hissed. "I'll kill both of you."

"No you won't," Levi corrected. Tim sprayed him some more. Lancaster writhed on the floor. "We're going to kill you."

"You can't kill what's already dead." Lancaster gasped through noises of pain.

Levi stepped closer. "Not quickly, anyway—"

"We could show you mercy and speed up the process in exchange for some information." Tim glanced at Levi. Levi gave him a look of disapproval.

"What...information?" The vampire heaved, his skin swelling.

"Where is St. Hubert's Key?" Tim asked.

"The Keys...of Saint Hubert?" Lancaster blinked.

"You're telling me you don't know where they are?" Tim took a step toward the prostrate vampire.

Lancaster's laugh filled the house. "They were...melted...long ago...completely destroyed."

"Who destroyed them?" Tim held the steam cleaner to Lancaster's head. In a blur, the vampire grabbed Tim's ankle, flipped him onto his back, and sank fangs deep into his leg. Levi drove a stake through Lancaster's back over and over again as Tim screamed. Suddenly the vampire turned to powder, his skeleton disintegrating into a pile of dust on the wood floor.

Levi wiped his forehead. "Fifth time's the charm."

"Levi, Levi..." Tim pulled up his pant leg and looked at his calf. Blood ran down his leg. "He bit me! I'm bleeding everywhere!"

"Relax," Levi said, his voice unsteady. "Let me look at it."

"Am I going to turn into a vampire?" Tim's face filled with panic. "I'm going to become a monster—"

"Calm down, you infant," Levi grumbled. "You're not going to turn into a vampire."

"Are you sure?"

Levi tore a scrap of cloth from his shirt. "Positive. You'd have to drink his blood. That pile of dust is the least of our worries now." He pressed the cloth into the pair of gaping holes where Lancaster's fangs pierced flesh. "You're in luck. He didn't bite an artery."

"Let me do it." Tim moaned as he took over applying the pressure.

"You're alive." Levi sat on his haunches. "That's more than we can say for our Homecoming Queen." He turned to look at the dead girl on the floor. A stench wafted from her body.

Tim winced. "Smells like her bowels released."

"She smelled like that before."

Tim wiped his face. "Now what?"

Levi stood up, allowing himself a moment to process his surroundings. "Time to clean up. No one can know we were here."

SAMANTHA ENTERED THE HOUSE, the sound of her mother and brother laughing made her shame more potent. She shut the door behind her.

"Is someone home already? I heard the door." Mrs. Symanski entered the foyer and stopped in her tracks. She looked Samantha up and down. "I hope the other girl looks worse."

"Mom, I'm so sorry." Samantha burst into tears. "I got in trouble."

"It's okay Samantha, I'm here." Her mother walked up and embraced her, patting her ruined hair. "I figured tonight was going to be a disaster, one way or another."

"It was." Samantha cried into her mother's sweater. "I found out Micah toilet-papered Barb's house."

"Who? You gotta compose yourself. I can't understand you."

"Micah Schuh toilet-papered Barb's house. I thought you did it." Samantha tried to speak. "I saw that launcher in the trunk and I thought you were the one who hit Barb's house."

Mrs. Symanski laughed out loud. "You can't be serious. I got her so many times in high school, it was cruel! I haven't toilet-papered since my senior year. I'm a full-fledged grown-up." She stroked the back of Samantha's head. "Besides, I'd be in jail if I did that sort of thing now."

"Or in a mental institution." Ken loomed in the doorway to the living room. "Sorry to see you had a bad night, Samantha."

Samantha hugged her mom tighter, unable to shake the feeling of intimidation that accompanied Ken. A little man dressed in black appeared at his side, the white of his collar making Samantha's eyes widen.

"What happened?" Mrs. Symanski asked. "Based on how bad you look, we better prepare for legal action."

"Kaeli Edwards happened." Samantha blinked back more tears, her mind scrambling as she processed the short man in the cleric's clothing. "I'm such a mess."

"Hormones and stress." Mrs. Symanski waved it off. "You'll probably get a few zits from this. Scrub your face before going to bed tonight." A telephone rang. "I bet that's Barb." Mrs. Symanski disappeared into the kitchen.

Samantha looked up at Ken. "Who is that?"

Ken looked down at the little man, who looked back up at him with dark eyes. "This is Father Pedro Montes, the key to my success."

"You mean—"

"He's an exorcist. He's performed hundreds of cleansings and exorcisms. He does it in real life, and I re-enact it on camera. We're sort of a team."

Samantha stared at the little man with the bronze skin and jet-black hair. "Is the house—?"

"Cleansed? Not entirely." Ken shook his head. "You're right. You're mother's job depends on this place and its supernatural properties. We can't make them all disappear."

Samantha put her coat in the closet. She looked back at the little priest, noting how he gazed around, oblivious to their conversation. "Does he speak English?"

"Not a word." Ken shook his head. "This little fellow's from Salvador City, down in Brazil. A beautiful little place on the Bay of All Saints."

"He travels with you? Does the Church allow him to do that?"

"He's on vacation. Why do you think I have to schedule so far in advance?" Ken smirked.

Samantha bit her lip. "Alright...what *did* you do?"

"After some convincing, I worked out a deal with your mother. There's a barrier in the bedrooms now," Ken explained. "You and your brother will be able to sleep through the night without any ghouls in your beds."

"That's a start." Samantha wiped her cheeks again, mascara smudging onto her hands. The tears were no longer flowing, but the damage was already done.

"You're underwhelmed," Ken observed.

"I'm out of energy. I can't care about anything right now," Samantha murmured. "You're sure we'll be safe?"

"Safe enough." Ken pulled out a smart phone.

"Does my mom know I called you?"

Ken smiled. "Sandra thinks I found her. I'm content to let her keep thinking that..."

"Thank you," Samantha breathed. "She'd kill me if—"

"For a price," Ken interrupted.

Samantha froze. "You said there would be no charge."

"I said we'd worry about the cost later." His face hardened and he leaned over her. "Little tricks and manipulations won't work on me. You owe me one favor." He held up his index finger.

"What favor?" Fear gripped her spine.

Ken's face remained devoid of emotional tells, but his eyes were dancing. "Don't ask just yet. I get to decide what it is and when to call upon you to do it. I expect your complete follow-through when the time comes. Understand?"

Samantha nodded. "I understand."

"Good." Ken's mouth twitched. Father Pedro blinked at them.

Mrs. Symanski entered the foyer with her hands on her hips. "The Edwards will likely press charges. Samantha, you're going to have to find people who will testify Kaeli started the fight. And you're going to have to do it from home. You've been suspended."

McMillan Marsh was noticeably free of flies and mosquitoes as Levi and Tim sank their shovels into the moist, semi-frozen ground. The trench they dug was only two feet deep, the ground getting harder with every shovel.

"Let's not dig anymore," Tim muttered. "It's frosty out, I'm sweating, I'll catch a cold."

"Nikki deserves a proper burial—which is six feet. That doesn't look like it's going to happen. The least we can do is give her another six inches."

"That's what he said." Tim cracked a smile.

Levi couldn't allow himself a grin, or even a moment to react with disgust. The dirty, pale feet of the Homecoming Queen poked out of the plastic tarp they wrapped her in. She lay on the ground near the truck, shielded from any eyes that might come down the road in the predawn hours.

Levi's back ached. His head pounded. His neck was sore, but his arms and hands were worse. Finally, he allowed himself a moment to catch his breath. "I think...I think this is good enough," he said.

"If you say so." Tim jumped out of the trench.

"Let's put her in." Levi set the shovel aside and grabbed one end of the tarp. Tim grabbed the other end. They half-carried, half-dragged the body into the trench, and laid her face-up, sealed in her plastic sheet. Levi took a moment to gaze at the sight, the plastic reflecting the moonlight, the undulating wrinkles of the tarp hinting a human being might be under there.

"Should we say anything?" Tim rubbed his leg and winced.

Levi shifted his balance from one foot to the other, trying to shake off the pain that filled his body. "Nikki Becker...I never learned your middle name, or what you liked, or what your plans were. But you were never cruel to me, or made me feel like a lesser person. And for that I'm thankful."

"Nikki Becker," Tim began, "I didn't know you either, but I knew your boyfriend's drug habits, and I guarantee you that relationship was going to end soon anyway. I hope you find peace, wherever you are."

Levi shoveled the first bit of dirt back into the trench. It made loud crumbling sounds as it hit the plastic. Tim put in the second shovelful. They continued to bury her without exchanging words. Eventually, the plastic couldn't be seen. Then the sound of the plastic couldn't be heard. When they finished, the sky was brightening. They set the shovels in the trunk and Levi made a mound of gravel pebbles at the head of the grave. They got in the truck and drove back to town.

"What do we do about the blood in the fridge?" Tim rubbed his eyes. "And the organs in the basement freezer?"

Levi yawned. "I don't know, Tim. What do you think?"

"I wanted to give the blood to a blood bank, but come to think of it, how creepy would that be to have that much blood dropped off anonymously? They wouldn't take it anyway…they would turn it over to the police."

The truck rattled around them as Levi pulled into town, the lights on Central turning off as the sun rose. He broke the heavy silence as they passed Target. "When the police look into Lancaster's disappearance, they'll find the blood, the organs, and they'll put it together. The less we do, the better." Levi parked outside the apartment. "Here you go. I'll head home."

Tim blinked with some difficulty, as if his eyelids were stuck together. "You can crash on the sofa. You look awful."

Levi felt physically numb, the rough skin of his hand like sandpaper as he wiped his face. "Thanks." He reached behind his seat and grabbed his duffle bag. It yowled until they got inside and the door was locked behind them. Levi unzipped it, and a black shadow sprang out and bounded around the room.

"He better not poop everywhere," Tim mumbled, cracking his neck as he zombie-walked to his bedroom. "Good night, Levi."

Levi squinted as sunlight erupted in the windows, horizontal and golden. He collapsed onto the sofa.

Chapter 13

The One I Need

The wood-paneled walls seemed to close in around Samantha as she sat in the chair in Barb's office. Despite her mother standing behind her, hands gripping the wooden back, she felt like she was being thrown to the wolves. She kept her knees together, elbows to her sides, and tried to be as small as she could without looking weak or afraid. Kaeli sat next to her, picking at her nails. Her father was behind her, a fat man with salt-and-pepper hair and a handlebar mustache. His glasses belonged in the 1970s. Barb sat in the chair behind her desk, clearly perplexed at the amount of people crammed into her coffin-of-an-office.

"I'm not happy about this course of events." She leaned back.

"Neither am I," said Mr. Edwards. "I'm not happy about what my daughter had to go through. As a teacher, I'm shocked this could even happen."

"I'm stunned that Mr. Edwards is stunned." Mrs. Symanski cocked her head. "It's clear he doesn't understand what kind of girl his daughter is."

"Mrs. Symanski, I'm going to ask you to please remain quiet while I sort this out." Barb's look of disapproval wasn't going to be enough to shut her mother up. Samantha reached up and grabbed her mother's hand. Mrs. Symanski relaxed and nodded.

"This tape recorder is for *our* records, and will be supplemented by eyewitness accounts. It's imperative we hear the story from both sides." Barb looked down at the papers on her desk then hit the record button. "So, we'll start with Kaeli. What happened on Prom night between you and Samantha?"

Kaeli sniffled and took a deep breath. Samantha waited with a mixture of loathing and fear as she began talking. "It…it all happened so fast. Samantha insulted my friends. I told her she can't talk to people that way. Then she hit me. I had to defend myself. It just spiraled out of control…she obviously has anger issues—"

"I do not!" Samantha snapped.

Barb cleared her throat, staring Samantha down before turning her attention back to Kaeli. "Are there other details you'd like to provide? The manner of insult you allege to have heard? The way you claim Samantha attacked you?"

"She said Matt and I were beneath her," Kaeli sniffled. "Matt Stauber, that is. He's a longtime friend. I was so offended. It was rude and pretentious. What kind of a person does that—treats people like garbage?"

"I see." Barb seemed unimpressed as she took notes. "And is that all the information you can provide?"

"Yes." Kaeli was on the verge of tears that Samantha doubted were real. Her father patted her on the shoulder. "It's so difficult for me, being in the same room with her again."

"That's enough commentary, Ms. Edwards." Barb snapped her fingers. Kaeli fell silent. "Now, Samantha. What happened on Prom night between you and Kaeli?"

"She threw punch on me," Samantha said with open revulsion. "Matt and I…Matt and I basically broke up." She sensed her mother tensing behind her and knew she'd be lectured later. "I was angry, upset…he didn't help me clean up the toilet-paper at your house. Instead he was hanging out with the person who did it. And Kaeli. I was furious with him. I still am, in fact." Samantha crossed her arms and thought for a moment. "I haven't seen him since Prom…Kaeli kissed Matt when he was my boyfriend on New Year's Eve. She always called me New Girl. Stuff like that. I was so mad at Matt for always backing her up and defending her…I told him he was beneath me because he is. I can do better." She sensed her mother's nod of satisfaction. "I turned to go into the gym, to get my stuff to leave…Kaeli threw punch down my back. Liquid punch, I mean. I was stressed, I was angry, and she was already getting what she wanted…Matt and I were done. Then she threw punch on me! I lost it. It was…it was stupid…done in the heat of passion. I defended myself."

"I never threw punch at her!" Kaeli pointed at Samantha. "She's lying!"

Barb's lips pressed shut. She turned to Samantha. "Any other details? Who was it that threw toilet paper all over my house?"

"Micah Schuh. Matt and Kaeli are friends with him." She waved her hand in the air. "After I got her back, Kaeli came at me. We wrestled on the floor—I ripped my dress."

"You ripped mine too!" Kaeli shot back. "You owe me a new dress!"

"Kaeli Edwards, stop talking. Right now." Her dad barked the words. Kaeli huffed and pulled a nail file out of her purse.

"We definitely need eyewitness testimony to get a better understanding of what *actually* happened." Barb shuffled through her papers. "Matt Stauber's testimony would have been valuable, but since his parents pulled him out of Columbus—"

"Matt's gone?" Samantha leaned forward. "Why?"

"Mr. Stauber mentioned a medical condition. It's their personal business." Barb switched off the tape recorder. "I'll have you all leave the room now. The suspension will remain in effect until this issue is resolved."

"But that could take months," Mr. Edwards scowled.

"The length of time it takes to resolve this issue is entirely up to you." Barb stood and nodded, forehead red behind her straight-cut bangs. "I'll be in touch." They filed out of Barb's office one at a time.

As she emerged in the hallway, Samantha spotted a redhead waving at her from the lobby. She ran up and held a cellphone to Samantha's nose. "I'm going to testify for you," Natalie squealed. "I was called into Barb's office!"

"You have pictures?" Samantha squinted at the tiny display screen.

"Even better." Natalie pressed a button. "I have *footage*."

Samantha felt her stomach bottom out. "I...how does it look?"

"It's, umm." Natalie put a hand on her hip and looked at her phone suspiciously. "It's a bit blurred, to be honest. You two were moving so fast. But I got a great shot of when she kicked you in the head."

"Great," Samantha moped. Natalie smiled before going into Barb's office. Samantha sighed and walked to the SUV with her mother.

"You went with Matt." Mrs. Symanski turned the key. "You went with Matt and you didn't tell me."

"I did...just in a different way." Samantha shifted and looked out the window, avoiding her mother's eyes. "I said you were right...about Matt."

Mrs. Symanski pulled onto the street. "Never have I ever pictured my daughter getting into a brawl at my old high school over some boy."

"It wasn't about him, mom." Samantha watched a robin land on a branch of a passing tree. "I never pictured myself getting into a fight either." They shared a brief glance and a laugh.

"It's going to hinge upon what eyewitnesses say." Mrs. Symanski let out a long breath. "Whether we get sued, you go to Juvenile Detention, or you walk away from this." The air was so thick with tension Samantha thought she could choke on it. "This isn't fun and games. It's an incredibly serious matter. The only thing you've got going for you is your record will be expunged when you turn eighteen, no matter what happens."

"Don't worry." Samantha heard the lack of conviction in her own voice. "Natalie has footage."

"Have you seen it?"

"No."

"Depending on what's on it, you could look like the aggressor. It may hurt you more than help you. You should call her. We should take the video to a lawyer and have him look at it. For now, you're still in the thick of it, honey." The click-clack of the SUV rolling over seams in the road filled the silence.

"I'm scared, mom." Samantha looked at the floor.

"Your fate rests in Natalie's hands. You should be scared."

IT WAS IN THE MOMENTS when he was sliding into sleep, that Levi saw Nikki Becker. She was still in a tattered, stained nightgown, staring at him from Arthur Harris's side. They were familiar companions. Though not welcome, they refused to leave, and he grew accustomed to their presence. They waited on the fringes of his mind, along with several other blurred faces he couldn't get rid of. Often, he found himself pretending to sleep, holding still, regulating his breath, wishing darkness would take him, and he wouldn't have to see them anymore. That never happened. Especially when people were whispering back and forth next to him.

"It's been a long time since I've seen Matt," Tim muttered. "What do you suppose happened to him?"

"Rumor has it he was pulled out of school due to his prognosis." Jennifer snapped her gum. "Whatever that prognosis was...even Dylan couldn't get it out of him. Speaking of which, that blonde bastard is graduating this year."

"That's coming up soon."

A loud slam startled him. Levi bolted awake at their table in study hall. "Did you hear that?" He looked around and realized it was Tim closing a textbook. "Thanks a lot." He sidled down and rested his head on his arms again.

"That's all anyone knows about Matt?" Tim shuffled papers in a folder and clipped some into his binder.

"That's all there is to know at this point," Jennifer replied. "Why so curious about him anyway?"

Tim stared at her.

"Not even a 'thank you' for the info? I was hoping for a little something for my trouble." Jennifer's voice was low. Levi opened his eyes. Through a crack, he could see her foot sliding up Tim's leg under the table. "Are you interested in reopening our...relationship?"

Tim laughed then grabbed her foot and pushed it off his lap. "I've been considering it for a while now. Maybe—yes. Looks like I'll have more supply anyway."

"Because Matt's no longer hogging the market?" Her voice was coy, almost a purr. Levi shut his eyes again, hoping it would help close his ears. "I'm joking, Tim. You need to relax."

"I am relaxed." Tim's voice climbed an octave. "I'm perfectly fine, babycakes."

"Alright then," Jennifer laughed a little. "When can we...meet up and make a transaction?"

"I'll text you," Tim coughed.

"You better not be toying with me." Jennifer's voice went ice-cold. Her chair shuffled as she stood. "I won't wait for you forever Kerner." She left the school library, heels clicking down the silent hall.

"She's so great," Tim sighed.

"You're disgusting." Levi covered his ears with his hands.

"I wonder what's up with Matt. Nobody gets pulled out of school this late in the year. It's pointless."

"The Clinic probably found a better way to manage his condition." Levi shrugged. "Let's not jump to negative conclusions."

"Levi, he was on silver supplements and wolfsbane pain killers. And they weren't working. He can't legally have pot here. What other solution might there be? They'd be experimenting on him— best case scenario."

"Maybe he moved to Colorado," Levi snickered.

"Suddenly you're an optimist." Tim glanced at the clock and packed up his books. "It's unbecoming. Stop it."

SUNLIGHT WARMED her face. The wind blew and brought no chill. Leaves rustled on the branches of the trees again. The last remnants of massive snow piles lined driveways, ditches, and a few select roofs in thin squiggles of white. The black helicopter gleamed gray in the sun. Samantha could feel her skin tanning as she sat on the bench in Veterans Park. It was a relief to see winter withering away, slinking back to Canada, or wherever it went.

"Hey Sammie!" Samantha looked to her right. A red car pulled up and parked. Becca, Laderia, Natalie, and Jennifer walked up to her.

"Hey." She sat straighter on the bench. "What are you guys doing here?"

"Rescuing your sorry ass, for serio," Laderia grinned. "I even broke away from my boy toy to come see you."

"What's the occasion?"

"Kaeli's parents dropped the charges against you!" Natalie bounced in place. "Jennifer found out this afternoon!"

"Mr. Edwards was on speaker phone in my father's office." Jennifer raised her chin. "Natalie's video made him change his mind."

"Oh...oh..." Samantha blinked. "So..."

"So you get to come back to school!" Becca sat down next to her. "Of course, so does Kaeli, but you two should be able to avoid killing each other. Especially now that Matt's gone. Of course, the Rockets really needed him, but that's life."

"Has anyone heard from him?" Samantha asked. "At all?"

"You can't possibly want to speak to him," Natalie frowned. "Not after all the drama."

"No...I guess not." Samantha turned her attention back to the helicopter.

"Your mom said we should take you somewhere and get your mind off of it." Becca smiled. "Laderia had a bright idea...a party at her casa."

"As long as no one winds up on the floor getting bitch-slapped," Laderia shimmied. "We can order pizzas and make margaritas. Nonalcoholic, of course—at least until my madre goes to bed."

"How does that sound?" Natalie pleaded. "Say yes."

Samantha looked at the helicopter one last time. She had a fleeting thought of running up to it, opening the door, and trying to make the thing fly. Then she remembered it was mounted in the park as a memorial. "Why not?"

"HAVE YOU SEEN HER FACE?" Tim was on the sofa staring at the ceiling. Levi was on the living room floor, trying once more to sleep.

"Whose face?"

"Nikki's."

"What do you mean?"

"I keep seeing her face. I see it in school a lot. I remember seeing her walk the halls, and then suddenly she changes. She gets all emaciated and bald. It's screwed up, man. I do double takes and triple takes. Then I blink…and she's gone."

Levi rolled over and stared at the ceiling as well. "Why do you think you see her?"

"I think she's haunting me…because she died…and we didn't save her."

Levi swallowed the lump in his throat.

"I thought it might be PTSD, but I looked it up…and I don't think I feel *that* bad, but it's still pretty glum."

"We didn't fail her, Tim." Levi pictured her body crumbling after Lancaster broke her neck. "*I* failed her. I could have killed Lancaster the day before school began. I let it drag out. I let my fear get in the way."

Tim let out an uneasy chuckle. "You're the bravest person I know. I can't even believe I'm hearing this from you."

"We're all just human here."

"Somehow, you seem much more than that. You're so level-headed."

"Only because of you, man."

"That's not true," Tim replied. "I've got an addictive personality and low self-esteem. You don't have to try to make it better."

"Even with your problems—you keep my head clear…you kept

438

pushing me on the Reinhart thing…I'm thankful for all your help. Really. I couldn't have done it without you."

"Kiss-ass." Tim sat up. "You should move back in."

"What?"

"We're stronger as a team—no matter how bad it's gotten between us. Besides, I recently rediscovered that it's lonely living alone." Tim laughed at his words.

"You're not alone." Levi stroked the back of a pointy black ear poking above his arm pit. "You've got Buttons."

"That cat hates me." Tim shook his head.

"Why would you say that?"

"I keep him locked in your old room all day."

"That's not cool," Levi's expression darkened.

"Hey, he's got a litter box, food, and water. I can't have him running around shedding. Besides, it's kind of creepy. He was a vampire's cat."

"Who helped us find Nikki. You should be nicer to him, Tim."

"I sincerely doubt he was trying to help you. He's a cat."

"You volunteered to take him."

"Well—things have changed."

"What do you mean?"

"Turns out I'm allergic to cats," Tim sniffled. "I can't share a pad with Buttons. No matter how adorable he is. He'll kill me."

"When were you planning on telling me this?"

"I wasn't." Tim shrugged. "I hear him moving around in there sometimes. Makes it feel less lonely."

"He needs contact, and play—"

"We do play. When he whines, he sticks his paws under the door. I get a spoon and mess with him. We have a blast."

Levi shook his head. "That's not enough."

"I'm sure it's more than Lancaster ever gave him. Don't make me sound like some sort of monster, man. I'm doing my best!"

"Alright, alright. We gotta find him a new home…find out if anyone wants a cat."

"SO, HE'S ALL LIKE, 'Vat is a cheese cuhd?' And I'm all like, what, Dylan never took you for cheese curds?! What kind of a Wisconsinite is he?" Laderia poured the cup of ice in the blender. "Give me some watermelon slices and tequila."

"Don't you want the margarita mix?" Natalie slid the bottle of mix across the granite countertop.

"That'll make it weaker. Don't be such a lady." Jennifer rolled her eyes, bouncing her crossed legs as she sat on the counter playing with her glass.

Becca tossed her hair. "You could stand to be more of a lady. Samantha, you look so bored. Come on, you're blonde. At least pretend you're having fun. Drink your margarita."

Samantha's head was propped up on her hands as she leaned on the counter, gazing around at Laderia's expansive home. The kitchen was so large Laderia looked small in comparison. Yet here they all were, in four feet of space, huddled around the blender while Mr. and Mrs. Valdez slept in their suite somewhere in the myriad of bedrooms upstairs.

"Samantha! Are you even listening?" Becca snapped her fingers in front of Samantha's face. She swatted at them in defense. "Come back to the present."

"I'm here, I'm here," Samantha grumbled. "What do you want?"

"We're discussing my hombre troubles." Laderia poured the freshly blended concoction into a margarita glass. "You know, differences in taste, language, nationality—all the big ones."

"You're a big one," Jennifer quipped. "When do I get seconds?" She held up an empty glass.

"Lightweight bitches don't need more than one," Laderia sneered. "I *got* more than you, so I *get* more than you."

"Don't sell yourself short. You've got a hundred pounds more than I do." Jennifer ran her tongue around the rim of the empty glass. "And you have a hot foreign guy. Muscle-bound and European. And you want to dump him."

"I do." Laderia puckered her lips and furrowed her brow. "He won't change his last name for me."

"What, you don't want to be Laderia Willfahrt?" Jennifer raised an eyebrow.

Laderia looked at her in blatant shock. "You *knew?*"

"Of course I knew. That's why my hair's so big. It's full of secrets." Jennifer smirked.

"I can't believe you didn't spread it all over the school." Laderia shook her head.

"I can be discrete when it comes to my friends." Jennifer seemed bored by the sound of her own voice.

"You're *not* very good at keeping secrets." Natalie grinned, her eyes glazed. "You told me just the other night about your parents' divorce—" She gasped at her own slip and slapped a hand across her mouth. "Look what you made me do! You can't confide in me, you know better!" she wailed.

Samantha felt a wave of relief wash over her as she looked at Jennifer. The brunette's face was a mask, composed even through the blush of alcohol.

"Silencio, chica," Laderia grabbed Natalie's wrist. "You'll wake my parents."

"It's a big deal though! And it's her fault I blabbed," Natalie pointed at Jennifer. "She knows better than to—to tell me things like that!"

"What are you staring at, Symanski?" Jennifer narrowed her eyes and Samantha looked away with a little smile. "I saw that smirk. You're happy about it, aren't you?"

"I think...I think it will be a better situation for your parents," Samantha replied.

"Well, I'm glad to hear your positive outlook," Jennifer snapped. "It's just peachy to know some girl that's met my parents once thinks they should split and is finally getting her wish."

"It's not my wish—"

"It sure as hell isn't your place, either," Jennifer's eyes were on fire. "You're not allowed to have feelings about it, one way or the other! That goes for all of you! Got it?"

"Got it," Natalie said.

"Girl, you're on my shit list." Jennifer tipped her glass in Natalie's direction. "And in case any of you were wondering, my mother's stint in rehab has done nothing for her. In fact, she's drinking more now. Thank you for your concern these past few months."

"But we haven't been concerned—" Natalie hiccupped.

Jennifer held up her hand. "Exactly. Zip it."

SAMANTHA WALKED THE HALLS of Columbus, ignoring the glances and whispers of the student body. Ever since she returned to school, people looked at her differently. Not with the fascination of a new toy, like at the beginning of the year, nor with the suspicion of Matt's first disappearance after Homecoming. Not even with the admiration when she took the heat for toilet-papering Barb's house.

It was fear.

No, maybe fear was too strong a word.

She couldn't decide what to call it, but she liked it the best. There was extra pep in her step, a bounce of energy finally returned. It must be the sleep she was finally getting. She hadn't heard a voice, seen a strange shadow, or heard creaking footsteps in weeks.

She finally found Laderia, Natalie, Becca, and Jennifer clustered in the hallway by the doors to the parking lot. "What are you guys doing back here? We need to get seats in the gym if we want to see the graduation ceremony."

"We're not here for the graduation ceremony." Natalie adjusted her blue and white sundress. "We're here to watch Laderia break it off with Stefan."

"I don't know if I can do this," Laderia gasped. "I thought I could, but I can't destroy him."

"Sure you can," Jennifer said. "The best part of a relationship is when it ends."

"That's easy for you to say. I have a soul," Laderia hyperventilated. "Ay caramba, here he comes."

"You can do this," Becca whispered.

"You chicas get out of here," Laderia said as the German boy walked up to the doors from his car, his blue graduation gown blowing in the warm wind. He entered the lobby and smiled at Laderia. The girls ducked around the corner and listened.

"How is mein liebchen?" His voice was a low rumble.

"Your liebchen has bad news."

"Vat bad news?"

"…We'll always have Marshfield."

"Vat? Are you dumping me?"

"Yes. I'm dumping you nicely."

"You are not dumping me."

"Yes I am."

"No you are not. Ve are not over."

"But you're leaving, Willfahrt. You and I can't last. We're on different continents."

"That vill change. You can alvays come visit me. Come to Germany."

"…you guys *do* have great sausage…"

"The best in the vorld."

"You two better be talking about breakfast meat!" Natalie yelled.

"Ve vill talk online. Text. Skype. Ve can last," Stefan said desperately.

"Like the Berlin Wall, we won't last forever."

"Like Dresden, ve vill rise from the ashes," he countered. There was a long silence. Finally Laderia came around the corner, shame coloring her face.

"We're staying together," she said. "Not coolio."

"HE'S A DOCTOR, and all those records we found were for people who passed through that funeral home. If he wasn't an active part of this, he wouldn't have those records. And let's not forget there's an operating room hidden in the basement. I bet this scheme is going to continue somehow." Levi shook his head.

"I know," Tim agreed. "But right now I just want to finish finals." He pulled another textbook out of his backpack.

"We'll have to monitor it," Levi continued. "See who the new players are. Whatever comes, we have to keep in mind what that pile of ash said: the next one will be worse."

"He was lying, no one else is coming." Tim shrugged. "He had no other card to play. He knew he was about to be dusted."

"Maybe you're right." Levi closed his eyes and tilted his face to catch the warmth of the sun. "I forgot what spring feels like."

"I forget it every year," Tim donned some shades. "Winter comes and I wonder why people live here. Then the snow melts and suddenly I remember."

Levi stole a glance at Tim's cell phone. "Graduation ended twenty minutes ago. She should be home by now, right?"

"Did you see her mom pull up?"

"No." Levi looked down West Park Street. "But that doesn't mean she didn't."

"Are you sure she'll like him?" Tim nodded to the crate between them on the bench.

"She seems like the type." Levi stuck a finger into the hole in the crate and stroked a black ear. "I feel this is right."

"HE'S OUT." Samantha gestured at her brother slumped over in the backseat.

"You've been sleeping a lot less during the day lately." Mrs. Symanski said.

"It's easier to sleep at night without creaking and voices and a little brother hiding in your bed." Samantha looked out the window at the passing houses.

"I'll have to thank Ken sometime. He really made a difference." They turned onto West Park Street. "It was lucky he stopped by when he did."

"Yes. Lucky."

They pulled in the driveway and parked in front of the garage. "I wonder how he found us."

"Coincidence," Samantha suggested. "Serendipity."

"I don't believe in coincidence," Mrs. Symanski unbuckled. "Wake your brother. He's too heavy to carry in." After rousing Brandon, they went inside. As soon as Mrs. Symanski set her purse

444

on the kitchen counter, the doorbell rang, echoing through the house.

"Samantha, can you answer that?"

Samantha passed through the dining room to the foyer and opened the front door. "Levi."

"Hey." His leather jacket gleamed in the sunlight.

"What are you doing here?"

"I have a question for you. Are you allergic to cats?"

Samantha blinked. "No. Why?"

"I'm looking for a home for a certain feline. I figured your house might be a good place for him."

"I'm not sure." Samantha glanced into the foyer behind her.

Levi picked up a crate from next to the front door. He tilted it up. Samantha peered inside. Two green eyes stared at her from the darkness. "He sets off allergies where I live. I don't want to give him to the pound. They might put him down." Levi opened the door to the crate and pulled out a sleek black cat. "His name is Buttons."

"Buttons? Did you come up with that?" Samantha took the cat and smiled.

"No."

"Who's at the door?" Mrs. Symanski appeared behind Samantha.

"Levi wants us to take in his cat." Samantha explained over her shoulder.

"Oh, what glossy fur! Is it litter box trained?"

"He uses the litter box." Levi looked between Samantha and her mother. "You want him? I can't keep him."

"I..." Samantha looked at her mother with pleading eyes. "I don't know."

Mrs. Symanski smiled and rubbed the cat behind its ears. "Brandon needs another male in the house." Buttons purred as he rubbed his face on Samantha's arm and Mrs. Symanski's fingers. "We can give it a trial run."

"That's great," Levi's smile appeared and vanished like a ghost. "Thanks." He handed the crate to Mrs. Symanski and she took it into the house.

"I can't believe she just did that." Buttons yawned in Samantha's arms. "I guess we have a cat now."

"I hoped you'd like him. Thanks Samantha. I'll see you around." He walked off the porch, then jogged down the sidewalk in the direction of Veterans Park.

Samantha watched Levi go, then noticed a bag of cat food and a litter box next to the front door.

About the Author

Lee Michaels moved to Marshfield, Wisconsin from the Washington, D.C. metro area in 2005. *Marstown, the beginning,* is the first book in his five-part series. A graduate of the University of Wisconsin Stevens Point, with a degree in Communications, Michaels is an award-winning artist and actor, with a particular bent and fondness for theater. Watch for his next novel as the story continues: *Marstown, the ghost and the butterfly.*

www.ingramcontent.com/pod-product-compliance
Lightning Source LLC
Chambersburg PA
CBHW060805030726
47503CB00002B/341